Land of Dreams

A dark and sinister carnival comes to a small California town, where dreams—good and bad —can come true . . .

"Beautiful . . . bizarre . . . a wonderful real-life fantasy."
—Orson Scott Card

"Unique, delightful . . . as unpredictable as rain."
—*Fantasy Review*

"Marvelous."
—Patricia A. McKillip

Homunculus

In the darkest alleys of London, a mad hunchback tries to raise the dead—and much more . . .

"The fastest, funniest, most colorful and grotesquely horrifying novel that could ever be written about Victorian London."
—Tim Powers, author of *The Anubis Gates*

The Digging Leviathan

An Edgar Rice Burroughs fan—with the power to make his fantasies come true—plans to journey to the center of the earth . . .

"Blaylock is an original author grounded in the quintessential classics, yet ready without notice to astonish."
—Philip K. Dick

"Wonderful . . . colorful . . . delightfully entertaining."
—Tim Powers

Ace Books by James P. Blaylock

THE DIGGING LEVIATHAN

HOMUNCULUS

LAND OF DREAMS

THE STONE GIANT

THE LAST COIN

THE PAPER GRAIL

THE PAPER GRAIL

JAMES P. BLAYLOCK

ACE BOOKS, NEW YORK

THE PAPER GRAIL

An Ace Book / published by arrangement with
the author

PRINTING HISTORY
Ace hardcover edition published May 1991
Ace mass-market edition / February 1992

ISBN: 0-441-65127-5

Ace Books are published by The Berkley Publishing Group,
200 Madison Avenue, New York, New York 10016.
The name "ACE" and the "A" logo
are trademarks belonging to Charter Communications, Inc.

10 9 8 7 6 5 4 3 2 1

To
Viki

and this time,
to
Tom and Venta Streff
Here's to friendship, food, philosophy, and the future

and to the memory of
Roy Squires

The author would like to thank some people for their help and their friendship:

Dorothea Kenny, Merrilee Heifetz, Randal Robb, Kirk Schumacher, and Tim McNamara, the Secret King of the North Coast. And especially Lew Shiner, the no-holds-barred story doctor. And Tim Powers, from whose tin shed full of plots, images, and ideas I've always stolen ruthlessly.

. . . that harmony is now broken, and broken the world round: fragments, indeed, of what existed still exist, and hours of what is past still return; but month by month the darkness gains upon the day. . . .

—JOHN RUSKIN

. . . to draw out the soul of things with the syllogism is as impossible as to draw out Leviathan with a hook.

—G. K. CHESTERTON

His body is perfectly spherical,
He weareth a runcible hat.

—EDWARD LEAR

THE PAPER GRAIL

1

THE skywriting in his dream wasn't a word or phrase, it was five white clouds drifting in a blue sky. There was no airplane gusting out smoke, only the five clouds very gradually appearing, exactly positioned, like a constellation growing visible in evening twilight. This time there was the heavy, rhythmic sound of the ocean in the distance, and Howard confused it with the sound of the seasons turning like a mill wheel. He knew in the dream that it was autumn. The pattern of the cloudy skywriting was always the same, and always suggested the same thing, but the seasons kept changing, following the course of the waking year.

In the dream, Howard walked into the mill, which was built of stone, and he stood before the fire in the hearth. A cold wind off the ocean blew at his back. There was no heat in the fire at all, and so he stirred the coals with a stick that he found in his hand, only half surprised that leafy green tendrils sprouted from the stick and twined up his arm in the few moments that he held it.

The fire popped and leaped, throwing embers onto the hearthstones. He knew he was dreaming, and he knew that in a moment he would kneel on the hearth and burn his knee on a hot ember, and that he would feel the pain of the burn even though it was a dream and the fire was cold. And then he would touch the clear fluid that seeped from the burn and taste it, only vaguely surprised that it had the piny smell and flavor of tree sap. There would be a message in the five clouds now, spelling out his fate, but when he walked back outside to read it, the mill wouldn't be a mill any longer. It would be a stone house on a cliffside with the ocean pounding on rocks below and the sky above dark with impending rain.

He woke up this time to the sound of waves breaking along the Point Reyes coastline. It was just dawn. He had slept that night in the back of his camper, parked at Stinson Beach, having driven the few miles from the campground at Mount Tamalpais

1

yesterday morning. Already the dream was fading from his mind. As always, he couldn't remember why it had seemed so vastly important to him, but it had left him with the ghostly suggestions of urgency and dread, and with the peculiar certainty that the five white clouds hadn't been real clouds at all, but had been painted by some unseen hand on the sky above his dream.

AFTER driving north out of Point Reyes, Howard stopped at Inverness for breakfast and then used up the rest of his half-frozen anchovies fishing in a big tide pool north of town, throwing chunks of bait at wheeling sea gulls and thinking about his job as assistant curator at a small and dusty museum in southern California. He had come north to pick up a single piece of artwork—what he understood to be a nineteenth-century Japanese woodcut sketch, perhaps by Hoku-sai.

He remembered the sketch as having been faded, with heavy crease lines where some idiot had folded it up, trying to construct, or reconstruct, an origami object. That had been nearly fifteen years ago, when he had spent a rainy weekend at the cliffside house built by Michael Graham, the old man who owned the sketch. Graham had kept it in a curious sort of box, hidden behind the stones of the fireplace, even though there had been prints on the wall, in plain view, that were more valuable.

Howard's cousin Sylvia had been there, too. She had guessed that the rice paper sketch had actually been folded into any number of shapes, and had wondered if a person could refold it, using the creases as a sort of road map. Every now and then, and especially lately, after his dreams about the mill wheel and the fireplace, it occurred to Howard that the road map metaphor fit better than either he or Sylvia had guessed.

Hanging from the rearview mirror in Howard's truck was an origami flower, a lily that had yellowed to the color of old ivory. It was dusty and torn, but too delicate by now to clean up or reshape. Young and romantic, he had given Sylvia a lily on the night they decided against making love, and she had given him the paper flower the following morning, folded up out of paper pressed from linen and leaves.

They were just twenty years old then, and the fact of their being cousins meant that they had very nearly grown up together. It also meant that when their feelings for each other began to grow romantic, there was something that made such feelings troublesome, if not impossible. In her junior year at college Sylvia told him she had decided to move north to Fort Bragg, where her parents lived, and against his own desires he had let her go without arguing.

A month ago he had found the paper lily in a box full of old college memorabilia, and had hung it in the cab of his truck. It turned out to be a sort of catalyst, suggesting Sylvia to him, stirring in him the desire to travel up the coast after all these years and pay her a visit. He told himself now that when he arrived in Fort Bragg today or tomorrow he would take it down before she saw it and misread his intentions—or, perhaps, read them correctly. Who could say what either of them would feel these many years later? Nothing had changed, really.

He thought about this as he fished in the pool above Inverness. Either there weren't any fish in the pool or else he was a lousy fisherman. A pelican landed on a nearby outcropping of rock and watched him with a dreadful eye. Howard said hello to it, and the bird clacked its beak open and shut, then cocked its head and fixed its eye on the remaining anchovies. One by one Howard fed them to the pelican, finally showing it the empty carton. The pelican stood there, anyway, watching him past its ridiculous beak, until Howard reeled in his line and picked his way across the rocks toward where his truck was parked on the roadside. Then the bird flew north, following the coast, disappearing behind grassy bluffs and then reappearing out over the ocean, skimming along a foot above the swell, while Howard followed in the pickup, driving at erratic speeds in order to keep the bird in sight and trying to remember whether signifying seabirds were good omens or bad.

He wasn't due in Fort Bragg until tomorrow, but there was no reason at all that he couldn't drive the few hours north today, maybe stop at Graham's house this very afternoon and get business out of the way, after which he could head on up to his Uncle Roy's house and get on with his vacation. He wondered idly whether Sylvia still lived there or had gotten a place of her own, and whether she still saw anything of the man she had very nearly married. What had he called himself then? An animal name of some sort—skunk, maybe, or weasel. Stoat, that was it. Howard had got the news roundaboutly, through his mother, and had insisted to himself that he was happy for Sylvia, that there were no hard feelings. How could there be, after all these years? He was a good deal happier, though, when he heard that Sylvia hadn't married, after all. So much for taking the long view.

On Highway One, above Point Arena and Elk, the road was cut into the cliff face, barely wide enough for two cars to

3

edge past each other. He slowed down, hugging the side of the highway, occasionally looking for the pelican, holding out hope even though he hadn't seen it for two hours. Tangled berry vines snaked down almost onto the asphalt, massed around the bleached pickets of rickety hillside fences. Above him the hills were dry and brown except for stands of cypress and Monterey pine and eucalyptus. Below him were hundreds of feet of rock-strewn, almost vertical cliffs that disappeared into the fog that was drifting ashore now. Here and there, when the road skirted the cliff, he could see the gray Pacific churning below on cathedral-sized rocks.

Occasional mailboxes appeared along the ocean side of the road, marking the driveways to isolated houses on the bluffs. Uneasily Howard started watching for Graham's house, matching landmarks along the highway with the little symbols on the pencil-sketched map on his dashboard. He remembered the house fairly clearly from his stay there years ago, and even more clearly from his dreams, where, because of some trick of dream architecture, Graham's house and the old stone mill were in some subtle way the same thing.

He drove straight past it, not seeing the fence-post mailbox or the weedy gravel drive until it was too late. Immediately the highway twisted around and began climbing, making it impossible to turn around. Somehow, missing the driveway didn't bother him. It was almost a relief, and he realized that the house filled him with an indeterminate sense of foreboding, like heavy weather pending on a muggy and silent afternoon.

He slowed the truck, though, and turned off the highway, up Albion Ridge Road, stopping at a little grocery store with a pair of rusty old gas pumps out front. Far below the ridge, the Albion River wound down out of the coast range. The north coast was in the middle of a long drought, and the river was a muddy trickle. On the bank sat a campground, nearly empty, with a dirt road running through it, leading beneath the bridge and down to a deserted beach that was strewn with driftwood and kelp. It looked like a good place to go shelling, especially this time of the year, when the first of the big north swells dragged the ocean bottom and threw seashells and long-sunken flotsam onto the rocky beaches.

He thought about spending the night at the campground. Maybe it was too late to stop and see old Graham that afternoon, anyway. The old man might easily be doubtful about strangers in pickup trucks appearing out of the fog so late in the day.

Howard would call back down to the house in order to make an appointment—for tomorrow noon, say. He felt grimy and salty, and his clothes smelled like fish bait. Tomorrow morning he could find a laundromat in Mendocino, and then backtrack the ten miles to Graham's house. The plan sounded fine to him, very rational, except that he knew he was simply avoiding things, and was beginning to feel as if the north coast, like the two poles of a magnet, was conspiring to attract and repel him about equally.

The gas station was actually a sort of country store, covered in rough-cut redwood planks and with a few chain-sawed burl sculptures out front that had turned gray in the weather. Old macramé and bead curtains covered the windows, which were dusty and strung with cobwebs and dead flies. The junk food in the rack on the counter was a little disappointing—carob brownies and sticky-looking granola bars in plastic wrap, all of it sweetened with fruit juice instead of sugar. It was guaranteed to be organic, put together by a local concern called Sunberry Farms. It certainly *looked* organic, especially the carob, which might as easily have been dirt.

There wasn't a Twinkie in sight, so he grabbed a pack of gum and one of the brownies and laid them on the counter. Gas was nearly a dollar and a half a gallon, and his old Chevy Cheyenne drank it like champagne. The attendant stood out by the truck, talking to a man carrying a tackle box, who set the box down and held his hands apart, obviously telling a fish story. Nobody was in any hurry up here, which satisfied Howard entirely. It seemed to be the first time in months, maybe years, that he wanted to be exactly where he was, drunk on the weather and the solitude and the sound of the sea.

He found a wire rack of postcards and window decals, and he sorted through them, pulling out a half dozen decals that advertised north coast sights—the Skunk Train, Shipwreck Aquarium, the Winchester Mystery House, Noyo Harbor. It didn't matter to him that he hadn't been to most of these places. What he wanted was to glue decals all over his truck and camper shell windows. He had a couple dozen of them already, from places in Arizona and Nevada and New Mexico. Soon he'd be out of room, and would have to start layering the decals, perhaps covering just the inessential edges and corners at first, and then ultimately losing one after another of them altogether. Once he had gotten started on it a couple of months ago, it had become a sort of compulsion, and he had come to believe in the virtues of excess, almost as if someday he would reach a sort of mystical decal threshold, and something would happen.

Normally he avoided any decal that didn't advertise a place. He didn't want slogans or political statements or any indication that he meant anything consistent. Obvious meaning would subvert the entire effort, and he'd have to scrape the whole mess off with a razor blade. Up until now he never bought too many at one time. The thing shouldn't be rushed. There was something about the air up here, though, that overrode that instinct, and he found that within moments he was holding a whole sheaf of the things. He picked out one last decal of a comical pelican, which he bought as a souvenir of the bird he'd shared his anchovies with. If there was any meaning in that, no one except him would be able to guess it out.

He wandered up the center aisle of the little store, toward a display of fishing tackle and rental poles on the back wall. Thumbtacked to a piece of corkboard beneath the carded fishing tackle was a faded and dog-eared bumper sticker advertising a local roadside attraction. It had holes in the corners so that it could be wired to your bumper while you weren't looking. In small letters it read, "Honk if you've seen," and then below, in larger letters, "The Museum of Modern Mysteries." Alongside was a sketchy illustration of ghosts flitting through a redwood grove with a shadowy automobile running along below, the front end of the thing lost in the foggy night. Howard unpinned it, instantly losing interest in his hand full of decals.

There was the scraping of shoe soles at the door, and Howard turned to find the attendant sliding in behind the counter. The man looked doubtfully at the brownie, pushing it with his finger. "This yours?" he asked, as if he couldn't quite believe it.

Howard nodded, suddenly regretting it. The thing cost nearly a dollar, the price of two decals. "Is this bumper sticker for sale?" Howard held it up for the man to see.

"Oh, that," the man said, sitting down on a stool. "That's a couple years old. It ain't no good. Place went broke."

Howard wondered for a moment whether his question had been answered and then decided that it hadn't been. "Don't want to sell it, do you?" He tried not to sound too anxious. The man was right, from his point of view, and was clearly having a hard time putting a price on a scrap of old faded paper.

"Used to have a decal, too." He leaned heavily on the first syllable of the word and nodded at the wire rack.

"Don't have one now, do you?"

"Nope," the man said. "Place went bust."

Howard widened his eyes, as if in surprise that such a place as a spirit museum could go bust. "People don't much believe in ghosts anymore," he said, trying to make it sound noncommittal, as if he were ready to believe in whatever the attendant believed, and blame the rest of the world for believing something else and causing trouble.

"People don't know from ghosts." The man switched on a portable television behind the counter. A game show appeared on the screen—a family of six wearing funny hats and jitterbugging furiously in front of a washer and dryer hung with enormous price tags.

The sound of the television ruined the atmosphere, and Howard was suddenly desperate to leave. He set his credit card down on the counter along with the decals and made one last try at the bumper sticker. "I'd be glad to buy the sticker," he said.

"Won't do you no good." The man stared hard at his credit card, as if Howard had handed him something inexplicable—a ham sandwich or a photograph of the Eiffel Tower. He read the name several times, looking at Howard's face, and then checked the number against a little book of bad-risk numbers shoved in alongside the cash register. "Barton," he said. "You ain't any relation . . ." He looked closely at Howard's face again and then smiled broadly. "Sure you are!"

"He's my uncle," Howard said. "On my father's side." It was no good to lie. Now he would have to pay triple for the bumper sticker. Howard's Uncle Roy had founded and owned the Museum of Modern Mysteries and then had gone broke with it. Howard had never even been there, although he had always loved the idea of it. And now, these years later, here was a long-lost bumper sticker advertising the place. Clearly he had to buy it as a memento. The man knew that now. He sat there as if thinking about it, about soaking Howard for the rectangle of sun-faded paper.

"Roy Barton," he said, shaking his head. "That old son of a gun. Hell, *take* the damned thing. You going up to his place now?"

"That's right," Howard said, surprised. "I'm up here on business, mostly."

"Roy Barton's, or your own?"

"My own, actually. I haven't seen Roy for a few years. I don't know what kind of business he's in now."

The man gave him a curious look, as if Uncle Roy were in some sort of business that didn't bear discussion. Then he said, "Roy Barton's pretty much in business with the world. Nobody'd be surprised if your business and his business didn't cross paths down the line. He used to call himself an 'entrepreneur of the spirit.' And by God he ain't far wrong. He'll liven up your day."

"I hope so," Howard said. "I could use it."

"Give him a howdy from me, then, will you? Tell him Cal says hello. He used to come in here pretty regular when he was working the ghost angle up to the museum. He had a lot of idle time. It wasn't but a half mile up the road. Building's still there, sitting empty. Ever been up there?"

"Never was," Howard said. "Always wanted to, but I put it off. Then he went under and it was too late."

"Too damned bad, too. He's a character, Roy Barton is. He *seen* some things out in the woods . . ." The man laughed, shaking his head, remembering something out of the past, some sort of Roy Barton high jinks. "Hell, I believe him, too. I'll be damned if I don't." He turned around to a glass-fronted drink cooler, opened it up, and pulled out a six-pack of Coors. "Take this along for him, will you? Tell him Cal Dalton says hello and why don't he stop in." He handed Howard his credit card along with the beer, and Howard signed for the gas and decals. Cal shook his hand. "Look for it on the right, three or four bends up. You can pass it easy if you aren't looking out."

Howard thanked him and left. Fog had settled into the campground below, making it look inhospitable and cold. Somehow the man's carrying on like that had lifted Howard's spirits, making him feel less like an outsider. The idea of having a look at the abandoned spirit museum appealed to him. There was a couple of hours of daylight left.

He had heard all about the museum from his mother, who had done her best to make the whole cockeyed thing sound reasonable. His mother was fiercely loyal to Uncle Roy, who had looked after them, in his way, in the years following Howard's father's death. Howard had picked up bits and pieces of family gossip lately about the museum's sad decline and about how Uncle Roy had borrowed himself into lifelong debt to make a go of it. The rotten thing about it was that his poor uncle had believed in it, in the ghosts. Despite the gimmicky bumper stickers and decals, he had been convinced that he had seen a carload of spirits appearing out of the north coast dawn and gunning away up the highway, dressed in out-of-date clothes and driving a Studebaker.

Why a Studebaker? That's what had torn it, had wrecked the museum, just as surely as if the Studebaker had driven through the wall. It was a car that lacked credibility. The ghosts might as well have been pedaling unicycles and wearing fright wigs. If only it had been some sort of generic Ford or Chevy, people might have bought the idea.

For Uncle Roy, though, the ghost museum had been a scientific study in the paranormal. He didn't care what sort of car the ghosts drove. He didn't require a ghost to follow fashion. The public ridiculed a Studebaker, largely because it had a front end that you couldn't tell from the rear; it was a sort of mechanical push-me pull-you. But if such a vehicle was good enough for the ghosts, then to hell with the public; it was good enough for Uncle Roy, too. That's what made it about ten times as sad when the museum closed down—Uncle Roy's sincerity.

Realizing that he wasn't very hungry, Howard opened the glove compartment in order to put the brownie away. A glass paperweight lay inside, dense with flower canes and ribbons that looked like Christmas candy. He meant it to be a gift for Sylvia, who had always loved pretty things. It had cost him a couple hundred dollars, though, and it might seem like an ostentatious gift. He would have to be subtle with it.

A half mile north of Albion there was a turnout on the land side of the highway. Howard slowed the truck and bumped off onto the shoulder, which widened out behind a line of trees into a gravel parking lot that had been invisible from the road to the south. Sitting at the far edge of the lot, overhung by fir and eucalyptus, was a long bunkhouselike building, empty and boarded up. There was a fence of split pickets running along in front, with three or four cow skulls impaled on random pickets. A painted, weathered sign over the front porch read, "Museum of Modern Mysteries."

He cut the engine and sat on the edge of the lot, just able to hear the muted crash of breakers through the rolled-up windows. So this was it. He had known it was out here somewhere, sitting lonesome and empty along the highway. Somehow he had expected more, although exactly what he had expected he couldn't say. He was tempted at first to climb out and have a look, but the windows were shuttered, and the longer he sat there, the sadder the place seemed to be. Some other time, maybe. He was planning on spending a couple of weeks; he

9

could always get Uncle Roy to drive him back out and show him around, if his uncle was up to it and still had a key.

Howard thought about the Hoku-sai sketch, hanging on the wall of Graham's house, back down the road. It was time to have a look at it. To hell with laundromats and appointments. He had waited long enough. It was almost two years ago that he had written a letter suggesting that Graham give the sketch to the museum in Santa Ana on what was called permanent loan. Graham could write it off on his taxes. Howard would use it as the focus of a new wing of oriental artwork.

Two years ago that had sounded enterprising—something new. But for nearly a year after he sent the letter he hadn't heard anything in return, and had almost forgotten about the sketch. Then, unexpectedly, he had got a letter back, agreeing to the permanent loan business. Graham wouldn't ship the piece, though; Howard would have to come after it. He had done nothing about it for most of a year. Then a month ago something shifted in him— the dreams, the accidental rediscovery of the origami lily—and he began to feel like a man whose spirit was beginning to recover from a long dry spell.

He came up with the idea of going up north, of taking a slow, zigzag route, driving back roads out of obscure beaches and primitive campgrounds. It would be nothing less than a matter of sorting out his life. He would visit Uncle Roy and Aunt Edith in Fort Bragg, get to know Sylvia again. He would take a month to do it, just like in the old days. Mrs. Gleason, his boss, hadn't liked the idea of month-long vacations, but Howard showed her Graham's letter, and that had done the trick. He had kept his thumb over the date.

Fog settled around the pickup truck as he sat on the roadside now, and water dripped onto the roof of the cab from an overhanging tree limb. The sea wind gusted around the doors, and Howard started the truck in order to fire up the heater. Once the engine was idling, his sitting there seemed pointless, so he rolled up to the edge of the asphalt and peered downhill into the gloom. A pair of headlights swung around the curve of highway below, the car itself still invisible in the fog. It was impossible to tell how far away it was, so Howard waited it out, letting it have the highway to itself.

Howard recognized the characteristic cheese-grater roar of a Volkswagen engine before the microbus actually materialized out of the wall of fog. It was moving slowly, even for a Volkswagen, like a deep-water fish prowling through submarine canyons. One moment it was a ghost, obscured by mist; the next it was solid. Howard thought suddenly about his uncle's Studebaker, full of top-hatted spirits, and on impulse he shifted the transmission into reverse, as if he would escape it by hurtling backward into the forest.

As it drew near, it appeared at first to be covered with sticks and leaves, like something that had driven up out of the deep woods. But it wasn't leaves; it was stuff from the ocean that had been glued onto the body of the bus in layers, so that only the front windows were clear. Dried kelp and sea fans, starfish and barnacles, clumped mussels and fish skeletons and seashells covered the bus in layers so that it looked like a tide pool on wheels. It was impossible to be sure it was a car any longer, except that it ran on tires and had a windshield. Even the rumbling engine might have been a cobbled-together mechanism of tube worms and starfish gears and pumping seawater. It growled uphill, lit within by the strange green glow of the instrument panel. The driver's face was a shadow.

Howard shifted back out of reverse, realizing that his mouth was open in disbelief. He watched the bus disappear into the fog around the curve of the hillside, noticing that a big patch of stuff had evidently fallen off the outside of the engine compartment—too much heat, probably. The effect was suddenly one of shabbiness, something like a ghost story ruined by missing paragraphs.

Still, something about the bus, about seeing it, reminded him of his uncle's museum and of Michael Graham's stone house, with its passages and turrets. The very atmosphere of the north coast was compulsive—the overgrown countryside and the perpetual mist, the strange appeal of a wire rack full of gaudy decals. It struck him that there was something right and natural about the deep-sea bus, as if it stood to reason. He laughed uneasily, reminding himself that eccentrics were common on the coast. They must issue cards, like a Mensa ID. After another week of solitude and fog he would be ready to apply for one himself.

No wonder Uncle Roy had been possessed with notions of ghosts. The foggy air seemed to be thick with them. For the first time since he'd left home a week ago he wanted company—even old Graham's company. He rolled out onto the highway, heading south again. He would make it to the stone house with an hour's worth of daylight to spare.

2

THE limousine crept along through the San Francisco traffic, down Grant Street, through Chinatown toward North Beach. It was July, and the streets were full of tourists, the heavy stream of cars barely moving in either direction and people cutting warily back and forth between bumpers. Why the fool of a driver had missed his offramp and tied them up in crosstown traffic, Heloise Lamey couldn't fathom. Stupidity, maybe. Some sort of smart-aleck malice—wasting the time of a poor old woman out alone, at the mercy of the world.

She said nothing, though. It was already spilled milk. She could rant and rave and it wouldn't get them to their destination one moment sooner. And the hired driver wouldn't care anyway. She could buy the limousine service and have the man fired and he wouldn't care. Her insisting on justice would simply provoke abuse. Despite his snappy uniform, he was sullen and dull and false-looking. She could see it in his eyes. She could take the measure of a man in an instant. In her sixty-eight years on earth she had learned to do that with a facility that she was proud of. It was the key to her success as a businesswoman.

People weren't what they used to be. The tradespeople didn't keep to their stations. Duty was a thing of the past. Everywhere she went people were full of abuse. There was trouble of some sort from almost everyone she ran into. She seemed to remember a time in the distant past when that wasn't so, when people and life were simple and direct. When that had changed, she couldn't at all say.

Before the war she had almost married a sailor. She remembered how handsome he had looked in his uniform on the day he shipped out. On the night before, they had danced to Benny Goodman. Now his bones were on the bottom of the ocean somewhere, and that's what life had to offer you ultimately—death and disappointment. The world hadn't changed in that respect. People had, though. Now there was nothing but grasping, people

12

clawing their way through life at your expense. A person had no choice but to get in ahead of them. There was no middle ground. She stayed home as much as she could, but even there she was forced to carry on a war with a lot of backwoods hicks who didn't know progress when they saw it, or destiny, either.

Her mouth set and her eyes narrowed, she sat in the center of the backseat and stared straight ahead out the front window, trying not to see the awful gaggle of people swarming on the sidewalks and in the gutters. She believed that there was a certain dignity in her face, which was long and thin and with a prominent chin and the eyes of a monarch—the sort who saw straight through her subjects and their pitiful little games. There was nothing weak in her face, nothing watery. It was the sort of face that wasn't easily forgotten. She peered at herself in the window reflection now, refastening a strand of hair that had come loose.

Her attention was broken by the high-pitched shouting of an old Chinese news vendor, arguing, probably, over a nickel. At the curb the rear door of a van swung open and a man stepped out carrying a flayed goat over one bloody shoulder and a string of plucked ducks over the other. Life, like so much scurrying vermin, went on around her. She thought for the sixth time how necessary it had been to hire a limousine. Then she realized they were stopped again, and she checked her watch. "I'm *very* late," she said to the driver, who said nothing in return.

The traffic cleared just then, as if it, at least, were paying attention to her. The car moved forward slowly, making nearly a half a block's worth of headway before stopping again. The lights of a tow truck whirled in front of them now, blocking oncoming traffic while the tow truck driver walked around an illegally parked Mercedes-Benz, looking in the windows. He pulled a clutch of flat plastic slats out of his coat and slipped one in along the edge of the front door of the parked car in order to jimmy it open, a policeman directing the cars around it, holding the limousine at bay with an upturned hand.

Skeptically Mrs. Lamey watched them work. Nothing was safe from them. Even the police would steal your car. "Honk the horn," Mrs. Lamey said to the driver.

"At the cop?" He turned and looked at her.

"Just *honk the horn*, young man. I've been patient with you up until now, but this takes it too far. Honk the horn."

The driver squinted into her face. "You gotta be kidding," he said.

"I never *kid*, if I take your meaning. I assure you I'm very serious. Honk your horn. I've hired this car, and I demand it."

"Why don't you climb up here and honk it yourself, lady? Then *you* can talk to the cop." He turned forward again, ignoring her. Opening the glove box, he found a pack of gum, pulling out two sticks and shoving them into his mouth, settling into his seat contentedly to wait out the tow truck, even if it took all afternoon.

Mrs. Lamey leaned forward, unable to believe it. She had expected grief of some nature, but this sort of outright impudence from a driver . . . "I *insist*. Honk the horn or I'll have your job."

"You can have the fuckin' job, lady, and the horn, too. Calm the hell down. Where you going, anyway? Just up to North Beach. It's easier to *walk* from here. If I was you, that's what I'd do. I'd get out and walk. You'd have been there twenty minutes ago."

"Your advice is worthless to me, young man. Here, look, they've gotten out of the way. Pull around these cars, for heaven's sake." She waved a limp-wristed hand toward the street.

He shrugged and edged the limousine past the tow truck, which had straightened out now and was towing the Mercedes out into traffic. They stopped and started a half dozen times down the last two blocks to Portsmouth Square, slowing in the press of cars swinging up onto Broadway and Columbus. Small gangs of youths lounged on the sidewalk along the square, shouting and smoking cigarettes.

Mrs. Lamey carefully kept her eyes straight ahead. There was nothing here that she wanted to see. She felt vulnerable, even inside the limousine, but with a little bit of work she could ignore the world outside utterly. As they turned up Columbus, though, she saw three young men with weirdly miscut hair bend toward the limousine and make obscene gestures with both hands, all three of them laughing and hooting. Mrs. Lamey concentrated hard on the windshield, on the car ahead of them, on the tip of her nose, blocking out their existence, eradicating the whole brief scene.

"That's rich, ain't it?" the driver said, chuckling in the front seat. "What it is, is the limo. Happens all the time. Can't go nowhere without people flipping you off. You know what I mean? It's a social statement is what I think." He shook his head, clearly pleased, able to take the long view. "You got to admire it, though." He looked at her wide-eyed in the rearview

14

mirror, as if inviting her to admire it as much as he did, to talk a little bit of philosophy.

Mrs. Lamey was silent. There was nothing on earth she had to admire. Where she came from limousine drivers spoke when spoken to. They weren't street-corner sociologists. He shook his head after a half minute of her refusing to speak, and they drove in silence up Columbus to Vallejo.

She directed him up an alley between graffiti-scrawled brick façades. Midway down, the alley opened onto a courtyard. "Stop here," she said suddenly.

"Here?" He turned and looked at her incredulously, having expected, perhaps, some more reasonable destination.

"That's right. Here. In the alley. I won't be needing your services any longer. I'm getting out here. *Can* you fathom that?"

He shrugged. "Suits me." He got out and went round to her door, opening it and gesturing gallantly at the littered asphalt.

"I won't be giving you a tip of any sort," she said to him, staring at his chin with a look of determination. "I don't know what you're accustomed to, but I'll tell you right now that I had thought at first to give you two dollars. You can ruminate on that for the rest of the afternoon. I'm moderately certain that I would have gotten quicker, more courteous service from a taxicab. One expects a certain amount of gracious behavior from a driver, a certain level of professionalism and expertise."

She took two steps to distance herself from him, then turned around to face him squarely. With an air of someone having the last word, she showed him the two crisp one-dollar bills that might have been his. She tucked them away finally and irretrievably into her pocket, turning away into the courtyard without a backward glance.

She hadn't gone three steps, though, when a horn honked. Without thinking she looked back at the alley, where the limousine accelerated slowly past the mouth of the courtyard. The driver was bent across the front seat, waving out the open passenger window. He shouted a parting obscenity which somehow involved eating. Mrs. Lamey closed her ears to it just a second too late, continuing across the courtyard and resolutely listening to nothing now but the *tap, tap, tap* of her shoes on concrete, blocking out the whole filthy world round about her.

There was a breezeway at the corner of the courtyard, opening onto another small, winding alley that ran steeply uphill. At the top she crossed a small parking lot and went in through the side door of a white concrete building with red letters on the side

15

proclaiming itself to be the "Whole Life Mission." Below that, in italic lettering, was the legend "The Church of the Profiting Christian."

Inside the church the air was heavy, still, and musty. The building was bigger than it appeared to be from the street, and Mrs. Lamey walked through the nave, past rows of empty pews built of wood-grain Formica. She peered into the empty sacristy and then into an adjacent chair-lined room, also empty of people, and containing a glass-fronted, water-filled tub. Heavy-looking television cameras and big reflecting lights hung from the ceiling and stood in the corners. She went on, pausing to knock on an office door and listen at the cloudy glass window. A sign on the door read, "Reverend White, Ministry Office." There was nothing but silence inside. Reverend White, apparently, was somewhere on the second floor.

She climbed a stairs and with a key from her purse let herself into a kitchen. Beyond it was a corridor with rooms leading off to either side. There was the smell of carbolic acid and alcohol in the air now, and the floors were tiled in white linoleum. A chrome pole on wheels stood in the corridor, hung with an IV bottle and with plastic tubing and clamps. Through one open door she glimpsed a gurney and a surgical table. A thrill of fear and anticipation surged through her, and she was struck with the notion that in the air of that room her destiny hung like a rain cloud.

She knocked twice on the window of the next door down, then pushed the button on an adjacent intercom.

"Who is it?" asked a man's voice.

"Heloise."

The door opened an inch and a man peered out, as if to ascertain whether it was really Mrs. Lamey standing in the hallway or somebody playing a trick. Satisfied, he smiled broadly and waved her in. He wore a white coat over a red shirt and black trousers. His patent-leather shoes matched his shirt. "Heloise!" he said, as if he'd been waiting for this moment for weeks. "I half expected you wouldn't come."

"Well, I'm here, Reverend," she said sarcastically. "Let's get this over with."

"It would be better to call me 'doctor.' I'm a minister downstairs, a doctor upstairs."

"An abortionist, maybe. 'Doctor' is a weighty word."

He shrugged. "I don't perform abortions anymore, actually. I was an abortionist when it was illegal and more profitable. Now

I perform elective surgery—reconstructive surgery, mostly."

Mrs. Lamey made a face, imagining what he meant despite herself.

He grinned at her for a moment and then put on a serious, bedside, medical-man face. "It's a fact," he said. "People come to me from all over the city. Up from Los Angeles, too. Men and women both. In fact, half a block up the street, at a bar called the Cat's Meow, there's a dancer who owes her entire career to me. You'd be surprised what people will pay to see. Enormous breasts are a dime a dozen in North Beach. People are tired of that sort of thing. But there's a certain fascination for—what can I call it? Alien results, let's say. For anatomy that's . . . physiologically wrong." He watched for her response, but she stood stony-faced. He couldn't phase her. He shrugged. "Anyway, even that's going by the boards. They're turning the Cat's Meow into a dinner theatre, and my client is out of a job. Your case is comparatively simple, though, isn't it? You've got too low an opinion of my talents, Heloise, which is a mystery to me."

"A mystery? A back-alley surgery like this. Performing whatever sorts of ghastly operations fifteen years after your license was revoked. And my opinion is a mystery to you?"

"Oh, no, not that. I don't have any problem with that at all. What mystifies me is why you seem to want my help and yet insist on insulting me." He lit a cigar and sat down, leaning back in his swivel chair, shifting the cigar from side to side in his mouth.

Mrs. Lamey brushed the heavy smoke away from her face. "Because I pay you not to ask questions," she said. "And I'd rather not hear about your loathsome work, thank you. How long will this take?"

He shrugged. "Moderately simple surgery. No exterior cutting at all. One just hauls the plumbing out through—"

"Save the filthy talk, Mr. White. How long will this take—until I'm home again?"

"A week in bed, under observation. You'll need a nurse, someone trained. Then four or five weeks before a full recovery. There's the threat of infection, of course. This is a moderately risky surgery, you know. I can't fathom why you'd elect to have it unnecessarily at this . . . late age." He smiled at her.

"Business," she said. "That will have to suffice."

He nodded. "You undertake the strangest sort of business, Heloise, don't you? I have faith in you, though. Our business efforts always seem to end satisfactorily. And, of course, I make

17

it a point not to pry into my patients' affairs."

"Don't, then. There's the matter that we discussed over the telephone, too. Can we take care of that right now, do you think, before we carry out this surgery?"

"That requires a different coat," he said, standing up and gesturing toward the door. They went out, back through the kitchen and down the stairs into the church. He unlocked the door to the ministry office, letting Mrs. Lamey through first and then locking the door behind them.

The office was large and ornately decorated, with oil paintings on the walls and an oriental carpet on the parquet floor. A six-panel Japanese screen covered half of one wall, and on a low, gaudily carved table in the center of the room sat a glass-encased collection of Franklin Mint coins. The Reverend White stepped straight across to the wall opposite the door where he lifted and took down a Norman Rockwell painting. "This is an original," he said, nodding at it and squinting. "Cost me plenty."

"I'm sure it did."

"I love Rockwell, though, don't you? He captures a sort of spirit, a sort of . . ." He lost track of the thought as he turned the dial of a wall safe that had been hidden behind the painting. The safe door swung open, and he carefully removed a velvet-wrapped bundle, laying it gently on the edge of the rug. He untied a ribbon at either end and unrolled the bundle, revealing two long, pale bones, streaked with brown and black. The bones themselves, looking porous and dry, seemed to have crumbled partly away at both ends.

"And these are what we discussed?" she asked, looking at the bones doubtfully.

"Yes, they are. They come with papers detailing their history over thousands of years, and not a particularly complicated history, either. I got these at a bargain-basement price, I can tell you. I've dealt in relics for years, and I know the man I bought these from personally. Here's his affidavit." He held out a signed paper, insisting that the bones were from the fore-arms of Joseph of Arimathea, the first of the so-called Fisher Kings, according to some of the Grail legends. The bundle included the two radii, recovered from beneath a church in Lithuania.

Mrs. Lamey looked the document over. It was signed by four different people, the signatures unreadable and full of flourishes as if the document were intended to be framed and hung on the wall alongside spurious doctoral diplomas. "This is certainly worthless," she said. "But then what isn't? I have moderately sure methods of proving their authenticity. And I'm entirely certain that you wouldn't defraud me, Reverend. You wouldn't sell me a couple of old monkey arms, not at a hundred thousand dollars." She paused and looked hard at him, waiting for his response.

"No," he said, as if surprised that she'd suggest such a thing. "Of course not. You have my word on it as well as this affidavit of authenticity."

She smiled at him and stood up, moving toward the door. "Keep the affidavit of authenticity," she said. "Line the birdcage with it. Leave the bones in the safe for now. We'll settle my account after my recovery. Any news of the Ruskin skeleton? I want him, too. All of him."

"No news at all. I've got feelers out, though. If it's available, we'll get it. You've got my solemn oath on that. My man in England has confirmed that the bones aren't in Coniston."

"I don't give a tinker's damn what your man in England confirms. If the bones aren't in Coniston, then they've got to be somewhere else. John Ruskin, for heaven's sake. It's not like the man was unknown. Don't they keep track of the corpses of great thinkers and writers? I can't believe they'd be so careless as to misplace such a thing."

The Reverend White shrugged. "It appears as if the bones were taken ages ago. Maybe he was never interred at all. My man can recover his flowered shroud, though, if that will be of any use to you. There was a claim made once that vines grew out of the shroud when it was sprinkled with holy water. If my man can recover it . . ."

"Tell your man to recover his wits."

"I've got him pursuing the matter. As I said, you've got my solemn oath . . ."

She interrupted him. "Your solemn oath. That's very good. There's no chance, is there, that the gentleman we spoke of has the skeleton? He might have had access to it, you know."

"In fact, I do know. I make it my business to know. Someone would have heard of such a thing. This gentleman you refer to is a noted lunatic, isn't he?"

"He's very subtle. A deceptive man. It's hard to say what he is."

"Well, he isn't the owner of the Ruskin skeleton. I'll make further inquiries, though, if you're serious about this."

"I've never been more serious, I assure you. And I would be very disappointed if you had dealt with him instead of with me. Don't play games with me."

"I'm impervious to games, I assure you."

"Then let's get on with the afternoon's business, shall we?"

"Happily," he said. "That'll require a different coat, though." He put the bones back into the wall safe, rehung the painting, and led the way back up the stairs to where, in the surgery, a gowned nurse was already laying out instruments.

HOWARD turned down the gravel drive, which dipped steeply into the darkness of the woods. It must have been nearly impossible to navigate right after a heavy rain. As it was, the truck wheels spun a little in the gravel and the pickup wallowed from side to side, in and out of deep ruts. He crept along, taking it slow through the ghostly, overgrown cypress trees, which ended abruptly on the meadow's edge, fifty yards or so from the cliff.

There was the house itself, half cloaked in fog, the whole thing a beautiful driftwood gray, the color of the ocean, with moss growing between the stones and with the meadow wild around it. Howard was amazed at how clearly he remembered it—how much it was like the house in his dreams. It was uncanny—troublesomely so. It was fifteen years ago that he had last driven down this gravel driveway, and yet it seemed to him that he could recall even the shapes of individual stones in the walls of the house and the weathered ends of exposed roof rafters.

He had been climbing the stairs in his dreams, the old mill having turned into Graham's stone house. The stairs hung to the outside wall of the turret, wrapping around to a landing and second-floor doorway. The steps were built of irregular, chunked concrete, sledgehammered out of a sidewalk and reinforced underneath with lengths of angle iron from an old bed frame torched into pieces. There was an iron pipe handrail along the wall where the steps were mortised into the stones of the turret, but the other three edges of each step hung in the air, and now it made him dizzy just to look at them.

In his dream he had climbed slowly, looking hard at the wide lines of cleanly troweled mortar between the stones. He had seemed to be looking for something, but he didn't know what. Abruptly he realized that odds and ends of things had been shoved very carefully into the wet mortar: cheap, colored-glass perfume bottles laid sideways, tiny iron toys, a faded ceramic

Humpty Dumpty wearing a polka-dot shirt and a green tie with a stickpin and with a broad, leering, know-it-all grin.

One moment he had been halfway up; the next he was at the top of the stairs, facing the weathered door, his heart hammering in his chest. He had turned and gone back down, taking the irregular steps two at a time, thinking that something had come out of the door and was watching him, had noticed him for the first time. He had gone straight out onto the bluffs, where the driveway ended in weeds, and had nearly stumbled headlong into an old truck from which two workmen were off-loading straw-stuffed crates of the ceramic Humpty Dumptys.

It was a ridiculous dream, that part of it was. He could see that clearly in the daylight. At night, though, at two in the morning . . . Darkness tended to multiply the significance of dreams. Dream mathematics acquired its own logic after dark. And night was falling quickly now. In twenty minutes there wouldn't be much daylight left.

Howard watched the house for a moment longer, waiting for the door to open, for someone to peer out. Anyone in the house would have heard him rattle up. Berry vines grew so dense as to nearly cover the west-facing downstairs windows, and had been hacked away to let in sunlight. Split shingles lay in a pile on the meadow, alongside a telephone pole that had been sawed into foot-and-a-half lengths. There were piles of sand and gravel with sun-shredded plastic tarps staked over them, and an old cement mixer hooked up to a rusty gasoline generator on wheels. Heaps of size-sorted stone lay stacked along the wild edge of the vines, most of the stones covered up by new growth. Beyond the open door of a long, low, lean-to barn in among the cypress and eucalyptus trees, a chain-saw mill sat in the middle of a mountain of wood chips.

The place seemed empty, deserted. He climbed out of the truck, taking his keys with him. There was a heavy odor of cedar and moldering vegetation and fog, and the thick silence was cut only by the low sound of a foghorn moaning somewhere to the north. He walked around the house toward the cliffs, stopping next to a prefabricated tin shed, probably bought out of a catalogue from Sears and Roebuck. The house appeared to be dark.

The fog cleared momentarily, and there was enough daylight left to see the black rocks nearly a hundred feet below the cliffs. Waves broke across them, surging up the cliffside and then washing back down. On one of the rocks, partly submerged and crumpled up, sat an old car like a piece of statuary on a plinth. It had obviously gone off the cliff. What was it? Something peculiar; he couldn't tell at first if he was looking at the front end of the car or the back end. A Studebaker? The ocean rushed out to feed an incoming wave, exposing the car entirely. It *was* a Studebaker—an old one, from some year in the early fifties. What a coincidence; it might have been the ghost car itself.

Howard chuckled to himself. He loved the whole idea of ghosts driving around in oddball cars, getting into trouble, maybe robbing a liquor store or setting fire to someone's shoes. Then he thought about the empty spirit museum and Uncle Roy's sad bankruptcy, the loss of his house and his having to rent it back from one of his creditors who had come to own it as a piece of collateral. What with all that and the fall of night, the subject of ghosts wasn't very funny at all.

The ocean raced in again, parting around the smashed front end of the Studebaker, water streaming off the fenders. The car hadn't rusted much, either, from what Howard could see of it. It must have gone over pretty recently.

Straight behind him, uphill, was the garage end of the barn. It looked as if someone hadn't set the brake, and the car had rolled across the grass and off the cliff edge. It would have continued to roll for a long ways, down the steepening slope, which was strewn with scree and loose boulders. There was a gnarled old piece of scrub half torn out of the cliff face some twenty feet above the beach, and hooked to it was the car's rear bumper, which had no doubt slowed the car's descent and explained why it wasn't an utter ruin now.

A pelican appeared from around the headland, angling along the back of a swell, into Howard's line of sight. It pulled up when it neared the beach, and perched on the front of the car like a hood ornament. Howard stepped back away from the cliff edge, suddenly dizzy, the sound of the waves becoming disturbingly rhythmic, like the sound of the mill wheel in his dream.

He wondered what he should do. Stay? That seemed presumptuous to him—to hang around the foggy meadow when no one was home. He would feel like a sneak. And it was very possibly pointless, too. Graham might easily be gone for the night. Howard would drive into Mendocino and find a hotel room, after all. In the morning he would wash his clothes, then call Fort Bragg to announce his arrival to Uncle Roy, explaining that he happened to be in the area a couple of days earlier than he had thought, and . . . It was weak, but it had the advantage of taking Sylvia by surprise and therefore not scaring her off. Howard could easily check into a local hotel if things weren't looking up at his uncle's house.

He was still watching the ocean when he heard footsteps behind him. He turned around, expecting to see Graham, after all. A stranger stood there, though, smiling slightly. Surprised, but not wanting to seem to be up to something, Howard stuck out his hand, salesman-like, and the man immediately shook it very heartily, one big shake before dropping it.

"Mr. Jimmers," the man said, introducing himself. He didn't look happy as he waited for Howard to explain what he was doing there, prowling around the premises. But then he didn't really look like trouble, either. His face was broad and fleshy, like a comical drawing of a gentleman toad, and he had a mess of salt-and-pepper hair. He wore a comfortable-looking wool sweater, a pair of old dungarees, and down-at-heel bedroom slippers, as if he had just been reading by the fire. He was short and squarely built, although not really fat, and might have been sixty or sixty-five.

"Howard Barton," Howard said. Then there was a silence. "I'm looking for Mr. Graham, actually. I'm from the museum, down south."

"About the Orientalia?"

"That's right." Howard was happy at that. The man knew about him. He was expected. "Roy Barton is my uncle, up in Fort Bragg." There wasn't much chance that Mr. Jimmers would know his uncle, perhaps, but it made Howard sound a little less dubious, his having an uncle in Fort Bragg.

"You don't say! Roy Barton of the spirit museum? The ghostly automobile Barton?"

Howard nodded. Apparently there was no escaping his uncle's reputation.

The look on Mr. Jimmers' face suggested that he found the whole business suspicious. He turned his head, fixing Howard with one eye and looking him up and down, as if taking his measure. "Haven't gone into the shed, have you?" Mr. Jimmers drummed his knuckles against the wall of the red and white metal shed. The car must have come very close to taking it out when it went over the cliff. In fact, there was a big crease in the side of the thing, about bumper height. It had a pair of cockeyed sliding doors, half rusted by the weather and secured by a ridiculously big lock. The idea of Howard's having "gone into" it was foolish, although a burglar with a can opener could have done it in an instant.

"Not me," Howard said. "Is Mr. Graham at home?"

Mr. Jimmers was pretty clearly off his rocker, an eccentric rustic. But despite that, Howard instantly wondered what was in the shed that he wasn't supposed to have meddled with. It sat dangerously close to the crumbling edge of the bluffs, resting up on wooden skids in the weeds. Surely they wouldn't store anything but garden tools in such a run-down shed.

A flurry of raindrops plinked down onto the metal roof, the sound reverberating hollowly inside, and for a moment it sounded as if voices could be heard within—the voices of surprised ghosts, maybe, arguing with each other. It must have been a trick of the echoing raindrops. Abruptly Mr. Jimmers squinted at Howard again, as if vaguely surprised and seeing him in a new light. Then, shading his face against the rain, which had already ceased to fall, he turned around on the path and trotted off toward the house, gesturing for Howard to follow.

When they got around to the front, Howard discovered that the truck door on the passenger side was ajar. He pulled the door open and saw that the glove box was open, too, and nearly empty. His paperweight was gone along with almost everything else: a box of fuses and odds and ends of spare change, nuts and bolts, an air gauge, pencils, an unopened package of Mr. Zog's surfboard wax, and ten years' worth of useless kipple— most of it completely worthless to whoever stole it. He'd very nearly been cleaned out, although none of it was valuable except the paperweight. They'd left him the brownie and the decals— most of them, anyway; the pelican was gone.

Mr. Jimmers held the arched door of the house open, and Howard slammed out of the truck and hurried up the curving walk toward the porch. "Shoes not allowed," said Mr. Jimmers. Howard took his off and left them by the door, sitting neatly alongside three other pairs.

"Someone stole everything in the glove compartment," Howard said, "including a glass paperweight that cost me nearly two hundred dollars. Can you believe that?" It occurred to him for the first time that Mr. Jimmers himself was suspect, but he took another look at the man and gave the notion up.

Mr. Jimmers wasn't paying attention, though, but was looking out at the evening sky. "I thought you'd brought rain with you for a moment," he said, sighing afterward and giving Howard one of his shrewd, sideways glances. "My advice is to keep your car doors locked. They'll rob you blind—like crows. They've got a fearful appetite for any kind of junk, especially little things. Steal the buttons off your coat if you let them. They go through the local parks carrying paper sacks, picking up all manner of stuff—bottle caps, bits of colored glass, anything they find on the ground. They'll steal your kitchen utensils right off the table, too."

"Who?" asked Howard.

"The whole damned crowd of them," Jimmers said, polishing his glasses on his vest. "They stay away from me, though. I'm a mean outfit, and they know it. 'Give Mr. Jimmers the road'— that's what they say when they see me coming. 'No quarter,' that's my motto. It's a good one, too. I recommend it to you. You're from down south, aren't you?"

"That's right," Howard said, wondering what in the hell the man was talking about and whom he didn't want to give any quarter to. "Who is it again?"

"Gluers is what they're called. They work a couple of communes back in the woods, up above the fog line. They put out the Sunberry products, natural foods. Very healthful. Always building, too. They built half of this house." He gestured at the stone walls and the open beamed ceiling. "They were . . . fond of Graham, you might say. Very nearly worshipped him. Looked after him like he was royalty. You won't see much of them, though. They don't come into town much. But leave your car door unlocked and see if they don't rob you blind. They've got a crow's eyesight for any damned kind of bauble and nut."

"Thanks for the warning," Howard said.

"Well . . ." Mr. Jimmers shook his head darkly. "You've got a lot to learn, my boy. You people from down south . . . It's not like that up here. My advice to you is to learn it quick, too, because there's those up here that will give you less quarter than I will. Gluers aren't the worst of them, either. Far from it. You might find friends among them before you're through, depending on who you *really* are. Take me, now. I've got a wooden keg, down in the shop. I toss in any old thing—the odd screw and washer, bent nails, the broken-off heads of tin toys. First Sunday of every other month, starting in January, I leave it out on the meadow. Next morning it's empty. They respect me for that. I'm hard, but I treat them right if they let me."

Howard nodded. "I think I see," he said, although he didn't, really. The heads of tin toys? It wasn't like *what* up here?

Mr. Jimmers put a fatherly hand on his shoulder. "You'll see a lot more before you're done. You can take my affidavit on that. You can put everything you know into your hat, and still have room for the rabbit. And don't for a moment think you can swindle me, either. Did I tell you I was an astronomer? I believe there to be a flat constellation—two-dimensional—made up of five stars in the shape of a chalice. Nobody's made out the shape of it because it's tilted exactly perpendicular to the rotation of the earth. The dog star, Sirius, is at the base, and points the true direction of the celestial mill wheel. There's a cosmic wind, though, that's about to blow it around edgewise, and when it does . . ." He shook his head. "Do you believe me?"

"Of course," Howard said, thinking to himself that the man was pretty clearly a fourteen-carat loony. Mention of the celestial mill wheel might have thrown Howard pretty hard, except that it was too mixed up with nonsense. That's what was in the shed, probably, the two-dimensional constellation. Mr. Jimmers didn't seem dangerous, though. "Is that your observatory? Out in the shed?" Howard smiled, thinking to humor the man, but realizing too late that what he had said might be taken for an insult.

"What do you know about the shed?" Mr. Jimmers asked, suddenly wary. "Did you go into it?"

"No," Howard said. "I don't know anything. Not a thing. I just got here." The conversation had gone off down a foggy tangent. He decided to take a stab at changing it. "So where is Mr. Graham?" he asked again.

"Dead," Mr. Jimmers replied.

 3

"DEAD?"

Mr. Jimmers nodded seriously and sadly, but still with an air of suspicion, as if to suggest that Howard, maybe, knew more about the business than he was admitting. "He went over the cliff just a couple of weeks ago. That's his car down on the rocks. A man can't survive such a fall as that. Body was never found. It's my notion that he was thrown clear of the wreckage. Longshore currents probably swept him down south by now. You'd have done better to stay home and waited for *him*."

Dazed, Howard followed Mr. Jimmers into an ill-lit sort of living room. "You don't have such a thing as a drink around the house, do you?" Howard asked. This was no time for being polite. His stomach was curiously hollow. His plans had been thrown for a loop, and he was somehow certain that his entire life had altered course on the instant.

Mr. Jimmers looked a little puzzled about the mention of a drink, as if he couldn't quite see the point in it, but he nodded after a moment and stepped along, disappearing into yet another room. Howard heard the satisfying clink of glass against glass. At least that sounded right to him—almost the only familiar sound he could remember having heard in a week.

The house was cold, with a stone floor and roughly plastered stone walls. Candles guttered in little hollows, making the room look like a shrine, but not lighting it up enough to do any real good. The fireplace was built of stone, too, and clinker brick, and all of it, the whole room, was stony cold, despite the hearty-looking fire. Howard stepped up closer to it, wondering if he could remember which of the stones disguised the cavity where the sketch had been hidden fifteen years past. Nothing was visible, though, no cracked joint or missing mortar.

His feet were nearly frozen, and he held them in front of the fire, wiggling his toes. He would have liked to keep his shoes on or else go out to the truck now for a second pair of socks. It was dark and foggy outside, though, and the truck was invisible through the murk, and there were odd thieves lurking in the woods.

He thought again about the paperweight stolen from the glove box—a two-hundred-dollar lesson. And now Graham was dead, too . . .

He patted his coat pocket, where he had Graham's letter. Thank God he hadn't left it in the cab of the truck. He half wanted to show it to Mr. Jimmers straight off, before the probate courts, or whoever it was, hauled Graham's possessions away and the sketch was forever lost. But then who the hell *was* Mr. Jimmers, anyway? The man was tolerably comfortable there. Or at least he went around with the air of someone who had made himself at home. And then there was the strange business of the shed . . . Suddenly Howard wanted very much to get a glimpse inside it—just a little peek.

But that was childish, wasn't it? If he were caught fooling around in either the shed or the fireplace, it might botch up the whole business of the Hoku-sai sketch, which had already gotten pretty shaky. He noticed right then that the walls were full of paintings and photographs and no end of wall hangings of one sort or another. In the dim light it was impossible to make any of them out clearly. Howard stepped over to have a look at a few of them.

Most of what hung on the walls wasn't of any note—reproductions of hunting scenes and of women with flowing hair and dressed in clothes that couldn't have been worn seriously during any historical era. There were some grisly-looking African masks and some wooden puppets and a wall-hung china cabinet crammed full of depression glass. Where in the world was Mr. Jimmers? Or more to the point, where was the drink?

He wandered into the next room, taking the direction that Jimmers had taken. This second room was brighter, having an honest-to-goodness electrical lamp burning in it. He wondered what the point of the candles was. Maybe Mr. Jimmers was the atmospheric type. He remembered this room all at once— the oriental carpets, the confusion of oak furniture, the wooden chandelier.

There on the wall were three badly framed, collodion photographs, antiques, hanging in a vertical row. He remembered those suddenly, from a class in Pre-Raphaelite photography that he had taken in graduate school. The photos had been taken by John Ruskin—when? 1855? 1860? They were very old, anyway, and, if they were authentic, might be worth a fortune to the right collector. He peered at them, unbelieving. He knew what they were now, although he hadn't known when he saw them years ago—three of Ruskin's Tintern Abbey photographs.

Ten years ago Howard had eyes for nothing but the work of the Pre-Raphaelite Brotherhood, and he had struggled through Ruskin's *The Seven Lamps of Architecture* and his rambling lectures on the Pre-Raphaelites. He was fascinated at least partly by his knowledge that Michael Graham himself was the great-grandson of James Graham, the Pre-Raphaelite photographer. But there had been more to his study than that. John Ruskin had been a curiously enigmatic figure—a sexually impotent genius surrounded by a cabal of artistic zealots who were strangely loyal to him and to his fierce esthetic desire to embody nature in art.

Anyway, it made sense that Michael Graham possessed these photographs. He had probably been willed them. Fancy them

28

having hung on the wall all these years, gathering dust. The house was a treasure trove of collectible stuff.

He was suddenly aware that Mr. Jimmers was regarding him from the doorway. He held a glass in one hand and a wine bottle in the other. Howard would rather it was a beer bottle, but right now that didn't seem to matter half as much to him as did the letter in his pocket. "I was wondering about the Japanese sketch," Howard said, getting straight down to business. Mr. Jimmers knew why he had come; he might as well say what he meant.

"So was I," Mr. Jimmers said. "What do you know about it?"

"Nothing. Not beyond Mr. Graham's having offered it to the museum." He pulled the letter out of his coat and held it up.

"And you've come up after it, have you? After all this time? What compelled you? Was it greed, or something else? I've always been a student of compulsion, and I see something in your eyes that intrigues me."

Howard gave him a look that wasn't meant to be intriguing. What was this? Suddenly he was being interrogated. Suspicions were being aired.

"This thievery nonsense," Mr. Jimmers continued, "this imaginary glass bauble gone from your pickup truck—that could easily be a clever ruse, couldn't it? An effort to throw suspicion elsewhere, to make it look as if you, too, were the victim of these thieves." He nodded shrewdly and then nodded again in the general direction of the wall. "It's been stolen, hasn't it?"

"What? My truck?" Howard took a panicked step toward the door before realizing that Mr. Jimmers wasn't talking about the truck or the paperweight. He meant the sketch. "Stolen? When? I've been a week on the road . . ." Howard found himself speaking in a tone of denial, explaining himself, laying out an alibi.

"A week? Driving up from L.A.? A day would have done it. Eleven hours, say. What if, my mysterious stranger, you've been skulking around up here for days?" Mr. Jimmers raised his eyebrows theatrically. "I'm thinking that you might be the one to shed some light on the business of the missing sketch, and perhaps on poor Graham's murder, too."

"Murder!" Howard almost shouted.

For the space of twenty seconds Jimmers stared at him, letting the idea soak in. Then suddenly he laughed out loud, bending a little at the waist and slapping his knee. Apparently he had only been fooling, playing a little game with the bumpkin from down south. He was suddenly cheerful. He ran his hand through his hair, frazzling it, and then strode toward Howard, holding out the glass, his face stretched into a toad-like grin.

"Cheer up," he said. "You can't trust anyone nowadays, can you? They'll rob you from east to west if they get a chance. 'Beard them in their den,' that's the byword around here. And if you can't, then beard them somewhere else." He winked like a conspirator and pulled at the strap of his suspender, letting it snap against his chest. "Come along upstairs," he said, taking the bottle and glass with him. "I've got something to show you."

Howard wondered if he'd ever get a chance at the wine. He was vastly relieved, though. The sketch must be all right, after all. Mr. Jimmers had hidden it upstairs, fearing thieves. The man was a crank, a joker, but he was wily. There was no use getting mad at him or trying to second-guess him. But how about this business about old Graham? *Had* he been murdered? And if he had, why? Who would bother to murder a ninety-year-old?

He followed along up the stairs, winding around past a second-story landing and then onto a third, where there was a stained-glass window looking out into the darkness. The window depicted what might be a wall built of salmon-shaped stones, or else a dry river littered with flopping fish. In front of it lay a broken Humpty Dumpty, and racing down out of the wooded hills beyond were two strangely shaped automobiles, pieced together with delicate ribbons of copper foil and jeweled with bits of faceted glass.

That's where I got the Humpty Dumptys from, Howard thought, relieved just a little bit. He had no doubt seen the window years ago and had carried the Humpty Dumpty around with him since, hiding back in the shadows of his mind. He reminded himself that there was almost always some reasonable, day-today explanation for even the weirdest aspects of one's dreams. The notion satisfied him for about fifteen seconds, and then it occurred to him that this window might just as easily be another mystery and not any sort of explanation at all.

He hadn't any time to study it out, though, because Mr. Jimmers opened a door into the attic right then, and leaned in to switch on the light. He stepped back to let Howard into a broad room with exposed rafters and roof sheathing and the undersides of shingles. Two big leaded windows were boxed into the roof, serving as skylights, and there were two more windows in the wall that looked out on the ocean. There was a seven-inch telescope on wheels in the corner and star charts on the wall around it. An oak desk and a couple of comfortable-looking

Morris chairs with low footstools sat in the center of the room. Books lined the walls, stacked up sideways and endways and ready to tumble off the edges of shelves. The room was heavy with the smell of pipe tobacco.

"Keep the bottle," Mr. Jimmers said.

"Sorry?" asked Howard, turning around.

Mr. Jimmers still stood outside in the hall. He had set the wine bottle and the glass on the floor just inside the room. He waved, wiggling his fingers by his ear, and then shut the door. Howard heard the click of the lock being thrown before he'd taken half a step forward. A tiny panel opened in the door, and Mr. Jimmers peered back in. Howard could just see his nose and eyes. "Ham sandwich suit you?" Mr. Jimmers asked.

Howard didn't answer. He stood there mystified and furious. "Think of this as a credentials check," Mr. Jimmers said. "Imagine that you've just made a border crossing into eastern Europe and you're being detained while the authorities have a look at your papers. Is everything in order, they wonder, or do we beat him with rubber hoses?"

Laughing, Mr. Jimmers shut the panel, and there was the sound of his footsteps descending the stairs. Then there was silence. Howard waited for him, expecting the door to open again at any moment. Certainly this was another joke. Mr. Jimmers had a sense of humor that had been honed in outer space.

When the panel opened again, though, ten minutes later, Mr. Jimmers clearly wasn't in any mood to let Howard out. He shoved a ham sandwich through the hole, and then a bag of Fritos and a too-ripe banana. Then he poked the comer of a quilt through, and Howard gratefully enough hauled the whole thing into the room, like a magician pulling an immense scarf through the mouth of a tiny bottle. "Watch the heater," Mr. Jimmers said. "Might blow a fuse if you're not careful." Then the panel slid shut and he was gone.

Apparently Howard was being kidnapped. He *had* been kidnapped. That part was over and done. What should he do? Threaten? Scream? Bang against the door with a tin cup? He didn't have a tin cup. And anyway, the entire adventure was so monumentally crazy that he almost certainly didn't see the whole picture yet. Mr. Jimmers was up to something subtle. Surely in a few minutes . . .

He waited, but Mr. Jimmers didn't return. The man was gone. Howard *was* kidnapped, shut up in an attic in an old stone house perched on a lonely cliff. Abruptly he was stricken with fear. It washed over him like a sea wave, and he walked across to the door and pounded on it. "Hey!" he shouted. "What the hell!" His voice was loud and foreign-sounding, and he immediately fell silent, not liking the noise. He listened, but could hear nothing except the pounding of the waves out on the reefs. He strode back and forth, furious with Jimmers, clenching and unclenching his fists at the utter irrational helplessness of things and wishing in his heart that he was home again, sitting in his own living room with his stereo going. He wondered why on earth he had left; what had possessed him?

He tried shouting again, but it was no good, and after a half hour passed and Mr. Jimmers hadn't reappeared, Howard resigned himself to his fate. There was no dignity, anyway, in screaming and flailing and demanding things. His best bet was to play the role of someone utterly confident but getting a little tired of it all. Surely Jimmers wouldn't keep him prisoner long. There was no point to it. But then what point had there been to anything lately? He was starting to feel a little like Alice, lost in a north coast wonderland.

He stood up suddenly and tried the two doors in the east wall. One was a half-full closet; the other was a bathroom with a toilet and a sink. He turned the water on and off. There were soap and a drinking glass on the sink and an electric space heater on the floor, which he pulled out and plugged into the only wall socket he could find. To hell with blowing a fuse; it was better than freezing to death.

The attic was well equipped, anyway. A man could pass many a pleasant month there, what with Mr. Jimmers pushing food through the door panel and all. Howard walked hurriedly to the windows, pulling one open. Foggy air blew in, smelling of wet rocks and the ocean. It would be easy enough to slide out through the window, except that it was a hundred and fifty feet to the rocks below. The back edge of the house was a mere continuation of the rocky cliff. In a pinch he could cut the quilt apart, using his teeth, maybe, and fashion a rope ladder. He would contrive to steal a spoon and would sharpen it on the stone walls, devising a weapon. Of course if he were only fed sandwiches, he would never get hold of a spoon . . .

He laughed out loud, shutting the window and then wrapping himself in the quilt. This was too bizarre to be believed. He shuffled across to the door. Thank heaven for small comforts, he thought, picking up the wine bottle and examining the label.

Almost instantly his spirits plummeted again. "Wild Blackberry Wine," it stated proudly, "Sunberry Farms." Below that was a Norman Rockwell-like drawing of a woman in a patchwork gown picking blackberries from vines that grew out of the engine compartment of a Studebaker turned into a sort of garden. Roses sprouted from the backseat and daisies grew out of the roof. The fenders were spiked with the suggestive tips of asparagus, thrusting from the tires. A peach tree shoved up out of the trunk, its branches heavy with fruit. Below the drawing was the legend "Natural and Healthful."

"Curiouser and curiouser," Howard said out loud. Then, steeling himself, he tilted the bottle back and tasted the wine. He grimaced and put it back down by the door again, his mouth filled with the sour taste of weeds and unripe berries. Clearly this was another of Jimmers' little gags. This wasn't wine at all; it was some sort of fluid used for polishing pan bottoms.

He went into the bathroom to fill his glass with water. Then he sat down on one of the Morris chairs to think things through. Even then he half believed that the door would swing open and Jimmers would let him out. His plans had disintegrated at a startling rate, only to be replaced by oddly disconcerting patterns and implications and dreamlike suggestions, and he felt a little like a fish swimming in a dark river and just getting its first startled glimpse of the slowly encircling net. He thought up explanations for Mr. Jimmers' behavior, abruptly remembering the oceanic Volkswagen bus and how weirdly compulsive it had seemed. Along with everything else—the stained-glass window, the wine label, the ubiquitous Studebaker, the glove-compartment theft— it argued that the north coast was its own universe, hidden by weather and isolation and mist, and working according to its own set of natural laws. Thinking about it was unsettling.

Years back there had been a lot of serious cult activity along the coast—severed heads perched on guardrail posts, disappeared hitchhikers, blood rituals on deserted beaches. He wondered uneasily what had happened to all of that, whether the cultists had gotten day jobs and were working at the pulp mills now, or whether they were still out there, lurking in the deep woods.

And who *had* stolen the stuff out of his truck? What had Jimmers called them? Gluers? What the hell was that? And when you came right down to it, who was Mr. Jimmers? Maybe the high priest of some fungal religion. No, Howard thought. That was unlikely. He was clearly too settled in here, with his books and telescope and all. He had lived here for years, and old Graham wouldn't have put up with any oddball shenanigans from his boarders.

Howard couldn't remember having gone into the attic when he stayed in the house fifteen years ago. Maybe Mr. Jimmers had been living here even then, holed up, searching the skies for his unlikely constellation. There had been other boarders at the time, besides him and Sylvia. He remembered an herbalist, very proud of his profession, and the Bay Area artist who drew underground comics—the man Stoat, whom Sylvia had nearly married years later.

Howard hadn't liked the man even then, before Sylvia had anything to do with him, or at least Howard told himself so. He was artsy and theatrical in the worst way. He had worn a single black glove back then and had called himself by a different alias. What the hell was it? Something idiotic. Morc, that was it. Morc of Fomoria. Black Hand Comics. The adventures of the Kings of the Night. He was a Norwegian, tall and blond and handsome— Aryan to a fault.

Besides him and the herbalist, there had been a crowd of standard-issue coastal hippies who worked for Graham as day laborers, coming and going out of the hills and along Highway One. Hadn't one of them driven a car that was glued over with something? Howard searched his memory. Clock parts. That was it—gears and springs and lenses. All manner of dismantled clocks and watches. The hood ornament was a brass sundial.

Thinking of his stay there reminded him of Sylvia—her face mostly. Howard had been timid back then, a tendency that was often mistaken for standoffishness. He wasn't so timid anymore, and couldn't afford to be if his stay in the north coast was going to amount to anything at all. His hanging around Sylvia certainly hadn't amounted to anything, although both of them had agreed on the night he brought her the lily that all was for the best. You didn't carry on with your cousin. Or did you? There wasn't any law against it, strictly speaking.

He realized abruptly that the passing years hadn't settled anything at all, hadn't made anything clear to him. He wondered idly whether she was as pretty now as she had been then, and whether she was still as full of momentary passions. She had been able to find almost anything and anybody interesting and worthwhile—one of those people who were so essentially good and honest that they thought everyone else was, too. Howard always expected to hear that she had bought real estate in a Florida swamp.

Stoat himself had been a sort of Florida swamp, Howard thought. Sylvia was like her father when it came to being gullible. Uncle Roy had been a moderately successful salesman when he was younger because he always believed so completely in whatever he was trying to sell, no matter its flaws. People and things were allowed to have flaws.

Perhaps that's why Howard had always found it so easy to be around Sylvia. She gave him the same break she gave everyone else. Also, she had always made plain things nice, somehow. She was a knockout in thrift-store clothes. He would have flown coast-to-coast to eat the plainest sort of casserole if she had made it. There would have been a flowered tablecloth on the table, and cut flowers, and there wouldn't have been any trace of self-consciousness in any of it, or in her cook-with-honey, mother-nature ways that made the simplest chores seem like a sort of dance. He wasn't the only one who saw her like that, either, and that had bothered him. He had always wished that she was his secret, but she wouldn't submit to being anybody's secret.

Howard sighed. He let his mind spin, feeling a little guilty about dredging up old jealousies and passions. All that was water under the bridge, wasn't it, no matter what he ran into on the north coast? Or who. He got up abruptly and walked across to where the wall plaster was discolored or smudged. It wasn't just a smudge; it was something set into the plaster, its color showing through.

He rubbed at it, curious, and the thin coat of plaster covering it chipped off. Underneath was a small, convex bit of metal, painted red. He hesitated for a moment and then decided that prisoners were allowed, even expected, to chip away at the walls of their cell. Following tradition, he dug around the metal with his pocket knife, discovering it, strangely, to be the fender of a toy car. There were other objects, too, under the curve of the fender, as if the collection were meant to be a tiny shrine.

He cleaned the plaster away carefully, like an archeologist at a dig, exposing first a carven Japanese god. Howard recognized it. It was Dai-Koku, the god of luck, carrying the tools that he used to dig out the treasures of the earth. There was a steel dog, too, out of a Monopoly game, and a clay marble and a little stoppered perfume bottle, stained purple by the sun and containing what looked like a sprig of dried violets.

Hastily he considered what he knew about Michael Graham—not very much, obviously. Plastering these odd miniatures into the wall couldn't have been his work, though, not unless Howard had misjudged him wildly. Graham hadn't been frivolous in any way at all. He worked from sunup to sundown, ate plain food, read his Bible, went to sleep. Howard had seen him fish once, off the rocks in the cove, but that seemed to have been the only lighthearted sort of activity he allowed himself. There was no way on earth that he would have been so full of momentary fun as to plaster toys up in a wall.

And if they hadn't been so near the surface, they would have remained hidden forever, until the house fell down. They weren't meant as decoration; they were meant as something else entirely.

Howard ran his hand across the wall below them, suspicious that there might be more buried there. There was a suggestive bump, and immediately he chiseled away at it, scraping the plaster off in a little dusty cloud. Underneath, still half hidden, were the red-glazed soles of Humpty Dumpty's shoes.

4

THERE was something about lilies that was attractive to Heloise Lamey—their heavy, fleshy flowers, perhaps, or the way the flower stalks thrust up through the earth, reminding her of a certain kind of lush scene in a D. H. Lawrence novel, although she would never admit this to anyone. They were easily susceptible to mutation, too, and color alteration. Their odor, when they had any, was most often intense and repulsive, as if they were dense with the stuff of decay, of excretion and death.

Her front-yard garden was laid out in orderly rows. It wasn't the sort of garden she would have chosen to lay out if she were gardening for the mere enjoyment of it. She did almost nothing, though, for the mere enjoyment of it. She had come over the years to lead a life of purpose, void of mere entertainment.

Across the street, nailed to the roof of a house, sat a plywood Humpty Dumpty the size of a man. It was still and inanimate in the windless morning—a small blessing. Onshore breezes would stir it up in the afternoon, and it would undertake its eternal waving, along with all the other wind-driven gewgaws in her neighbor's front lawn. Movement for the sake of movement, that's what it was. His wooden gizmos had no object that she could fathom, other than simply to drive her mad. They were utterly frivolous. She would contrive to deal with them, though, and with him, sooner or later.

For the moment she concentrated her energies on her garden, which was a geometric copy, row for row, of the vegetable garden planted somewhere by her half brother, Michael Graham, a man with an authentic green thumb. Lord knew where his garden lay. She hadn't actually seen it, just as she hadn't ever seen his garden at the cliff house. But she had understood the design of that garden, too. She had felt it in her joints, as a person with arthritis feels pending rain. She had never felt it so clearly, though, as she had since her recent trip to San Francisco.

She had planted eight rows of flowers, all hybrid tubers and bulbs. There was still more to plant. On her porch sat a half dozen pots of dye, all of it mixed up out of things of the earth—berries and roots, autumn leaves and iron filings and blood. Two sea hares nosed around in a bucket of clear ocean water. She had hauled them out of a tidal pool a half hour ago. Carefully she picked one of them up, holding it by the head over a clean glass bowl, and began to squeeze it, gingerly at first and then harder when it wouldn't give up its ink. A rush of viscous, vivid-purple fluid gushed out into the bowl. She let it drip for a moment, then tossed the creature into a clean ceramic jar. She picked up the second sea hare and milked it of its ink, too, pitching it into the jar along with the first.

Then, very carefully, she unstoppered a jar of hydrochloric acid, sizzling the liquid in over the writhing bodies of the two sea hares. Within moments they were still, their soft flesh disintegrating in the shallow pool of acid. She had no idea at all what would come of cooking the two creatures down, but the acid was already turning an interesting color of greenish brown. Traces of the purple ink trailed out of the things, deepening the color nicely.

Nearby lay the two forearm bones she had brought back from San Francisco. When she told the Reverend White, very truthfully, that she was going to turn them into a dowsing rod, he had shrugged. He hadn't understood it, but he knew her too well to doubt her. The bones were connected now at the elbow end, lashed together with strips of animal hide and ivy vine. He had supplied some of the animal hide, too—the more interesting fragments—although necessarily in strips too small to do any real tying up. She had contrived to weave them into the lashings, though, along with the rest. The result wasn't pretty, and for a week it had smelled worse than almost anything she could think of, but the awful smell had faded as the object dried out.

Picking up the V-shaped dowser, she limped into a clear spot in the garden, focusing her concentration on the earth, on dirt and humus and worms and percolating rainwater. She closed her eyes and pictured the symphony of movement in the soil—roots unfurling, creeping downward; billions of grains of earth shifting, settling, giving way; rock decomposing; leaves and dead roots rotting; seeds opening and pushing toward the surface; ants and moles and gophers and earthworms creeping along in the darkness; the entire surface of the dry world stirring, crawling, heaving with motion just as steadily and surely as the surface of the sea.

The tip of the dowser bent downward, drawn toward the soil, twisting in her hands so that she could barely hold on to it. "Cabbages," she said out loud. It was as if she had seen them herself, like slide film played against the back of her eyelids. He had put out cabbages. She opened her eyes and swayed there, nearly losing her balance and blinded by the bright sunlight. With an effort she managed to clear her mind, bringing herself back around to her own garden. She marked the spot with a piece of stick, and then using the dowser again, she traced out the row, some twelve feet of it, wondering what to plant there, what sort of maleficent vegetation might wither his cabbages.

She worked by instinct. Someday soon she would know where his garden was hidden, where *he* was hidden, and she would have a look at her handiwork. It struck her as funny that she was engaged in a vegetable war, probably the first in the history of the world. It was a war she must ultimately win. He was old and feeble and dying, and his power was dying with him.

She fetched a trowel from the porch and began to dig holes in the dirt, humming now and laying a tuber in the bottom of each. A sea breeze ruffled her hair, and she scowled, looking without wanting to at the thing on the roof across the street. Its plywood arm caught a gust and slowly straightened out in a long, sardonic salute, jerking upright in order to repeat the gesture, probably over and over for the rest of the afternoon. She hummed louder, drowning out the world, pausing to pour sea hare ink over each tuber in turn and then filling in the holes with dirt.

HOWARD woke up stiff. Sleeping on the Morris chair had required a certain degree of exhaustion and it had taken him half the night to attain it. He had slept hard in the early hours of the morning, though, and now he felt disheveled and drooly and wrinkled, and his neck was kinked and stiff.

Abruptly he knew what had awakened him—his name had been called. A key rattled in the lock, the door swung open, and there stood Mr. Jimmers and, for God's sake, Sylvia. Howard pulled himself up and hurriedly wiped his face and ran his hands through his hair. He unwrapped himself from the quilt and stood up, the pain in his spine nearly arching him over backward. "Sylvia!" he said, trying to sound cheerful and robust but actually just croaking. He tried to clear his throat. Like a proud father, Mr. Jimmers stood beaming at Sylvia, the look on his face seeming to assure Howard that although he had waited a long time for this moment, the wait must clearly have been worth it.

He was right. Sylvia seemed not to have aged. Her skin had the same pale cast to it, almost a translucence, and her hair was full and dark and an absolute sculptured mess. She wore red lipstick, too, which was gaudy, but right at the moment she seemed custom-built for gaudy, even though it wasn't what Howard remembered or expected. And her eyes were larger than he remembered them, too. She reminded him of a woman out of a Rossetti painting, modernized with twentieth-century makeup and natural, handmade-looking clothes. She would have looked terrific even in a flour sack or a mu-mu. Almost laughing at him, she said, "You look awful."

"Do I?" he managed to say. He was flattered, somehow, that she would say such a thing to him, willing to joke around when they hadn't seen each other or even spoken in years. He tried to think of a way to quit looking awful, but there wasn't any.

"Utterly awful. It's my fault that you had to sleep in a chair all night, too. Mr. Jimmers couldn't get through to me until this morning, because I was out late. He said that he had a man locked into the attic who might be a thief and murderer but claimed to be my cousin. We didn't expect you until the end of the week, actually."

"I got impatient. Solitude wears you out after a while."

"And you've had years of it, haven't you? No wonder you look like you do." She smiled at him, clearly assuming that his sense of humor had held up. She might easily have seen him last week. It was as if there were nothing about him that she had forgotten, which either was a good thing or wasn't. Howard wasn't awake enough to tell yet, but he remembered that this was another reason he had never gotten rid of his memories of her.

He dropped the quilt and managed a smile. He was a fairly ridiculous sight. The whole adventure in the attic was funny as hell if you looked at it right, through the Sylvia spectacles, so to speak. He realized that he was staring at her, and he looked away, bending over suddenly to pick up the quilt from the chair. He folded it carefully.

"And I'm awfully sorry about all this," Mr. Jimmers said to Howard. "There's been dirty work recently, though, what with Mr. Graham going off the cliff and all. Things along the north coast are . . . unsettled, you might say, and your sudden appearance, I'm afraid, was fraught with suspicion. I hope you forgive me."

"Sure," said Howard. "Not at all. Of course I do." Forgiving him was easy all of a sudden. He was a friend of Sylvia's, after all. Howard wondered exactly how he was a friend of Sylvia's, and whether he could use that friendship to pry the sketch out of Jimmers. This was no time for that sort of selfish thinking, though. He would tackle Mr. Jimmers some other time. He'd had enough of the man for the moment.

Mr. Jimmers hurried across the room just then and pulled the plug on the space heater, looking skeptically at the frayed cord. He threw open one of the windows. "Close in here," he said, wrinkling up his face. Then he caught sight of the chiseled wall, blinked at it in surprise, started to say something, and fell silent. He picked up Howard's pocket knife, which still lay open on the desk. "Burrowing out through the wall?" he asked, gesturing at the hacked plaster. Sylvia looked at it, seeming mildly surprised. "This man is a curious man," Mr. Jimmers said to Sylvia. "You must always be a tiny bit vigilant around a man who suspects that things are hidden in the walls." He closed the knife and handed it across carefully.

Sylvia peered more closely at the plaster now. "Things *are* hidden in the walls," she said to Mr. Jimmers.

"I wonder if this man didn't put them there himself," Jimmers said.

"I . . . Of course I didn't. How would I have done that?" Howard found himself fumbling again. Mr. Jimmers couldn't seem to stop pummeling him with nonsense.

40

Jimmers shrugged, as if he would believe Howard mainly out of politeness. "Well," he said. "I'm nearly certain that you *would* have put them there, if you'd been given half a chance. Don't you think so, Sylvia?"

"Of course he would have. So would I. I think right now, though, that I have to get back to the shop. Some of us have to work. Where are you going?" she asked Howard.

"Why . . . I thought I'd drive up to Uncle Roy's," he said. "Up to your place. You're still there, I guess."

She nodded.

He felt a little like he was inviting himself, despite his having sent the letter telling them that he was coming—which is to say, the letter inviting himself.

"It isn't any sort of palace," she said.

"I don't need a palace, really. I'm not the palace type."

"You never were," she said, and she stepped across and kissed him on the cheek in a sisterly way. "Father is a little down on his luck right now. He's not what you'd call solvent. I think you two will hit it off, though."

Howard couldn't remember a time when Uncle Roy *wasn't* down on his luck. He was a *businessman*—something that he would tell you proudly, making the word sound less generic than it really was. But as a businessman he was a spectacular failure. He had done moderately well as a salesman when he was younger, then managed to force a living out of the pet store trade for a few years. But then he had sold the business and borrowed heavily to open the spirit museum, which had cooked his goose financially.

"I want to help out," Howard said. "I haven't done anything for the last two years but squirrel money away."

"Father isn't fond of charity," Sylvia said flatly. "I wouldn't bring it up to him."

"I didn't mean that. I meant that I don't want to mooch off him or anything."

Mr. Jimmers appeared to be uncomfortable listening to the two of them talk. He edged toward the door, as if to hurry things along. It was checkout time for Howard.

Sylvia beamed her smile at him again and fingered the quartz crystal that hung around her neck on a copper chain. "Duty calls," she said, turning to leave. "Can you find the house all right?"

"Sure," Howard said. "No problem. I've got the address." Suddenly he wanted nothing more than to be out of there—out of the attic and out of the house. He wanted elbowroom and space to think, to rearrange what he knew about the world. He realized that his shirt was half untucked, so he shoved it back in, excusing himself and heading for the door of the bathroom. Mr. Jimmers went out, following Sylvia, and when Howard appeared downstairs a few moments later, Mr. Jimmers asked him if he wanted breakfast. "My hospitality hasn't been worth much so far," he said, looking abruptly downcast. "I'm a scientist, in my way, an inventor, and I'm afraid that I overlook the niceties sometimes. I live rough, you see, with no one to care for but myself . . ."

This was a new Mr. Jimmers. Howard hadn't thought of that. It must be terribly lonely, living out on the deserted bluffs like this. And now with Graham dead, maybe murdered, Mr. Jimmers was alone and pretty clearly frightened of strangers, and rightfully so.

"I'm afraid that all I've got are these cans of chop suey," Mr. Jimmers said, hauling one of them out of the cupboard. "You can scramble them up with eggs. It's not bad, actually, on toast. Pity we don't have any toast. The sandwiches last night were the end of the bread. I've got salt, though. I don't eat breakfast myself. It runs my metabolism ragged, breakfast does. I take a cup of Postum, actually, with hot water out of the tap in order to flush the system."

"Thanks," said Howard, trying to sound sincere. "I've got to get up to Fort Bragg, though. I'm not a breakfast man, either."

Jimmers put the chop suey away. "Cup of Postum, then?"

Howard held up a restraining hand. "System's fine. I'll just run, I think. The ham sandwich last night was tip-top, though."

"You're too kind," said Jimmers, ushering him through the room with the fireplace and out toward the front door, where Howard fetched his shoes back. Having sat outside through the foggy night, they felt damp and sticky to the touch. The truck heater would dry them. "Goodbye, then," said Mr. Jimmers, starting to close the door as soon as Howard stepped out onto the front stoop. "Nice of you to drop by."

The sky was clear and blue and the air was cold. Out over the ocean the fog lay like a gray blanket, but it was a long way off. The day would be a warm one, and Howard was almost cheerful, anticipating breakfast in Fort Bragg. He went around to the camper door, thinking to throw his jacket into the back. On the window, dead center, was the pelican decal. These were *gluers*, all right, just like Jimmers had said. They'd stolen the damned decal and then stuck it onto the first window they'd come to. Oh, well, Howard thought. That's pretty much where he would have put it, anyway. They'd saved him the work.

After a moment he drove away north, mulling over the last twenty-four hours. Mr. Jimmers had told him nothing. *Had* the sketch been stolen? Or had Mr. Jimmers put it somewhere for safekeeping? Is that what he had in the mysterious tin shed? Howard hoped not. The thing wouldn't be worth hanging in an incinerator after a week outdoors in a misty climate like this. You might as well throw it in the ocean. Howard would have to deal with Mr. Jimmers again soon. He would get Uncle Roy to help him. Maybe he could fake up some sort of story about the museum paying a commission so as to be able to slip poor old Uncle Roy a couple of hundred dollars. He'd have to be canny about it, though.

He thought momentarily about being trapped in the attic last night, how he had been scared half witless and then had been furious with Jimmers. It still wasn't funny. Not really. But it wasn't a matter for the police, either. There was too much that he didn't understand, too much mystery hovering on the fog. Maybe he was done with it; maybe not. He would ask Sylvia, appeal to her inherent honesty. Sylvia wasn't the cipher that Jimmers was.

Sylvia. Things had started off unevenly there. It seemed to him suddenly that he had made an off-key, Blinky the Clown impression on Sylvia. On an impulse he sucked his stomach in a little and sat up straighter, regarding himself in the mirror. He wasn't hopeless, anyway. His face was still pretty lean. Some people developed moon faces when they gained weight, but he had never had that problem. He had a rapid-fire metabolism that let him eat anything at all without regret, and he took that to be a sign of good health. At times, when he really overdid it, he developed a moderate spare tire, which, unless it got out of hand, was easy to hide. At least the north coast beaches didn't lend themselves to sunbathing. He could keep his shirt on and his stomach pulled in.

Maybe he would start jogging again, too. And no more junk food, either—no doughnuts or Twinkies. It would be a new regime, the Sunberry Farms approach, starting after breakfast, which he'd eat in Fort Bragg and which would consist of a hell of a stack of pancakes. An hour a day chopping wood for Uncle Roy wouldn't hurt him any, either. He would earn his keep is what he would do. He rolled down the window and inhaled hugely. The air was full of the ocean and the musty smell of autumn vegetation. He was surprised at how good he felt, despite having been tortured in an attic. It was a brand-new day.

Maybe he'd be better off if the Hoku-sai *were* gone. It would almost sever his connection with the museum. Over the past week the sketch had become a sort of carrot on a stick. Its having disappeared would free him, wouldn't it? If he managed to get hold of it, he'd have to haul it back down south, out of duty, and actually put together the display of Japanese artwork that he'd been mouthing off about. He had worked hard at selling the idea to Mrs. Gleason, although now he didn't know quite why. The museum seemed a long, long way off. If he walked back into it today, it would seem utterly alien to him. Before long he would forget where the paper clips were kept and how the coffee-maker worked. Maybe he had come north to stay, and he was just now realizing it.

He flicked sand out of the corner of his eye, which looked almost unnaturally blue because of the reflection of the sky in the rearview mirror. His hair was cooperating, too. It was a little long, but what the hell. He would have to shave, though. His beard, when he tried to grow one years ago, had looked like something bought cheap at a swap meet. It was getting gray, too—a constant blow to the vanity, and a reminder that the years were flying past, that he was older now. The thought sobered him just a little, and suddenly he was cold from the sea wind blowing in through the open window.

He passed the first turnoff into Mendocino and looked back into town, and there was Sylvia standing next to a yellow Toyota parked at the gas station. In an instant he lost sight of her. That's where her store was, on Main Street in Mendocino. He had heard all about her opening it up, running it on a shoestring, half her stuff selling on consignment. On impulse he turned back down Lansing Street, driving toward Main.

The gas station was empty now, which was just as well. He didn't really want her to see him and think he was skulking around, spying on her. He was just curious about her shop, about what her life had become during the years that he hadn't known her. He drove slowly down Main, surprised at the number of cars on the street. It was as if Mendocino had become a sort of shoppers' amusement park. There was the yellow Toyota, parked along the curb. He slowed, wondering which store was hers. Too many of them qualified as "boutiques."

Suddenly there she was, standing on the sidewalk in front of an ice cream store. She saw him and widened her eyes, starting to wave, actually looking happy and surprised to see him. Howard grinned, made a waving gesture of his own, and then looked away stupidly, pretending he was just passing through. He would have stopped, to explain to her that he was curious to see what she was up to, to thank her for having come to rescue him from the clutches of Mr. Jimmers. But he couldn't. Standing next to her, shaking his head and gesturing, was a tall, blond man, nicely dressed, fit-looking. He didn't wear a single black glove anymore, but Howard knew who he was.

"Shit," Howard said out loud, mad at himself for having been so utterly incapable of dealing with things. Intending to circle back toward the highway, he turned right down Albion and nearly drove straight into an oncoming car. The driver honked, shouting incoherently out the window. Shaking, Howard pulled to the shoulder, staring in disbelief at the roof of the house across the street. Fixed to the shingles, gazing placidly down at him, was a tremendous wooden egg man with a by-now familiar face. After a moment the thing waved at him. Howard drove slowly away, looking back at it once in the rearview mirror just to make sure he hadn't imagined it.

His hands shook on the steering wheel, and not entirely from the near accident. He had never before felt so cut adrift, so entirely out of his element and broken off from everything he was familiar with. He had fallen among pod people. Yesterday he had whistled a tune while he fed that pelican his fish bait and then innocently followed it up the coast. He possessed dependable road maps drawn up by the Triple A. And in his pocket, folded like a passport, was a signed letter from Michael Graham. The headlights on his truck were new and so was the battery. He had the receipt from the Pep Boys to prove it.

So what the hell had happened? He had apparently turned up the highway to Loonyville by mistake, because he was watching the pelican instead of the road map. His worries and his troubles hadn't vanished into the landscape, after all; they had merely taken new faces, and for a few idle days they had been harder to see because of the shifting shadows of north coast vegetation. He watched the cars whiz past on the highway, thinking that with a flick of his hand he could trip the right-turn blinker instead of the left and simply go home.

Opening the nearly empty glove compartment, he pulled out the Sunberry brownie, unwrapped it, and bit the corner off, unprepared for the dirt-and-ground-weeds taste of the thing. There was nothing at all in the flavor that suggested food. Even the pelican wouldn't eat such a brownie. He bundled it back up in plastic wrap and dropped it onto the floorboards. This was it—the last insult he would take. He had half a mind to drive back into town and throw the brownie at Stoat, take him straight out of the contest.

He had a pretty good picture all of a sudden of the way things had fallen out in Mendocino. A week ago Michael Graham had heard Howard's engine start up, way down in Orange County. "Let's move," he had said to Jimmers. "Break out the Humpty Dumptys." He had tottered to his feet, leaning heavily on his cane, and as one last arcane joke, he had made his way out to the garage, climbed into the old Studebaker, released the hand brake, and rolled straight off the cliff into the sea. Like the faithful subject he was, Jimmers had waited Howard out, watching through the window, giggling over the idea of giving the high sign to the gluer boys and then locking Howard into the attic, feeding him on old bananas and on wine fermented out of root mulch by the selfsame lunatics who had robbed him, finally staging the rescue by Sylvia at precisely the moment that Howard, slumped into his attic chair, had begun to drool and snore. But that hadn't been the end of it. Howard had driven off happily enough despite it all, and what had Jimmers done? He had called Stoat, probably on a car phone. "Here he comes," Jimmers had said. "Comb your hair, for God's sake, and get out there onto the sidewalk."

There was something deep going on. Howard could see that much even if he couldn't yet make out the shape of it. He watched the smoke billowing like overweight ghosts out of the Georgia-Pacific mills on the edge of Fort Bragg and realized that he was hungry. Maybe that's the trouble, he said to himself. He would attempt the patented pancake cure.

Right then, flapping its big, fateful wings, a pelican flew overhead, perpendicular to the highway, and Howard immediately turned down Harbor Drive, in order to follow it, admitting out loud that he was a born sucker.

He pulled into the parking lot of a restaurant called the Cap'n England, stopping alongside an old stake-bed truck and climbing out, noticing with a start that a waxwork dummy with a staved-in head sat on the truck bed, leaning tiredly against a half dozen cinder blocks. "Me, too," its face seemed to be saying to him as it looked sadly out at Howard from between the slats, its hair clotted with fake blood and one of its eyeballs dangling from tendrils of stretched putty. Howard gaped at it for a moment, surprised to discover that he wasn't at all surprised. Of course, he said to himself. It was the sort of thing you came to expect after a day on the coast. Locking the door of his truck, he went inside to eat.

 5

UNCLE ROY'S house lay at the end of Barnett Street, backing up against a fir grove that seemed to run on forever, up into the hills. It was a tumbledown Victorian that needed paint. Pieces of its gingerbread trim had cracked and fallen apart over the years, and here and there bits of it were broken off or hanging by rusted nails. Someone had started to patch the place up, sanding and repairing the wooden fretwork, but the work was sketchily done, a long time ago by the look of it, and the rickety two-by-four scaffolding nailed to the west side of the house where someone had once been scraping eaves had turned gray in the weather. The yard was brown and overgrown, with old yellowed newspapers, still in their rubber bands, lying discarded in the weeds.

Howard shut the motor off and sat there. He was still full of pancakes and bacon, and he had managed that morning to wash and dry a load of clothes. All his errands were finished. He had arrived at his destination, ready to knock on Uncle Roy's door and introduce himself—the long-lost nephew from down south. He felt relieved at last. He was among family again, and as run-down as the house was, there was something comfortable in the very notion that it was a shelter from the crazy hailstorm that had been pounding him since yesterday afternoon.

He eyed the house a moment longer, slowly changing his mind about it. It didn't just look run-down, he decided—it looked haunted. Uncle Roy could have opened *it* up as a spirit museum and no one would have scoffed. Ragged lace curtains blew out of an open upstairs window, and on the front porch a willow rocker tilted slowly backward, then slowly forward. Somewhere, around in back maybe, a door slammed shut in the wind. The neighborhood was quiet otherwise—empty of people.

Howard climbed out of the truck, leaving his suitcase for the moment, and stepped up the front walk to the wooden porch, where the paint in front of the door had long since been trodden away. He knocked hard. There was no use being timid about it. The door creaked open slowly on its own; there was no one there. Inside lay a dark room of heavy, shadowy furniture. Beyond the entryway stood a turned newel post at the bottom of a stairs. There was a brass lamp fixed to the top of the post—the head of a dog with illuminated glass eyes.

Howard waited, wondering who had opened the door. No one appeared. He knocked again on the casing. Maybe the door hadn't been latched, and he'd knocked it open himself. It hadn't felt like that, though; the door was too heavy. Beside him, the rocking chair creaked in the breeze. "Hello," he said, although not too loud. There was something hushed and still about the place, as if it were abandoned. It wasn't a place for shouting.

The first notes of somber organ music drifted down from upstairs somewhere, and there was a sudden banshee wail, distant and tormented like the sound of something muffled in a locked closet. A faint patch of gauzy brightness lit the stairs, and for a moment someone seemed to be standing there, halfway up. It was a woman in a lacy dress or shroud, her hands held out in supplication, her eyes wide with a sort of horrified passion.

Howard found himself backpedaling into the yard. His heart chugged like an engine. The door of the house slammed shut, and laughter echoed out of an upstairs window—the deep and throaty stage laughter common to ghosts with a sardonic sense of humor. Heavy chains rattled and the laughter turned to a tormented moaning. Then there was the amplified scratch of a needle scraping across a phonograph record, followed by a curse. "Damn it!" a voice said.

A head appeared through the lace curtains of the window just then. It was Uncle Roy, with a face like a melon. Howard hadn't remembered him as being fat. "Nephew!" he shouted, then knocked the top of his head on the window frame. "*Damn* it!" he said again. "Don't stand in the yard. Come in!"

He disappeared, and Howard climbed the porch stairs again, happy and puzzled. Clearly Uncle Roy had been expecting him. Home at last, he said to himself, and nearly laughed out loud.

Again the door opened, but it was his uncle this time, rubbing his head. He pumped Howard's hand, dragging him into the house and turning on a light, cheering the place up considerably.

"What did you think of it?" Uncle Roy asked.

"Very impressive," Howard said. "The woman on the stairs did the trick. Knocked me right back onto the lawn."

"Cheesecloth. You drape a few single layers of it across the stairs and then play a bit of film across it from a projector. You don't get much of an image, but then you don't want much of an image, do you?"

"Not for a ghost, no. That one was about right."

"It's the *effect* that's paramount here. You either have it or you don't—effect or nothing. I've learned that from studying business. I've got rubber bats, too, on pulleys, and a skeleton from the university in Sonoma. And look at this." Howard followed him into the kitchen. Uncle Roy climbed onto a step stool and pulled open a high cupboard, hauling down a jar. "Eyeballs," he said. "Honest-to-God eyeballs in alcohol."

"Really?" Howard looked at the bizarre things. They were eyeballs, all right, of various sizes, clearly not all taken from the same sorts of creatures. "What are you going to do with them?"

"Game of marbles between corpses. I've got a couple of waxwork dummies on their hands and knees. They're obvious corpses—hair all grown out and stringy, skin like a burn victim, ragged old suits of clothes . . ."

"Really?" Howard said. "I think I met one of them this morning."

His uncle nodded at him, apparently not finding the idea crazy in any way. "The trick is to have them shooting eyeballs into a ring drawn in blood. Very nice effect again. Repellent, too. Makes the public veer off, I can tell you, when they see the eyeballs. They'll pay you for it, though, and come back again and pay you some more. There's nothing the public won't pay for if you trick it out in the right kind of hat." He put the jar back into the cupboard and shut the door.

Howard reconsidered the notion of the spirit museum as a "study in the paranormal." He had been led to believe that his uncle was serious about the ghost business, that the museum had failed because he refused to ham it up with waxwork corpses and projected dead women. He had stuck by the Studebaker because it was true and right. Now here was Uncle Roy, loaded with tomfoolery and with a jar full of eyeballs in the cupboard.

49

"My boy," Uncle Roy said, turning to him suddenly and grabbing his hand again. Howard felt like the prodigal son, guilty for having stayed away so long. "How is your poor mother?"

"Very well, actually. She's feeling absolutely fine. Happy, I think."

Uncle Roy shook his head, as if Howard had said she was living in the street—on a grate, maybe, with her possessions in a bag. "I'm certain she never recovered from your father's death. None of us did. He was my brother, after all. He had his faults, but . . ." He looked at Howard suddenly, as if reading his face. "In a way it was lucky you were so young. I don't mean it's easy growing up without a father, but sometimes it's harder on an older child, one who's come to know his father. I tried in my way to make up for it, at least until we moved up here. Can you ever do enough, though?"

Howard nodded, surprised at his uncle talking like this. Uncle Roy was obviously sincere, and Howard was moved by it. He hadn't expected this. "I know you did," he said. It was true, too. It was Uncle Roy that had taken him to ball games and driven him to the beach and told him jokes and winked at him covertly on serious occasions. Now he sensed that his uncle doubted all that. He had clearly been worrying, maybe for years, that he ought to have done more for Howard. On impulse, Howard put his arms around his uncle's shoulders and hugged him, and after an awkward moment Uncle Roy hugged him back, wiping at his eyes afterward and sighing heavily. "Time passes," he said.

"That's the truth." Howard sat down in a stuffed chair. "You don't look much different, though."

"I'm a fat man now," Uncle Roy said. "I used to be fit. There was a time when I could work like a pig in the sun, all day long, and then get up the next morning and start in again. You remember those days."

Howard nodded.

"About your mother, though? How is she? Her letters sound melancholy sometimes—between the lines, if you follow me."

"No, really," Howard said. "She's doing well—working at the library, actually, putting together stock for the new bookmobile." Uncle Roy put his hand on Howard's arm, to console him, perhaps. Conversation fell flat. "Sorry just to stop past early like this," Howard said, changing the subject after a moment's silence. "I didn't mean to surprise anybody, but—"

"Not at all. We got your letter and all. This is no surprise. Sylvia called up this morning and said she'd found you in

50

Jimmers' attic, tied into a chair. That damned Jimmers . . . It gave me plenty of time to set up the woman on the stairs, though. How long can you stay?"

Howard shrugged. "My plans aren't definite yet. I don't want to put you out . . ."

Uncle Roy waved the idea into oblivion.

"Do you know this Mr. Jimmers?" Howard asked, anxious to get on to new subjects. "I'm not sure I understand him. Tied into a chair, did she say?"

"Jimmers is a case. Completely sideways, if you know what I mean. He'll be coming when the rest of the world is going. Did he tell you about his tin shed?"

"A little," Howard said uncertainly.

"What did you think of the door opening all by itself?" Uncle Roy broke into another grin.

Howard tried to fathom it, to recall one of Jimmers' doors opening all by itself. Did he mean the door of the shed?

"Sorry . . ." he started to say. Then he caught on—he meant the front door of Uncle Roy's house, just five minutes ago. "I give. How did you do it?"

Uncle Roy opened the refrigerator door and bent over to haul something out—a pickle bottle full of severed fingers, maybe. "Mechanics. Leave it at that. What did you study in school?"

"Art history, mostly. Some literature."

"Both worthless. Can't earn a living with them. Don't know anything about magnetism, do you? 'The country that controls magnetism controls the earth.' Who said that?"

Howard shook his head again. "I don't know."

"Diet Smith. I thought you read literature. Sandwich?"

"No, actually. Thanks, anyway, but I just ate breakfast."

"Not down at the Jersey Deli?"

"No, someplace down at the harbor. Captain somebody."

"That would be the Cap'n England. Owner's a pal of mine. Not a bad breakfast. Skip the Jersey Deli, though. It's last year's grease. I got a spoiled egg in there once that nearly killed me. Location's bad, too. They'll be out of business inside the year, just like the last nine jackasses that opened up there. Anyone can see it. Location is paramount." Uncle Roy slathered mayonnaise on two slices of white bread and heaped on six or eight layers of packaged cold cuts. "Pickle?" he asked, unscrewing the lid from a jar full of kosher dills.

Somehow the eyeballs were too fresh in Howard's mind. "No thanks. You go to town, though. Do it justice."

"It's early for lunch, but my life doesn't run according to schedule, if you know what I mean. No liquor before four, though. Can't have your vices wear you down. They've got to be harnessed, controlled. 'Every excess carries within it the seed of its own decay.' Sigmund Freud said that, when he was sober. The rest of what he said was dope talking. Have you read psychology?"

"Not much, I'm afraid."

"Good man." He walked back out into the living room and sat down heavily in a chair, sighing deeply, as if he'd been at it since dawn and was only now getting a rest. His jacket, which years ago might have fit him, was too tight now—a shabby tweed coat bunched tight under his arms and with the buttons in opposite hemispheres. He wore baggy cotton trousers with it and a pair of scuffed penny loafers that actually had pennies wedged in under the leather bands. He worked at his sandwich in silence.

"Hey," Howard said, suddenly remembering. "I ran into another friend of yours down in Albion. Wait a sec." He went out the door, hurrying to the truck. Uncle Roy's talk of being sober had reminded him of the beer, which he had iced up down at the laundromat. He pulled the six-pack out of the cooler, locked the camper door, and went back in. "It's a gift from Cal, at the Albion grocery. He said to tell you to stop in sometime."

"That old horse thief," Uncle Roy said, jiggling with laughter. "He used to tell the damned stupidest jokes." After a moment's thinking he said, "What do they get when they cross an ape and a mink?"

Howard shook his head.

"A hell of a coat, but the sleeves are too long." Uncle Roy laughed twice, slapping his knee hard. Then he cut it off, nearly choking on his sandwich. "Beer?" he asked, yanking a Coors out of the six-pack. He pulled the pop top and took a long swallow.

"No thanks," Howard said. "I'm full of coffee and pancakes."

"Normally I don't drink before four, like I said. But I don't look a gift horse in the mouth, either. There's bad luck in that."

Howard acknowledged that there was. His uncle finished the first beer, bent the can in half with his hands, then stomped it flat on the rug and opened a second can.

"It *has* been a while," he said finally, smoothing his hair down, although it was already straight and smooth and combed flat across the crown of his head, where the hair was thin. Getting fat had given his face a jolly and genial man-in-the-moon look, which was perfect for him.

Howard nodded. "Nearly fifteen years."

"That long? No! Really? I always wondered about you and Sylvia. Did something happen there? Is that what's kept you away?"

"No, nothing, really." He blushed despite himself. He was talking to Sylvia's father, after all, and his own uncle to boot. It didn't matter what he told himself about Sylvia, the truth had a way of making itself known. "You know how that is," he said. "Four or five hundred miles might as well be a million. You write, you quit writing. There's no excuse for it really, and no reason, either." He gestured uneasily.

Uncle Roy and Aunt Edith had come to live in Los Angeles after Howard's father died. Howard and Sylvia had been toddlers then, and for the next eighteen years had been down-the-street neighbors. Then his uncle and aunt had moved north to Fort Bragg, where life was less expensive and where, his uncle had been fond of saying, a man could carve his niche. Uncle Roy had done that, in his way, although it was a strangely shaped niche.

"What about all of you?" Howard asked. "How's Aunt Edie?"

"She's well." Uncle Roy jerked his thumb toward the door. "She's downtown, doing the grocery shopping. Damn crust," he said, dangling the edge of his sandwich over his plate. He pulled the two strips of crust apart and liberated a bit of lunch meat still glued to the mayonnaise, then stepped across to the front door, opened it, and threw the remains out onto the lawn. "Squirrels," he said. "They love a crust."

Almost at once the door opened again and Aunt Edith stood there, looking in uncertainly past a cardboard carton full of groceries. "Was that you throwing something out onto the lawn?" she asked.

Uncle Roy winked at Howard. "The boy did it," he said, jamming the crushed beer can under his chair cushion and nodding at the half-drunk beer, then winking at Howard. Howard caught on and picked it up just as Aunt Edith pulled the door shut, looking bright-eyed at him. Surreptitiously Uncle Roy shoved the six-pack across the floor with his foot so that it sat next to Howard's chair, and at the same time he took the carton out of his wife's arms so that she could rush at Howard and hug him. "Look at you!" she said, thrusting Howard away and standing back in order to do just that. He set the beer down.

"You're a long, tall drink of water, aren't you? How tall?"

"Six three," Howard said.

"I can remember when you were like this." She held her hand out, waist-high, and shook her head. "You should put on a little weight, though. You were always thin."

"If you ate my cooking you'd be thin, too," Howard said.

Uncle Roy went into the kitchen and laid the box of groceries down on a Formica table. Then, dutifully, he set about putting things away.

"There's more in the car," she said to him, giving Howard another quick hug. "We're letting Howard cook, Roy. Maybe he can thin us both down."

"Let me get the stuff in the car," Howard said, wanting to help. He went out into the front yard again, past where the crusts lay in the weeds now, and found the family station wagon in the driveway. There were two more cartons of groceries in the back, and he set one of them awkwardly on top of the other.

He noticed several books of food stamps slid down along the side of the carton, next to a loaf of bread. So that's how it is, he thought sadly. He was doubly determined to help out somehow, to solicit Uncle Roy's help in getting the sketch away from Mr. Jimmers. He would broach the subject that very afternoon. He picked up the boxes, balanced them with one arm, and slammed the cargo door of the wagon, then carried the boxes into the house. Aunt Edith was just then hurrying out the back door, carrying a sandwich on a plate. Howard was certain that she had shut the door quickly, as if in order to hide something.

Uncle Roy put away the lunch meat and bread and mayonnaise, mopped up the counter with a tea towel, and hung the towel back up from a peg on the wall. "I like to help out in the kitchen," he said. "Some men don't like that kind of work, but I don't mind. Any work is good work, that's the byword around here. We'll get help in when things click for me." He began uncrating more groceries, half pulling out the loaf of bread and then dropping it back down into the box. "What's that?" he asked suddenly, peering out the window.

Howard looked out, expecting to see something going on with Aunt Edith. She was gone, though, perhaps out of sight around the side of the house. There was nothing out the window but fir trees, the forest floor overgrown with berries and lemonleaf and poison oak. The pointed leaves of wild iris grew in clumps along the edge of the trees beside a little path that ran out into the woods. For a moment Howard thought he could see his aunt's red jacket moving along the path, some distance through the trees. He couldn't be sure, though.

When he turned back around, Uncle Roy was putting away the bread. The leftover food stamps were gone from the box. One of them, in fact, protruded from where it had been shoved into his uncle's coat pocket. Howard glanced away, turning on the water in the sink as if he wanted to wash his hands, and out of the corner of his eye he saw Uncle Roy push it down farther into the pocket and then hurriedly shove the balance of the stamps into a kitchen drawer and shut it. "Just dry them on the dish towel."

Howard nodded, pulling the towel from its peg. They talked for a time, Howard telling him about his trip north, omitting any mention of the past twenty-four hours. There was no use sounding like a paranoid nut. Uncle Roy listened, nodding his head. He took the towel and began swabbing down cupboards and mopping up spots from the floor. Then, abruptly, he shot a glance out toward the front window, as if he'd just then seen something wonderful or puzzling out there. Howard followed his gaze, not able to help himself even though he suspected he was being hoodwinked again. Uncle Roy headed into the living room, gesturing at Howard, indicating that Howard should follow him along to the door. When he opened it, though, nobody was there. There hadn't been any knock; Howard was certain of it.

"Must have been the wind," Uncle Roy said, and at that moment, as if to prove him right, there was the sound of a door slamming—the same that Howard had heard when he first arrived.

"Toolshed door." Uncle Roy stepped outside and down the front-porch steps, continuing around past the side of the house, past the abandoned scaffolding. Tilted against the back side of the garage was a lean-to shed with a plywood door, which wobbled open in the sea wind. It hung there for a moment, as if deciding something, and then banged shut. "Damned latch," Uncle Roy said, shoving the hasp shut and driving a pointed stick down through it to keep it tight. "This is my current project." He waved at an immense pile of old weathered lumber, full of nails, as if it had all been pried off the side of dilapidated houses. "Barn lumber. There's a fortune to be made in it if a man's got any gumption. Gumption's the thing, you see, out here. This is like the frontier."

"What do you do with it?" Howard asked.

"Clean it up. Sell it. Yuppies buy it for twice the price of new lumber in order to make new houses look old. It's all fakery, of course. The only people they fool are each other. Still, it's good wood. They did a study—concluded that hundred-year-old redwood planks, pulled off a house roof, hadn't lost more than two percent tensile strength."

"Really?" Howard reached down and pulled up the end of one of the boards. A grisly-looking spider darted out, scampering away into the weeds as the board slammed down again. "Beats bulldozing the stuff, doesn't it?"

"That's it," said Uncle Roy. "Conservation is what it is. Recycling. Pull out the nails, trim the ends, stack it up, and wait for the trucks to roll in. I'm just now getting started on it. My back's been acting up, though, and I've had to take it easy."

Howard looked at the old dry Bermuda grass, curling up through the heaped wood. Clearly no one had touched it for months, perhaps years. "Maybe I can help you with it. I can pull nails and trim ends easy enough. I'd like to do that."

Uncle Roy hesitated, thinking it through, as if he had talked too much and gotten in too deep. "We'll buy another six-pack and draw up plans," he said, winking. "Tonight. After four."

A telephone rang. "Roy!" came a shout from the kitchen.

"That's Edith. Come on." He hurried past the garage, up onto the back stoop, and into the service porch. There was an old washer and dryer there, vintage twenty years ago, and one of those fold-up doweled-together wooden clotheslines with underwear hanging on it. A door led into the kitchen, where Aunt Edith was just then hanging up the phone.

"What?" said Uncle Roy. "Who was it?"

"Syl."

"Why did you shout? Did she want to talk to me?"

"No. She might have, though. I wanted you to be ready at hand."

"What did she want? Is she all right?"

"Heavens, yes, she's all right. Why shouldn't she be all right?"

"Then why on earth did she call? We were just discussing the issue of the barn lumber. Howard's got an idea for selling it down south. That's where the housing market is. We were just starting in on it."

"Dressed like that? Howard's just arrived. Don't make him work until he's had a chance to sit down for a moment. That wood's been lying there since who knows when. Let it be until after lunch, anyway. Give the boy a breather. Sylvia's coming for lunch. She's upset about something, I think."

Aunt Edith went on about Sylvia, for a few minutes, about the store and her making things to sell in it. They were dependent on the tourist trade in Mendocino. It was easy for a shop to founder and sink. You got around it by diversifying. Tourists loved a trinket, and they were certain that the north coast was a haven of creativity. They didn't want a shirt that they could buy in a mall down south. They wanted whales and wool and driftwood and natural foods.

"That's her now," Uncle Roy said. There was the sound of an engine cutting off out on the street.

Edith nodded. "She called from right down at the Safeway. She's picked up some salmon for dinner tonight, in honor of Howard being here. I told her—"

"Good," said Uncle Roy, interrupting her. "It's time we had something high-toned for dinner. I'll cook it up myself. A little dill weed, a little white wine. Have we got any wine?"

"No," Edith said.

"We'll remedy that. Always cook with the wine you intend to drink," he told Howard seriously.

The front door opened and Sylvia walked in. She might easily have been crying. Howard was suddenly furious, ready to murder someone—Stoat, the dirty pig. He forced a smile, thinking that it would be a disaster to fly off the handle now, even in Sylvia's defense.

"What the hell's wrong?" Uncle Roy asked, seeing the same thing in her face.

"I don't think they're going to renew my lease. I'm going to have to move the shop, probably back off Main Street."

"The sons of bitches!" Uncle Roy slammed his fist on the kitchen table.

"Roy!" Aunt Edith said, glancing at Howard, pretty clearly embarrassed for him.

"They're talking about redevelopment along Main," Sylvia said.

"What the hell is that, 'redevelopment'?" Uncle Roy looked disgusted. "Of all the damned things . . ." he said.

"That's when they tear down whatever's interesting and put up something shabby and new," Howard put in. "They're always up to that down in my neighborhood."

"Is this certain?" Uncle Roy squinted at her. The look on his face suggested that he read an entire plot into the notion. "Who told you, the old lady?"

"No, Stoat. This morning. I saw you drive past," she said to Howard. "I'm kind of glad you didn't stop, though. I wasn't in any mood to talk."

So Stoat, somehow, had become—what? Her landlord? A landlord's agent? Guiltily he found that he was wildly relieved. Happy even. This explained the sidewalk conversation. Stoat was a backwoods Simon Legree, twisting his blond mustache.

Uncle Roy paced up and down, dark looks crossing his face. "They're moving," he said.

"Oh, Roy." Aunt Edith started putting together sandwiches on the counter.

Howard wondered what his uncle meant—who was moving? What did the word mean, exactly?

Roy stopped. Looking hard at Howard, he asked, apropos of nothing at all and in the cryptic manner of Mr. Jimmers, "Are you a man who likes to fish?"

6

Uncle Roy brooded while Sylvia and Edith ate their sandwiches. Looking nervous, as if he had nothing to do with his hands, he got up finally and opened the refrigerator door, staring in at Tupperware containers full of leftovers. He hauled out an open tin can, holding it up and widening his eyes at Howard. "Peach?"

Howard shook his head. "Still full from breakfast."

"Anyone else?" Sylvia and Edith shook their heads. "Don't mind if I do?" No one minded. Uncle Roy poured milk into the peaches, fishing a clean fork out of the drawer. He waved for Howard to follow him and took the can out into the living room and sat back down in his chair, sipping milky peach syrup out of the open can. Howard could hear Sylvia and Aunt Edith talking between themselves, having cranked the conversation up once the men were out of the room.

"Slippery little devil," Uncle Roy said, biting into a peach, eating it off the end of the fork. Howard waited for the subject of the unrenewed lease to surface again, but it didn't, and he became aware that Uncle Roy was studiously avoiding it. After a couple of minutes Sylvia left, heading back down to Mendocino. Uncle Roy assured her that nothing would happen, that he would work things through. "Don't worry," he said to her, but it was unconvincing.

Then Aunt Edith came in, wiping her eyes with a handkerchief and immediately climbing the stairs. Howard sat there uncomfortably. His uncle had sunk into his chair. He sat now with his head pulled down into the flesh of his neck and chin, as if he had turned into a sort of human pudding. There was more in his face than sorrow or worry. He was thinking hard about something, making plans. He started to speak, but was interrupted almost at once by the sound of footfalls on the front porch and then a heavy knock.

Uncle Roy shook his head, meaning for Howard to stay in his chair.

After a moment a woman's voice spoke from outside, very loud, as if she were shouting through a bullhorn. At first Howard thought it was Sylvia come back, apparently in some sort of rage. "I know you're in there!" the woman shouted, and then banged on the door again. It was an old woman's voice, though, loud and thin like the voice of the Witch of the East.

"Ssh!" Uncle Roy put a finger to his lips. The house was silent for a moment. There was no movement from upstairs.

"Open this door!" came the voice from the porch, followed by a rapping on the window. "Your car is apparent! Don't pretend! You'll find yourself living under the bridge!"

Howard sat very still. He heard the sound of something scraping on the porch—the rocker being hauled aside—and then someone's face, just a slice of it, appeared in the window beyond the one-inch gap between the curtains. "I can see the back of your head, Roy Barton!"

"That's not me!" shouted Uncle Roy. "I have my *lawyer* in here! He's a bulldog when he's riled up! He's come up from San Francisco, and he means business. With a *capital B*!"

The woman laughed, high and shrill. "Send him out!" she shouted, banging on the window again. Howard saw that Aunt Edith had descended the stairs now, carrying her purse.

"Put that damned thing away!" Uncle Roy hissed. Then to Howard he said, "Never let them see the color of money. Drives them wild—like the scent of blood to a shark. They won't rest

59

till they've torn your belly out." He nodded toward the porch. "It's the landlady."

Howard nodded. "Wait here," he said, getting up and heading for the door.

Uncle Roy grabbed his pant leg. "Just let her rant," he said. "She'll tire out and go away. We've got to hold her off until after Halloween. I'm going to make a killing on the haunted house, and then we can pay her."

"I see," Howard said, although actually he didn't see anything at all. What haunted house? He found that he didn't have any faith in the notion of his uncle's making a killing, in haunted houses or otherwise. "Let me deal with her. I've handled her sort before."

"She's a bugbear . . ."

"Let me at her."

"Go to town, then," Uncle Roy said, letting go of Howard and sitting up a little straighter. "It's all right," he said to Aunt Edith, who still hesitated on the stairs. "Howard's got a line on this woman. He's just been telling me about it. He'll settle her hash."

Howard smiled and nodded at his aunt, mouthing the words "No problem" and opening the front door.

On the porch stood a tall thin woman in a red dress. She had the face of a pickle with an aquiline nose, and she glared at him from behind a pair of glasses with swept-back frames dotted with rhinestones. Immediately she tried to push him aside, to rush into the house. Howard forced her back out, weaving across in front of her and pulling the door shut as if he would happily crush her sideways if she didn't move quickly. She folded her arms, seeming to swell up there on the ruined porch.

"If you're a lawyer," she said, looking him up and down, "I'm a Chinese magistrate."

"Mr. Barton is willing to make a partial payment," he said in a low voice. "I've advised him not to let the issue go to court."

"Wise," she said, eyeing him steadily. "A partial payment against what?"

Howard hesitated. He wasn't sure what. Uncle Roy had said that this woman was the landlady, but what did that mean? Did this have something to do with Sylvia's store, or with the house? It didn't matter to him, really. "What do you recollect the total to be?"

"*Recollect!* There's a payment of four hundred-odd dollars a month against a principal of forty-two thousand at twelve

60

percent amortized over thirty years. The house is mine, my smarty-pants lawyer, unless he empties his pockets, which he can't do, because they're full of moths!"

"Calm down," Howard said gently, laying a hand on her arm. "Try to relax."

She whirled away, as if his hand were a snake. He smiled benignly, trying to put just the hint of puzzlement into his eyes, as if he were confused and sorry that she'd gotten so carried away. "Breathe regularly," he advised her, using a soft, clinical psychologist's voice—the sort of voice designed to drive sane people truly mad.

He pulled the rocker back over from where she'd shoved it aside, adjusting its position carefully, wondering what the hell to say to her. He gestured at the rocker then, as if she might be anxious to sit down, to take a load off, and he widened his eyes like a happy dentist coercing a child into the tilting chair. Uncle Roy, he could see, was watching through the gap in the curtains now. The curtains moved, parting another couple of inches. His uncle grinned out at him and wiggled his hand in a sort of coy wave, and then whirled his finger around his ear, making the pinwheel sign.

The woman took another step backward, nearly to the edge of the porch. It was clear that she wouldn't go anywhere near the chair and wouldn't settle down, either. Howard's theatrical patience had worked her into a fury. Her eyebrows were arched and her forehead furrowed, as if she had eaten a slug.

Then abruptly she caught herself, her face instantly composing. It seemed to have taken an effort, though. "I sent Mr. Barton a notice that I'd no longer accept late payments. I meant what I wrote in that letter. It's incontestable. The law is the law."

"Surely two or three more weeks . . ." Howard said, calculating when Halloween was.

"In two weeks Mr. Barton will be living out of the back of his automobile," she said, interrupting him. "I pity his poor wife, but she's brought this upon herself, marrying the likes of him."

The front door squeaked fully open just then, and a rubber bat as big as a pigeon dropped down into the doorway, flapping on the end of a black thread. His uncle stood hidden inside somewhere, probably manipulating a pulley. Howard could hear him stifling his laughter in the palm of his hand. The woman made a rush for the open door again, but Howard was there before her, pulling it shut, trapping the bat outdoors. It dangled in front of the closed door, its nose thumping against a panel like a rubber knocker.

She cast Howard a faint grin and shook her head tiredly, as if the rubber bat trick had very nicely illustrated exactly what sort of man Roy Barton was. Which of course it did, to Howard's way of thinking. "My client is willing to offer you ten cents on the dollar," he said. "Right now. Instantly." He pulled his checkbook out of his jacket pocket, took out a pen, and opened the book, as if ready to sign it.

"Tell Mr. Barton he can park his car behind the Texaco station at the corner, in back along with the other wrecks. He can utilize the gas station rest room that way." She turned around and stepped off the porch, heading for the curb. The sound of chains and recorded laughter echoed out of the upstairs window, very slow and throaty this time, as if played at a too-slow speed. Howard saw the back of her neck flush pink, but she didn't turn around.

He caught up with her on the street as she was climbing into her car. Keeping his back to the house, he talked through the open passenger window. She started the car right up, as if she meant to drive off. "Four hundred even?" he asked.

She gave him an assessing squint, her eyes traveling to his checkbook, as if a little disappointed to see it. "Four hundred forty-two. It's already three weeks late. There's another payment due within eight days. Precisely. Or I'll take action."

"Here then." He tore off the check and handed it through the window. She hesitated for a moment, but finally she took it, as if she couldn't stand not to.

"You're a very small boy," she said. "And it's a very big and badly designed dike that you're trying to stopper up." She blinked rapidly, but her voice was slow and studied now, like the voice of an aged and nearly psychotic schoolmarm delivering a standard lecture on behavior for the ten thousandth time. She suddenly changed her tone, though, looking him in the eyes. For a moment it looked to Howard as if she had gone into trance, and then she gave him a sideways look and asked, "Who are you, really?" She seemed to be seeing him clearly for the first time, and for a moment he was overwhelmed with confusion, as if he had just been caught stealing something.

Howard fought for something to say. She obviously hadn't swallowed the lawyer gag. "Just a friend from down south," he said. "He's in pretty tight straits right now, but he'll pull out of it. He's got a couple of irons in the fire."

She gazed at him, smiling faintly, as if he had said that Uncle Roy was really a Persian prince, just about to inherit the kingdom.

"The water you're swimming in is deeper and darker than you can imagine," she said. "And you won't be able to find the bottom when you tire out, which you will, very shortly. I don't know who you are, but if you've come out here to challenge me, you've made a fatal error. I'll see that old fraud on the street. See if I won't. He won't stand in my way, and neither will you." She gave him a pitying look then, as if what she was telling him was purely for his own good. "Mark me, he'll bleed you dry, too, if you let him. Go back home. Don't throw good money after bad. There's nothing for you here. You don't understand anything."

She pulled away from the curb just then, and Howard had to step back quick to avoid being clipped. He ditched the checkbook in his coat, and after pulling his bags out of the truck, headed back into the house, wondering at her strange speech. It hadn't sounded as if she were merely talking about finances.

"What came of it?" asked Uncle Roy. "Did she react to the props?"

"Infuriated her."

"Good, good. So much the better. Will she hold off until the end of the month?"

"Yes, but I had to threaten her," Howard said. "I guess the lawyer scam worked on her." Howard didn't like to lie to his uncle, except that Uncle Roy would feel good about the ruse, and that was worth something and would explain why the old woman had gone off without any money. "These landlord types want the check," Howard said. "They don't want to foreclose. They can't afford it. They're in the business of being paid, not of renovating houses. I guaranteed her the money come November. It was as simple as that."

"And we'll get it, too. This haunted house business can't fail. You've seen what I've got going here—the corpses, the ghost woman, the bats."

Howard nodded. "The eyeballs," he said, finishing the list. He realized that his hands were shaking. The meeting outside had worked him over pretty thoroughly. Now he had involved himself in a lie, and in the end it would probably be impossible to hide it from Uncle Roy, who, regardless of what sort of deadbeat he was, wouldn't put up with Howard paying his bills for him. Sylvia hadn't made that part up.

"Who is this woman?" Howard asked.

"One Heloise Lamey. She owns half the coast. Part of a consortium of some sort. This man Stoat is part of it. They're an octopus—a finger in every damned sort of pie."

"So she's Sylvia's landlady, too, down at the shop?"

"One and the same. Stoat wasn't a bad sort, years ago. Money is the root, though. Don't ever let anyone tell you different. Money is the stinking root."

"What's their problem?"

"They're millionaires, aren't they? Rough crowd, millionaires. All this talk of redevelopment . . . There's oil in it for them, too—offshore. They'd pave the ocean if there was money in it. Take your man Stoat. He's drunk my beer, dated my daughter. He was always a little slick, of course. But I don't hold that against a man. That's all appearances, and we know what those are worth. But then he fell in with the old woman and made a couple of bucks. That frosted it. He turned into a damned chameleon, changed the color of his scales. Started to live for his bank account."

Howard found the anti-Stoat talk very pleasant, and he wished that he knew more about the man so as to be able to run him down even more expansively. His mouth was dry, though— probably a nervous reaction from his bout with the landlady. "I'm going to grab a glass of water," he said, leaving his uncle in the living room. Aunt Edith had gone back upstairs. He circled around into the kitchen, working things over in his mind. He had been there about an hour and a half and already the complications were descending on him. He might have expected it. Nobody told him it would be easy. There were never any guarantees. He drank a glass of water at the sink, staring out the window at the woods, lost in puzzled thought. The sound of a voice made him jump.

"That's not a friendly place, those woods." It was Uncle Roy, who had slipped into the kitchen. He nodded at the window, at the forest beyond. His face was serious, almost fearful. "There's bears in them. Can you believe that? Mountain lions, too. Those woods are stalked by carnivores."

"Really?" Howard said. "Right out there?"

"Can't tell by looking, can you? Trees are too dense. The creatures might be watching us right this moment, hiding in the shadows. They don't take well to civilization. It ruins them. They develop a taste for garbage over the years. They'll tear a man's head clean off, too, and eat his entrails."

"Not often, I hope."

"Doesn't have to happen to a man more than once, does it?" Uncle Roy smiled at him, having deliberately misunderstood. "Nope, those are inhospitable trees—nothing but poison oak in there. The poison vapors get into the lungs, finally. Throat closes up tight. Death by constriction, the medical men call it." He shook his head darkly, not relishing the idea of a man's throat closing up. "Cultists, too. All varieties of them, but not half as bad as the dope farmers."

"I hear they're a dangerous crowd," Howard said. "I can understand it, I guess, price of dope and all. Must be profitable."

"Oh, there's money in it. Yes indeed. Money's paramount in a backwater like this. Guns, dogs, trip cords, Claymore mines, razor wire, spike pits, bear traps—you name it; the dope farmers have the lot of it, the whole megillah. I wouldn't go into those woods on a bet."

Howard shook his head, as if he wouldn't either, for the moment anyway. Aunt Edith had gone into them quick enough, though, and carrying a sandwich, too.

"Then there's the logging roads. They'll run you right down, loggers will. They'd take a man like you for an environmentalist. Nothing they hate worse. They'll shoot you on sight. The only crowd that won't shoot you are the cultists. They want you alive."

Uncle Roy seemed to have gone crazy, rattling off his catalogue of forest horrors. He peered into the refrigerator again, pushing things around, trying to find something that appealed to him. "Coke?" he asked.

"Thanks. Shall we ask Aunt Edith?"

"For permission? Or whether she wants one, too?" He looked angry all of a sudden, as if the question had set him off. "She's retired, actually. Taking a nap. You won't see her until it's time to cook dinner." His face softened a little then. "She's worried about Sylvia, to tell you the truth. What she wants is more faith. Things iron themselves out. She's got the usual motherly instincts, though, and they run her ragged. Survival is paramount in a business like Sylvia's. If she survives the winter . . ." He shrugged and then grinned abruptly, as if having thought of something more cheerful. "Edith is ticked off about the rubber bat, actually. She wasn't keen on my putting on the laugh record, either. She takes the old woman too seriously."

Howard couldn't think of anything to say about taking the old woman seriously that wouldn't irritate his uncle, so he changed the subject entirely, trying to force Uncle Roy to slip up and be a little bit candid for a change. "Tell me," he said. "What are they, these gluers I keep hearing about? Mr. Jimmers mentioned them to me. They seem to have stolen a bunch of junk out of my glove compartment. Are they some kind of cult?"

"Nobody knows, really. Almost nobody. Live back in among the trees. Anarchists to the last man jack of them. Won't wear matching socks to save their mortal souls. Won't cut their hair. Spend their days gluing stuff up, layer on top of layer, usually on their cars. Coral reef syndrome; that's what I call it. Kids all ride skateboards—break into churches and schools. Won't work. Some people think it's primitivism, the decline of man. They distill a hell of a bottle of whiskey, though, just between the two of us."

"I can tell you that their wine isn't worth anything at all. I tried some last night. I was forced to drink water instead."

"That bad?" Uncle Roy grimaced, as if finding it hard to imagine. "They don't drink the stuff themselves, that's why. They don't know a lick about wine, except that all these natural-sounding fruit wines are big with the tourists, especially the teetotalers. They bring home a bottle of herb wine and offer it to company as a joke. It's like taking the cure. The gluer elders can drink whiskey, though. They smoke the malt over fires like the Scots do, only they don't use peat; they use green redwood skived out of root balls with an adze."

"Root balls?"

"That's right. Got to be done that way. Hand me down a couple of those glasses."

Howard reached into the cupboard over his head, pulling out two green tumblers. Behind them, sitting in the back corner of the cupboard, was a collection of salt and pepper shakers—ten or twelve pairs. Sitting among them, smug and leering, was a porcelain Humpty Dumpty. Howard was stricken speechless. Here, too, he thought.

"Do you know what the oldest living thing in the world is?" asked his uncle.

Howard shook his head, unable to guess.

"A root ball from a stand of redwoods. They've got redwood trees out there that are two thousand years old if they're a day. Where do they come from? you might ask. Not from seeds, mostly—from root balls. One tree puts down roots and then one day another tree comes up from the roots of that first one. Then along comes another, and all of these new ones putting down new roots. First tree grows old and dies, finally—falls over. Maybe it's a thousand years old, maybe two. And this goes on for twenty thousand years through God's own generations of trees, all of them growing and adding roots to this root ball. *It* doesn't die, though. Fires don't touch it. Bugs can't get at it. How old is it? How big is it? You tell *me*. Nobody can guess. Bigger than the pyramids, older than the woolly mammoth."

He squinted at the unopened Coca-Cola cans. "Anyway, that's what they use to smoke the whiskey. Older the root material, the better the spirits. That's paramount. You're a literary man. Have you read Morris' essay on age?"

It seemed to Howard as if he must have, but he couldn't calculate it right now. The coincidence of the Humpty Dumpty still played in his mind. He reached into the cupboard again and pulled it out, waving it at his uncle. "What *is* this, anyway?" Howard asked. "I seem to be running into a lot of them lately."

His uncle eyeballed him, as if he were trying to fathom the question, or, perhaps, as if he were considering how much he could safely say on the subject. "That's Humpty Dumpty," he said. "One of Edith's dust collectors. Nothing you need to worry about."

"Right. It's just that they seem to *mean* something, don't they? Maybe it's the look on his face. He's such a know-it-all."

"Mean something? I'm not sure . . . They've got a fascinating history, I suppose. They're an incredibly ancient business involving fertility and reproduction. Sort of a metaphoric root ball, aren't they? Nobody knows how long they've been around. That lad is one of your vegetation kings; that's my notion. Early incarnation of the thing. Your friends the gluers are fond of him. They revere a fat man. Consider themselves to be the king's men, if you know what I mean."

"I'm not sure I do," Howard said, putting the little porcelain egg back into the cupboard. "Who's the king, then?"

Uncle Roy hesitated for a moment before speaking. "Maybe you're putting too fine a point on it," he said. "Safer to think of it as a myth. It's easy in this climate to get swept up in the wind and rain and forest, to start thinking in terms of weather. Things up here can be supernaturally green, and would be, except for the drought. People drift north talking about 'getting back to the land.' But they don't know what that means. Not really. That's what I was telling you a moment ago—that business about the woods. They're a dangerous place. Do you follow me?"

Howard shook his head. He didn't follow anything except that his half-innocent question about the Humpty Dumpty had sailed the conversation straight into the realm of the mystical. What was wrong with people up here? Everyone was a puzzle waiting to be solved. First Mr. Jimmers and then the landlady. Now Uncle Roy. And what the hell *was* Aunt Edith doing out in the woods with a sandwich on a plate?

"Look here," Uncle Roy said, suddenly animated. "It's nearly four o'clock. Forget the Cokes. Let's make a little run down to Sammy's. I usually drop in about this time. We've got a couple of hours to kill before dinner. We can work out the elements of the barn lumber scheme."

What scheme? Howard wondered, following his uncle out the door. Now suddenly there was a scheme, although nobody on earth could lay out the particulars of it. In his mind, Uncle Roy was probably certain that Howard had given serious thought to the barn lumber angle. He hoped the haunted house plans were less imaginary.

"We'll take your truck," Uncle Roy said, climbing heavily into the passenger side and looking down furtively into his jacket pocket.

Howard went around opposite and fired up the engine, driving down Oak Street toward the highway, swinging south finally, and then back up Cypress. "Across the street there," Uncle Roy said. "By the warehouse."

The tavern was long and almost windowless, sided in dark redwood with the name "Sammy's" painted on it. Its roof was a shambles of different-colored composition shingles in layers—strips and pieces having broken or blown off over the years. A neon cocktail glass stood atop a rusted steel post outside, lit dimly despite it being daylight. Only a couple of cars were parked in the gravel lot when they pulled in, including what might have been an old Chevy from around 1965. Only you couldn't quite tell now, because it was utterly covered in layers of cheap religious icons—Day of the Dead skulls and bleeding Christs and robed Virgin Marys made out of painted plastic and plaster of Paris.

"Gluers," Uncle Roy whispered.

7

"TROUBLE?" Howard asked, and almost at once he felt a little foolish, a little childish. He realized then that he was full of a vague, bulk-rate uneasiness. There was a shadow lying across the landscape, and he suspected that it had some sort of fearful shape and that he was on the verge of making it out. Here was another piece of that shadow, he had thought, seeing the car parked beneath the neon sign.

Uncle Roy shook his head. "No," he said. "You can relax about that. You won't be running into any trouble from them. I'd guess just the opposite. Follow my lead, though. There might be profit in this. You do the knocking, I'll do the talking."

Howard followed him into the bar, suddenly unable to see in the darkness. There were illuminated beer signs on the walls and a light over a pool table in one corner, but it was dim and cool and smelled like spilled beer. He stood for a moment just inside the door in order to let his eyes adjust. Uncle Roy moved off, negotiating the furniture easily—from long practice, probably. In a moment Howard made out the bulk of shadowy tables and chairs and the long bar against the wall.

The place was almost empty aside from a couple of hunched men drinking beer at the bar and talking to each other about basketball. One of them turned and gave Uncle Roy the high sign, saying, "What's new?"

"Easy livin'," Roy said, and the man laughed, going back to his beer and basketball. In the back corner, a man who must have been a gluer sat talking to another man in a shirt and tie and with the face of a grocery store manager. This second man stood up as Uncle Roy angled toward the table. He picked up a carton of bottles and took it with him as he moved away, heading toward the bar and nodding to Uncle Roy.

The gluer looked like an old hippie—the brother of the Patchwork Girl from Oz. His clothes resembled a quilt sewn by a drunkard, and he had a mess of graying hair that hung halfway down his back. Howard stood for a moment, wondering whether to join his uncle or order something from the bar. The gluer didn't look like a happy man, though; he looked like a zealot, like the Holy Man of the Moab, maybe. And so going after a drink struck Howard as a better idea. He wouldn't meddle in his uncle's affairs any more than he had to—for the moment, anyway. He stepped across and asked the bartender to draw two draft beers.

When the man turned around to pull the tap, Howard slipped one of the bottles out of the cardboard carton and glanced at it. It was unlabeled, but the amber-colored liquid inside, and its seeming to have come in with the patchwork man, convinced him that the bottle held the fabled Sunberry Farms whiskey that his uncle had talked about. No doubt about it.

"What's that to you?" the bartender asked suddenly, surprising him.

"What?" asked Howard. "Nothing. Just curious. Wondering what it was. Can I order a glass of this?" Sheepishly he slid the bottle back into the case.

"I don't know what you're talking about," the bartender said. "Why do you want a glass of it if you don't know what it is? This belongs to that man over there." He nodded toward the corner. "It's urine samples that he's running up to the lab. Terrible outbreak of hepatitis around here. Some new San Francisco strain. You know how that goes—disease capital of the world. Health department's hired these poor bastards to collect samples."

"By the quart?" Howard asked.

The man shrugged. "Who the hell are you, anyway? Do you want something to drink, or are you just here to ask questions?" He picked up the box and set it on the floor behind the counter. Then he stood up and looked Howard straight in the face, not smiling at all.

"Roy Barton's my uncle. I'm visiting from down south."

"Barton family, eh? So you're here with Roy. That's all right, then. Where you from, L.A.?" He relaxed, smiling again and turning around to pull a bottle of Scotch off the shelf. He poured a couple of ounces into each of a pair of Old-fashioned glasses, talking all along about the last time he was down in L.A., about the smog and the dirt and the freeway killings as if he wanted to bury Howard's interest in the gluer whiskey beneath a dump truck full of words. He put the bottle away. "Tomatin, this is called. Not a bad whiskey. You aren't going to find it just anywhere."

70

Howard took a polite sip, turning around to have a look at what his uncle was up to. The gluer was just then handing him a couple of bills—tens, it appeared—and Uncle Roy handed over a few folded food stamps. The whiskey was raw and fiery and Howard nearly choked on it. He took the other three glasses from the bar, croaking out his thanks, and headed for a table near a half-dead potted palm, wondering whether he would have to pay for the Scotch. He didn't want the damned stuff. Maybe the potted palm wanted it. Clearly the bartender had poured it in order to take Howard's mind off the gluer bottles.

Uncle Roy was walking back across toward him. He tipped Howard a huge wink, as if he'd just done a pretty bit of business. Howard wondered what the going rate for food stamps was—sixty cents on the dollar? The gluer walked out of the bar, without his case of whiskey. Howard heard gravel scrunch outside as the car crept out of the parking lot.

"What's this?" asked Uncle Roy, nodding at the Scotch glass.

"Scotch. On the house, I think."

His uncle nodded. "You tried to order some of the Sunberry malt, didn't you, and he talked you into this? What did he tell you was in the case?"

"Urine samples."

Uncle Roy chuckled. "This Sunberry whiskey isn't exactly aboveboard, if you follow me. They don't serve it down at the Hungry Tiger. Sammy took you for a cop. He knows you aren't a local. You must have thrown him, walking up to the bar like that and hauling one of the bottles out."

"I didn't mean to. It was all that talk about root balls, I guess. The whole idea's pretty astonishing."

Uncle Roy nodded. "Anyway, I figure to have the haunted house open by next week," he said, as if they'd been talking about the haunted house scheme all along. "That'll give me seven days to run kids through before the thirty-first. Once we pass Halloween the thing'll be a dead bust. Everyone's gearing up for Christmas by then. I've been toying with the idea of doing a sort of Santa's village, too, with reindeer and all—maybe hire a little carnival to dress it up with. I make a hell of a Santa Claus."

"Quite a bit of work, isn't it?" Howard asked. "Converting a haunted house to a Santa's workshop, or whatever it is, in just a couple of months?"

"It's just a matter of imagination, of picturing the details. 'God dwells in the details.' Mies Van Der Rohe said that. I wrote it down on my hand with a ballpoint pen once. That's the way to remember a thing—write it on your hand. Or else write it in mirror writing on your forehead."

Howard suddenly became aware of a framed photograph on the wall near the table. At first he couldn't make it out, because it was full of unfamiliar shapes. He peered more closely at it. It was a picture of the Watts Towers, built by Sabatino Rodia starting around 1920 in south-central Los Angeles. Rodia had spent years building the towers out of old, found materials— rebar and pipe, China plates and seashells and trinkets and pieces of colored glass—until he had put together a cluster of tall spires in junkman-Gothic style. The truth struck Howard forcibly, like a stone in the back of the head.

"Rodia was a gluer!" he said to Uncle Roy.

His uncle nodded, as if it were common knowledge. "He was touched by the instinct," he said. "And do you know what else?" He looked furtively around, as if he were about to reveal a secret. "Under each of the feet of those towers, there's a pair of 1938 Buicks with reinforced roofs and frames. Welded steel I-beams. Banks of steel-belted truck tires on quadruple axles. Eight-speed gearboxes. All of it underground, where you can't see it."

Howard looked again at the photograph. "What do you mean 'under' them?"

"They're built on top of automobiles—the towers are. Engines are ready to go. Tanks topped off. One of these nights, when the weather's right and the wind's blowing out of the east and the constellations are set just so in the sky . . ."

Uncle Roy sat back and widened his eyes, waving his right hand with a sort of flourish that reminded Howard of Mr. Jimmers talking about his two-dimensional constellation, which was just about as unlikely as this. The two must belong to some sort of fabulists' club.

"So why are they built on top of cars?" asked Howard. "They're going to drive off or something? This fleet of Buicks? Where to? Up the coast?"

Suddenly laughing, Uncle Roy tilted forward and slapped Howard on the shoulder. "That's rich, isn't it? Up the coast highway in the night! You've got a hell of an imagination for a nephew. Here, let me buy you another beer." And with that he stood up and walked off toward the bar, leaving Howard to wonder what sort of an imagination nephews usually had— nothing that could touch the imagination of an uncle, apparently. How much weight *could* a bunch of old Buicks stand? Even reinforced . . . He looked more closely at the photo. They were immense. What—a hundred feet tall? He couldn't make out the base of the towers, which were buttressed with arched steel—tons of it—rising out of a fenced backyard. His uncle returned with two fresh, full glasses.

The door opened just then, flooding the floor with sunlight. Stoat walked in. One of the men at the bar stood up hurriedly and went out through the back, not even looking around. The other man at the bar nodded over his beer, keeping to himself. Stoat squinted for a moment in the dim light before heading across to the table. "Mr. Barton," he said, cheerfully enough.

How on earth can he know who I am? Howard wondered, and then realized that it was Uncle Roy that Stoat was talking to. The man's hair was perfect, as if it had been shaped with a laser scalpel, and he looked both well off and comfortable in his clothes. Howard didn't trust his looks—too chiseled, too careful, with no hint of eccentricity and no humor in his face at all even though he was smiling. He had changed over the years, lost the affectations that he had sported back in his underground-comics days, which was the way with all affectations. You either lost them or came to believe in them, and Stoat was obviously too clever for that. Success and his own cleverness had worked him over, perhaps.

Howard could see that his uncle was sweating. He looked nervous and he smiled self-consciously. His left eye twitched just a little as he took a long pull on the new glass of beer, drinking half of it off at a single swallow.

"Mr. Barton," the man said again.

"Are you addressing me, my good fellow?" Uncle Roy asked. Howard tensed, knowing that here was another piece of the mystery, about to be unveiled. His uncle was pretending, and Howard wondered what he would have said if Howard hadn't been there. Abruptly Uncle Roy looked surprised, as if he'd just then recognized Stoat. "Well," he said, gesturing toward an empty chair. "My good friend Stoat. What brings you into a dump like this? Must be woefully important business."

"That it is," said Stoat, looking at Howard as if he wondered whether he could discuss such business in front of a stranger.

"This is my nephew," Uncle Roy said. "Howard Barton. He's an assistant director at the Getty Museum. Expert in oriental artifacts. He's up here for a little breather, a little constitutional, if you know what I mean. He was a special forces agent in Southeast Asia, highly connected."

"I think we've met," Stoat said. "Southeast Asia? I thought you'd managed to avoid that part of the world. Now you're with the Getty? That must run you in and out of elevated circles."

Howard nodded again. "That's right. I'm doing a little trouble-shooting."

"Troubleshooting? Up here in the woods?"

"Vacation, really."

"Well," said Stoat, "this is the country for that. Nothing but peace and quiet."

"I've gone into the barn lumber business since I talked to you last," Uncle Roy said to Stoat. "With any luck I'll be able to cut a deal with the Getty. They're going to build a new wing, out of my lumber, I hope. It's a hell of a project, but they're loaded. Swimming in green. There's a bunch of old houses coming down up Eureka way, part of a downtown bypass. I've got *bracero* labor up there right now, prying the places apart. Howard's acting as my liaison down south. This kind of deal is delicate."

Howard kept silent. His uncle had pretty clearly leaped in with his wild tale in order to keep Howard from talking. Howard had explained his trip in his letter. It had been no sort of secret—up until now, anyway.

Stoat was sucking on a eucalyptus drop, and he shifted it back and forth in his mouth when he talked. It was his only mannerism that was less than magazine-photo quality. "The world is full of delicate deals," he said. "I talked to Sylvia today. I guess you know that by now."

Uncle Roy stared at him, not trusting himself to speak, perhaps. Howard had plenty to say, but he forced himself not to say it now. There was too much room for error, for making things worse.

"What I mean to say is that I'm afraid she's overreacted to what I told her. I didn't mean to be making threats. To be truthful, I don't like the idea of redevelopment along Main any more than she does. As an artist I appreciate the beauty of that little town. I want to see it preserved. I'm not the only member of the consortium, though, and I was only passing on to her what was in the wind. I don't want her to be taken by surprise. I'm going to do what I can to head things off." He hesitated, letting this sink in. Then he said, "Heloise Lamey and I don't always see eye-to-eye on these issues."

"Heloise Lamey doesn't see eye-to-eye with anyone," Uncle Roy said. His face didn't betray what he was thinking, though, and what he said sounded like a flat statement rather than an acceptance of what Stoat was telling him.

Stoat sat back in his chair. "A certain amount hangs in the balance," he said. "Nothing's certain."

"True enough," Uncle Roy said, not giving an inch.

"You know she's wild for that . . . object we discussed."

"I remember the object in question. It's disappeared, apparently. Gone from the face of the earth."

"I almost wish it were," Stoat said. "You don't have to come cheap, you know. You can take her straight to the cleaners. And she doesn't care about the old man, either."

"The cleaners couldn't help her," Uncle Roy said. "Too much dirt. Too many years of wallowing with pigs."

Stoat sighed deeply, as if he took this last statement to be a personal insult, but would swallow it in order to maintain the delicate balance of things. He produced a pen, though, and wrote a number on the bottom of a bar napkin, five or six figures—not enough for a phone number, but plenty if it had to do with dollars and cents. Howard caught only a glimpse of it before Uncle Roy tucked it into his coat pocket.

"Another round of drinks here," Stoat said to the bartender as he stood up. He widened his eyes at Uncle Roy. "Think about it," he said. Then he nodded to Howard, walked across and laid a five-dollar bill on the bar, and walked out.

Uncle Roy sat still for a moment, as if waiting for Stoat's return. A car started up outside, though, following the labored, metallic whine of a bad starter. Uncle Roy relaxed then, all in a heap, producing a handkerchief and mopping his brow. The atmosphere in the bar seemed to ease just then, and Howard could smell the wind off the sea, tainted with candy-drop eucalyptus.

"Put that in the tip glass, Sammy," Uncle Roy said, waving at the bill on the bar. "Let's go," he said to Howard. "I won't drink on that bastard's money. Go ahead—I'll meet you in the truck."

Without asking about it, Howard went outside, squinting in the late-afternoon sunlight. He sat in the truck for a moment warming up the engine before his uncle came out, carrying a paper sack. Uncle Roy winked at him after he hauled himself in and waved the paper bag. There was a bottle of Sunberry Farms whiskey in it. "No need to tell Edith about any of this," he said.

"Not a word," Howard said. "I'm not sure what went on myself."

Uncle Roy gave him a sideways look. "There's nothing to tell, really. Damn all creditors," he said. "There's nothing worse than a landlord. Bunch of vultures. Money's not enough for them, they want your soul, too. Give me a psychotic with a loaded gun anytime."

"Anything to do with that sketch I'm after?" Howard asked, working on a hunch.

Clearly his uncle didn't want to discuss it. Let the matter slide, his face seemed to say. And the sketch wasn't Howard's in any real way, despite Graham's letter. Although if he, or rather the museum, wasn't going to get it, someone owed him an explanation—some story he could take back south with him.

"Don't worry about Stoat," Uncle Roy said, as if that answered Howard's question. "I've already forgotten him. He draws pictures of copulating machines. What can you say about a man like that? Steer clear of him. That's the advice I gave Sylvia, and I'm going to give the same advice to you. I'll show him a thing or two if he comes meddling around us again."

Uncle Roy went on in a more determined voice. "Look, I won't pretend here. You've come up north at a . . . tenuous time. Things are shaky. The ground's rumbling. Pressure's dropping. Do you follow me?"

"Yeah," Howard said. "The haunted house and all. The landlady. I'm willing to help, though."

"I know you are. God bless you. But it's not just that. There's some of this business that you ought to steer clear of. This man today . . . this Stoat—he's a dangerous character. And you come up here on vacation and run straight into him."

"And Sylvia was crazy for this guy."

"After a fashion. She's fond of a handsome face and she trusts damned near anybody until they give her reason not to. He's not her sort, though. And if she knew he was hounding me . . . !" Uncle Roy shook his head at the thought of what Sylvia might do.

"Well, look," Howard said, pulling in at the curb in front of the house. "I've got a sort of proposition for you. A business deal. It wouldn't mean much money, I'm afraid, only a couple hundred. And I wouldn't ask you at all if I thought it might be wasting your time. It seemed like a sure thing to me yesterday, but after visiting with Mr. Jimmers last night, I'm not so sure anymore."

"Sure about what? I'm happy to help. I don't need any commission, though—not from my nephew."

"Of course, of course. It's the museum, though, that's offering the commission. They've sent the money up with me—part of an expense account. It's this bit of artwork that I'm supposed to obtain—I don't know how much I told you about it in my letter. It's a piece owned by Michael Graham, a sketch for a Japanese woodblock print. But now Graham's dead, and I can't get anything sensible out of Jimmers. I'm a foreigner up here, and what I need is a local—someone these people trust. You, actually, if you'd tackle it. I've pretty much come to the conclusion that I can't accomplish it alone. I hate to foist this off on you, what with the haunted house and all . . . ."

His uncle was as pale as one of the Studebaker ghosts. Abruptly he held up the paper bag and pulled the cork out of the bottle with his teeth. He offered the bag to Howard, who immediately looked into the side mirror, a little bit uneasy with the idea of opening the whiskey in the car.

"No thanks."

"That's the stuff," his uncle said, after swallowing a mouthful. "That's the feathers on the bird." He replaced the cork with a shaking hand. "My advice to you is to forget this—what did you call it?"

"It's a sketch by an old Japanese artist. Hoku-sai, I think. Graham had it hidden. Jimmers claims that it's gone now, but I can't make out whether Jimmers has made off with it or if the piece has been stolen. I don't mean to accuse him, of course."

"Well, you know how it is up here. Lots of mysteries. Jimmers is one of the biggest of them. It'll probably surface in one of the oriental antique shops down in San Francisco, and Jimmers will be in groceries for a couple of months. I'll level with you. This is nothing you want to be involved in. If the thing's gone, it's gone. I'm certain that if Jimmers still had it, he'd ante up. Think of it as spilt milk."

"Maybe," Howard said. "I've got to try to recover it, I guess. I've got to have something to tell them back at the museum. I'll need advice, though, from someone who knows the territory. But I won't take it for nothing, so this commission business still stands. If you won't help, I'll have to go elsewhere, which I don't want to do."

"I'm telling you that I can't do you a shred of good. You're pumping money down a rat hole."

"Fair enough. I've been warned."

"Of course if push comes to shove," Uncle Roy said cryptically, "then I'm your man. You won't be working alone."

Howard nodded, grateful for the promise but wondering how to apply it. He pulled in at the curb in front of the house and the two of them got out. Howard decided not to press it any further, not to mention the "object" that Stoat had referred to back at the bar. Easy does it, he told himself.

"Follow me," Uncle Roy said, heading toward the back, past the scaffolding again. He stopped at the lean-to shed, pulling the splinter of wood out of the hasp, then stepped inside. There was a trouble light hooked up, hanging from the ceiling, a heavy orange extension cord leading away beneath the house. Uncle Roy turned the light on, pulled open a drawer, hauled out an inch-thick stack of sandpaper, and shoved the bottle in under it.

"Edith's not much on hard liquor," he said. "I've got a house bottle, too, but I'm pretty sure she keeps a weather eye on it. She's a fierce one when she's got a measuring stick in her hand. Doesn't mind a couple of bottles of beer gone, but a bottle of whiskey had better last a man six months; either that or he's a rummy. Better to humor her than to argue the case, though. That's paramount in a marriage. Argue for fun, if you want to, but not for profit."

Together they strolled toward the back door, Uncle Roy telling Howard about his plans for the haunted house, calculating ticket prices and overhead and then going on to the barn lumber issue, and from there into talk about video game arcades and the profit to be made hauling chicken manure, carrying the conversation farther and farther away from landlords and rice paper sketches and the manifold mysteries that rode on the evening sea wind.

 8

HOWARD found himself that evening in Sylvia's yellow Toyota, riding down the coast highway toward Mendocino and Sylvia's shop. Dinner had been a little rough. Uncle Roy talked so seriously and optimistically about the haunted house that he might have been soliciting investments in it. It was set up in an abandoned icehouse down on the harbor, behind the Cap'n England. His friend Bennet was "working on it night and day." It wasn't clear to Howard whether "Bennet" was the man's first name or last name. Uncle Roy was the business end of the thing and the creative genius behind it. The man Bennet could use a hammer and nails and had been willing to work "on spec." Uncle Roy promised to haul Howard down there tomorrow, first thing in the morning, and show him a thing or two.

Uncle Roy's cheerful and convincing notions about the haunted house did nothing to enliven things, though. Aunt Edith had a look about her that suggested she found the haunted house tiresome, or worse—that she saw it as another looming financial disaster. Howard knew that they were in such straits that the loss of a couple of hundred dollars qualified as a financial disaster.

Sylvia said little. The subject of haunted houses seemed to embarrass her slightly, as if she had her opinion but couldn't state it without causing trouble between her parents. Howard smiled and nodded, uttering pleasant statements in a sort of oil-on-the-waters way. It had been a strain, though, and when he had suggested, after dinner, that he and Sylvia go out for a drink, she had accepted without hesitation.

Now Howard tried to make small talk while driving into Mendocino, but she seemed depressed and was untalkative. "This haunted house business might just work," he said. "Those are popular things down south. Kids line up for blocks."

Sylvia glanced into the mirror and shrugged. "Maybe," she said. "Mr. Bennet's sunk most of the materials into it. They're mostly salvage. If it fails, there won't be too much loss, financially speaking."

"Right. That's what I was thinking. Uncle Roy's got some nice props, anyway—the eyeballs and ghost woman and all."

Sylvia looked at him as if she thought he was kidding. "It isn't money, though, that's bothering Mom. Not mainly. I think she can't stand to see him make a fool out of himself. She believes in him like crazy, and so every time he jumps on a new idea she suffers for it. She's seen him fail, and she doesn't want it to happen again, for his sake."

"I talked to the old landlady today, what's-her-name."

"That would be Mrs. Lamey. She can be awful. Sometimes I think that it isn't just money she's after."

"He gave her a thrill with the rubber bat."

Sylvia smiled just a little bit, as if there were something about Uncle Roy's eccentricities that pleased her, after all. Then the

79

troubled look came into her face again. "If I lose the store," she said, "we lose the house."

"That's too bad. The store floats the house?"

"In the spring and summer, when the coast is full of tourists, but the rest of the year it's a matter of squeaking by. Dad gets a Social Security check, but you know what that's worth these days. Anyway, I'm squeaking now. I operate these private New Age parties on the side, selling catalogue stuff, and that helps. That's what I was doing last night. That's why Jimmers couldn't find me. Mother and Father were out playing pinochle. Anyway, Father has the capacity to sort of fritter money away when we get a little ahead. Before the haunted house it was an aquarium down at the harbor. He got hold of a lot of heavy window glass and had the idea of gluing up aquariums and piping water in out of the ocean. He even applied for a grant to study marine life. He was going to sell fish and chips on the side."

"It didn't work?"

"No." She shook her head.

"He means well."

"Of course he means well. And he's optimistic, too. He's always on the verge of making a killing. The spirit museum was going to make a killing, and it bled him nearly dry. It's almost a blessing that he doesn't have any real money to invest anymore."

"He's got a certain innate genius, though. I'm sure of it. If he'd only find out how to put it to use."

"Before we all go broke."

"As I understand it, he believed pretty strongly in the museum."

Sylvia looked hard at him. "Why shouldn't he have?"

Howard shrugged. "Sounds a little implausible, that's all. He was in competition with all those other roadside attractions, where gravity abdicates and water runs uphill and all. Hard to imagine tourists stopping at any of them, unless maybe their kids force them at gunpoint. What sorts of gimmicks did he have?"

"Gimmicks? None, if I understand what you mean. It wasn't fakery. He had a historical interest in the paranormal. He was sure there was something out there, along that stretch of highway. He was picking mushrooms early one morning, and . . . He's an amateur mycologist, did you know that? He used to be very well thought of, actually."

"No," said Howard, "I didn't know. Anyway, he was out picking mushrooms . . ."

"And he saw a car full of ghosts drive past in the early-morning fog. They were apparently in Michael Graham's car." Sylvia looked straight ahead, down the highway.

"I heard about that. He wrote a letter to my mother. How did he know they were ghosts?"

"He said they just evaporated there, while he was watching. The car was sort of drifting up the highway, and there were three men in it, wearing out-of-date hats. The car was slowing down as it passed him, and the three inside just . . . the car disappeared in the fog. It was Father that drove it back down to Graham's after it rolled to a stop against the guardrail. There wasn't anyone in it and not a soul around."

"These ghosts were car thieves?"

She shrugged. "I guess they were."

"And so on the basis of this he invested twenty-odd thousand dollars?"

"That's just what he did."

"You know, maybe he opened the place too close to town. If it was out in the middle of nowhere, people would stop in hoping to buy a snack or just to stretch their legs. But there's no use stopping when there's restaurants and motels five miles down the highway. They'd breeze right past him. He's big on location. I wonder why he didn't see that."

Sylvia didn't say anything for a moment. Howard realized that what he was saying wasn't new to her. She and her mother had agonized over all this for years. His dredging it up now wasn't helping to cheer her up.

"You still don't understand it," she said. "Dad believed in these ghosts, and he thought that there was something out there that accounted for them. That explains the location problem. Why on earth would he have set up the museum anyplace else?"

"Sure," said Howard. "I wasn't thinking. I guess it's just that I wish he would have made a go of it. I'd like to go out there sometime. See what it's all about. Building's still there, I see. I passed it on the way in yesterday afternoon."

"Yes, it's still there. Mrs. Lamey owns it. It's pretty worthless, though. The roof leaks and there's termites in the walls. It's too small for a restaurant, and there's a moratorium against new building out there, so no one can do anything with it. There was talk of it being opened up as a gift shop, to sell redwood products, I think—lamps and carvings and all. Nothing's come of that, though."

They pulled off the highway into Mendocino. There was the hint of mist in the air, and a fuzzy red-tinted ring around the full moon. A scattering of cars was parked along the sidewalk, but almost no lights shined in any of the shops except at the Mendocino Hotel, where the bar was fairly quiet.

"Can I have a look at the boutique?" Howard asked.

Sylvia nodded, fumbling in her purse for her keys. They clomped down the boardwalk and opened up the darkened shop. It was neat and sparse, a sort of study in minimalism, with blond fir paneling and a pine floor and what seemed to Howard to be almost no clothing at all on the wooden racks. It looked very high-toned, being empty like that, but there couldn't be much money in it. He fingered a roughly woven wool scarf, taking a peek at the price tag that dangled from it. Eighty-nine dollars, it read.

"Sell this stuff?"

"In the summer. Local folks can't quite afford most of it." Sylvia slipped behind the counter and began to fiddle with papers while Howard looked around.

There was a pile of wooden bowls turned out of burls, a couple of rugs, a few pieces of art glass, and two Plexiglas trays full of folksy jewelry. All of it was expensive, backwoods designer stuff. There didn't seem to be a lot of anything but space. At one side of the counter were half a dozen books on origami art as well as patterned paper, cut into big sheets and slipped into plastic bags along with step-by-step folding instructions. Alongside lay an origami bird standing next to an origami egg, the egg so finely folded and faceted that there seemed to be almost no hard edges.

Hanging overhead were a half dozen more folded creatures, most of them fish. They were startlingly intricate—thousands of tiny folds in what must have been enormous sheets of paper to begin with. "Still folding paper?" Howard asked.

"Yeah," Sylvia said. She seemed distant, angry perhaps at what she had conceived Howard's attitude to be, or upset about the lease business and about the tense dinner.

Howard wondered if this was the time to bring up having found the paper lily, but he decided against it.

"It's therapy of a sort."

"Ah," said Howard. "Therapy." Somehow the notion of therapy spoiled things just a little. Sylvia opened the cash drawer and banged a roll of pennies hard against the edge, breaking the roll in half. Howard noticed that the several bills in the drawer were folded up, too, into bow-ties and stockings and elfin-like shoes. He reached across, picked out a bow-tie dollar, and widened his eyes at her.

She shrugged. "Lots of time to kill, I guess."

On the other side of the counter lay a couple of Chinese baskets full of crystals—mostly quartz and amethyst—as well as big copper medallions and bracelets and small vials of herb potions and oils. Alongside were racks of books full of New Age advice on the mystical properties of rocks and about reincarnation and out-of-body travel. There was some Rosicrucian flapdoodle on a throwaway pamphlet and a calendar of local events starring self-made mystics and seers and advice-givers of nearly every stripe.

Howard put the folded dollar back into the drawer and picked up the Rosicrucian ad. On it was a drawing of Benjamin Franklin seeming to be impersonating Mr. Potatohead. The legend below read, "Why was this man great?" Howard grinned, thinking up a couple of possible answers.

"You don't have to stand and sneer at it," Sylvia said suddenly.

"I wasn't sneering, was I? I didn't mean to sneer. Look at Benjamin Franklin here, though." He held the paper up so that she could see it. "What's wrong with this man's face?" he said in what he hoped was a sufficiently serious and compelling voice, and then puffed out his cheeks and crossed his eyes. He started to laugh, but Sylvia's frown deepened, and so he controlled himself with an effort.

"Really," he said, gesturing at the crystals and books. "It's very . . . modern, isn't it? Very up-to-date. I like all of this sort of New Age stuff. It's so easily replaceable, like a paper diaper. This year your piece of quartz crystal cures arthritis or summons up the spirit Zog; next year it's a mantelpiece ornament, and you can't sleep until you own a three-thousand-dollar Asian dog. What was it last year, Cuisinarts and biofeedback? Or was that the seventies? I thought the Rosicrucians went out with *Fate* magazine." He caught himself then. He had started out thinking to be funny, but now he was being something else. Uncle Roy would advise against the truth, or at least his version of the truth. There was no profit in it. It would make things worse.

"You see through things so clearly," Sylvia said.

He shrugged, deflating a little but stung by her getting ironic with him. "Well," he said. "I guess I wasn't taking the long view. People can't afford a hundred bucks for a hand-knit pair of gloves, but they can fork out twenty easily enough for a copper bracelet that lets them talk to the dead." He tried to look cheerful, full of play.

Sylvia looked steadily back at him, though, and he realized that he had messed up, perhaps fatally. Sylvia didn't seem to have any sense of humor about this sort of thing. Like her father, she had probably developed a rock-steady belief in her products. She was too honest to do anything else. Howard reminded himself that he hadn't known her for fifteen long years. She might have come to believe in anything. Back when they were younger she had accused him once of despising whatever he couldn't understand, and there had been some truth in that. He hadn't forgotten it, but maybe he hadn't changed much, either. Life was safe and restful that way. You didn't have to tire yourself out developing new interests, and you could feel virtuous about being narrow-minded, too.

"I don't care about turning a profit. Not like you mean it," Sylvia said. "I'd like to make things a little easier on Mom and Dad, though."

"Sure." Howard felt a little ashamed of himself now that she had put it like that. "I didn't mean . . ."

"And besides, you seem to think this is all a fake. Everything's a fake to you. I was thinking you might have outgrown that sort of cynicism by now. And what's worse, how do you know what *I* think? How do you know what I believe and don't believe? Don't go around insulting people before you know what they're all about." She paused for a moment and then looked him straight in the face, glaring just a little bit. "In fact," she said, "there's evidence that I've lived past lives—lots of them. If you'd open your mind, instead of closing it down like a trap, you might find out a few things about yourself that would interest you."

"What sorts of lives?" Howard was suddenly defensive again. He couldn't help himself. Maybe it was because she'd let him spend the night locked in Jimmers' attic while she hustled crystals to New Age loonies. He knew what she would say, too, about these past lives—that she was some sort of princess, Egyptian, probably, maybe Babylonian, or a serving girl who had caught the eye of the prince. There must have been a raftload of them back then, all waiting to die a few times in order to have a shot at being modern girls.

"I was a servant in the court of Ramses III, if you're really interested. Once, about a year ago, I underwent trance therapy and drew hieroglyphic figures in the sand with a stick. They had meaning, too. They weren't just scribbles. My therapist translated them. I had never seen any such things before, either. So you explain it, Mr. Skeptic; nobody else can." She still stared straight at him, waiting for him to scoff.

He widened his eyes at her. "Do you mean like bird-headed men and ankhs and people doing that bent-handed Egyptian dance? I always loved that stuff. I had an elementary school teacher whose name, I swear it, was Rosetta Stone."

"Seen enough?" she asked, heading toward the door.

"I guess. Look, I'm sorry. I was just being funny."

"You're a riot. You don't believe in anything and so you make fun of people who do. Are you frightened of something, or what?"

"I don't know. I haven't thought about it that way."

"Well, think about it. You don't half understand what's going on up here, do you? Maybe you ought to go back down to L.A. and leave us alone. Get lost on the freeways or something."

Howard followed her out of the store, into the moonlight. His mind whirled. He'd been stupidly facetious, even though he could have predicted it would cause trouble. If he were utterly confident that he *did* understand some central mystery, then maybe he could put up with that sort of behavior from himself. But truthfully he had come to think, over the last couple of years, that he understood almost nothing. And the last two days had pretty much made him certain of it.

"I'm sorry," he said. "Actually I'm a little nervous. I *don't* know what's going on, just like you said. Everybody's telling me that, and I think it's getting to me. I don't know anything about anybody's past lives, and I'll admit it. I promise I won't make fun of it anymore. Let's get something to drink, like we set out to do. A bottle of wine."

"I'm pretty busy," she said, clearly still miffed about his attitude.

"What busy? What's there to do?"

They stood on the boardwalk near the duck pond. The full moon shone on the weedy water. It might have been romantic under other circumstances, but at the moment it was just cold and windy and uncomfortable. It occurred to Howard that he and Sylvia had gotten remarkably familiar with each other in the last two hours. The fifteen years had simply disappeared, like Uncle Roy's ghosts. Somehow, though, it had gone just as quickly sour. And it was Howard's fault, mostly. He tried to think of why it was partly Sylvia's fault, but he couldn't come up with anything good except for the reincarnation nonsense.

"I'm sorry I got smart," he said.

She nodded. "I think you say that too often."

"Say what?"

"That you're sorry. Quit saying it. Just do something about it."

"Right. Bottle of wine?"

Without saying anything more she headed up the street. He followed along, catching up to her at the corner, where she turned, angling across toward the Albatross Cafe. The bar upstairs was nearly empty, only a couple of people playing darts and eating popcorn. Geriatric-sounding New Age jazz played softly over hidden speakers. After being careful to consult her, Howard ordered a bottle of white wine and two glasses, and they sat in silence for a time.

"Mr. Jimmers tells me you were robbed yesterday," she said finally.

Howard nodded, then went on to tell her about the adventure at the turnout on the highway, about the gluer microbus and the stolen paperweight. The news didn't seem to surprise her. "Did you tell Father about it, about the paperweight?"

"Nope. Subject never came up."

"I'll see if he can get it back for you," she said. "It might be sold by now, or traded away. There's a fairly hot black market operating up here. Lots of bartering and contraband. Father's had a hand in it. He's got connections that might have seen it. You might check out the antique stores downtown, too, or right here in Mendocino."

"Good idea," Howard said. "I wouldn't mind buying it back." He paused, thinking hard. Seconds passed while he stared into his glass. Finally he spoke, taking his chance on the wine and on Sylvia's inherently romantic nature. "Actually I was bringing it up as a gift for you." He gazed into his glass as the moments slipped past, hoping that the silence was underscoring his meaning. When he looked up in order to meet her eyes, she wasn't there; she was standing at the popcorn machine, holding the empty bowl from the table.

"I can't stand not to eat popcorn when it's around," she said, returning with a full bowl.

"Me neither." He snatched up a big handful and munched on it, trying to think of how to rephrase the statement about the paperweight. He topped off their wineglasses, noticing that the level in the bottle had gone down quickly. That wasn't a bad thing, except that if he were depending on the wine to loosen the evening up, a single bottle might not do it. And yet if he ordered a second, she might think he was up to something, or else drank like a fish along with the rest of his vices and bad attitudes.

"Anyway, this paperweight was a Mount Washington weight. I'm not sure how old, but nineteenth century for sure."

She nodded at him and said, "I almost feel like an appetizer. What do you think?"

"Sure," he said, putting the lid on the urge to make a silly joke out of her statement. "I mean, I'm pretty full of salmon. Something light, maybe. You choose it."

"Be back in a sec." She stood up and moved away, studying a menu that lay on the bar and then talking to the bartender for a moment. Howard could hear her laugh, but she was speaking too low for him to make out any of the conversation. Clearly they knew each other well. He felt like a tourist as he pretended to watch the dart game. Now he would have to bring up the paperweight a third time. That was almost impossible.

"Want anything to drink?" Sylvia asked from the bar.

"A beer," he said. "Anything local, thanks." He turned back to the dart game. He might as well leave the rest of the wine to Sylvia.

She sat back down, smiling and with his beer and a glass. "The bartender's a friend of mine," she said. "His name is Jean Paul. He's a martial arts expert and owns—what do they call it?—a dojo up in Fort Bragg. He has to moonlight here four days a week in order to keep the dojo open. Martial arts is a spiritual thing with him, a way of life."

Howard decided to say nothing. He couldn't tolerate Jean Paul. Clearly it was a fake name. The subject of Jean Paul would just get him into trouble. The man had probably been a ninja assassin during the Ming dynasty. Wasn't a dojo some sort of aquarium fish? Martial arts stank on ice. It was another New Age phenomenon pretending to have lived exotic past lives.

"Say," he said. "I ran into Stoat down at a tavern in town."

She was silent on the subject of Stoat.

"What's he up to these days along artistic lines? Does he still paint, or is he mostly a financier?"

"He paints pictures of complicated-looking microcircuitry, with bits yanked out of it. It looks sort of . . . physiological.

Fleshy, I guess you'd say, but it's cold and empty and nasty. Very nasty. To my eye it's just dead on the canvas. He's heavily into cybernetics."

"You two aren't . . ."

"Aren't what?"

"Seeing each other."

"I saw him this afternoon. You drove past, remember."

He nodded. "Of course. I just . . ." Howard let the subject die. Somehow the jovial bartender had made him jealous, and the jealousy had reminded him of Stoat. He had caught himself, though. There was no percentage in taking that line. "So anyway, this paperweight . . ." Howard started to say.

"Oh, yes," Sylvia said, interrupting. "You were worried about getting it back."

"Well, no. Not exactly. You see, I remembered back when you used to have a couple. Remember that French one that you had—the St. Louis weight with the little running devil in it?"

She nodded, but the conversation was interrupted by the arrival of the food—two plates, a tray full of potato skins, and a wire rack full of condiments and a couple of spoons. Sylvia studied her wineglass, her eyes distant, her mind troubled again. The paperweight subject had evaporated.

On the theory that desperate times called for desperate measures, Howard picked up the two spoons and wedged one into each eye so that the handles thrust away on either side of his head like dragonfly wings. He stared in her general direction, his face screwed up to keep the spoons from falling out. He swore to himself that he wouldn't relinquish the spoons, no matter what, until she did something—hit him, walked out, asked to use a spoon, anything.

She let him sit for a long minute, until he began to think about the other people in the bar and the spectacle he was making of himself. He started to wish he could see something past the edges of the spoons. What if she had left—gone to the popcorn machine or the rest room? What if she slipped out and drove home? Finally she laughed, though, as if she couldn't help herself, and shoved the end of a potato skin into his mouth when he tried to say something.

"Cheer the hell up," he said, swallowing the thing.

"*You* cheer up. Better yet, don't talk. You keep getting into trouble when you talk."

"I won't. I promise. I mean I will. Anyway, this paperweight . . ." He wanted more than ever for her to know that he had brought it as a gift.

She pursed her lips and nodded. "I'll see what I can do. I can see that it's really bothering you. Like I said, if it's still around, maybe Father can get it back. You'll just have to be patient about it. It's really got you worked up, hasn't it? That's probably why you're on edge, why you're so catty about things."

It was hopeless. Giving her the paperweight now, even if he had it, wouldn't work. He had made too big an issue of it. He decided to cut his losses and drink his beer. He poured the rest of the bottle of wine into her glass.

"I'm warning you right now," she said, "that if I drink that, you're going to have to drive home."

"Fine. I'm sober as a judge. It's still early, though."

She checked her watch. "Just nine o'clock." She drank her wine meditatively for a moment. Then she said, "You know, for a minute there I thought you were going to tell me that you'd brought the paperweight up to give it to me."

His eyes shot open. "That's what I did," he said. "That's what I've been trying to tell you."

She laughed. "That's okay," she said. "You don't have to say that now. I know what the thing means to you. You were like that when you were a kid, too. Remember?"

"I guess I was." He wondered what she meant, what she was up to. "Like what?"

"Remember you had that one marble, the one with the red and blue swirls? That favorite one? What did you call it? 'Martian Winter.' Remember that? You were sure cornball sometimes."

"I . . ." He shrugged. He *had* actually made up names for his marbles, but how on earth had she remembered them?

"You went absolutely stark when it disappeared. Remember? You cried for about a week."

"Me? I never cried about that." He'd been about eight at the time. He could still remember it clearly. It was one of those disasters that loom monumental in the mind of a child. He certainly hadn't cried about it, though—not in public, anyway.

"Did you ever figure out what happened to it?"

He shook his head. "Lost it under the couch or something."

Now she shook her head. "Nope. I stole it. I gave it to Jimmy Hooper." She smirked at him, finishing off her wine.

"I knew you did."

"You *liar*! You never knew anything about it."

"And I never drew bird men in the dirt, either, and had my trance therapist scope them out."

"Neither did I. I was lying about that. I knew it would about kill you. I really didn't steal your marble, either."

"I knew you didn't," he said. "And I really did bring that paperweight up here to give it to you."

"You're sweet," she said, still not believing him. "I know what let's do, let's go out to the museum."

"Now? In the dark?" Suddenly he regretted letting her finish the bottle of wine by herself.

"I've got a flashlight in the car. Don't forget that I'm pretty familiar with the place. I grew up there, nearly."

"Would tomorrow be better? Tomorrow afternoon—I'm supposed to work on the haunted house tomorrow with Uncle Roy, but not all day."

"You're scared," she said. "Just like when you lost the marble. Tell me your pet name for it again. I've forgotten. I want to hear you say it just once, just for the sake of old times."

He sat like a stone idol, smashing his mouth shut, and then made the motion of turning a key in front of his lips, locking them tight.

"Remember when you set marbles all over the floor and said they were the 'ice planetoids,' and then you went to the bathroom and I brought Trixie into the house and played 'deadly comet'? I think that's when the Martian one disappeared, don't you? It went down the heater vent in the floor."

"No. Forget the marble. We were talking about going down to the museum. I can't believe you're serious about that." He found himself hoping that she was, though. He could picture them hand in hand in the moonlit museum, waiting for the arrival of the ghost car. It was something they might have done in high school.

"Why not?" she said. "What are you afraid of, ghosts?"

"What the heck," he said. "Not me." Not for the first time, it struck him that Sylvia looked astonishing in her sweater. It gave him a new appreciation for the overpriced clothes in her shop. "Let's go," he said. "I'll drive."

9

THANK God for the moonlight, Howard said to himself as they wound their way down the highway, south through Little River. The road was empty save for one set of headlights a half mile behind them. Howard was ready to pull off the road and let the car pass rather than drive with its lights shining into his rearview mirror, but it stayed well back—always one or two bends behind them, pacing them evenly.

Without the moonlight it would have been utterly dark. As it was, there were patches of silvery light, illuminating here and there a bit of road or beach cut by the shadows of rocks and trees. The wind and the darkness had sobered Howard up quickly, but Sylvia leaned against his shoulder with her eyes closed, softly humming. The wine had relaxed her and she had managed to forget the day's troubles. Howard wished that it had been something else that had relaxed her—him, specifically. But he hadn't been able to.

This was home to her, this wild stretch of twisting ocean highway. He was in strange territory, though, and it made him nervous. No, that didn't entirely explain it—even as kids she had twice his sense of adventure, half his sense of fear. He watched for the headlights behind them. There they were, right on track. He couldn't see the car, even with the moonlight. "Slow down," she said, sitting up straight in the seat. "Here it comes."

He turned off the highway, past the picket fence with its cow skulls and across the weedy gravel parking lot where he pulled up against a wooden berm and shut the engine off, leaving the keys in the ignition. The windows in the building were tightly covered with plywood shutters, and even in the darkness, maybe especially so, the place had a long-disused look about it that somehow made him skeptical about going in.

Sylvia climbed right out, though, pulling a parka out of the backseat along with a flashlight. Howard reached for his corduroy coat, wishing he had brought something warmer. The ocean wind rushed straight up at them from across the road, and he could hear the crash of breakers, unnaturally loud in the silent night. They scrunched across the gravel toward the rear of the building, back into the shadows of the forest. The smell of eucalyptus leaves was heavy in the air along with the smell of the sea.

Sylvia shifted a little pile of granite rocks beneath an electrical circuit-breaker box, carefully lifting the grapefruit-sized rocks, as if wary of bugs, and shining her light in among them. "There's a key here somewhere," she said. Beyond, at the end of the building, was a padlocked door.

On an impulse he stepped back around into the parking lot and waited. Nothing. There wasn't a car in sight. He thought without meaning to of the gluer microbus on the highway and of the Chevy in the parking lot at Sammy's. Where was the car that had been following them? It should have gone past while they were fishing out their coats, but it hadn't. It had vanished.

There were driveways off the highway, of course, dirt roads leading down to houses on the bluffs or else up into the hills, up to the land of the cultists and dope gardeners. That would explain it. The car had turned off. It was as simple as that. It wasn't the fabled ghost car making a run down the coast. Graham's Studebaker was smashed to scrap on the rocks, anyway. Even ghosts wouldn't care to drive a wreck like that.

Cutting off the urge to whistle, Howard walked hurriedly around back, to where Sylvia ought to have been searching for the key. She was gone.

"Syl!" he whispered, suddenly terrified. There was no answer. He looked around wildly for a rock, a stick, anything. He hunched down and scuttled across to the pile of rocks she'd been messing with, picking one up and hefting it. Then he stood still, listening, and very slowly edged toward the building to get his back to a wall. He gripped the rock. There was nothing—no sound at all.

Until the door swung open and Sylvia stepped out onto the little wooden stoop, shining her flashlight into his face. He shouted—something between a scream and a groan—and threw the rock straight at the ground, as if he wanted to pulverize a lizard.

"What on earth is wrong with you?" she asked in a normally pitched voice. It sounded insanely loud. "What were you going to do with that rock?"

He stood blinking at her, his heart pounding against his ribs "I thought you were gone," he gasped out. "I thought there was some sort of trouble." He whispered this last bit, knowing that there was no reason to and that it made him seem twice as terrified.

"Aren't you gallant?" she said, laughing. "Coming to my rescue like that. There's nothing out here." Then she was silent, listening, as if to let the night provide its own evidence. There was nothing but the low rumble of breakers from across the road and the sound of the wind sighing in the trees.

The stillness didn't make Howard feel any better. That was just the trouble, wasn't it?—that there was nothing at all out there. He would have been more comfortable surrounded by the familiar noises of a southern California suburb.

He picked up the rock and tossed it back into the pile, calming down enough to be embarrassed at having thrown it like that. Sylvia went back into the darkened museum, playing the flashlight around on the walls. Howard followed, expecting— what?—ghosts, maybe, the Studebaker crowd in their top hats playing chess.

The place was dusty and deserted. It looked as if even in its heyday it had never amounted to much. He had expected some kind of fun house—with a mysterious cellar, maybe, and with different rooms and passages—but there was only the one big room and what looked to be a tiny office and bathroom off to the side.

Because of the darkness, nothing was particularly visible. Faint moonlight shone through the open door, but there was almost no light at all through the shuttered windows. Only the little beam of Sylvia's flashlight illuminated the room. She shined it across low tables built of redwood planks, like picnic tables. They were covered with dust, but nothing else.

"He used to sell literature on the supernatural," she said. "All kinds of stuff, some of it serious, some of it completely nuts. It was all over two of these tables. I used to keep it straight, which wasn't hard, since there were hardly any customers to mess it up. There was a wonderful model of the Studebaker, too, with the ghosts sitting in it. Mr. Bennet built that. It had a table to itself. I kept it dusted. Father's got it somewhere, in a closet at home or something.

"Wait," she said, "there's a picture." On the wall was an enlarged photograph, out of focus, of a Studebaker on the highway. In it sat a trio of half-evaporated men. One of them was looking out the window at the camera, his face indistinct.

"Uncle Roy took this?" Howard asked. "I thought he was out picking mushrooms when it drove past."

"He was out photographing them, actually. It was pure luck. There he was with the camera in his hands. Impressive, isn't it?"

Truthfully it looked to Howard like a bunch of dressed-up guys in a car, driving through the fog. "It's weird, all right," he said, not wanting to cross her. "I wonder who was driving. This crowd would be more at home in a coach-and-four."

Sylvia shrugged. "I was always so astonished just at their being there in the car that I never worried much about who was driving."

There were a number of other photographs on the wall, mostly bad ones in dime-store frames. Most were faked-up pictures of ghosts with a couple of paragraphs alongside by way of explanation. Sylvia shined the light on each in turn. There was a photograph of the ghost dog of Tingwick and another of the ghost dog of Garden Grove. Farther along was the Brown Lady of Raynham, descending a set of stairs, just like Uncle Roy's ghost woman, except that his was more convincing.

There were several artist's renderings of ghost cars and carriages, along with a dim photograph of a sort of Gumby vehicle parked behind a barn. Howard was happy to see that ghosts were as up-to-date as anyone, that early in the century they'd given up carriages and horses and taken to the highways in what were usually very fashionable cars—Daimlers and Austins and Rolls-Royces—all except Uncle Roy's ghosts, who had stolen a shabby old Studebaker. Beside a drawing of the ghost bus of North Kensington there was a photograph of the ghostly image of Dean Liddell, which had mysteriously appeared on the whitewashed wall of Christ Church Cathedral sometime in the early 1920s.

"Dean Liddell . . ." Howard said. "Wasn't that Alice Liddell's father?"

"Might have been," Sylvia answered, giggling just a little. "They have the same last name."

"Ssh!" Howard cocked his head and listened.

"I was just joking . . ." Sylvia started to say, but he clutched her arm and held it, and she was instantly quiet. They stood listening to the faint sound of the wind. "What was it?" she whispered after a moment.

"I heard someone walking—on the gravel outside."

"Just a squirrel," she said, but she didn't sound convinced. They could see nothing through the shuttered windows. Both of them listened, but there wasn't a sound that there shouldn't have been. Sylvia started to giggle again. "Where's your rock?" she asked.

He relaxed a little. It was his imagination again. He forced himself to ignore it, and then he wondered suddenly what he was doing out there in the woods in the middle of the night. Clearly he wasn't there to discover anything about the place. Daylight would be necessary for that.

Sylvia stood about a foot away from him now, still shining her flashlight on the sketchy visage of Dean Liddell. Howard put his hand on her shoulder and immediately felt a little less jumpy. She let it lie there, saying nothing and holding the light steady.

"Alice Liddell was Lewis Carroll's Alice—Alice in Wonderland," Howard said.

"Really. And her father's face appeared on a wall? The family hogged more than its share of fame."

"This is the only one of the ghost photos that doesn't look fake, isn't it?"

"How about Father's?"

"I mean besides his. Neither one of them looks like trick photography, anyway."

"I'm ready to believe it," she said. "You're the doubting Thomas, remember?"

"Listen!" He had heard it again—the scuffing of shoe soles, the crunch of gravel. They stood absolutely still, but there was only silence again, as if something were waiting. And then, whisper-quiet, the back door of the museum swung closed.

"The wind," Sylvia said as Howard stepped toward it, following the beam of her flashlight.

But there was a quick metallic clicking and the sound of the padlock snapping shut. There were clear footsteps outside now— someone hurrying—and low voices talking, maybe arguing.

Howard had a quick insane notion that it was Mr. Jimmers, come around to lock him in for the second night in a row. Crazy as it had to be, the thought made him furious. He banged on the locked door, and then, in a rage, kicked it with the bottom of his foot. "Hey!" he shouted at the darkness, but no one except Sylvia was paying any attention to him.

"Shut up and listen," she whispered, grabbing him by the arm now. "Someone's going through my car."

It was true. They could hear a car door close, followed by the sound of the trunk slamming shut. Howard went from one window to another along the wall, trying to see out past the edge of the shutter, but it was no good. Through one he could see a sliver of moonlit ground, but that was all. Another door slammed.

He slid one of the windows open. "I can kick the shutters out," he whispered. "They're just held in by a screw or a nail or something."

"Why?" she asked.

"You're being robbed. What if they're going to steal your car?"

"What are you going to do, chase them up the road? Let them have the car and everything in it. Who cares? It's insured. Don't be a hero. This isn't worth getting beat up over."

She was right. He saw that right away. He was still smarting from when she'd scared him outside, when he had thrown the rock into the dirt, and it seemed to him that kicking out the shutter would redeem him somehow. He listened again, to the sound of someone walking, probably two people. The footsteps receded now, fading into nothing. They hadn't stolen the car.

"Where are your car keys?" he whispered.

"In the ignition."

That was puzzling. Why *hadn't* they taken the car? Clearly because they weren't garden-variety thieves.

"Are they both gone, do you think?"

"I don't know," she said. "Why wouldn't they be? Probably someone on the road, looking to steal a jacket or a blanket or something."

He wondered. Somehow it felt as if it were something more sinister than that. "What if they light the place on fire? With us locked inside?"

"Will you shut up about that!" she said, talking out loud. Then she whispered, "Why would they do that? Don't invent things. This is bad enough. And if they do, then you have my permission to kick out the shutters—all of them."

"Wait!" He held his hand up. There was the sound of a car engine trying to catch—except that the starter was bad, and it whined for a moment before the engine rumbled and the motor noise evened out.

"Stoat!" Howard said, and leaning back, slammed the edge of his forearm into the bottom of the shutter. It popped loose, but it was hinged at the top, and so it flopped back down into place, a nail in either corner bumping against the window casing. Hurrying, he bent the nails over sideways and then pulled one of the tables across. "Come on," he said, climbing onto the table and holding the shutter open. Sylvia climbed up next to him and handed him the flashlight.

"Careful," he whispered. "Check first."

She stuck her head out, looking up and down the building. The parking lot was deserted. "They're gone," she said, and climbed through, dropping easily to the ground below and then standing up to grab the shutter. He gave her the flashlight and then climbed out himself, heading for the car. The keys were lying on the seat. The thief had taken them out to open the trunk and then tossed them back into the car. He could as easily have tossed them into the bushes, and Howard and Sylvia would have spent the next hour walking up the highway into Little River. This was very slick—carried out like a business venture, without any malice or larking around.

"Wait," Sylvia said, hurrying back toward the rear of the building again. Howard went with her, watching carefully, trying to be ready if someone was hiding in the shadows. There was no one—only the scattered rocks and the door locked shut. Sylvia put the key in among the rocks and built the pile back up on top of it. "Let's get out of here," she said, sounding frightened now.

"Gladly."

"How did you know it was him?" she asked. "It might not have been Stoat. What do you have against Stoat?" She gazed at him evenly, and he had the notion that she was baiting him, being playful.

"His car engine," Howard said. "His starter's bad. It sounded just like that down at Sammy's this afternoon. You'd think a guy like that would be on top of things, would worry about being identified. Either he's sloppy or he doesn't care. Why should he? Apparently he didn't steal anything."

She shrugged. "Nothing that I can see. What the hell was he after?"

"You don't know?"

"I don't know. And quit looking at me like that." She climbed into the car and started up the engine.

"I'm not looking like anything." He shut the door and sat back in the seat, feeling easy at last. "Let's go."

"So what was he after?" she asked again. "Can't you tell me? Is it a government secret or something? What are you, CIA?"

"No, I can't reveal my true identity. You can call me Agent X."

"I'll call you brand X if you don't tell me what in the hell he was looking for."

"*They*," Howard said. "They wanted the Hoku-sai sketch. The one that I came up after."

"Where is it, then?"

"You tell me," he said, "and we'll both know. Could be that Jimmers has it. He's about the most suspicious person I've ever met."

"He's pretty shady, all right," Sylvia said. "But he's just an eccentric. He's not up to anything—what?—illegal or something. Is this trouble with the sketch illegal?"

"I don't know. It may have something to do with Graham's murder."

She looked at him, driving carefully along the dark highway, past the Little River Inn. "Maybe Graham wasn't murdered," she said. "Word has it that he committed suicide."

"Who told you that?"

"Who told you he was murdered?"

"Mr. Jimmers . . . I think." But *had* Jimmers told him that? Or had he only been joking? Jimmers had laughed like a prankster after saying it—hardly the response of a man who believed his friend to have been murdered. "I don't know, really. Anyway, you mean he *wasn't* murdered?"

"They found a suicide note in the car."

"He wrote a suicide note and left it in the car? Then drove the damned thing into the ocean? What did he want, for the fish to read it?"

"I don't know. I'm just telling you that they found a suicide note—Mr. Jimmers did. He gave it to the police in Fort Bragg. It was Mr. Jimmers that found the car and all."

"How'd he get down to the ocean, by boat?"

Sylvia shrugged. "He got down there, that's all I know. The tide was up and the car doors were open—the fall knocked them open, I guess. Graham's body was gone, washed out with the tide, but the note was still in the car, clothespinned to the rearview mirror."

"Uh-huh." Howard realized that he didn't half believe in Graham's suicide. He didn't believe in murderers, either; what he believed was that he still knew almost nothing about what had gone on. But he had an idea, though, that he could find a way in the morning to learn more, and he determined to get up early, before the rest of the house was awake. "I might as well tell you that Stoat threatened your father at the bar this afternoon. He pretty clearly was after something—the sketch, I think. And he implied that the problem of your lease could be fixed if Uncle Roy could come up with it. He offered him money for it, too. A lot, I think."

"Father doesn't have any sketch. At least I'm pretty sure he doesn't."

"That's what he said. Stoat didn't believe it, though."

They drove in silence into Fort Bragg. It was almost midnight, and he was tired out. Sylvia was, too. He could see it in her face, which, this late in the evening, revealed her age just a little bit. He could see the strain of the passing years in the lines beside her eyes. "Thanks for holding it together like that out there," he said. "I was pretty shaken up."

"I was, too."

"You were thinking. I was lurching around." He patted her knee, not really meaning anything by it except that the physical contact, the warmth of her leg through her jeans, made him feel a little more solid. The world had been too full of ghosts.

"It's late," she said, answering an unspoken question.

"Yeah, and I'm beat." He moved his hand away, as if he had to in order to rub his eyes. They turned up Barnett Street, angling toward the curb in front of the house, in behind Howard's truck. Abruptly he sat up straight in the seat, peering out through the window. "Shit," he said.

"What, what's wrong?"

"The camper door's open. I left it locked."

 10

HOWARD awoke in darkness, jarred awake when the iron clock in the living room tolled five. That had gone on all night, and he had finally gotten off to sleep by smashing the pillow over his head and then had awakened two or three more times when the bell tolled. He rolled over, deciding not to get up, after all. Sleep was more important to him. Then he lay there thinking, waking up a little more each minute, starting to worry about trifles, as he always did when he woke up in the early morning.

Only now what he worried about seemed to be more than mere trifles, and it seemed to be more and more certain to him as the minutes dragged past that he didn't have very much idle time. He was being locked up at every turn, and his truck had been burgled twice—once by the gluers and now by Stoat and whoever else had gone through Sylvia's car. They hadn't taken anything this time, but the act itself was ominous. Things were happening in pairs and in triplicate, and somehow at five in the morning that seemed to signify. He climbed out of bed after another few minutes of mulling things over and pulled on his clothes.

Fog had drifted in during the night. It was gray-dark outside, and still. He went out silently through the kitchen door, trudging through the wet grass around to the front of the house, where he got Sylvia's flashlight out of the backseat of her car, eased the car door shut, and headed for the backyard again.

When he passed Uncle Roy's workshop, he hesitated for a moment and then pulled the splinter of wood out of the hasp and opened the door. He turned on the light and looked around, wondering what he could carry with him out into the woods. He only half believed Uncle Roy's horror stories, but somehow the fog and the early-morning twilight had started to work on him. He found a two-foot length of closet rod in among a stacked-up pile of scrap lumber. He swung it into the palm of his hand a couple of times, deciding that it would do the trick as well as anything. It was a bit of security, anyway— something to balance the fear that was seeping into him even as he stood there.

He went out again, leaving the door unlatched, and headed straight for the misty line of fir trees. The yard sloped up into them, fenced off by berry vines, which had been hacked away along the north edge so that there was a path into the woods. On the other side of the path lay a vacant lot, overgrown with vines and scrub.

Up close, the woods weren't quite as thick as it had seemed from a distance. Even with the fog he could see a good ways through the trees—far enough so that he was unlikely to come upon anyone unawares. He switched on the flashlight, but the glow was feeble because of the dawn leaking through the tops of the trees. In among the deep shadows the light helped more, though, and he was happy enough to have it. He suspected that he didn't have far to go.

He walked along for a time, conscious of the smell of evergreen and fog. You didn't often get that sort of thing down south. Here he was, up at dawn, trudging through the primeval woodlands. It wouldn't be a bad thing to make a morning ritual of this—in any sort of weather. He could buy some sort of oilcloth raincoat and a pair of galoshes, too, and try it in the rain, carrying a thermos of coffee.

Just when that pleasant notion occurred to him, the path forked. He stopped and listened to the stillness, a little bit wary now. The fog had thickened and seemed to be settling in rather than lifting. How far *had* he walked? He had been enjoying himself and not paying attention. There was a rustle back among the trees just then, and his heart leaped. He stood still, thinking of Uncle Roy's bears and lions. It hadn't been much of a rustle, though—barely enough for a rabbit or bird—just enough so that his hearty, up-at-dawn mood utterly evaporated and he was filled with unease. He told himself that the forest wasn't any different in the fog and the darkness than it would be in the sunshine. Then he tried to convince himself that surely the fog would begin to burn off as the sun came up.

He looked behind him, though, and saw nothing but a wall of murk and trees. He had no idea how far away the city lay or in which direction he had come. He had wanted to go straight on up the path, roughly along the property line—but which of the two paths confronting him now was the main path and which one branched off? Neither one was well traveled. For no reason at all he stayed to the left, going along quickly and quietly for three or four minutes until the path forked again.

Again he angled left. That ought to be safe. If he failed to find anything at all, he could at least make his way back by—what?—taking all the left forks again. Or was it all the right forks?—he would be returning after all. Would there necessarily be any forks at all? He would be coming back, but then he wouldn't be coming *backward*, would he? Most of these sideline trails would be leading away behind on his return, anyway, deeper into the forest. It would just muddle him up to pay attention to them.

Somehow it had gotten darker; either that or the forest was more dense. He was sure now that he had come too far, but he went on slowly, anyway, determined to turn back soon. There was something up ahead; he could see it dimly through the mist, a sort of clearing. Just then there was another path, too—this one leading away behind. It couldn't do him any good now, but it was the one that would cause trouble on the way back. There was a lot of autumn-colored poison oak, he noticed, climbing all over the stump of a tree, right there at the fork. He would remember that easily enough.

He walked on, as if hurrying now would get him out of the woods sooner, and within moments he found himself standing at the edge of the clearing he had seen through the trees. It was overgrown with grass and wild iris and skunk cabbage. The path ended there, just like that. Clearly he was deep into the woods—far deeper than Aunt Edith could have ventured yesterday afternoon. She had been gone for maybe ten minutes and seemed to have made a round trip of it—although now that he studied it out, he couldn't really be sure that it was *her* red jacket he had seen through the trees. It might have been anybody, kids maybe. This might easily be a wild-goose chase.

Someone had been using the clearing as a junk pile, too—so much for the primeval woodland idea. There were a couple of old car fenders tilted against each other toward the far side of it, although it was too weedy and misty to make much else out. There was something about the way the fenders were tilted together, though, as if they were meant to form a little shrine . . .

Suddenly he was both curious and terrified. He ducked back behind a tree and stood listening. There wasn't a sound. Clearly this was too far out into the forest to be a mere junk pile; no one hauls car fenders into the woods just to throw them away. A child might haul them out there to build a fort, of course, although scrap lumber would have made more sense. He quit trying to make sense out of what he saw. This had something to do with what he had found embedded in the attic plaster night before last. There was no getting around it.

He stepped out from behind the tree, satisfied that there was no one around, and walked to where the two fenders stood, sunk six inches or so into the soft loam. There was freshly dug soil scattered across the top of the weeds. Someone had been working at the thing recently. Beneath the arched, mismatched fenders, someone had built a clever little wall out of odds and ends—small stones, an old glass inkwell, doll-sized lipstick tubes, a broken pocket knife, a rubber puppet head, half a dozen ivory dice, a couple of broken tin toys, and, among more of the same, his stolen paperweight.

Sitting on this junk-pile wall, his short legs dangling, was a ceramic Humpty Dumpty, its paint nearly weathered off and the white of its shell the color of an old meerschaum pipe.

Howard reached down to pick up the paperweight, but then stopped himself. Something in him didn't want to disturb it, any of it. There was something child-like about the collection— like the careful arrangement of small toys and collected objects, say, on top of a child's bedroom dresser, arranged just so for reasons that only the child could fathom. He was struck with the certainty, though, that the oddball little wall wasn't the work of a child. There was a magic in the arrangement and choice of objects. He could feel it in the air of the clearing. He had stumbled into an open-air cathedral, and he felt suddenly that he didn't belong there and didn't want to run into anyone who did. To hell with the paperweight.

He was determined now to head straight to the house. He would find a way to slip out that afternoon, maybe, when the fog lifted and the sun shined. He slowed down in order to make less noise. There seemed to be paths everywhere around the clearing, and the fog had settled in so that even nearby trees were ghostly and dim. He stumbled on a root and nearly fell on his face in the grass, dropping the flashlight to catch himself. He sprang up at once, shaking his hand and looking around, half expecting a patchwork zombie to materialize out of the fog. He had wandered straight off the path somehow, out onto another little patch of meadow.

This was no good at all. He was utterly lost, and had been within five minutes of leaving the house. The whole concept of direction, of north, east, south, and west, was imaginary. It meant nothing, had no application. Realizing it made him mad. He would sit down and wait. Wasn't that what someone advised? Sooner or later they would discover that he was missing and—what? Follow him into the woods, track him with dogs? It wasn't likely. He could wait out the fog, perhaps—unless it didn't lift for two or three days. It was almost funny. He was thirty years old and lost in the damned woods. He didn't feel like laughing, though, or sitting, either, so he found the path and started walking again, searching futilely for his own footprints coming the other way.

The trail narrowed and weeds grew up through it. Clearly it wasn't very often traveled. There wasn't any sign of his footprints on it, or anyone else's, either. A fallen tree loomed out of the fog, blocking the trail and making it certain that he'd gone wrong. He turned around, took ten steps back, and found another trail, this one broader and well traveled.

Don't get frantic, he told himself, half out loud. Then immediately he understood that to be evidence that he was getting frantic. He felt the urge to run up this new path, just in order to get somewhere different, and so he consciously slowed his pace and forced himself to pay attention to his surroundings—to remember oddly shaped bushes and trees. It was daylight now, and the fog was ghostly white where the sun shined through. It was wet, too. Water dripped down the back of his coat from overhead branches. *Were* there bears in the woods? He asked himself that, wishing immediately that he hadn't thought of it.

Again the path forked, this time to the right—a better path, it occurred to him, although he couldn't have told himself why. He had to duck beneath low branches, hunching along through the gloomy twilight. There was suddenly an ocean breeze— just the hint of one, as if maybe he had found his way back toward the edge of the woods, after all, and he hurried along, wondering how long he'd been out there—a half hour, anyway, maybe longer.

The path ended at the clearing with the shrine again. He had blundered in a sort of zigzag circle through the woods, coming upon the clearing from the other side. At once he plunged back into the trees, with no idea where he was bound, and stumbled within seconds into a patch of forest partly clear of fog. He found himself atop a ridge, its overgrown slope running down into a weedy little pond, and then another hill beyond it, very steep and grassy. He clambered down the slope toward the pond, standing after a moment in marshy grass at the edge, watching water striders flit across the top of the water while he caught his breath, utterly lost.

Across the pond, floating on the shallow water and tied to a half-submerged tree, lay an old rowboat with a couple of trout poles and fishing tackle in the bottom of it, partly covered in a piece of oilcloth. Leading away from the boat, along the edge of the pond and then through the grass and up the opposite slope, was another trail. Through the trees he could just make out what looked to be the shingled roof of a cabin, the rest of the cabin hidden by the hillside. He picked his way down and around the pond, slogging through mud and wet grass until he reached the path on the far side.

He crouched along, moving slowly, watching the back of the cabin appear above the crest of the hill and ready to duck into the bushes at the sight or sound of anyone at all. There was a light on inside the cabin and smoke from a chimney. It occurred to him that he ought to have been happy, stumbling back into civilization like this, but he wasn't. This was hardly civilization. Likely as not, this cabin had been Aunt Edith's destination yesterday afternoon. He had come too far not to find out now.

Now that he needed it, the fog had mostly disappeared. He crept forward, toward the rear of the cabin where a long pile of split logs reached nearly to the windows. The intelligent thing, of course, would be simply to knock on the front door and announce that he had gotten lost in the woods and needed directions. Except that there was clearly something secretive about Aunt Edith's furtive trip, and at the moment he felt like being equally furtive. And there was the shrine in the clearing, too, not a hundred yards away, that lent the whole business a strangely dangerous air.

He peered in at the rear window, into a small bedroom containing little more than an unmade bed. Through the open door he could see into what was maybe a living room, just making out the edge of a stove and the corner of a small wooden table. Shadows moved across the edge of the table, but no one stepped into view. He would have to find a more useful window.

He edged down toward the corner of the cabin, ducking low behind the woodpile in order to take a peek before stepping into the open. He could feel the ocean breeze again, blowing uphill toward the cabin, and it struck him that if the breeze held up he could take a stab at following it toward town. A well-traveled path angled away in that general direction, and although the trees were too thick for him to be certain, that path must surely lead toward Uncle Roy's house—toward the city instead of deeper into the woods.

His footsteps were noiseless on the soft, weedy ground as he slipped past two curtained windows, neither one of which gave him any view at all of the interior. At the corner of the house there began a broad, wooden front porch, and the ground ran away downhill steeply there, so that in the very front of the porch there were four or five wooden steps. He would have to clump across the porch in order to see in.

He crept back down to the woodpile and from there back down the hill toward the pond, so as to approach the house from some little distance. It wouldn't do to seem to have been snooping around. Should he whistle? He squashed the idea as too theatrical. He would yell "Hello" instead, a couple of times, and then head up onto the porch and knock heartily so that no one on earth could think him a sneak.

Putting on his best look of pleasant surprise, just for the sake of anyone looking out the window, he cupped his hands over his mouth and stopped cold, cocking his head to listen. He had heard the sound of a door slamming. There wasn't any doubt. It must be well after six now. He had been mucking around in the woods forever. He jogged away in a crouch again, back toward the woodpile. Inside of three minutes, here came Aunt Edith, carrying a foil-covered plate of food and a pot of coffee. She hurried along, although she didn't look ill at ease; she looked attentive, as if she wanted to arrive with hot food.

She passed out of sight, and then momentarily he heard a screen door slam shut and then another door shut more softly. This time he hurried around the opposite side of the house, the side that fronted the deep woods, so that if his aunt went back out directly, she wouldn't catch him in the open.

A red wheelbarrow stood tilted against the house, surrounded by garden tools and piles of mulch and stakes and pots. The nearby garden was made up of moldery little rows of withered cabbages and anemic onions, all of it blighted somehow. He pulled the wheelbarrow away, settling it down onto its bed, and silently climbed up onto it so as to see in through a window just beside the edge of the front porch. Luckily the curtains hung a couple of inches apart—plenty far enough for him to get a quick glimpse inside.

There stood Aunt Edith next to an old black potbellied stove. Her plate of food sat on the table. Sitting in a chair, just getting ready to tie into the food, was old Michael Graham, thoroughly alive, although incredibly old and frail-looking. A walking stick leaned against the back of an adjacent chair.

Howard clung to the windowsill, lost in thought. What did this mean? The old man was hiding out here, certainly. That was clear. So he wasn't murdered and he hadn't committed suicide. The car-over-the-cliff business had been a ruse, a red herring to confound Stoat and his associates. Who knew that, besides Uncle Roy and Aunt Edith? Jimmers? Sylvia, clearly. Why hadn't they told Howard? Because he was from out of town—a casual guest. For his own good, obviously, they would attempt to keep it secret. There was no use him getting involved. So where was the sketch? It was a good bet that the old man had it. His mind spun, trying to add things up, to work out the mathematics of the puzzle.

Aunt Edith turned to leave, and Howard dropped off the wheelbarrow and scuttled back toward the rear of the house, hunching along past the woodpile again. In a couple of minutes, after she had plenty of time to get home, he would follow her. There was nothing more to learn—not without breaking into the cabin and searching it, which was utterly out of the question. He was sliding into deep waters, to be sure, and his best bet would be to wade ashore while he still had his feet under him, and give up any notions of being an amateur detective. He didn't owe the museum anything, anyway, and no one, certainly, owed him the Hoku-sai sketch.

He crouched there for one more moment, just to be safe, and in that moment he felt a tap on the shoulder.

11

FOR a moment Howard crouched silently, knowing that trouble stood at his elbow, but asking the universe for another ten seconds of relative comfort before he had to look doom in the face. He tensed himself and turned around. Doom had taken the form of Uncle Roy, who stood there in a heavy jacket, holding a field guide to West Coast mushrooms and a little basket covered with a handkerchief. He shook his head as if advising Howard not to talk and then nodded back toward home. Howard followed him down the path, feeling sheepish and still shaking a little from the fright.

Uncle Roy ambled along, stopping every now and then like an Indian tracker to examine the ground. He picked up a limp little mushroom and dangled it there for Howard to see. "*Panaeolus campanulatus*," he said. "Don't eat this one."

"I won't," Howard said.

Roy pitched it into the bushes, wiping his hands on his pants. "I've got a bunch of crap at the house that I've got to haul down to Bennet's. I figured you'd want to come along. You seemed keen on it last night. We'll run it over to his house this morning."

"Sure," Howard said. "I was out for a walk. You don't get this sort of opportunity down south. There's no place to walk to, really."

"That's a fact. That's why we got out of there. These woods, though . . . You're lucky you didn't just disappear into the fog, wander up into the coast range somewhere. It's a dangerous place. They've found the bones of hikers up there, picked clean." He said nothing for a moment and then, matter-of-factly, said, "You've found the cabin."

This took him by surprise. "Yes, I guess so."

"I knew you would. I knew it yesterday afternoon in the truck there, when you brought up the subject of the sketch again. 'There's no hiding anything from a lad like Howard,' I said to myself. And then when I couldn't find you around the house this morning even though your truck was still out at the curb, I waited for Edith to go out with the old man's breakfast and I came along after her. Sure enough, there you were. 'Howard's a shrewd one,' I said to myself. 'We've got to come clean with him.' Look here. Look at this."

He bent over and pointed at a brown, corky-looking fungus coming out of a rotted stump. "That's a pretty specimen, isn't it?"

"Nice color at the end there," Howard said, pointing to the pale blue edge of the thing and waiting for Uncle Roy to come clean with him.

"That's one of the pore fungi. What they call 'artist's fungus.' Believe it or not, it's tough enough to carve. You can make attractive household articles out of it—matchboxes, candlesticks. Not much market for it, though."

"Lots of mushrooms out here in the woods, aren't there?"

"More than you'd suppose. You can just eat the hell out of most of them, too. You wouldn't want to, maybe. Half of them taste like rotten dirt. Take a look at these." He lifted the cloth from the top of the basket. Lying in the bottom was a handful of small purplish fungi, misshapen and evil-smelling. "I'll bet you a silver dollar that these are uncatalogued. Never seen or heard of them. I've been finding them over the last few days, growing out around the cabin. I call them witch flowers. Look at the shape."

Howard peered closely at them. Sure enough, they looked like little disfigured lilies, as if someone had set out to make imitation flowers out of crayons and snail slime but hadn't seen enough real flowers to get the shape right. "Smell like hell, don't they?"

Uncle Roy looked shrewdly at him. "You don't know how close you are to being right," he said, putting the cloth back over them.

The two of them set out down the trail again, still going slowly, Uncle Roy on the alert for mushrooms. "About the cabin," he said. "We're putting up a guest there."

"Right. Michael Graham. That's where Aunt Edith goes with the food."

"Breakfast, lunch, and dinner."

"I guess that means he's not dead, then."

"No, he's not dead. That was a ruse that didn't work worth a damn. Might have gained us a week."

Us? Howard wondered about that. Maybe Uncle Roy was coming clean at last.

"He's lame, though. He's old. Do you know how old he is?"

"No," Howard said, and the phrase "older than the woolly mammoth" sprang into his mind.

"Ninety-something. He has the right to be lame."

"Lame, though," Howard asked. "From the accident? The car going over the cliff?" He felt abruptly foolish for having said such a thing. He hadn't been in the car at all. Maybe he was lame from some old war wound.

"He can hardly get around any longer without his cane. Does a little fishing when he's up to it, but most of the time it's all he can do to eat. He and I are old friends, you know."

"Are you?"

"Oh, yes. Old friends. We go way back, to before Edith and I married. When it got bad for him . . . Well, he was too easily gotten at, if you see what I mean, out there on the bluffs and all, with no one around but Jimmers. We thought we'd better hide him. The woods are full of our people, too, coming and going."

"I saw some evidence of that. But what do you mean 'gotten at'? More creditors?" That was a safe word, one of his uncle's favorite euphemisms.

"Worse than that, actually. This sketch that you're keen on. You aren't the only one, you know."

"Is that right?"

"Yes, and it's not just the money, either."

"I can see that," Howard said. "The piece can't be as valuable as all that."

Uncle Roy stopped for a moment. They were in sight of the house now. "There's value and then there's value," he said, nodding back uphill in the direction of the cabin. "It's a rare piece, all right. I know why you've come out here, but let's not bother the old man as early as this. He's tired. Spends his time just holding his own. He usually comes down to fish around dusk. If we can swing it, we'll bring down a couple of poles and stop off for a chat, maybe this evening. I'm going to level with you, though. Your being here is a liability, of sorts. Don't mistake my meaning, either. I want you here. I think maybe you *have* to be here. It's entirely possible that you don't have any choice in the matter. You better brace yourself for that. But you're a suspicious character, aren't you, riding in like Perceval on a horse. What's his game? they're thinking." He looked hard at Howard, clearly waiting for an answer.

"I don't know what my game is," Howard said truthfully.

"I believe you. Maybe you don't have one. Maybe you do. No matter what we like to think, we don't always get to choose what games we play in this world. Sometimes they choose us."

Uncle Roy set out again, and said nothing more until they were out of the woods. When he stopped again in the backyard in order to finish their talk in private, he had the look of a man who was choosing his words carefully.

"Anyway, you're something of a liability. What I mean is that word's out that you've come north, after the sketch, looking for Graham. Who are you, they're wondering, one of us or something new? It's pitched the balance all haywire, hasn't it? Now, we supposed that they thought Graham was dead, but from what Stoat was saying yesterday afternoon, they didn't fall for the wrecked-car trick. Stoat could as easily have been fishing, of course. But he's gone through your truck, hasn't he? And through Sylvia's car, too—undoubtedly because she was with you. He's onto you, then, and no denying it. What I'm saying is that I don't want you leading him or any of his people into the woods. That's paramount. You understand that, don't you?"

"Sure," Howard said. "I didn't know . . ."

"You couldn't have. I should have told you, but I didn't want you dragged along, either. I'm beginning to think it's a whirlpool, though, with all of us in the same boat, going round and round together. We'll pull through if we look sharp, all engines full. Maybe you're the captain of this damned tugboat— the dread Captain Howard from down south. Time will tell. We're not alone in this, either. We've got confederates."

"What did you mean 'his people'? Is there a whole crowd of them, then, trying to put their hands on the sketch?"

110

"Too many of them for my taste. Stoat's not the most formidable of them, either. It's Heloise Lamey that we've got to watch. Say, I'm half starved. Let's hit the Cap'n England for breakfast—some of those million-dollar pancakes and bacon. You can buy. Edith cooked the old man a couple of eggs, and she'll want to fix us up, too. But I want to talk a bit—set you straight on some of this, if you know what I mean. Secrecy is paramount."

"Surely Aunt Edith . . ." Howard made a stab at protesting, but Uncle Roy cut him short.

"True enough. She's a party to this, but not in the way you and I are. She's been looking after Graham, and so has Sylvia. I like to call them the 'tent maidens.' "

He grinned at Howard, finding this clever. Howard didn't get it, though.

"Like in the Grail romances."

"Ah," Howard said. "Sorry. I'm ignorant of most of that."

"Well, no matter," Uncle Roy said. "Live and learn, as the old saw goes. Anyway, they're both on the boat, too, but they don't come out on deck very often, and so maybe they haven't taken a good look at the sky lately. It all makes Edith pretty seasick, is what I'm trying to say, so we'll let her rest in her stateroom for the moment. But you and I can't sleep, boy. Not a wink. The barometer's dropping, and it's up to lads like us to haul on the bowline. That's paramount. We can't be slackers, or they'll catch us out."

"I'm your man," Howard said, trying to decide if he had learned anything particularly useful or new. Uncle Roy seemed to live in a world of euphemism and metaphor, and it left Howard with a hundred practical questions, all of them clattering around, colliding with each other. Maybe over breakfast . . .

"My advice right now," Uncle Roy continued, "is to lie low. You know nothing at all. That's the byword. Don't tip your hand. Forget the sketch for the moment. It'll be there right enough when the time comes. Or else it won't. I don't know quite where it is, and that's the solemn truth. Jimmers reported it stolen to the police, and for all I know that's gospel. He's a deep one, though, and in a business like this it's better if the left hand doesn't know what the right hand is doing. Do you follow me? They don't know which way to jump when you work it like that.

"This business of Jimmers' shed . . ." his uncle was saying as they trooped in through the back door. He cut off the sentence, though, at the sight of Aunt Edith washing dishes. "Ready in five?" he asked Howard.

"Easy," Howard replied, and went up the hallway to change his clothes, hearing his uncle in the kitchen saying something to Aunt Edith about them "making a connection on the barn lumber."

AT midmorning, Howard found himself pulling into the parking lot of the ghost museum again, along with Uncle Roy, two propane lanterns, and a heavy flashlight. Uncle Roy had a "hunch," and he couldn't rest until he'd taken a look at the museum. But they must try to be back up in Mendocino before noon, he said, in order for Howard to meet Bennet, who spent his mornings working on his house. Howard intended to ask Sylvia out to lunch today, too. Time was short.

The place seemed doubly deserted in the wind that blew off the ocean, whipping the tree branches. A little flurry of pine needles and autumn leaves whirled across the gravel lot, pinning Howard's pants to his legs, and the hollow-eyed cow skulls on the pickets stared straight into the wind, watching the whitecaps through the trees. The whole place was inhospitable, geared to frightening people away—a perfect habitat for ghosts but a bad one, perhaps, for customers.

The rocks beside the rear steps were scattered over the ground. "Sylvia piled those back up last night," Howard said, suddenly tense.

"Of course. They came back is what they did. It's just as well you got out of there, although I suppose they gave you a chance to do that so as to avoid confronting you. They don't want outright trouble. Not yet. Key's gone, of course, the bastards."

"No, it isn't," Howard said, spotting the key in the dirt along the concrete foundation where someone had tossed it. "Why did they lock it back up, do you think? Why bother?" He handed his uncle the key.

Uncle Roy shrugged, stepping heavily up the stairs. Now that they were around out of the wind and into a little bit of sunlight, he had started to sweat. "Maybe they didn't find what they wanted but are afraid it's still here," he said, unlocking the door and pocketing the key. He lay the propane lanterns on one of the tables and fired them up, adjusting the flame.

What there was left of the place had been dismantled. The framed photographs, one by one, had been pulled off the walls, taken apart, and lay now scattered over the tables and floors.

Nothing was smashed or wrecked. The intruders hadn't been in any sort of fury. Again, the whole business was methodical, painstaking—something that Howard found troubling. It seemed to argue that their adversaries, "the enemy," as Uncle Roy had referred to them during their cryptic talk at breakfast, were calm and organized and moderately sure of themselves.

In the little bathroom, the lid had been removed from the top of the drained toilet, and the medicine cabinet had been pulled entirely out from its niche in the wall and yanked apart. They'd taken the steel band off from around the mirror and pulled it away from its backing. They'd even looked into the hollow chrome-plated bar of the towel rack.

Out in the main room, the floor vents were pulled up. Howard looked down through the hole in the floor at the old gravity heater below, sitting in an open concrete box. With the flashlight it was easy to see where the dust had been disturbed on top of the dark metal. Someone had hung through the hole and had a look around down below.

"So they were looking for the sketch," Howard said, helping his uncle gather stuff up. "They thought it was framed up behind one of these photographs or rolled up and shoved into the towel bar or something. Thorough crowd. As I read it, though, their being here means they don't have it. Not yet."

"Don't be so sure. If they have it, they need time, and this could be a ruse. Throw us off the track with a lot of tom-foolery."

"Why would they have been so careful about it, though? I guess because paper is delicate, and they didn't want to tear it up, to damage it."

"Or to *pretend* to care about not tearing it up, of course. The trick is to separate illusion from reality here, isn't it? This is a powerfully tricky lot of scum. Their purposes are never apparent. Nothing is."

Uncle Roy squinted at Howard, making this last statement seem to apply to everything, to the north coast in general, to the wide world.

"Too bad about these pictures," Howard said. "They don't seem to be ruined, though. We can put them back together again."

Uncle Roy smiled at him, as if he'd said something funny. "That's the way to talk," he said. "These are all copies, actually. I took everything valuable along home two years back, when the place folded. You can only keep so much stuff."

"How about the police?" Howard asked suddenly. "The place has pretty clearly been ransacked. Let's call the police and put them onto Stoat."

"Let's not," Uncle Roy said. "Let's not even think about the police. We don't want institutionalized help." With that he shut the lanterns down, picked them up, and headed for the door. Five minutes later, after ditching the key in a new hidey-hole, they set out for Mendocino, Uncle Roy directing Howard through town and up onto Albion where they parked at the curb in front of the house with the Humpty Dumpty on the roof, the very house where Howard had nearly wrecked his truck yesterday morning.

The front lawn of the house was a wonderland of miniature windmills and whirligigs. A small, dark-haired man in a string-sleeve T-shirt worked out front, shoveling concrete out of a galvanized tub. Across the street, dressed in a sort of red kimono and a pair of Wellingtons, Mrs. Lamey watered her roses.

Howard was surprised to see her there, in public, just like that, living across the street from the Humpty Dumpty house. It meant that she had a life of some sort, a favorite chair that she sat in, maybe a family. Up until then he had defined her entirely in terms of mortgages and percentage points. It surprised him even more sharply when she recognized him and waved, as if she were happy to see him. Well, he thought, business is business. Maybe this is watering the roses, and business doesn't apply.

He waved back. There was no use being troublesome. Then he gave his attention to Mr. Bennet, who nearly broke Howard's fingers when they shook hands. He spoke with an accent, but just the trace of one, and Howard couldn't place it.

"I build things," he said, hosing wet concrete off his shovel and seeming to sum up his life in that one statement. He gestured at the yard. It was a pincushion of gimcracks, all wind-operated: little men sawing boards in two, ducks flapping their wings, fish on wires swimming around posts, Dutch windmills and whirligig cows slowly cranking away in the wind off the ocean. "They never stop," he said. "Something's always moving." He lit a cigarette and puffed hard on it.

Bordering the house were beds full of wooden, painted flowers—tulips and daisies cut out with a scroll saw and complicated roses glued up out of individual wooden petals. There were wooden animals behind the wooden flowers, with heads that tilted and wobbled continually. The entire lawn was alive with movement, up and down and back and forth and sideways. The roof of the house was spiked with weather vanes, too, swiveled toward the east, and in the midst of them, with his legs crossed and wearing high-water pants and the familiar red-soled shoes, sat the plywood Humpty Dumpty, like a judge on a bench, leering across the street toward where Mrs. Lamey sprinkled the roses. A strong gust blew straight off the ocean, and one of the Humpty Dumpty's arms lowered in a solemn sort of wave and then was jerked back upright by a spring.

Mr. Bennet turned off the hose, ran his hands through his hair, and stepped onto the porch and then into the house. Uncle Roy followed, saying to Howard, "I think he planted this whole passel of whirlibobs just to drive the old lady nuts. That's part of why she hates me, because I'm friends with Bennet. She thinks this place is a disgrace. Tried to burn him out two weeks ago, too. That's when we put the egg man on the roof. She can't stand to have the damned thing waving at her day and night. She tried to get an injunction against it."

"Really?" asked Howard, honestly surprised. "She tried to burn his house down?"

Uncle Roy nodded slowly and decisively, like Oliver Hardy, while grinning with the same sort of raised-eyebrow expression that had betrayed him when he was talking about the fleet of underground Buicks yesterday.

Mr. Bennet pulled a steel coffeepot off the stove and poured coffee out into three heavy porcelain cups that were stained brown on the inside. The coffee was tepid and bitter and full of grounds, but Mr. Bennet drank it with relish, as if it were the last cup he'd ever see, and smoked on his cigarette between sips. The place was only sparsely furnished, with plain wooden furniture, and the old area rug in the living room was pulled back across the red pine floor and rolled up onto itself. An oak dresser lay dismantled in the middle of an ocean of wood dust, and a belt sander sat inside one of the drawers along with three or four loaded-up sanding belts.

"Little project," Mr. Bennet said, nodding at the dresser. "Woman up near the harbor owns it. I'm cleaning it up for her. Poor old lady." He shook his head. "Mrs. Deventer," he said to Roy.

"Oh, sure, Mrs. Deventer." Then to Howard he said, "Mrs. Lamey's trying to run her out of her house, too. Lamey owns the land on either side. They want to put up a bank, and Mrs. Deventer's smack in the middle of the project. She'll hold out, though. She's Dutch, just like me."

"What he means is a German with his brains kicked out," Bennet said, nodding broadly. "You ain't a Dutchman," he said to Uncle Roy. "Last week you were telling me you were—what was it?" He looked at Howard, as if he needed help sorting things out. "A South Sea Islander of some nature. A Fiji, I think it was."

"What I said," Uncle Roy said, shaking his head tiredly, "was that my grandfather *lived* in the South Seas. He wasn't any kind of native. He was in the hotel business."

"That ain't how I remember it." Mr. Bennet pursed his lips and then changed the subject abruptly. "I've been studying numbers," he said.

Uncle Roy nodded in assent. "He's going to crack the lottery."

"It's something I call the Principle of Universal Attraction. Numbers are just like people, just like you and me. Do you know what I mean?"

"Like people?" Howard asked.

"Just like that. Like people going to a banquet, going down to the VFW for a fish fry. They walk in the door and they don't know nobody. Not a soul. Think about it. Hold it still in your mind. They mill around, don't they, and sit down somewhere, on one of them folding chairs. Pretty soon they strike up a talk with someone they don't know from Adam, and what does it turn out but that both of them like baseball. They can't get enough of the Giants. Or maybe they got the same kind of dog or their wives are up to the same damned foolishness. You with me so far?"

"Sure," Howard said. Through the window he could see Mrs. Lamey sitting on her porch, which was sheltered from the wind. She was reading a book now and drinking something hot out of a cup. Howard began to think that he'd sold Mrs. Lamey short. Still, though, if she'd really tried to burn Mr. Bennet's house down and if she was the sort of monster that Uncle Roy seemed to think she was . . .

" 'Nother cup of coffee?" Bennet gestured at their half-filled cups.

"Not unless you've got a pack of Rolaids to sweeten it with," Uncle Roy said, nudging Howard in order to illustrate how funny the remark had been. "Your coffee tastes like rat poison. What the hell do you do to it?"

"You don't know from coffee," Mr. Bennet said, waving at him in disgust and then ignoring him and talking straight at Howard. "So anyway, numbers are like that, too, like people.

You dump them in a box and away they go, searching out someone to have a chat with. Birds of a feather is what it is. Shake them up, spin them around, and here comes number forty-three, sitting down with number eighteen, and then number six and number eight, maybe, and number twelve making a third, feeling more and more comfortable with each other as the night goes on. Next Tuesday there's another fish fry, but this time, as soon as they're in the door, they're searching each other out straight off. The trick is to watch them, figure out who it is that's attracting who. That's all it is—attraction. Simple attraction Not like love. I don't mean like that. This is a casual thing, day by day. You've got to study it hard if you want to peg it."

"Mr. Bennet went out to Vegas ten years ago and nearly beggared them," Uncle Roy said. "Went to town on keno, day and night. Wouldn't stop. They nearly had to shut down. Brought the whole damned town to its knees. Where was it?" he asked Mr. Bennet.

"Place called Benny's."

"Penny's, wasn't it? I thought you said it was Penny's.'

"That's because you don't listen worth a damn," Mr. Bennet said, draining his coffee mug. "You and your Samoan grandfather." Then to Howard he said, "It ain't one of your Strip hotels, nor downtown neither. You don't want to draw attention to yourself, you see, in one of the big spots. They'll work you over in the alley if they catch on. Small joint, though, doesn't pay any attention. They think it's a run of luck. I took them to the cleaners, too. I'm going back again someday, when I've got the goods, the particulars.''

"How much did you soak them for?" asked Howard.

"Nearly five hundred bucks," Uncle Roy said.

"I bought that truck with it." Mr. Bennet nodded out toward the curb. There was a flatbed truck with stake sides parked there, half on the grass. It looked like it had been through some rough times.

"We used it to haul a load of chicken manure up from Petaluma just last week."

"That was two weeks ago," Mr. Bennet said. "Nothing like chicken manure for the rosebushes. Put too much around them, though, and it burns the roses right up.''

Uncle Roy stood up to pour himself another cup of coffee, shaking his head sadly at the pot, as if it were a crime against the gentle art of cooking. "People around here are big on organic gardening," he said. "You can sell a truckload of chicken manure to the Sunberries nearly any day of the year. Leaf mold, too. You can drive out toward Ukiah for a load of leaf mold out of the oak woods." He shrugged. "It's a way to earn a couple of bucks. We're saving a little up in a joint fund, isn't that right?"

His friend nodded. "We need a stake for when we make the run out to Reno."

"Tell him about numbers some more," Uncle Roy said. "I can see that he still doesn't get it."

"The problem with numbers," Mr. Bennet said darkly, settling down to the task, "is that there isn't any end to them. Do you get it?"

Howard said he did. He knew that much about them, anyway.

"I mean to say that they'll trip you up that way. You'll chase them like a dog after a mechanical rabbit until you drop dead. That's the Babel effect."

"That's right," said Uncle Roy. "What he means is that you can't get there from here. There's no such thing as rich enough, nor anything else of the kind. Your man Stoat, now . . ."

Mr. Bennet looked up sharply at the mention of the name.

"Howard's all right," Uncle Roy said, waving his hand. "He's come in with us, lock, stock, and barrel."

"Well, then," Mr. Bennet said, and shook Howard's hand solidly again. "Good to have you."

"So people like Stoat," Uncle Roy continued, "and your woman across the road there, they *want* things, don't they?" He looked very serious. " 'I want more and more and more,' that's what they go around mumbling all day long. It's the song they sing. What do they *want*, though? They don't know. They can't put a name on it. It burns them up, though. It's a little taste of hell, isn't it, all this wanting. Is it another dollar? That's not it. They've got more than they can use. Another acre of land? What for? A mechanical eyeball in the middle of the forehead? What good would that do them?—they can't see a damn out of the eyes they've got. I know what it is, though, what they want. It's *apotheosis*. They want to be God almighty." He slammed his open palm against the tabletop, and coffee sloshed out of his cup. "Damn it," he said, "gimme a paper towel."

Bennet handed him a sponge off the counter. "The boy don't see the connection," he said. "He don't see the number business. You get too worked up to explain it worth a damn."

"I'm right, though, aren't I?"

"Right enough. It's a matter of patterns is what it is."

"Everything is," Uncle Roy said.

"Now take the gluers, for instance. What's their motto? 'No rules.' That's it, plain and simple. Look at them, wearing two different shoes, never driving into town by the same route twice in a row. And let me tell you something you won't believe. When one of the elders, one of the gluer saints, comes around, what happens?"

Howard shrugged.

"Everything goes haywire."

"That's a fact," Uncle Roy said. "Picture frame corners open up. Aquariums leak. Streets don't even meet perpendicular anymore. Believe it."

"Your table saw won't cut square," Mr. Bennet said. "Don't matter how hard you try to tune it up."

"It's anarchy, pure and simple—chaos, hanging around them like a magnetic field." Uncle Roy sat back in his chair, squinting at Howard. "It's elemental energy."

"But what is it," asked Mr. Bennet carefully, "when you've got anarchy written into the rulebook?"

"When you *compel* it?" asked Uncle Roy.

They waited for a moment, forcing Howard to answer. "Well," he said finally, "I don't suppose it's anarchy anymore."

"Give that man a cigar," said Uncle Roy. "There's more to it than that, though. Do you remember what Bennet was telling you about the numbers?"

Howard nodded again.

Mr. Bennet hunkered forward in his chair, dropping his voice. "What your Samoan uncle means to say is that there's *patterns in the chaos*."

"What you might call 'the Way,' " said Uncle Roy.

"The Dance."

"And the Hoku-sai sketch . . . ?" Howard started to ask, but his uncle stopped him by holding up a hand. He shook his head and jerked his thumb backward toward the window, toward where Mrs. Lamey once again meddled with her rosebushes. She seemed to have her head cocked, as if she were listening to voices on the wind.

"We're not like the others," Uncle Roy said, gesturing out the window. "We're the king's men, aren't we? Isn't that what I told you? The circle's been broken. We mean to put it back together again before they have a crack at it. We mean to put the pattern in order."

119

"And the lion will lie down with the lamb," Mr. Bennet said, with a note of finality in his voice.

"This is alchemy that we're talking about," Uncle Roy said, clearly worked up almost to a missionary zeal. "There's the one crowd, the Stoats and the Lameys who would turn lead into gold to line their pockets with, and worse. And there's another crowd . . ."

"Us," said Mr. Bennet.

" . . . who don't give a damn about metallurgy, except to drag this whole sorry world up out of the leaden age it's fallen to— back to a place that's a little bit sunnier, if you follow me."

"Won't it just fall again?" Howard asked. Clearly his uncle and Mr. Bennet were deadly serious, even though they'd lapsed into the mythological. They weren't talking platitudes and abstractions here. That was certain. They were driving toward some goal that they could see with their eyes, like the walls of El Dorado, perched on a meadow above the sea.

Uncle Roy shrugged. "It will, certainly. Just like your Humpty Dumpty. But the path to the garden is a crooked one, hid by mist. You've got to be walking on it to see it clearly."

"That's right," said Mr. Bennet. "Your man *will* fall off the wall, won't he? That's his nature, and God bless him. Then some damned old fool will try to put him back together again, sure as you're born, and God bless him, too."

Uncle Roy gave him a sharp look. "Who are you calling a damned old fool, you damned old fool?" Then to Howard he said, "But there's no choice in the matter, not really, not for men like you. That's paramount, isn't it? This matter of choice and no choice. You've got it and you don't. It sounds contradictory, and that's just fine. Sense is nonsense when you get around behind it, and the opposite, too. You can see that, can't you? I knew that when I saw you. Here's a lad who'll do his part. That's what I said. He's got the instinct. Like a salmon. That's why he's come north. Forget the damned museum. It's redemption you're here for. Break out that can of Glub's glue and start puzzling the pieces back together again. The other crowd's at it right now, hammer and tongs. Only it's the dark tower they're mortaring back up, piece by piece, and by God we mean to bring it down."

"Earthquake and thunder," Bennet said, putting down his coffee cup.

"Brimstone and fire," said Uncle Roy. Then he hooked his fingers under his coat collar, looking very much like Humpty

Dumpty himself, having had his say.

"Nearly noon." Mr. Bennet stood up abruptly and smashed out his cigarette into his empty coffee cup. "You got the wigs for the corpses?"

"In the truck," Uncle Roy said. And then he winked broadly at Howard. "Don't make too much of this, my boy. Don't lose any sleep. Take Sylvia somewhere nice. Here." He hauled an old, wrinkled ten-dollar bill out of his pants pocket and gave it to Howard. "Have a drink on me. Life goes on in the midst of the battle. Otherwise what's the battle for?"

"Really . . ." Howard said, trying to think of a way to refuse the ten. It was clearly leftover money from hustling food stamps.

Uncle Roy frowned. "Take it," he said. "Wasn't I just telling you about making a run out to Reno? This isn't all nonsense, you know. This is no time for doubts. The sand's running out. The king is wounded, but we mean to put him right, or bring the whole shebang down in the effort. Have a drink on your poor old uncle."

Howard nodded and stood up. "Right, thanks." He shoved the bill into his pocket. "I'll just catch up with you later, then."

The three of them went out, Mr. Bennet locking the door. And after hauling the wigs out of Howard's camper, Uncle Roy and Mr. Bennet shuddered away up the street in the flatbed truck. Howard watched them turn the corner, heading for the highway, and then stepped across toward where Mrs. Lamey sat on her porch.

 12

MRS. Lamey sat in an armchair, bent over and mixing up a potion of some sort in a ceramic bowl that lay on the floor of the porch. It was apparently fertilizer—fish emulsion from the smell of it. She glanced up at Howard as he came up the flagstone walk, between the tree roses. "Well," she said, standing up and wiping her right hand on her apron. Then she held it out so that he could shake it. Her face still had the pickle look, but it wasn't distorted by rage now, probably because there was no chance of being assaulted by rubber bats.

"I'm afraid I made a rather negative impression on you yesterday," she said, not in an apologetic tone, perhaps, but with some hint of regret and shared responsibility.

"It was a difficult business."

"Well, I oughtn't to lose my temper like that. But Mr. Barton can be an irritating man." With a momentarily bemused smile, she shook her head and said, "I'm afraid he's not what they'd call fiscally responsible."

Howard couldn't argue with that, although he hated the phrase "fiscal responsibility," because usually it meant nothing, and left everything out. He was intrigued, though, that Mrs. Lamey was apparently apologizing in her way, making amends. She was puttering in the garden now, carrying on like a human being. Obviously she had discovered that Howard's check was good. "Putting out a little fertilizer?" Howard asked. "What's this can of rusty nails for?"

"For the hydrangeas," she said. "Do you garden?"

"Not much, no. A few tomatoes in pots, some houseplants, that's about all."

"Well, if you bury rusted nails around the roots of hydrangeas, the pink blossoms come out blue. It's the iron in them. Sounds almost magical, doesn't it? You can change the color of roses, too, although not so easily. It's rather messy, but you get interesting results. I'm something of an amateur horticulturist, and put this together myself." She gestured at the ceramic pot, and Howard could see, now that he was standing next to it, that it didn't contain fish emulsion at all. It was full of a heavy red liquid.

"Don't shudder when I tell you that it's blood," Mrs. Lamey said, putting on a pained expression. "Any sort of blood works well enough, but fish blood is best. Wonderful fertilizer at the same time. And easy to come by, too, at the cannery. I put it around the white roses. You've got to soak the roots, though, and keep after them with it, if you want the full effect. I use safflower stamens to color white daisies yellow. I even raised a black orchid last year."

"A black orchid?" Howard asked. "How?"

"Squid ink and charred wood." She nodded at him, with a look that suggested she was telling the solemn truth. "The colors aren't natural, of course. But that's the beauty of it. Look here." She led him across the patchy grass to where a little forest of pink ladies was blooming against the wall of the house. They stood there alien and huge, thrusting up through the dark soil, their blooms an alien, fleshy color of brown-pink. There was a rotten smell in the air around them, as if there were a dead animal under the house. "These were a product of blood and rust," she said, "and a couple of other ingredients that I'll keep secret."

"Fascinating," Howard said. He couldn't think of any other word for it, except maybe "morbid" or "abominable" or some other word out of an old pulp horror story. The heavy blooms suggested something both human and unearthly, the effect heightened by a web of faint bluish veins beneath the flesh, reminding Howard uncomfortably of bloodstreams or, worse, tattoos. He thought of the "witch flower" mushrooms that Uncle Roy had been collecting in the woods around Graham's shack, and in his mind he saw Mrs. Lamey sowing fungal spores in the sea wind, watching them blow north across the road and into the forest.

"You're the curator of an art museum, I'm told."

"Well," said Howard, suddenly on his guard, "that's close. I'm not actually curator. It's a small natural-history museum that dabbles in art. I'm not even certain I'm going back to it. I like it up here."

"Do you? I'm so happy to hear that. I was afraid I'd rather put a damper on that. Here you were, newly arrived, and I lost my temper completely. I've been wanting to apologize ever since."

"Don't mention it," Howard said, walking back toward the porch. He didn't believe her suddenly. There was something in him that distrusted wide swings in temperament, and he suspected that she had come to some conclusion about him since their struggle at Uncle Roy's house yesterday. She had determined that he was important, and he wondered why.

Howard noticed the printed figures on her kimono for the first time: little squared-off mechanical gadgets and loose coils, blocked-out patches of computer circuitry and radio schematics and what looked like tiny robotic bugs. It was all highly stylized and hard to sort out, but the little figures seemed anatomical somehow—bits and pieces of internal organs reduced to webs or skeletons or very sketchy computer graphics. He was certain he knew who had designed the fabric.

Howard realized suddenly that if he were going to catch Sylvia in time for lunch, he would have to hurry. He checked his watch and looked surprised at what he saw. "I guess I'll be off," he said.

"So soon? I was rather hoping to show you my collection of miniatures. It's seldom that there's an expert in town."

"I'll have to take a rain check," Howard said.

"Good. I'll tell you what. I have a little . . . circle, I suppose you would say. A salon. We meet on Tuesday nights. You'd be surprised at the number of artists and writers living around here. It's not rare that people drive up from San Francisco and even farther south just to be part of my little circle. I'm a queen mother to them, you could say—their fiercest champion and critic both. They're my *real* collection of miniatures. All of them full of potential, like seeds that want a little water and soil. Why don't you drop past? The conversation is stimulating."

"I'm not any kind of artist," Howard said. "I only meddle with what other people do—try to talk learnedly about it."

"Learned talk is the order of the evening. Say around six."

"I'll try, certainly. I'll bet Mr. Stoat is a member of this circle."

She burst into laughter at the suggestion—cackling and waving her hand almost coyly as if he'd suggested something bordering on indecent. "Nobody calls him *Mister* Stoat except me. It's merely 'Stoat.' He's very defensive about that. You've met him, then?"

"Just briefly. Seems fascinating."

"He's a little bit nervy, too. Don't let him bother you. He's very glossy and hard on the outside, but a terrible pussycat inside who thinks he's a panther. I can keep him on leash, but I don't suppose anyone else can. He's a genius, really, and a man of many talents. A fearful decadent, I'm afraid." She winked at Howard and said, "I'm glad we had this little talk, then. You'd make a welcome addition to my little circle. You'd fit right in. And I hope you harbor no ill will toward me for my shameless behavior yesterday afternoon."

"Not at all."

She stood for another moment regarding him, and suddenly he felt self-conscious and a little embarrassed, as if something more were expected of him.

"Do you know," she said, "you look a little bit like someone I knew once, many years ago."

"Really?" Howard said. "I have a common face, I guess."

"On the contrary, it's . . . remarkable." For a moment Mrs. Lamey's features betrayed a look of profound longing and remorse, and it struck Howard, sadly, that this was the only honest expression that had crossed her face during their conversation. The rest was veneer. Even the gardening enthusiasm had sounded false, nearly demented. This wasn't false, though, even Uncle Roy would agree to that.

She smiled abruptly, dissolving the sorrow by an act of will. and said, "Tuesday night, then."

"Tuesday night."

She held her hand out, limp-wristed and palm down, as if she expected him to be gallant and to kiss it. He gave it a small shake instead and hurriedly crossed the street, climbed into his truck, and turned the key, letting the engine idle for a moment. This last exchange had unsettled him, and although he didn't want to hobnob with anyone's "little circle," he felt as if he had made a solemn and necessary promise to her, and he told himself that on Tuesday he would pay her a visit. He wouldn't have to stay long, and it would give him an opportunity to be a sort of spy for Uncle Roy.

Except that she was something more of a mystery to him now, and it seemed less likely that she and her salon were the "enemy" that Uncle Roy had talked about at breakfast. His uncle was full of exaggeration and wild metaphor, a habit which made jumping to conclusions a dangerous thing.

Sitting alone in the car, free of persuasions, it seemed entirely possible to him that all this north coast plotting might have a very simple and mundane explanation—greed, likely as not, or a consequence of a lot of backwater types nursing grudges over the long years.

Then he remembered the shrine in the woods and old Graham hiding out in the cabin, and his own truck having been ransacked, and the talk about the attempt to burn down Bennet's house. After a moment he admitted to himself that what he really knew was nothing at all yet. Just to keep things smooth, as he drove away he waved out the window to Mrs. Lamey, who was crouched in front of the hydrangea bush now, burying rusty nails. The Humpty Dumpty on Bennet's roof waved, too, as if in sarcastic imitation.

IT was still early afternoon when they bumped down the drive toward Graham's house on the bluffs. Sylvia had taken two hours off and had sent Howard out to buy sandwich makings so as to supply poor Jimmers with a decent meal. They had a picnic basket full of food and drink in the back of the truck. Howard meant to beard Mr. Jimmers on the subject of the Hoku-sai sketch. Either Jimmers had it or he didn't, and if he had it, then he ought to be willing to discuss Howard's claim on it. He was free to refuse to hand it over, after all; there was nothing that could be done to force him. Graham's properties were tied up by law for who knows how long from the date of his death—except that he wasn't dead, anyway, and so Jimmers had no business meddling with the old man's property. He no doubt thought he was protecting it somehow, which you had to admire.

Howard went round and round in his head, arguing all this out with an imaginary Mr. Jimmers. The wind off the ocean drove right through his sweater when he stepped out of the truck, and there wasn't much heat in the noonday sun floating orange and cool in the sky. They could see Mr. Jimmers out on the bluffs, hoeing in a little garden that was sheltered from the sea wind by a long lean-to of wavy squares of yellow fiberglass. They had clumped nearly up to him before he caught sight of them and stood up straight, resting against the hoe, still dressed in the shabby tweed coat but wearing a pair of heavy rubber boots now.

Off by itself stood the tin shed, locked and mysterious. Howard purposefully avoided looking at it so as not to arouse suspicion. Above them in the wall of the house, facing the meadow, was the mysterious door-that-led-nowhere, and the broken-off stairway built of stones that went two thirds of the way up the wall toward it.

"Swiss chard," Mr. Jimmers said, nodding down at the meager-looking greens poking up through the soil.

"Good, are they?" asked Howard.

"Wretched, actually, but easy to grow if you don't let the wind blow them to bits. Not enough sun, though, so you've got to grow a lot of them if you want to harvest enough to eat. You should have seen the garden in the old days, before Mr. Graham declined." He shook his head sadly, hacking at a weed with the corner of the hoe blade. "Now it's reduced to these few rows of Swiss chard. It's a disgrace is what it is. But a man can stay healthy on a diet of greens. Taken in sufficient quantity, with eggs, they'll provide a human being with a full range of nutrients, a complete diet. Postum is made entirely of vegetable matter. Did you know that?"

"No," said Howard. "Really? Vegetable matter?"

"Wheat, mostly."

"Speaking of eating," Sylvia said, "we've brought along this basket."

Mr. Jimmers dropped his hoe and set off toward the house, rubbing his hands together as if he hadn't eaten anything except Postum and Swiss chard in days. "I'll just put on a tablecloth," he said, prying off his rubber boots on the front porch. Sylvia slipped her shoes off, and Howard did, too, realizing too late that his socks had holes in the toes. Maybe it would make him look vulnerable, he thought, and would be a good ploy. He'd have to suffer cold feet again, though.

It was at lunch that he brought up the topic of the sketch. Awkwardly, and pretending not to care very much, he said, "About the Hoku-sai, Mr. Jimmers."

"That would be the sketch on rice paper?" Mr. Jimmers said.

"That's correct."

"It's damned rare, you know."

"I do know that. That's what explains my interest in it in the first place."

"I mean to say that Hoku-sai woodcuts abound, but original sketches, especially from the Mangkwa, are rare as hen's teeth. And items with this history, I should think, are rarer still."

"What Howard wants to know," Sylvia said bluntly, "is whether you've got the thing, Mr. Jimmers, and whether you're willing to fork it over."

Jimmers smiled hugely and raised his eyebrows at Sylvia. "Have another slice of this wonderful cheese, my dear," he said. "I'm in a precarious position, of course. Mr. Graham was never found, was he? Who's to say he's dead? He's *assumed* dead, of course, but the lack of a body rather complicates the dispersal of his property." He winked at Sylvia before going on. "And if I'm not really certain he's dead, beyond a shadow of a doubt, I can hardly go about giving his things away, regardless of quite possibly spurious letters." He held his hand up in order to put a stop to Howard's protests. "There are no end of awful people in the world, who would be entirely happy to think they've fooled Mr. Jimmers and gotten their hands on this curious—ah, sketch, as you put it. What makes you think it's a Hoku-sai?"

"Isn't it?" Howard asked.

"Of course it's not. You see the problem, then. You're blundering around, aren't you? You haven't any idea what you want. All you know is that you want it. Should you have it, though? That's the question."

"So my letter of acquisition, signed by Graham, means nothing to you?"

127

"On the contrary, my boy. It means ever so much. It means you might easily *be* the man who now or very shortly will own this valuable object that we've been discussing. For the moment, I mean to say, you are *not* the man. What we would like is not always what is, but it might be what will be, if I make myself clear."

Mr. Jimmers nibbled a piece of bread contentedly, as if it didn't take more than a good crumb or two to satisfy him. "I wish I could find something here to offer you two by way of dessert," he said regretfully. "I had a paper bag full of horehound drops somewhere. I can't remember quite where. I haven't seen them for the better part of a year. Wild horehound, put together by the Sunberry people."

"That's all right," Howard said quickly.

"It's not all right, not entirely. I've become a regular Mother Hubbard. Nothing to offer guests. You're the first I've had, though, in years. I promise that next time I see you I'll have something nice. I've developed a taste for canned-spaghetti sandwiches on a superior-quality white bread. Nothing fancy, just bread, margarine, and spaghetti—canned spaghetti. Doesn't really matter what brand."

So the subject of the sketch had been brought up and abandoned in the space of a single minute, buried beneath Mr. Jimmers' spaghetti sandwich. He had half promised something, but Howard couldn't be sure what. What was it he had said? That Howard might well be "the man"—as if Mr. Jimmers were waiting not simply for someone with a letter of requisition, but for someone who knew the answer to a riddle, or would know the riddle itself, or would have the secret password.

"About the sketch, then," Howard said. "I understand your hesitation, and I hate to keep bothering you with it. That's the problem. I don't want to make a pest of myself, but I've got the letter from Mr. Graham, which I believe to be perfectly authentic, and—"

"I'm certain of it," Mr. Jimmers said, interrupting. "Perfectly authentic. May I see the letter again?"

"Absolutely," Howard said, pulling it out of his coat and handing it across.

Mr. Jimmers studied it, nodding and squinting, and then abruptly tore it into fragments and threw the pieces over his shoulder.

"Wait!" Howard shouted, getting up out of his chair. It was too late, though: the pieces lay on the floor. He sat back down, his mouth open. Sylvia was smiling faintly, as if she thought the whole production was funny, but didn't dare laugh out loud.

"Now you've got one fewer scrap of paper to worry about," Mr. Jimmers said to him. "Avoid focusing your energies on trash. That wasn't worth anything to you. It was meant to draw you up here, that's all. This isn't a matter of museums. This is something more. You don't need letters of 'requisition,' as you put it. The whole world is tired of your letter of requisition. It makes them sick. Remember the promise in the adage—everything will be revealed in the fullness of time." Then he held his hand up again, as if he would prevent Howard from commenting. "The *fullness* of time."

He touched his mouth with his napkin and said, "Come along. I'll show you something noteworthy—something that will relieve your mind immensely." He tipped Howard a wink now, as if he were going to let the both of them in on a secret, and they followed him into the parlor with the fireplace, which was lit but had died down into a pool of embers. He threw in a handful of brown pine needles and blew on them and then laid a half dozen cedar sticks on top, which flared up immediately and began to pop and crackle, lighting up the little area around the hearth.

Mr. Jimmers stood very still, listening, and then tiptoed to one, then the other doorway, and stood listening at each for a moment. Then, putting a finger to his lips, he eased a stone out of the face of the fireplace, reached back into the recess, and pulled out a carefully folded bit of paper.

Howard caught his breath. Here it was, still in its hidey-hole but no longer in its case. Mr. Jimmers nodded at him and unfolded it with steady hands. "Not another of this quality in the world," he whispered. "Never again will be." Howard could see inked images through the paper.

"What do you think?" Mr. Jimmers asked, holding the sketch up so that the firelight glowed through it. The confusion of folds in the paper appeared almost to be Xerox reproductions—the shadows of folds—and not authentic folds at all. It was very fine work, the rice paper yellowed with age and frayed along the edges. "This," said Jimmers, gesturing at one of the images, "is the flowering staff. And these are meant to represent secret keys. This one is a cup and this is a coin and this is a tree by a river. And if you fold the thing in half twice, what you get is . . ." He folded it in half twice and said, "A broken egg. Now watch."

He folded the sketch again, warping it first and then shoving his hands together so that the center third of the paper disappeared behind the outside thirds, and then he turned it around diamond-wise and folded the top corner down. As if by magic the broken sections of eggshell became whole, and random spots and lines and shadings on the sketch formed a face on the patched-together egg. It sat now on the limb of the tree by the river and held the staff in its hand, its thin arms stretched out along smaller limbs on either side, almost as if it were crucified to the tree.

An electric thrill ran through Howard, and he was surprised to find that Sylvia had taken his hand, as if she felt that something was pending, some revelation. The firelight behind the rice paper made the images waver and jump as if they were seen through ocean water. Mr. Jimmers let go of one of the corners of the sketch, snapped his fingers, and the fire flared in the fireplace, throwing out a great wash of greenish-blue flame that seemed to consume the rice paper sketch even as he held it.

Looking dumbstruck with surprise, Jimmers shouted and waved the burning scrap dramatically, as if it were scorching his hand but he couldn't manage to let go of it, and then with a wild flourish he threw it onto the stones of the floor and trod on it until the flames were out and there was nothing but a few black fragments left, smudging the gray stones.

"Damn it," Mr. Jimmers said, looking morosely at the bottom of his stockinged feet. "It's that damned cedar—throws God's own amount of sparks."

Howard realized that his own mouth was open. He had meant to shout, but there hadn't been time, it had all happened so fast.

"*What* a tragedy," Mr. Jimmers said. "*What* an unbearable loss."

"You're joking," Howard managed to say. He was certain suddenly that Mr. Jimmers had pulled a fast one, with all the finger snapping and the whoosh of flame. He had pitched something into the fire to cause the flare-up and had pocketed the sketch and burned up a dummy of some sort. He bent over and picked up a fragment—one that still had a bit of unburned paper clinging to the black ash. There was a slash of brown ink on it—easily identifiable as the top of the flowering staff. So Jimmers had burned a *copy*. It couldn't have been the real one. Still, it had *looked* to be the real one. Howard waited for Jimmers to snatch it back out of his coat and laugh.

130

Instead he sat down heavily in a stuffed chair and buried his forehead in his hands. "Alas," he said.

"You can't really have burned it up . . ." Howard looked to Sylvia for support. She shrugged and shook her head, as if to tell him to drop it entirely.

"Not a word of this leaks out!" Mr. Jimmers said, almost frantically, jerking his head up and staring at the two of them. He wore a hunted look, the look of a man whose life was suddenly threatened by an unseen foe. He reached into his coat, hesitated, cocking his head. Howard nodded inwardly. Here it came . . .

But Mr. Jimmers merely pulled out a ragged old handkerchief and mopped his brow. "I believe a drink is called for under the circumstances. A strong one."

Howard couldn't disagree. He and Sylvia followed Mr. Jimmers back out toward the kitchen, where Jimmers pulled the cork out of the bottle of Sunberry wine that Howard had tasted two nights back. He poured out two tumblers full, nearly killing off the bottle and announcing that he never touched the stuff. Sylvia sipped at hers, but Howard couldn't bring himself to it and set his glass down untouched, pretending to be distracted for a moment by something out the window. Then Mr. Jimmers wandered off, seeming lost and depressed, and left the two of them alone.

"What about a walk along the bluffs?" Howard asked loudly, catching Sylvia's eye and jerking his head.

"You children go along without me," Mr. Jimmers said from the next room. "I've got to think this through. I've betrayed my trust. I . . ." He fell silent, and they heard him slump heavily into a chair. Sylvia folded up the tablecloth and repacked the dishes, leaving the remainder of the food for Mr. Jimmers. When they peeked into the parlor a moment later, he was nodding in his chair, asleep.

Howard still half expected him to spring up and laugh, but that didn't happen; instead he began to snore, his head lolling forward over his chest.

 13

"WHERE are you going?" Sylvia asked when they'd gone outside.

"For a walk on the bluffs, like I said."

"Now?"

"Of course now. What's the hurry? You don't have to be back for another forty-five minutes. We just got had, that's what I think."

Sylvia was silent, walking next to him with her arms folded across her chest. "It looked like a trick."

"Sure it was. He's got the damned thing in his coat. He's no more asleep than I am. What he's doing now is hiding the thing again, and I'll bet you a shiny new dime that it's not going back behind the rock, either." Howard looked over his shoulder, back toward the house. They had gotten around toward the rear now. A trail led away through the berry vines, down along the edge of the bluffs where someone had long ago erected a picket fence, to keep people well back away from the edge, maybe. Howard walked down the path until they were hidden from the house by wild shrubbery. He pulled a key out of his pocket.

"What's that?" Sylvia asked.

"A key."

"I can see that. What's it for?"

"Jimmers' shed. I'm going to see what's inside it. There were a half dozen keys on strings inside the back door. I slipped it off of the hook when he fell asleep in the chair. You were cleaning up the lunch stuff."

"How do you know it's the right one?"

"I looked at the lock. It's a regular antique. This key is old enough and cut right. It's the only one of the bunch that's anywhere near working. The way I see it, the padlocks on all these outbuildings are probably keyed the same. It wouldn't make sense to carry a dozen keys."

"What did Father tell you was in there?"

"A fabulous machine, actually."

She nodded. "It figures. What else would Mr. Jimmers have in a tin shed? You know what Jimmers told me was in there?"

"What?" asked Howard. The whole business was beginning to look pretty dubious to him.

"The Platonic archetypes."

"*All* of them?"

"That's what he said. He told me that nearly a year ago. Said the shed was packed with them—the archetypal bottle cap and chair and mustache and who-knows-what-all."

"The wing-tip shoe."

"The archetypal corkboard. Everything. He said he couldn't explain the physics, but it had to do with the sort of infinity you see in double mirrors, like in a barbershop."

"I bet it does. I bet he did that trick in the parlor with mirrors, too. Uncle Roy called it a ghost machine. He's pretty certain that it had something to do with the crowd that stole Graham's car. I promised him I'd have a look at it if I could. Apparently Jimmers won't let him anywhere near it. Tell me something—is there bad blood between Jimmers and your father?"

"Well, yes." Sylvia stood looking out over the ocean, her hair blowing back out of her face. She looked as if she were thinking of how to continue, so Howard waited for her, even though he was itching to have a look into the shed before Mr. Jimmers woke up.

"Mr. Jimmers and my mother were lovers."

"Jimmers?" Howard asked, trying not to sound too incredulous. He tried to consider Mr. Jimmers in that light, but it wasn't easy.

"Long time ago—shortly before I was born. You know who she wound up marrying, though."

"You might have been Sylvia Jimmers."

"Very damned nearly."

"You wouldn't have been as pretty."

Sylvia blushed just a little, which was encouraging. "Actually," she said, "he wasn't a bad-looking man when he was young. It wrecked him, though, breaking up with Mother. She's still guilty about it—more than makes sense, really I think she likes carrying guilt around like baggage. She wouldn't know what to do without it. She told me once that I had Mr. Jimmers' eyes."

"Really? I think Uncle Roy has them, in a jar in the kitchen. There was a lot of bitterness, then?"

"I suppose so," Sylvia said. "Nobody hates anybody, though. Same circle of friends and all—everyone winding up in the same place, finally. Mr. Jimmers had a difficult time of it, though. He was hospitalized in San Francisco at least twice for mental disorders. He was brilliant, too. An engineer until he gave it up and began living in a garage in Fort Bragg. Spent all his time working on a flying automobile."

"He was a gluer," Howard said flatly. "I'll bet you."

"After a fashion, I guess. The compulsion seems to move people differently. Anyway, he was put away, and when he got out he fell in love again. You wouldn't believe with whom."

"I give up. Anybody I know?"

"Heloise Lamey."

"Not old Landlady Lamey!"

"The very one. Lasted something under two months. Father says that she wanted to use Mr. Jimmers to betray Graham, but that he wouldn't knuckle under and she dropped him after some sort of scandal that resulted in Jimmers' disgrace. Jimmers disappeared for a time, back down to San Francisco, and then came back and has lived here at Graham's since. He came and went in the night, I guess, because nobody ever saw him. It was always assumed he was here, just sort of puttering around, watching the stars. Mother kept track of him. I remember coming out here with her once when I was a little girl, and her telling me that he was on a diet of sprouts and milk and vitamins. He even published a newsletter and started an organization, the Flat Constellation Society, but he was closed down for mail fraud. He was innocent, though. He believed it all."

Howard nodded. "I like that. An authentic crank is innocent of mail fraud, but a fake crank isn't. There's a certain logic to the idea."

Sylvia gave him a look. "You know what I mean."

"Actually I do. Was this some sort of religion or something?"

"I've seen some of his newsletters. They were full of articles about saucers and the hollow earth and especially about machinery. He had a sort of Jungian slant, though—not your usual nut literature, except that he claimed to be in contact with hundred-year-old spirits. He didn't capitalize common nouns or put everything inside of useless quotation marks or things like that."

"That's reassuring," Howard said. "I don't mean to be slighting or anything, but it sounds as if he and your father ought to have gotten along fine."

"Somehow that didn't happen. They were rivals when they were in love with my mother, and they just carried right on being rivals. They used to play pranks on each other once in a while after it was all settled and over, as if it weren't really over at all. Mr. Jimmers would have a truckload of manure delivered out to the museum, say, as a joke, and then Father would strike back at him by printing up a fake newsletter from the Flat Constellation Society, full of crazy limericks and psychotic illustrations. Then we moved south, of course, and they pretty much gave it up until we came north again years later. It's died down again now, but I think that Father is capable of starting it back up anytime."

"I would have thought that Jimmers was a fan of the ghost museum. What did he think, that Uncle Roy set it up to make fun of him or something?"

"No, not especially." She hesitated for a moment, pulling her hair back out of her face and tying it into a big knot. "I shouldn't tell you this, since you're such a terrible skeptic, but it's altogether possible that Mr. Jimmers rigged up the entire ghost car phenomenon. That was his crowd of hundred-year-old spirits driving the car. Don't ask me how. Don't even ask me how he fooled us with the sketch just now. Right before the museum failed, Father saw a glowing creature walking through the forest after dark. He was just closing up, getting ready to head home. He followed it, but it ran off up one of the lumber roads and disappeared. Father couldn't keep up with it. He drove straight to the newspaper office, full of excitement, and of course they treated it as a farce. The next morning a cow was reported stolen from a farm near Albion, and that same day it was found, right up behind the museum, sprayed with luminous paint."

Howard smiled. "Did Uncle Roy paint the cow? I love the idea of that—a glowing ghost cow terrorizing the north coast. That's good. A canny business move. It would have hauled the tourists in by the busload."

"Of *course* he didn't paint it. If he had, he wouldn't have been fool enough to let it get away up the lumber road. And he would have made sure a few other people saw it, too. He thinks Jimmers did it, as a prank, to make him look like a fool. It certainly worked that way. The museum was just then going under, and the luminous cow fraud is what broke the camel's back."

"I dare say it would. So did Uncle Roy strike back?"

"A couple of times. Nothing very inspired, though—not for a while. Sometime I'll tell you about his campaigns. I think he was

135

tired of it right then. The cow incident hadn't turned out to be very funny. Mother got a little bit shortsighted about his capers, too. You could tell that last night. I'm surprised that she hasn't put a stop to the haunted house. The only thing that I can figure is that she's more tired out than he is. She can't keep up with him anymore."

"She's fairly long-suffering, isn't she? In the best way."

Sylvia nodded. "In some of the best ways. Not always."

Then after a moment Howard said, "Let's make a move on the tin shed before Jimmers wakes up."

"If you stay up here," Sylvia said, ignoring what he said and growing suddenly serious, "I know just exactly what's going to happen to you."

Howard gestured at her, as if to tell her to go on, to reveal his future. "Read my palm," he said, holding out his hand.

"You're going to end up like Father and Mr. Jimmers— spending your life worrying about secret societies and outer space and ancient mysteries. You don't believe in anything, and what happens when you don't believe in anything is that you've got no defense against all this weird crap when it puts itself in your way."

"You're a fine one to talk, passing out mystical pamphlets and selling recipes for sun tea made out of rose quartz and stump water."

"At least I can take an objective look at it. I've got some basis for comparison. You're utterly ignorant of it, because you've never considered it, and when something that doesn't fit comes along, you don't begin to know where to put it."

Howard had the vague feeling that she was right, not because of any particular logic or nonsense about her being objective, but because right at the moment he was faced with a basket full of strange activities that he hadn't been able to fathom. This business about rivalries and wrecked love affairs put a new coat of paint on the horse, too, or on the cow.

"Thanks," he said.

"For what?"

"For worrying about me. I'm not much on secret societies, though. You don't have to let that trouble you. There's good reasons for me to stay up here. That's what I think."

"Uh-huh." She looked at him suspiciously and then out at the ocean, lost in thought.

He put his arm around her shoulder and pulled her close, feeling like a teenager in a darkened theater.

136

"What are you up to?" she asked, looking him in the face.

"Nothing." He didn't let her go, though.

She nodded. "For a moment there I thought you were making a pass at me."

"Maybe I was."

"Remember that girl who used to live in the house behind you? Jeanelle Shelly. You were out of your mind over her. And how old were you? About six? You started in early."

"I didn't 'start in.' "

She leaned against him, neither of them saying anything. Howard was struck by the feeling that they were still playing at being in love—him making his fumbling advances and her fighting him off with language, making verbal jokes, diffusing things by poking fun at him. Suddenly she looked at her watch. "I've got to get back to town," she said.

"I'm going to look at that shed. I'll hurry."

Sylvia nodded, as if it had to be done in order for Howard and her father to rest easy. "I'll take your word for it," she said. "What I'm going to do is head back to the house and keep Mr. Jimmers company. If he wakes up, I'll give you a holler so that you know he's up and about."

"Good." Howard whirled the string with the key on it around his finger. "It won't take a minute."

"Wait," she said. "Look at this first. It's been here for years." She led the way through brown, waist-high weeds toward three lonesome cypress trees growing in a clump halfway up toward the highway. In between the triangle formed by the three trunks sat a little gluer shrine, very much like the one set up in the woods by Graham's cabin. It was built of old junk again—perfume bottles, bits of ceramic tile, wooden dominoes, an old rusty fishing reel, a brass doorknob, all enclosed within a pair of arched automobile fenders, rusted and pitted to the point that they were almost lacy.

"This has been here for as long as I can remember," Sylvia said. "They just add new stuff sometimes and rearrange it."

"There's one like it back behind your house, out in the woods."

She nodded. "That one's new. It appeared the day Father moved him back there. Nobody was supposed to know where he was, but they knew."

"You wouldn't believe what I found in that one," Howard said, "back in the woods. My paperweight, sitting right there in plain view."

"And you took it back?"

Howard shook his head. "It'll be safe enough out there. I had the feeling, actually, that it had been put to good use. Don't ask me why."

"Not me. It's funny, though, the weird sorts of things Howard Barton is learning to take on faith. What's next? Membership in the Flat Constellation Society?"

"Next is the adventure of the tin shed."

"You're sure?"

"Too good a chance to pass up," Howard said, and the two of them tramped back up to the trail again and then along the bluffs toward the rear of the house. Sylvia went around toward the front, disappearing beyond the hillocks of berry vines.

Where the rear wall of the house became one with the cliff, there was no backyard at all, just a narrow shelf of rock far above the sea. High above was the attic window, beyond which Howard had spent the night, sleeping in a chair. He found that he could pick his way along the slender ledge, just as long as he didn't look down. The stones of the house wall were rough and the mortar was deep-set, so there were handholds. And someone, ages past, had cemented an iron railing into the rocks in order to prevent anyone from going over, but one end of the railing had long ago rusted through, and it dangled uselessly now like a broken tree root a hundred feet over the water. Even a seasoned rock climber would have found it impossible to scramble down the wet and mossy shale to the beach below.

Safely back on the meadow, he hurried past Mr. Jimmers' Swiss chard toward the tin shed, hiding behind it finally and peering back toward the house. It looked quiet enough. There was the chance that Mr. Jimmers was simply being subtle again, that he hadn't fallen asleep at all but was giving Howard a chance to betray himself, but Sylvia would have had time to get back in by now, and she hadn't hollered . . .

He crouched at the corner of the shed and took one last look. Then, staying low, he scuttled crabwise to the locked sliding doors. The key slid straight in and the lock opened easily, as if it were slick with graphite. In a moment he had slipped the padlock out of its holes in the door handles. He yanked on one of the doors, and it let out a screech of rusty protest, jiggling along its bent track just a few inches and then jamming tight. He pushed on the opposite door, along the bottom edge, wishing he had a can of sewing-machine oil to spray into the track and expecting momentarily to hear Sylvia yell.

The door jerked along a bit farther, and suddenly the opening was wide enough to slide through. He took the padlock with him, remembering his adventure at the spirit museum, and wafered himself through, easing the door shut again at once, all but about an inch so as to have some light to see by.

There was light leaking in under the eaves, too, enough to reveal Mr. Jimmers' device. It was built of wood and brass and copper and leather—a product, pretty clearly, of the Victorian age, of the early days of the Industrial Revolution. It had foot pedals and an organ pipe apparatus alongside a broad, spoked wheel, as if from an oversize sewing machine. A wavy-looking fishbowl lens was set in the top. The whole thing had a sort of Rumplestiltskin fairy tale magic to it, a backwoods cobbler's notion of what a "machine" must look like. There was a bit of writing carved into the wooden superstructure, which read simply, "St. George's Guild, 1872."

John Ruskin again, Howard said to himself, rolling back onto his heels and squinting in concentration. Knowing that it was Ruskin who had established the unsuccessful St. George's Guild didn't tell him anything at all about the machine. But the name of the guild itself was powerfully suggestive to him, and abruptly he thought of Sylvia and his just-ended conversation with her. How was it that she saw him and his desires so much more clearly than he saw them himself?

Here he was, hiding out in Mr. Jimmers' tin shed, turning quite possibly innocent artifacts into fourteen-carat mysteries in the spirit of Jimmers and Uncle Roy. He was infected, and no doubt about it. Knowing that didn't help at all either, though. And with an almost helpless curiosity he reached across and gave the brass wheel a spin. The wheel revolved effortlessly, frictionlessly, as though now that it was put into motion, it wouldn't be inclined to stop.

Suddenly there was a shift in the quality of light in the shed. A dim glow emanated from the lens atop the machine. Howard spun the wheel faster and the light brightened. The wheel whirred on its bearings, and Howard was momentarily torn between trying to stop it, to end whatever was happening before it had gone too far, and to see it through, into the heart of some deeper mystery. He let it spin. There was the sound of bees humming, which sorted itself out into the low babble of voices like a roomful of mechanical men talking excitedly.

A pale fog materialized in the air over the machine. Particles whirled in it like dust motes. Vibrations shook the shed, and the machine, rocking on its springs, began to bang against the tin wall with a slow, rhythmic pounding, like the spinning of an out-of-balance washing machine. The noise and the spinning made him dizzy, and he was aware suddenly that there were stars on the ceiling over his head, pale and diffuse like stars at twilight.

The mist from the machine congealed into a spinning blur like a tiny human head, and there was the loud sound of footsteps walking down a long wooden corridor. The misty face developed features now, and Howard's curiosity turned abruptly to fear. The thing blinked, as if vaguely surprised to find itself there. Then its mouth began to work, like the mouth of a ruminating cow. The machine banged away at the wall of the shed, easily loud enough to awaken Jimmers and throw him into a panic. The babble of voices combined to form a single voice, deep and commanding, but mostly lost in the banging and whirring of the machine.

Howard heard his name shouted, and he reached down to stop the turning of the wheel, which thumped against his hand, still spinning heavily and freely. There was a body forming beneath the head now. Howard could see a waistcoat, a dangling pocket-watch chain. The ghostly shape was growing, too, exactly as if it were approaching him from across a vast distance. There was the sound of wind rushing through a canyon and the flapping of bird wings and of pages rustling in an old book. Then, as the wheel slowed, the image began to fade and the light dimmed. The voice ran down until it was nothing but a tired whisper and then the sound of bees buzzing again, and Howard slumped back onto a gunnysack full of mulch, realizing that he was faint with the stuffiness of the shed, with the heavy, dusty air.

Someone tugged at the shed doors. There was a furious rattling and screeching as they skidded open. The machine still banged away, but not so heavily now. Afternoon sunlight poured through the open doors, and the night sky overhead dissolved into the daylight as Mr. Jimmers pushed past Howard's feet and slammed his hand against the hub of the brass wheel, stopping it dead. The ghost noises evaporated altogether and the foggy head was gone.

Left over, like a negative afterimage on the back of his eyelids, the floating, two-dimensional face still hovered there. Howard blinked, looked closer, and realized that the visage, somehow, seemed now to be painted against the corrugated tin of the shed wall, like an imprint taken with ghost-sensitive film. Slowly it faded and vanished.

14

Mr. Jimmers' hair and clothes were mussed from his napping in the chair, and he stared at Howard now like a schoolmaster thinking about birch rods.

"What on earth were you doing?" asked Sylvia, staring past Mr. Jimmers' shoulder at the now-still machine. Howard could see that she was smiling. She was taking on the job of scolding him before Jimmers had a chance to get going. "The whole shed was *vibrating*. We heard it inside the house. What is that, Mr. Jimmers, some sort of gramophone?" She looked at the device innocently.

"That's nothing," Mr. Jimmers said, waving them backward out of the shed. "I mean that's just what it is. A gramophone. It's an early sort of television, really, that skims energy out of the ether. It's a delicate instrument, though. I can't have people meddling with it. There's people who would misuse it . . . How on earth did you get in here?" he asked suddenly, squinting hard at Howard.

Howard handed him the key. "Sorry," he said. "It was breaking and entering. Curiosity, mainly. Better call the police."

"Curiosity," said Mr. Jimmers flatly as he padlocked the shed again and then dropped the key theatrically down his shirt. He smiled momentarily, as if to show that he had nothing against curiosity. "We don't need the police. Not this time."

Howard had begun to feel genuinely guilty. Now that he stood in the sunlight, with the workaday world clear and solid around him, the mystical adventure in the shed seemed suddenly to have happened in some distant time. What did he think he had seen? A ghost? "I really am sorry," he said again, and abruptly Sylvia grinned at him and mouthed the word "See?" He ignored her. "I didn't know . . ."

"You're right about that," Jimmers said. "You didn't know. What other keys have you stolen from me?"

"None. That's it."

"I'll vouch for him," Sylvia said cheerfully. "He means well, he's just a nitwit. He's always been like this. It's a sort of Dennis the Menace complex."

This seemed to make Mr. Jimmers happy. As if to celebrate, he kissed Sylvia on the hand and patted her head. "Ask next time," he said to Howard patronizingly and laying a hand on his shoulder. "I'll let you have a glimpse through my telescope sometime. Perhaps you'd like copies of some of my literature?"

"Sure," Howard said, relieved that he was being let off the hook.

Mr. Jimmers didn't produce any literature, though. Instead he said, "I've got nothing to hide, nothing at all. You can go through my effects with a flea comb. Nothing up *my* sleeve." He tugged his coat sleeve up, revealing the thin fabric of his mattress-stripe shirt and the pale flesh of his wrist. He nodded at his hand, turning it over slowly, and said, "Why did the turtle cross the road?"

Taken utterly by surprise at this lunatic question, Howard could only shake his head.

"Chicken's day off," Mr. Jimmers said very seriously. After making sure the padlock was secure, he picked up his hoe and began chopping at weeds again, working in his oddball garden. They left him there, Howard apologizing one last time and driving away miserably toward town. He hadn't been caught in any such stunts for twenty years and had forgotten how humiliating it was.

He tried to explain the experience with the ghost head to Sylvia, who made him repeat the more lunatic aspects of the tale. "Do you know what I think it was?" she asked. Howard didn't know. "A hypnogogic experience. A waking dream. You only *thought* you saw—who was it? John Ruskin's ghost? Talking like a swarm of wooden bees?" She nodded but had a perplexed look on her face, and he caught her looking at him out of the corner of her eye. She was evidently satisfied to know that Howard had been face-to-face with the Unknown, and had come away shaken and confused. It was as they were pulling up in front of the boutique that Sylvia remembered about the picnic basket. They had left it with Mr. Jimmers.

"Damn it," she said. "It isn't mine, either, it's Rosie's, the woman who works for me at the shop. It's expensive as hell, full of her plates and tablecloth and everything. What'll I tell her?"

"I'll go back after it," Howard said promptly, although not really liking the idea at all. He would have to confront Mr. Jimmers again. It was the only gallant thing to do, though. "It isn't ten minutes down the road. I'll fetch it back here inside of a half hour. Tell her . . . tell her that I drove off with it in the truck by mistake, and that surely I'll realize it and bring it back around. Then I will. Simple as that."

"You're sweet," she said, leaning over and kissing him on the cheek, then moving away before he had a chance to respond. With a mock-wicked look she said, "You should have seen your face when Jimmers was yelling at you."

"Pretty woebegone, eh?"

"Pitiful. I remember that look perfectly from when you were a child. Remember that time you got caught in the garage with Jeanelle Shelly? Don't deny it. Your mother sent her home and then gave you that lecture about being struck dead by God. Remember?"

"I . . . What? How did you . . . ?" Howard couldn't speak. He realized that he was blushing fiercely, confronted now with this old, mortifying sin.

"I was listening at the garage door, out in the driveway. You remember that I was there when you came out looking shameful. Anyway, that was the sort of look you had this time around, too. Mr. Jimmers and I saw the shed just vibrating like a tuning fork, and I said, 'What on earth!' and Jimmers said, 'My Lord!' and to tell you the truth I didn't know *what* we'd find. 'He's got Jeanelle Shelly in there,' I remember thinking. Actually I think I said it out loud, which must be what confused Mr. Jimmers. He's wondering right now who Jeanelle Shelly is and where you've got her hidden now that you've had your way with her in the shed."

Howard discovered that it was utterly impossible to respond, so he smiled crookedly, like a man struggling to be a good sport.

"Look at you," she said suddenly, pretending to feel bad about Howard's deflated condition. "I'm awful, aren't I? But you're such an easy target." She kissed him again, again unexpectedly, and then slid over and climbed out of the truck, keeping him consistently off balance. Poking her head in through the open window, she said, "Save the basket, will you? Before Jimmers turns it into a sanatorium for mice or something."

She stepped away from the truck and waved at him as he backed almost happily out onto the street. He waved back and

143

then drove off slowly, still able to feel a sort of electric tingle on his cheek where she'd kissed him. He looked into the rearview mirror, and there were red lip marks, which he wiped off with the sleeve of his sweater. Whistling now, he pushed his foot down on the accelerator and angled south onto the coast highway, feeling suddenly as if he were man enough, after all, to confront the curious Mr. Jimmers one more time.

MR. Jimmers wasn't hoeing in the garden anymore. The meadow around the house was windy and deserted, and afternoon shadows stretched away across it. Howard was tempted toward the tin shed, having learned only about half enough to satisfy himself. If it had only been full of gardening tools, he could have been happy and gone about his business on an even keel. He didn't have the key any longer, though, and he surely couldn't afford to be caught meddling around there by Mr. Jimmers, who *would* call the police this time, machine or no machine. Or maybe take a shot at him with a load of rock-salt.

So he strolled toward the house thinking hard about Mr. Jimmers himself. Who and what was he? A sideshow magician and crackpot professor of fringe science, or an artful genius of great power, toiling at a deep and authentic mystery? Too bad you couldn't just ask him. Howard stepped up onto the porch and slipped off his shoes, then raised his hand to knock.

The front door stood open a couple of inches. Howard paused, vaguely surprised. There was dirt on the sill and trailing into the house, knocked off of someone's crepe-soled shoe—someone who clearly hadn't been invited in under Jimmers' watchful gaze. Howard shrank back against the wall, out of sight of anyone inside who might see him through the open door.

Suddenly tense, he looked around himself. He saw the car now—a red Camaro pulled in behind the long wooden shed that housed the chain-saw mill and workshop. His first impulse was to leave—head straight for his truck and gun it the hell out of there, up to Albion where he could call the police from the store. His starting the truck, of course, would alert whoever was inside, and by the time the police arrived they'd be gone, and Mr. Jimmers would be what? Dead? Robbed?

And maybe it was nothing at all. Steeling himself, Howard listened at the almost closed door. He heard nothing. He pushed it open, waiting for it to creak or slam or rattle, but it was silent, helping him out.

Ducking down into a crouch, he peered around it into the shadowy interior hall. He wished it were earlier in the day instead of nearly twilight, because he could see almost nothing inside.

He slipped in, anyway, hurrying across and pressing himself against the wall, where he would be mostly hidden but could still see a section of the parlor. From the light playing across the parlor carpet, Howard could tell that a fire still burned in the grate. The fireplace itself and Mr. Jimmers' easy chair were both hidden by the intervening wall, though. There seemed to be nobody up and moving in the room—no shadows or noises.

He was halfway across the floor toward the doorway when he heard something heavy crash to the floor in an upstairs room, followed by the sound of a muffled voice. The place was being ransacked. He peered through the doorway into the parlor, and there was Mr. Jimmers, slumped in his chair—tied into it with a length of rope. He sat with his head on his chest. Blood oozed slowly out of a wound on his forehead. Howard stepped across, picked up Jimmers' hand, and found his pulse, which was steady and regular. Jimmers' eyes opened, blinked, and then opened wider, in confusion at first and then narrowing with anger. He grimaced, as if the effort had hurt.

Howard shook his head and put a finger to his lips. "It wasn't me," he whispered, looking into Jimmers' eyes to see if there was any sign of concussion. "Move your right leg." Mr. Jimmers shifted his leg, then moved his other leg and both arms in turn, without having to be asked.

"Did you see them?" Howard asked.

He shook his head once, slowly, and shut his eyes. "They're upstairs," Howard said. "I came back after Sylvia's picnic basket."

He felt foolish suddenly, explaining about the picnic basket, but he wanted to make very sure that Mr. Jimmers understood why he was there. Jimmers nodded weakly, keeping his eyes shut, and fumbled with Howard's hand, pressing it a little. "I'm all right," he whispered, opening his eyes then and seeming to summon his strength. "Leave now. They won't find it. They'll get out when they're through. Don't tangle with them. Leave me here. No police." He drifted off, then abruptly whispered " 'Mall right" again before giving up.

There was another crash upstairs, and the sound of heavy furniture being pushed around. Howard was helpless. His brain spun. Clearly he was involved in whatever was happening here, and not only because he had stumbled into it. This was what Uncle Roy had been talking about that very morning. This wasn't any sort of metaphoric vagary, like the business about the Tower of Babel or the attractions of numbers. Sides had been drawn in some sort of peculiar north coast war, and Howard had been drafted into it, on the side of Jimmers and old Graham and his uncle and aunt. And, of course, Sylvia.

But what did that mean? He had to take action—get Jimmers out of there. Except that maybe Jimmers was right. If Howard left him there, tied to his chair, the thieves would assume nothing and would go on their way, satisfied.

Or else they'd work Jimmers over. That was equally possible. And who were they? Was one of them Stoat? Would he stoop to this? Impulsively Howard bent over and went to work on the knots. It was thin nylon cord, though, pulled tight and knotted to each of the four legs. Whoever had tied Jimmers up hadn't known what the hell he was doing, and the knots were a mess.

Suddenly there was the sound of a voice again: the words "We'll *ask* him!" It was clear and loud this time, as if from halfway down the stairs.

Howard realized that Mr. Jimmers was mumbling something. Leaning closer, he heard the words "gun" and "closet." Looking around, Howard saw the coat closet back out in the hall, near the front door. He pushed the rope ends under the chair and leaped across to pull the closet door open. There, behind three or four umbrellas, stood an old, beat-up shotgun.

He jerked it out by the barrel and carried it across to the wall, where he waited silently, listening and catching his breath. No one appeared. The voices were arguing now, from upstairs again. Whoever had been coming down had gone back up.

He looked at the shotgun, realizing that the cold metal of the barrel repulsed him. There was something deadly and final about it, and instead of making him feel that much safer, it meant that he was that much closer to real trouble.

His hand shook, and he closed his eyes and breathed evenly, trying to control himself, to think things out. He had used a shotgun once, to blast skeet off the stern of a ferry on a two-day voyage from England to Spain. He had got his share of the little clay disks and from a hell of a lot farther off than he would be now. He told himself that this was nothing he couldn't deal with.

Only there was a moderate difference between shooting a lump of clay and shooting a man—a difference he couldn't allow himself to experience. Maybe he had fallen into the middle of Uncle

Roy's complicated troubles, but those troubles couldn't involve him in killings. Still, there was Jimmers hit on the head and tied into a chair. The gun was protection for both of them—better than nothing. It was a good prop is what it was. He wouldn't have to use it.

Having made up his mind, he hefted the gun again. It was wrapped heavily with old duct tape where the wooden stock joined the metal behind the trigger. The whole thing felt mushy, as if the tape weren't just to help with the grip, but actually tied the halves of the gun together. The tape was dirty and old, too, and sticky with glue, and the barrel was flecked with rust from sitting in the damp closet. The whole thing rattled, as if all the joints were loose. All in all it wasn't a very formidable sight.

So what? It would have to do. The mere noise of the shell being chambered would paralyze them with fear, especially if they were unarmed.

Feeling slightly more steely-jawed, he checked Mr. Jimmers again, who seemed to be resting as comfortably as a man might in his condition. His forehead wasn't bleeding anymore. Howard went on past him, listening hard, padding silently in his stocking feet. They were still at it up above, taking the place apart.

He edged up the stairs, pointing the barrel of the shotgun up the gloomy well and wedging the stock against his stomach so that he could jam the shell home in an instant—if the gun was loaded. He turned it over, and through a little open door in the bottom he could see the brass disk at the end of a shell.

No one met him on the stairs. He heard them talking now, oblivious to him. He hesitated on the second-floor landing, looking for cover, and jumped at the sound of a door closing. He gripped the gun more tightly, forcing the wobbly stock against him. His hand slipped across the duct tape, which had gone from sticky to slick with sweat. The tape moved under his palm, and he could feel that the wood of the stock was cracked. Never mind, he told himself. It's a prop, a gimmick. If he moved quickly and found a place to hide, they weren't going to see him, anyway.

It was easy to tell which room they were in. The door was open and the light on, and he could see through it when he'd taken three steps up the hallway. He would duck into an adjacent room, one already torn up, and follow them down when they left. That way he could see who they were, identify them. And if they tried anything further with Jimmers, Howard could stop them.

Better to let them get away clean, though, than to provoke any stupid confrontation.

"Shit!" a voice said suddenly. "It's not here."

"Can't be."

"What now?"

"Upstairs," the other voice said. "The attic."

Howard leaped toward the nearest bedroom door, but it was six paces away, and one of the two thieves was halfway out of the room and stepping into the hallway before Howard had his hand on the knob and was pushing it open. "Hey!" the man shouted, as if half in surprise and half to alert his friend, who was still hidden in the room behind.

The man in the hall wore a disguise, a cheap shoulder-length woman's wig and a black Lone Ranger mask. There was makeup on his cheeks—putty that was piled up and then cut with gouged-in scars. He wore a black T-shirt and blue jeans. Howard froze where he stood, trying to put on a steel-edged smile. It wasn't Stoat. "He's got a shotgun," the man said evenly. His companion was silent.

Stepping forward slowly, the man in the wig gestured at Howard, who shuffled back into the center of the hall, putting another yard between them. He set his feet, squinted, and aimed the shotgun straight at the man's chest. His hand shook on the gunstock, though.

The man stopped, not liking the look of Howard's shaking hands. He threw his arms into the air, grinning with false surprise. "Down, boy!" he said, laughing. "Chill out. You've got us."

Howard tensed, ready for him as the man took another step forward, gesturing with both hands and shaking his head as if trying to make Howard see reason. Howard didn't look like a killer; that was the problem. The man could smell it, like a wolf. Howard didn't have the instinct, and there was no way in the world to hide it. He should have made his move long ago; now it was clear he had no move to make.

"Give me the sketch," Howard said suddenly.

"What?"

"Give me the sketch. I want it. I'm taking it."

The man glanced hesitantly over his shoulder, but there was still no sight of his companion. "Sure," he said then. "Aim the damned gun at the floor, though. It's not worth killing anyone over. What are you? Friend of the old man downstairs?"

"To hell with the old man downstairs. He's out cold. He'll think you have it, won't he?"

The man grinned. "Smart," he said. He leaned forward, staring into Howard's face. Howard stepped back again, tightening his grip on the trigger and slide. Sweat ran down his forehead, and he told himself that it wasn't supposed to have gone this far. People were supposed to live in terror of shotguns. He pushed the stock tighter against his stomach, clicked the safety catch forward with his thumb, and jacked the shell into the chamber. There was a throaty *kshlack-shlack* as the gun levered away from his stomach with the force of the slide slamming forward.

And then, as if in a cartoon, without any warning at all, the stock simply fell loose from the rest of the gun, dangling for a moment on the end of the pulled-loose duct tape before clattering to the hallway floor.

At the sound of the gun being chambered, the man in the wig had jumped backward toward the bedroom door, which right then was slamming shut. The door clipped him in the back, and he sat down hard, knocking it open again. Howard got a brief glimpse of someone's backside, crawling in behind a pulled-apart bed. Howard gripped the end of the barrel in his right hand, threw his arm back, and flung the useless piece of steel wildly at the open door. The man in the wig ducked against the doorjamb, throwing his hand across his face.

The piece of metal whirled like a boomerang, slamming into the plaster wall three feet past the open door. By then Howard was running hard, back down the hallway. He heard the steel thud against the wall and then the explosion of the gun going off. He pitched forward, onto his chest on the floor, and slid out onto the landing. Chunks of plaster clattered against the walls behind him, peppering the back of his neck, and something sharp hit his hand and bounced away, leaving a bleeding cut—a fragment of green bottle glass. With a hasty glance behind him, he was up and running before he had time to think about it.

Howard leaped up the stairs two at a time, toward the attic, thinking that he should have gone downstairs instead, but at the same time wanting to lead them away from Mr. Jimmers for reasons that he didn't bother to think about until it was too late to change his mind. He heard a shuffling behind him and the thud of a knee hitting the stairs when one of them fell. Then he pushed through the attic door, slamming it shut and bolting it from the inside. He fastened the little panel window shut, too, before he began hauling furniture across in front of the door, panting and

149

gasping and yanking on the chairs and the library table. He threw his shoulder behind a stack of lawyer's bookcases and inched the heavy cases across the floor, too. Then he heard the outside bolt snap shut.

He was locked in. For fifteen seconds he had wanted desperately to be locked in, but now that he was, from the outside . . . He stood up and leaned against the stack of bookcases, trying to breathe evenly. He forced himself to think, willed himself to calm down. He was struck with the blind ignorance of what he had done—capering around with the ludicrous gun, nearly killing someone, himself maybe, out of stupidity. He should have got Mr. Jimmers out of there while the others were occupied upstairs. They wouldn't have guessed anything fishy was going on below. He could have helped Jimmers to the truck and been gone in minutes, and to hell with them—unless they had come down the stairs and surprised him at it . . .

He made himself stop. He had tried, anyway. Dwelling on mistakes wouldn't help now. When this sort of thing happened in the future, he would remember. Live and learn. If nothing else, at least these people would get the impression that Howard wanted the sketch as badly as they did. He had brought a gun along, after all.

The quilt still lay on the floor. There was the casement window. Hadn't he just determined that very afternoon that a man might risk climbing down? If the cloth ripped, of course, or if he couldn't hold on . . . well . . . there was precious little chance that he would fall straight down onto the little rocky ledge, merely to break his ankle, say. What he would do is tumble a hundred-odd feet down onto wave-washed rocks.

They were talking outside the door now, low and indistinct, arguing. The wigged man was accusing the other man of something—chewing him out for having tried to shut the door, probably, back in the hallway. Soon they would unbolt Howard's door and force their way in. They would deal with him as they had dealt with Jimmers. Probably worse. He was in the way, a dangerous obstacle, and competition to boot. That's what they were doing outside—deciding his fate.

He thought again about the quilt and the window. He picked the quilt up and tugged on it, unable to rip it. It was strong enough, certainly, and there was a scissors in the library table drawer. He could cut the quilt into six strips, tie them together. That ought to give him what?—thirty-five feet or so. He'd have to make it eight strips. What would he fasten the whole mess to? Something that couldn't be jerked through the window, that wouldn't come apart. The library table would do in a pinch. It would jam up against the open window, and its heavy oak legs would hold up fine.

It would work. He had determined that. But there was no way on earth that he wanted to try it.

The two outside were silent now, or had left. He hoped to heaven that there were other rooms for them to rout through, or that better yet they'd made their getaway, content to save the attic for another day. It was possible, too, that they had gone downstairs to murder Jimmers, or to rough him up, to make him talk.

Thinking hard, Howard strode across to the closet and threw the door open. He was struck again with the strange construction of the thing, built, as it was, into an odd little bit of outward-curving wall. The strangeness of it seemed to signify now, far more than it had two nights ago, when he was comfortable in his chair and eating a sandwich and there were no potential murderers lurking outside the door.

Clearly the rounded bit of closet wall that faced him now stood adjacent to the stairwell. He thought abruptly of the Humpty Dumpty window. What had been the point of that fishy section of window and wall? It had needlessly narrowed the stairs. Perhaps that window let out onto a room or passage behind the closet, a hidden turret. Clearly it was all part of the same secret structure. The closet itself wasn't more than twenty-four inches deep. The curve of the wall argued that the turret it formed was something much larger—eight or ten feet across.

He couldn't recall having seen it from outside the house, from the vantage point of Jimmers' garden or from where the back of the house was knit into the cliff. It was a secret room of some sort, and no doubt about it.

At once he began pulling stuff out of the closet—a boxed telescope, portable file boxes, dusty books, paper bags filled with receipts and scraps, cardboard boxes with the tops woven shut. He pushed it all behind him into the room, working frantically, warming up again with the exertion. He scooped out the last of the litter on the floor, so that the closet was utterly empty, and he stood staring at the walls of the thing, catching his breath.

There was nothing to see. It was just a closet, set in a round piece of wall. It was plaster on the inside, just like any other closet—dirty plaster streaked yellow with water stains.

If there was a secret passage of some sort beyond it, it must be accessible from some other part of the house. What was on the opposite side this far upstairs, though? Nothing. There was only the one attic room. He was certain of that.

Except there was the exterior door, the one you *could* see from Jimmers' garden, the one in his dreams that opened out onto nothing, with the broken stone stairs leading almost to it. That was it. There *was* a door, all right, and so arguably there was a secret passage, and it was an even bet that this was it.

But what good did it do him? Even if he was free and standing down on the meadow, without a twenty- or thirty-foot ladder he could get nowhere near the door, which was padlocked, anyway, just like Jimmers' shed—probably the same key.

He stepped out into the room again. The exertion had calmed him down. It was the quilt, apparently, or nothing.

Resolutely he found the scissors and hacked away, cutting as straight and clean as he could along the vertical seams and wondering whether the stitching would hold a man's weight or would ravel into threads when he was halfway to the ground. Cotton batting fluffed out from between the panels, deflating them, making the strips look flimsy and weak. He would roll it up and knot it in order to fake a little extra strength. He went on with it, growing more and more doubtful, each passing minute increasing his anxiety, the silence outside the room becoming more ominous.

When the quilt was cut apart, he stood up and stepped across to the casement, throwing it open, steeling himself before looking down. The tide was low, and the hulk of the Studebaker sat high and dry. The kelp-covered reefs were half dried out in the afternoon sunlight. There was a movement below, on the edge of Jimmers' garden. It was the man with the wig, working feverishly, digging up the Swiss chard with a spade.

Damn it, Howard thought. That might be it. What if they'd tortured Jimmers and he'd confessed to burying the sketch and covering the thing's grave with vegetables? If that was the case, maybe they would take it and leave. Maybe not. One way or another, Howard would be spotted in a second Rapunzeling down the wall. They would wait below and just give him a gentle push with the end of the shovel when he touched down.

The scissored-up quilt looked like hell to him, lying there on the floor. He stared at the closet again, thinking, for some strange reason, of Mrs. Lamey and her dyed flowers. What was it? The closet still intrigued him, still drew him. He shoved into it again, rapping against the plaster this time, knocking methodically. It echoed thin and hollow beneath his knuckles.

15

IT was a piece of wallboard is what it was, thin and flimsy, not plaster at all. Dollars to doughnuts it wasn't original. Graham wouldn't have had anything to do with wallboard back when he built the place, even if it had been available, which it probably hadn't been. Shoving his face nearly against it, Howard could smell the musty, dried mud odor of the recently applied joint compound and the chemical odor of new paint. There were brush marks where someone had painted-on the stains, probably with rusty water. It might have been done yesterday, last week. Whoever it was—Jimmers, probably—had made a thorough job of it.

Howard knocked again, listening close—rap, rap, rap along the entire length of the thin wall. There were studs at either end, with three feet of unsupported wallboard in the center, pretty clearly where a door used to be. It pressed inward half an inch when he pushed on it.

He leaned back, levered himself against the door frame, and kicked the wall with the bottom of his foot, which chunked through the wall, tearing open a ten-inch ragged hole. He kicked it again, widening the gap, and then grabbed the wallboard with his hands, slamming it back and forth, breaking out chunks and throwing them back through, into the dim antechamber beyond.

Along with the chalky smell of drywall dust, he could smell ocean air drifting up out of the passage. It led to the sea, then, probably to the base of the cliff, a cave through the bluffs themselves. Too bad about Mr. Jimmers' quilt; there had been no point in scissoring it up. Howard had become a sort of thorn in the poor man's side. But if he wanted to make up for any of the trouble he had caused Jimmers, then Howard had to hurry, to get back to Jimmers before it was too late to help him.

For a moment he hesitated, though. To do it right, a sort of Huckleberry Finn job, he should knot up the quilt strips, anchor

153

them to the table, and drop the end out the window. That would throw them off the scent. He should repack the closet, too, and then shut the door behind him when he made his escape. They would take one look into the room, see the tied-together quilt, rush to the window, figure things out wrong, and charge back down to see if he was outside somewhere, skulking around.

Either that or they would suppose it was all fakery and that he was hiding in the closet. They'd find the passage and be after him, if they cared about him, and he would have wasted twenty minutes screwing around being clever.

Without waiting another instant he bent through the hole, stepping on the pieces of drywall in his stocking feet, nearly slipping on them as they skidded across the floor. Jimmers' hankering after Japanese customs had begun to look something worse than silly, and Howard made a vow never again to give up his shoes. Still, socks were better than nothing, even if they had holes in the toes.

Now that his eyes had adjusted to the dim light, Howard could see that the tiny chamber beyond the closet was nothing more than the top landing of a spiral stairway. The Humpty Dumpty window hung in the wall adjacent to the first step. A diffused glow showed through it from the hallway beyond, and Howard could see the figure of a man just then moving across the window like a shadow—probably one of the two intruders, sneaking up the stairs. It might have been Jimmers, of course, free and coming to let him out, but Howard didn't think so. It was more likely that they had found nothing but Swiss chard in the garden and were looking to have a go at the attic. The bolted, barricaded door would hold them up, but not for more than a few moments.

Howard started down the stairs, taking them two at a time, hanging on to the handrail, which was an iron pipe that snaked down into the blackness. Within eight steps the night had closed around him and he couldn't see anything at all. He gripped the cold railing, stepping down slowly now, thinking of the ruined stairs that led to the high doorway above the meadow. What if someone, Jimmers, had done something to these stairs, too?— pried two or three of them apart with a crowbar so that a person coming along in the blind darkness would . . .

But that wouldn't make sense. Clearly the passage had been used, and recently, too. And someone had gone to some little trouble to hide the fact while sealing the passage off altogether. Why? Howard couldn't say, and didn't have time to consider the problem. There was a sudden, muffled banging from above, and then the sound of a voice shouting—the thieves yelling through the attic door, probably. He couldn't make out the words. The shouting stopped and the banging started back up, a loud, slow *thump, thump, thump* now, as if they were slamming at the door with something heavy, trying to batter it open.

Abruptly he found himself at the bottom of the stairs. Cool, wet air drifted up from below. The smell of the sea was stronger now, mixed with the musty odor of stone and decayed kelp, and he could hear the murmur of breaking waves echoing up through the tunnel. It was still utterly dark, and he felt around himself before going on, running his hands across rough timbers like in a shored-up mine. After a few feet of level ground, the passage ran off steeply again, with wooden steps set right into the dirt and rock. Howard followed them down, gripping the corroded pipe, listening for sound from above.

He just barely heard another distant thump and then heavy scraping—the table and chairs shoving away in front of the door. So now they knew. They could see the closet door standing open, the jagged hole torn in the wallboard. They would see the cut-up quilt, too, and know that he hadn't gone straight out, that he had wasted time first, that they were right behind him.

They wanted the sketch, though; they didn't want him. If they had already found it, they would profit by getting it out of there, simply taking off. He stopped and held his breath, cocking his head. Someone had come through the wall. He could hear them scrabbling around on the loose pieces of drywall. It was deadly silent for a moment except for the noise of his own heart beating, and then there sounded the thumping of shoe soles on the wooden stairs.

He hurried on, down into the ground, brushing the air above his head to try to find the tunnel ceiling. There was nothing, empty air. And then suddenly the steps ended, and his stocking feet slid on gravel, shooting out from under him so that he sat down hard on the ground, scraping the palms of his hands, his breath whumping out of his lungs. He pushed himself up, dusting the gravel off his hands, and took off again. He went carefully now, stepping gingerly on rocks, feeling his way, trying to hurry along in a sort of high-stepping caper. If he wore shoes, he might have run—the two behind him surely would—but the gravelly tunnel was too rough.

There they were. Howard heard a scuffling and a brief snatch of cutoff talk. In the echoing darkness of the tunnel it sounded like the disembodied voice of a ghost. There was no way to tell where it had come from. Thank God for the railing; he had something to hold on to, at least, and unless Jimmers was simply crazy, there ought to be nothing obstructing the passage at the bottom end, no boulders to stub his toes on. The sound of the ocean, clear and close now, argued against any sort of door across the tunnel mouth.

The passage leveled suddenly and he saw ahead of him a moonlit section of sand and rocks. He stepped outside, into the evening air, the sand beneath his feet crusty and damp from the receded tide. The cold sea wind blew straight onshore, into his face. The sun was low over the ocean now, almost swallowed up. A wall of tumbled rock on his right cut off the view of the smashed Studebaker and made it impossible for anyone to see the tunnel mouth from the meadow above. To his left the bluffs rose straight up toward the sky, loose and scrubby—impossible to climb. He might have been able to scrabble up a ways in order to drop a rock on someone's head, but he wasn't in a rock-dropping mood.

He waded straight out into a big tide pool instead, gasping at the cold water that swirled around his ankles and stepping up onto a dark shelf of rock that was a garden of limp, exposed sea palms. He slid on the slippery leaves, slamming his foot against a jagged bit of rock and then sliding sideways into a deeper pool, soaking his right leg up to the waist. His breath jerked up out of his throat, and he nearly shouted as he pulled himself out of the freezing water and scrambled in behind a table-sized angle of stone, gripping two handfuls of sea palm to hold himself steady.

Right then the two men appeared at the mouth of the passage, looking around themselves warily. One of them carried a stick— a table leg or something—and he held it out to the side, ready to bash someone. They turned to look above them up the bluffs just in case Howard was up there. Seeing nothing, they stood murmuring to each other, one of them shaking his head.

Howard kneeled in the shadow, hidden behind his rock. The ocean swirled in just then, rising to his waist, trying to push him forward. His breath shot up out of his lungs with the numbing cold of it, and he was nearly washed off into deeper water. The ocean rose higher, and his legs slowed around as he kicked to try to find a purchase against the rocks.

Then the ocean receded, leaving him sodden and hanging. He got his knees up under him, creeping toward higher ground, crouching to stay hidden while the two on shore still looked around themselves dumbly, surveying the cliff face once more and then looking hard out into the ocean—straight past him. They edged out onto the rocks, trying to get a glimpse across to where the Studebaker sat. But that meant taking a swim, or at least a wade out into the ocean, and their tiptoeing around made it seem as if neither one of them wanted to get wet.

They pointed Howard's footsteps out to each other and looked across the little bay. Howard stayed put, watching them between the rocks, thankful that the sun was low and the shadows were long. But if they came his way, they would see him, and he would have no choice but to turn and run—head for deep water and swim straight out to sea. The water was cold, but not cold enough to cause him any serious trouble, not for a little while, anyway.

They stood arguing now. One of them pointed oceanward, and Howard heard the other one say, "Who cares?" very loud, and then turn and walk away, back into the tunnel. The other stood there for another minute, evidently considering things.

The water swirled up around Howard's waist again, pushing him up the rock, spinning him in a lazy circle. He held on, waiting it out, cursing the man who still stood there hunting him. The ocean was colder than he had realized, and with the wind blowing now he would be colder yet before he was out of it. Then the second man was gone suddenly, back into the darkness.

Howard held on. What if they were crouched in the shadows, waiting for him to make his move? They might be more desperate than he thought. It was possible of course, from their point of view, that Howard had the sketch with him, that he had found it in the attic and taken it. He suddenly regretted all the tough talk in the hallway when he had confronted the man in the wig. He shouldn't have mentioned the sketch at all.

Minutes passed. The ocean rose and fell. Howard's feet were like blocks of heavy, numb sponge, wrapped in soggy socks that bagged around his ankles. He could see the silhouettes of the two men now, far above him, moving around in the attic, back and forth across the windows. There was no going back up the tunnel, not unless he wanted to hand himself over.

Without wasting any more time, he stood up, balancing carefully. Starting to shiver, he picked his way seaward from rock to rock, his wet pants sticking to his legs. It struck him that the cove must be impossible to navigate, even in a small boat at high tide.

Far outside he could see the white tumble of breakers.

He looked over his shoulder, back at the little bit of beach, where the tunnel mouth lay dark and silent. He could see only a black crescent of it now, and in a moment it was lost to sight completely beyond intervening rocks. He was safe. They would see him from the attic window if they cared enough to look, but by then he'd be too far off to chase. He had only to keep moving. In a half hour, he told himself, he would be in Jimmers' parlor; the fire would be roaring, and he would have his shoes back. By then, he hoped, the two men would be gone.

His socks were a ragged mess, pulled apart on the rough rocks. He couldn't feel much at all because of the cold water, which was just as well, because there were a couple of bleeding cuts on the bottom of his feet. He stepped along gingerly, forcing himself to slow down. He was tired and wobbly, and if he hurried he was sure to slip and fall. A twisted ankle would plunge him into deep trouble.

The tide seemed to be creeping higher, too. If he didn't want to find himself swimming against it, he would have to get out and around the long, rocky promontory that formed the south edge of the cove. It wasn't much farther to the tip of it—fifty yards, perhaps.

He could see where the water rushed out, leaving the low, kelp-covered shelf of the promontory high and dry, and then rushed back in again to cover it, slamming up against the vertical face of the upthrusting rock cliffs. He would have to avoid that, somehow—wait for a lull in the waves and run for it across the rocks; to hell with his feet. In ten minutes, probably, there would be nothing but ocean there, breaking waves, and getting past it would mean a long swim in rough water.

He set out across a bed of mussels and barnacles, hobbling gingerly on the things like a South Sea Islander across hot coals, his feet pressing them down. A broken shell knicked the soft arch of his foot, and he said "Ouch!" out loud, not caring who might hear him anymore, which was no one. The house sat on the cliff far above and behind him now, lit up from top to bottom. A faint wisp of smoke rose from the stone chimney.

He skirted the tip of the promontory finally, crawling up and onto a dark, stone shelf. The ocean washed through, deeper with each succeeding swell. Waves that had been breaking farther out in shallow water rolled right through now to smash against the ledge that he picked his way across, and he was knocked off his feet and had to scramble to keep himself from being swept back out with them.

He wasn't certain where the rock shelf ended and the next cove started but he knew there was another cove there, visible to the south of where he and Sylvia had talked on the bluffs that afternoon. He pictured it in his mind, as if to make it exist for him by sympathetic magic. There was a trail that led down to it from above, switchbacking along the bluffs, through the wildflowers and tall grass, and he imagined himself staggering up that trail, out of the water at last.

Another wave washed through, humping up over the ledge and quartering toward him across the now-submerged kelp and smaller rocks. He braced himself, but it slammed him over backward, pushing him helplessly toward the cliff face where the water roiled and leaped and blasted into the air in heavy geysers. He flailed with his arms, trying to turn himself around, waiting to be knocked senseless. His head scraped sickeningly across a mussel-covered rock, and he could hear his scalp tear for a stinging-cold moment. Then the face of the wave smashed against the cliff, and the wave's energy turned on itself as the sea rushed back, dragging him along, surging away from the rock wall and hauling him off the edge of the reef and into deeper water before relaxing its grip on him.

He struck out hard, swimming parallel to the shore, his sodden clothes dragging at him. They had saved him a thousand cuts and scrapes, though. Pulling any of them off now would be madness. They would do something to cut the sea wind, too, when he got to shore.

He kept that in mind—getting to shore—as he kicked over the top of a wave and down the back side of it, still swimming. Again he pictured Mr. Jimmers' stuffed chair in front of the parlor fire, and the fire itself, heaped with cedar logs, leaping and popping, orange sparks rushing up the stone chimney.

His arms and legs felt weighted, and he found that he couldn't easily open and close his hands, which he pulled through the water like frozen bricks. A wave broke, catching him by surprise and washing over his head. He fought to stay on the surface, coughing up ocean water and gasping for air, kicking his legs tiredly. He forced his arms to move, plodding along in a sodden crawl stroke and paying attention to the waves and to the rocks along the shore.

He could see that the cliffs moved slowly past him now. He was making headway—more than he ought to be making. He was being swept along in a current. Suddenly frightened, he began to swim straight in toward shore with fear-induced power, trying to pull a little energy out of the waves washing past him.

When he rose on one swell, he saw that he was straight off the next cove, which stretched lovely and flat and sandy for something like fifty yards. He kicked furiously into an onrushing wave, which sped him forward, picking him up and hurtling him past the black humps of exposed rock. He held his hands out in front of him and tucked his head against his chest, expecting to be slammed against the rocks as the wave jumped and foamed around him, carrying him shoreward now in a wild rush.

Then the wave abruptly dwindled, dumping him thirty feet from shore and washing out to leave him on his knees in the shallows. He tried to stand, but couldn't, and another wave tumbled through, sliding him in across the sand before rushing back out and leaving him there on the beach, sodden and gasping.

He rested for a moment before crawling farther up, the ocean licking at his feet. Then he lay there again, thinking that as the tide came up, the waves might easily submerge the whole beach, which was almost flat. He could see flotsam and seaweed scattered in the rocks above him, advertising the high-tide line. The sight of it compelled him to stand, and he staggered away toward where the dirt path joined the beach, trying to dust the sand off his hands against the side of his pants.

He plodded tiredly up the path some twenty or thirty feet before sitting down in the dirt to rest. His feet had started to thaw out, and it wasn't any sort of pins and needles tickling; it was a slow burning and itching, and the painful realization that they were cut up, and that he was walking now nearly barefoot through dirt. He still wore his socks, but there wasn't anything left of the bottoms of them except a few stretched bunches of thread. He stopped long enough to turn his socks over, so that the heel stretched across his ankle. At least his head, miraculously, was whole. There was a wash of watery blood across his hand when he touched his cut scalp, but the mussels, blessedly, had been just a little bit spongy, happy just to slice him up and tear out clumps of hair.

Twice again he stopped to rest, looking down on the cove and at the ocean that had both saved him and tried to drown him. Then he trudged upward, finally topping the rise and finding himself on the meadow, skirting the wooden fence where he had talked to Sylvia only a few hours earlier.

He was suddenly in dangerous territory, and he slipped along warily, boosted by the adrenaline rush of confronting the two robbers again. He couldn't afford to do that. But what would he do instead? Pitch their distributor cap into the weeds and drive like hell down the highway? Wait for them to leave peaceably and then go in after Jimmers?

He pushed through the vines at the side of the house, crouching behind the cement mixer and peering past it.

They were gone. The red Camaro simply wasn't there. Cautiously he hunched across the yard in the shadow of the house. The front door was shut, the house dark. Fearing that they'd moved the car and that he would blunder into them, Howard edged along the wall toward the garden. There was nothing— just the tin shed standing lonely in the moonlight.

He retraced his steps to the front door, opened it slowly, and listened for a moment before pulling off his socks and stepping in out of the sea wind. The house was silent, the fire nearly burned down. Mr. Jimmers sat in his chair yet, just as Howard had left him. He was breathing evenly, obviously asleep.

Without a backward glance, Howard eased the stone out of the face of the fireplace, reaching into the dark recess. The hidey-hole was empty, the sketch gone.

"Move and you're a dead man," a voice said, and Howard believed it, and stood very still, his nose six inches from the granite wall of the fireplace.

 16

A MINUTE passed in complete silence. Howard was aware of the cold stones of the floor and of the pitifully burned-down fire and of the stomach-wrenching truth that someone right now was deciding calmly what to do with him—shoot him, maybe, in the back, or merely beat him senseless with a club. He began to shiver again, violently now. Whatever energies had fired him when he was sneaking back into the house had waned, and it was with a growing sense of horror that he realized he was in no condition at all to put up a fight.

Still nothing happened—no blow, no further orders, not even a poke in the ribs. He risked standing up out of the semi-crouch he was in. No one protested. There was nothing but silence. He turned his head slightly. No one said a word. He had moved, and he wasn't a dead man. He had the eerie notion, though, that someone was standing directly behind him.

He couldn't bear it any longer, and he turned to look, ready to throw himself onto the floor, into the fireplace if need be. There stood Mr. Jimmers, wide-eyed but otherwise deadpan and staring at his pocket watch as if counting off the seconds. He had cleaned the blood from his forehead and wore a big, rectangular bandage on the cut. Howard hadn't noticed it, sneaking around as he had been.

"A little experiment in human behavior," Mr. Jimmers said, putting the watch away. "Taken a swim, then?"

"Yes," said Howard. "That's right. They chased me down to the cove, and I got away across the rocks."

"And came back around to rob me?"

"Not at all. I wanted to know if they'd got it. What were we fighting about, after all, if it wasn't to keep them from getting it?"

"I burned it this afternoon. You saw me. Disbelieve your own eyes these days?"

"I thought it was, you know—a prank, a trick."

"Ah! That's it. A prank, a trick, a cheat." He smiled suddenly. "They're gone. Empty-handed. I told them it was in the attic, after they locked you in. They came back down to rough me up. I'm not the sort, though, to be pushed around like that. I've got friends, and I warned them of it. Clever of me, wasn't it, telling them it was in the attic, hidden under the drawer in the library table? You should have heard me."

Mr. Jimmers waggled his eyebrows at Howard, and then said, "Ouch," under his breath, and touched his forehead gingerly, his face clouding over for a moment. Then he grinned again. "It could be they think *you've* got it now—that you found it and fled. I said you were a skunk, a thief, a poseur from down south. I'm free of them. They're yours now. Here, sit down." Mr. Jimmers gestured toward the chair, but then seemed to see for the first time that Howard was soaked through, and he shook his head, as if withdrawing the offer. Instead, he threw two logs onto the fire and blew at them with a bellows.

"You'll warm up faster standing up," he said. "Cup of Postum?"

"No thanks. You're all right, then—no ringing in the ears or faintness?"

"Not at all. I'm tip-top. They didn't want trouble, assault charges. You know what they wanted. How about you, though? You've taken a nasty scratch on your head."

"Assault charges?" Howard said. "You called the police?"

"No," said Mr. Jimmers. "Nor will you. You'll disappear south, back to the warrens of Los Angeles. I've thought this through, and I've come up with a plan that might save you. You'll leave your truck and all your belongings. They aren't worth anything, anyway. We'll smuggle you up to the Little River airport and fly you out in a private plane—to Oakland, where you can catch a commercial jet into Los Angeles. You can't return to work, of course, or to your living quarters, but I can't imagine that you'll suffer any for that. It's possible that we can arrange some little stipend to see you over. I have a cousin in the cordage industry down there. He could probably find you a position."

Mr. Jimmers paced up and down, his hands behind his back. Howard stood cooking before the fire, listening in astonishment. "Anyway, straight off you'll send someone in to steal your dental records. And when you don't reappear at Roy Barton's place, our thieves will be certain you've drowned with the sketch. Meantime, somehow we'll get a cadaver and soak it in a tide pool for a few days, let the crabs and fish have a go at it, then tow it a quarter mile out to sea and set it adrift. By the time it washes up on shore there'll be no one alive who can say it's not you if they don't have the dental records, which they won't of course, because you'll have destroyed them. No, cancel that. Forget the dental records. We've got a corpse, don't we? We'll break its teeth out. Wait! Better than that, and easier, *we'll cut off its head!* To hell with dental records. Don't bother yourself with them. This is foolproof! We'll pull the wool straight over their eyes. You won't have anything to fear from these men. I had to pitch you into the soup there with the shotgun and all, which I notice you ruined somehow, but I'm hauling you out again with the ladle. Dry yourself off and get back to the business of living. That's my last word on the subject, and it's a good one."

Howard said nothing during this appalling speech. The fire leaped behind him, throwing out a wash of heat, and he stepped forward and brushed at the back of his legs. He had no earthly idea

163

whether Mr. Jimmers was serious or playing Tom Fool. He didn't have the strength to ask and certainly not the strength to play along. Of course he wouldn't disappear south. If these thieves accosted him, he'd tell the truth—that he had seen Jimmers burn it. They could turn him upside down, empty his pockets, give him the third degree. What good would it do them? They hadn't killed Jimmers tonight. It stood to reason that they wouldn't kill him, either.

"Wait here," Mr. Jimmers said, hurrying away. He was back within minutes with a set of dry clothes, and Howard, suddenly, was itching to be out of there. Mr. Jimmers was safe. Howard could catch Uncle Roy at the haunted house. He would know what to do next. In fact, Uncle Roy and Sylvia might easily be the next victims. There was no time to stand and chat with Mr. Jimmers.

"Hold off on the cadaver," he said to Jimmers. "It's a good plan, but I see some bugs in it. I'll contact you."

He took the dry clothes with him to the next room, and, feeling ridiculous but almost warm again after cinching up the too-short and too-broad pants, he thanked Mr. Jimmers, latched on to the picnic basket, and went out into the evening, carrying his wet clothes in a plastic grocery bag.

"HONESTLY, Mr. Stoat. Think about it," Mrs. Lamey said. Stoat sat on her living room couch, his feet propped up on the table. A second woman sat across from him, scowling toward the window as if she were tired with the conversation. Mrs. Lamey went on, gesturing expansively. "Those old properties on Haight Street are worth millions. Your friend the Reverend has made a fortune renovating dilapidated flats. I mean to tap it myself—tie into them with a bulldozer. You get tiresome when you pretend to have a social conscience, Mr. Stoat. I know very well that you haven't any such thing. A conscience of any sort is like fetters, isn't it?"

"Dangerous talk," Stoat said, shrugging. "Never deny having a conscience. You might wake up one morning and discover you're right. And we're talking about the area around where the old Haight Street Theater used to stand, aren't we? Down around Haight and Cole? That's dangerous ground. The last developer got firebombed by urban terrorists, didn't he?"

Mrs. Lamey made a long face. "There's terrorists," she said, "and there's terrorists. It's all a matter of motivation. The good Reverend White, I believe, has some little experience with these terrorists. He has a great deal of motivation on call, pockets full of it."

"Are you saying that—"

"I'm not *saying* anything, Mr. Stoat, except that you need have no fear of urban terrorists, as you call them. All you have to fear is your bleeding social conscience."

"There's no point in talking in labels and definitions, anyway. I've never thought of myself as having a 'social conscience,' as you put it. When you politicize morality you lose it. That's what I think. A standard-issue conscience is enough for me."

"That's absolute shit," the second woman said, breaking in. "You're stone-scared, Stoat. Don't turn this into a study of philosophy. Face yourself."

"It's tiring to face yourself, Gwen, if you don't like what you see in the mirror."

The woman named Gwen wore a khaki dashiki, a necklace of wooden beads, a pair of old combat boots. She had long, straight, unevenly cut brown hair, as if she were working hard to affect the look of an urban guerrilla at a Halloween costume party.

"Let's ignore your conscience, then, shall we?" Mrs. Lamey said to Stoat. "What I'm talking about is some squalid empty lots and a run-down lot of flats occupied by human rubbish." She held up a hand to silence Stoat, who had started to speak. "What will happen, as it's happened time and time again in the past, is that one fine day a cigarette and a mattress will burn another half block to the ground and all those people will be on the street, anyway, if they're not dead. The entire area is an unsanitary warren of drug havens and bathhouses and human degradation. What I propose is to rebuild all of it, and human dignity into the bargain."

"What you propose is turning two hundred people out of their homes in order to profit by it. Let's keep all this motivation talk straight, just like Gwen suggested."

"It's a matter of perspective, isn't it?"

"It's a matter of something."

"Don't pretend to be above it, Stoat," Gwen said. "You're a fine one to talk about profit. How long ago was it that you sold out? And didn't I just hear you propounding a lot of shit about there being no such thing as a social conscience? Now you're coming in on the side of the huddled masses."

"On the side of the poor bastard who's trying to get by from day to day."

"Shit happens, Stoat."

Mrs. Lamey frowned. "My dear," she said pettishly, "could you try to be less fecal about this whole thing?"

"Shit, shit, shit!" Gwen said at Mrs. Lamey's face. "You and my goddamn mother. Let me give you a piece of advice. It's a couple of lines from my last poem. 'You've got to be able to shit and look at it. That's all that matters.' "

"*All?*" Stoat asked, blinking at her. "I would have thought something else . . . a good bottle of wine . . ."

"*Fuck* what you would have thought."

Mrs. Lamey recoiled, like a snail touched with an electric prod. After a moment's silence she said, "Forgive me if I try to get us back on subject. This little venture would return quadruple the investment within a couple of years. It's *quite* an opportunity. Now, here's a thought. If you want so badly to help the downtrodden, why don't you make them an offer—each and every one of them. Let them all be partners in this. For every hundred dollars each of them invests, we'll return two hundred dollars after two years, guaranteed. There's nothing more egalitarian than profit sharing. There's two hundred and fifty or so of them. Squeeze a hundred dollars out of them on the average and we'll have enough to rent a crane and wrecking ball." She smiled at the dashiki-clad woman, who frowned back at her. "You don't seem to want to agree with anyone today, do you, Gwen?"

"Agreeing doesn't agree with her," Stoat said. "I'd cut off her allowance if I were you, Heloise. Being a patron of artists and poets ought to give you a certain power over them. Here's one of them waxing obscene in your living room. Let's wash her mouth out with soap."

"You took my money greedily enough when you were drawing your disreputable comic books and living in poverty, Mr. Stoat. Leave Gwendolyn alone. She'll come into her own." Mrs. Lamey cast the woman a motherly look.

"Why don't you both suck on a gun barrel?" Gwendolyn said.

The door opened just then and in walked two men, one of them wearing a beard and dressed in a coat and tie, and the other in a fashionable knitted sweater and pleated pants and carrying a leather shoulder bag like a yuppie banker dressed for a country excursion. Mrs. Lamey stood up, looking sharp at them. "Did you locate it this time? Or did you simply tear the place up and hit the man over the head again?"

"Got a fix on it this time," the second one said. He reached into the shoulder bag and hauled out Mrs. Lamey's magical divining rod—the two lashed-together forearm bones. A rotten, musty smell issued from the bag and from the bones. The man held them gingerly, as a person might hold a loaded gun with a cocked hair trigger. It was clear that he found it a loathsome object and wanted to get rid of it as quick as he could.

Mrs. Lamey took the thing from him, then strode across the room to lay it on a distant table, out of harm's way.

"Can't you shift it farther than that?" Stoat asked. "Why does magic stink so badly?"

"Nearly everything stinks that badly," Gwendolyn said. "You've been holding your nose all these years. Let go of it once, you'll learn something."

"Where, then?" Mrs. Lamey asked.

"Near as we can tell, in the tin shed. Who would have thought he would leave it out there? We used triangulation to home in on it, just like you suggested. Took us straight to the edge of the bluffs. For my money it's either locked in the shed or thrown off the cliff."

"And you extricated it, then, from this tin shed?"

"No, we didn't. The nut—what's his name?"

"Jimmers."

"That's it. He spotted us out the window. Said he'd already called a cop. So we moved on. He might have been telling the truth. Shouldn't be any real trouble to get at it—pair of bolt cutters when the old boy's asleep."

"No, we'll get it now, before anyone else has a go at it. There's more in that shed than . . . what it is we're after." She stepped to the window. Across the street sat Mr. Bennet's house with its garden of wooden gizmos. Bennet himself had gone off with Roy Barton two hours ago. His truck sat carelessly at the curb. The street was silent and empty.

"You know Sylvia Barton, I think," Mrs. Lamey said to Gwen.

"I did once," she replied, speaking to Mrs. Lamey's back. "When she was sweet on Stoatie here."

Mrs. Lamey turned around, looking shrewdly at her. "Your voices aren't so very different. Hers is pitched just a little higher. Could you mimic it, do you think?"

She shrugged. "I suppose so. How's this? Hello," she said, sounding something like Felix the Cat, "I'm Sylvia Barton, raven-haired beauty."

"Too high. I don't want a cartoon imitation. I want something that will fool our friend Jimmers."

She tried again, modulating her voice until Mrs. Lamey told her to stop, that she had it at last. "Practice that," she said. "And you three, you're going back out to that house one more time. Please don't come back empty-handed this time. Bring me what I ask for or go home and make an honest living."

"What about Jimmers?" the man in the suit asked. "He'll be watching for us. What shall we do to him?"

"Nothing," Stoat said immediately. "There's no profit in violence here. If I'm going along, you can be damn well sure Jimmers is not going to get a glimpse of my face. I'm fairly well known around these parts. I'm not going in there waving a lead pipe. Sometimes it seems like I'm the only one around here that values subtlety."

"Or fear, for that matter," Gwendolyn Bundy said in the voice of Sylvia Barton. "How's that? Do I still have it?"

"Just right," Mrs. Lamey said proudly. "That's my girl. Mr. Stoat is entirely right in this case. Leave your lead pipes in your car and leave your car where it is. Better yet, move it around the corner. I don't want you parking in front of my house anymore. You've bungled this twice, and that sort of bungling leads to troubles."

"What, we're *walking* down to Elk?" the man in the sweater asked.

"I've arranged for transportation. You'll leave at once. When you get there, Mr. Jimmers' car will be gone, with him in it. You'll have a good half hour to do the job and then disappear along with the goods. Don't dawdle, though. I don't want any possibility of a slipup. Gwendolyn, you're to phone Mr. Jimmers. You're Sylvia Barton, and you've run out of gas—where?"

"Irish Beach," said the man in the sweater.

"Too close. Point Arena. Just north of Point Arena, on the side of the highway. That's safe. Poor Sylvia will have to walk three or four miles back into town if he doesn't bring her up a gallon of gas in a can."

"What if she can't convince him?" the man in the coat asked.

"She'll convince him. I promise you. I know Mr. Jimmers and I know his past. He's a born champion, or wants to think so, and he has a special place in his heart for our Sylvia. By the way," she asked Stoat, "has she been notified that her lease won't be renewed come January?"

"Sent the notice off in the mail this morning. I'm not certain, though, why she has to be punished for the obstinacy of her crazy father."

"The sins of the fathers," Mrs. Lamey said, "will be visited upon the heads of their daughters. I mean to bring the whole family down in the manner of the Chinese communists. Get at the cousins and the aunts and the grandfathers, too, if I can find them."

Stoat shrugged.

She turned back to the man in the coat. "If worse comes to worst," she said, "then Gwen will have failed to convince him, and Jimmers' car will still be in the drive. In that case you'll have to terminate the immediate plan and figure out more forceful methods, even if they discommode Mr. Stoat, who perhaps ought to wear an extra pair of socks to keep his feet from getting cold." She looked hard at Stoat until he looked away.

Gwendolyn Bundy smiled widely. "Poor Stoatie-Woatie," she said.

The man in the sweater didn't look entirely convinced. "What about this transportation business?"

"Simple as anything," Mrs. Lamey said, breaking into a grin and stepping across to the window again.

 17

HOWARD slept in late the next morning, but woke up feeling better than he would have expected. His cuts and scrapes were superficial, and twelve hours of sleep had done a lot to restore him. Chasing around in the back of his mind was the idea that he knew something now that he hadn't known before, but he couldn't say just what. It was more likely a feeling of having fallen in among people with a common interest—as if he had been baptized at last and was finally part of a congregation.

Uncle Roy and he took the morning off and drove up along the coast to fish. They caught nothing but seaweed, though, and came home early in the afternoon to an empty house. Aunt Edith was off doing volunteer work at the hospital, and so when Uncle Roy drove off to the harbor to meet Bennet, Howard stayed home to glue decals onto the windows of his truck. It was a frivolous way to kill an hour, but it gave him time to think, and somehow gluing on the decals seemed right to him, appropriately strange. He was caught up in crazy activities, and this was no crazier than the rest.

Afterward, he went to work on the barn lumber, cleaning a good part of it up and stacking it against the wall. At six it was time to meet Sylvia at the worrisome haunted house. He half dreaded becoming involved in the project. Aunt Edith would probably have him arrested for contributing to the delinquency of an uncle. There was no way on earth, though, that once he was asked he could decline to help with it, or that he could even say anything serious against it.

He drove down to the harbor, finally, and found the old wooden icehouse. It had been painted white once, but the white paint had faded to a sort of uniform gray in the weather. There was a sign on top that read "Snowman Ice" above a painting of a winking snowman in a hat. The place didn't look a lot like a haunted house, maybe because of all the activity going on around it—kids on bikes and tourists looking for fish restaurants and fishermen going back and forth in pickup trucks. It was run-down enough, though, with broken windows and a couple of old ground-draping pepper trees at the corner. Uncle Roy was hard at it when Howard arrived. Howard could hear the sound of a dull circular saw whining and burning its way through a piece of wood. Sylvia's car was there, too, parked in front.

The door creaked open when he pushed on it, and Howard walked into an entry hall gaudy with dark red, velvety wallpaper. The skeleton from the university hung from a noose tied to a brass chandelier fixture in the ceiling, its wired-together toes pointed at a threadbare piece of oriental carpet. The ceiling was high, easily twelve feet, but the skeleton's knees dangled at eye level, anyway, and Howard was tempted to give it a knock just to hear it clatter like a wind chime. It would be a mighty temptation on Halloween night.

Beyond the entry hall was a big, open room with a dirty wooden floor, littered and stained and water-warped. In the dark, maybe, the place wouldn't look too bad. Uncle Roy sat at a plywood table near a pair of tall windows, carving ornate pumpkins. A plugged-in circular saw lay on the floor next to a couple of little triangles of plywood that had just been cut off the corners of the table. The air smelled of sawdust and friction-burned wood. Uncle Roy scraped sticky orange strings and seeds onto a heap of newspaper. "I figure we need quite a few," he was saying when Howard walked in. Sylvia still had her coat on.

"Damn it!" Uncle Roy cried just then, and threw his knife down onto the plywood. "Look at this! Hell. I've screwed it up." He tilted his head back like an artist, regarding his pumpkin, and then sliced delicately at the corner of the thing's mouth.

"So you went fishing today?" Sylvia asked Howard.

Howard nodded, and she said, "That's good. You've had too much excitement. You're on vacation."

"Right. I'm feeling pretty good, really. Rested. My only regret is that I didn't get the picnic basket back on time." He examined Uncle Roy's pumpkin, shrugging at it. "Looks all right to me."

"I've cut its damned teeth out," Uncle Roy said, shaking his head. "This knife isn't worth a damn. A knife has got to be sharp. That's paramount. Now I've gone and wrecked it." He picked up the knife again and hacked the pumpkin into oblivion, sweeping it finally off onto the carpet and then slapping the knife blade back and forth across the plywood in an awkward attempt to sharpen it.

"Rosie forgave you," Sylvia said, pushing up her jacket sleeves and looking over the pumpkins.

"Take one of those that sit flat," Uncle Roy said to her. Then to Howard he said, "Traded eighty pounds of pumpkins from the Sunberries for a couple of boxes of scrap leather I got off a pal of mine who's an orthotist. He gave me these, too." He leaned over and picked up two rubber hands, which were surprisingly lifelike except for being dirty, as if they'd lain around waiting to be used for ten or fifteen years. Uncle Roy pitched the hands into a cardboard carton full of wigs and old clothes and said, "Haven't heard from Jimmers, have you?"

"No," Howard said. "I was outside, though, most of the afternoon, with the saw running. Aunt Edith was down at the hospital."

"She got her five thousand hours pin for volunteer work," Sylvia said.

"That's right," Uncle Roy said proudly. "She's worth five women. Take my word for it. You sure Jimmers didn't call? I thought he might have. I thought maybe getting beat in the head yesterday had knocked some sense into him."

"Nope."

Uncle Roy fiddled his knife blade into the plywood, prying out a long sliver. "They stole Bennet's truck today. Just this afternoon."

"His *truck*?" Howard said. "Why?"

Uncle Roy shook his head. "Prank, I guess. What it is, is Mrs. Lamey."

"Mrs. Lamey stole Bennet's truck?"

"She had the job done. Bet on it. It was revenge for us putting the Humpty Dumpty on the roof. He'll find it driven off a cliff down south somewhere." Uncle Roy sighed. "Poor bastard. And after he spent all his Vegas money on it. The whole kit and caboodle."

"And you didn't call the police, of course," Howard said.

Uncle Roy shook his head. "It isn't worth that." He fell silent. He studied a fresh pumpkin, scowling at it. "What can we do about it?" he asked, as if he expected the pumpkin to answer. And then to Howard he said, "Sure you don't know who they were yesterday? Not Stoat?"

"Not Stoat. Smaller man. Stoat might have been hiding in the other room, but I don't think so. That's not his style."

"And today they steal Bennet's truck right off the street, colder'n a duck. The dirty bastards." Uncle Roy squinted at his pumpkin and then thrust the knife blade into it, up near the stem, cutting out the lid. The knife caught and hung itself up. Cursing, as if he'd had enough trouble already with uncooperative knives and pumpkins, he yanked at it, jerking it entirely free of the pumpkin and lancing the blade across his thumb. "Shit!" he yelled, tucking his thumb into his hand and holding on to it. He threw the knife down onto the table, then peeked at the cut thumb. There was a line of blood on it. He opened his hand all the way, relieved to see that the blood didn't well out, that it wasn't much of a cut. "Lucky the damned knife wasn't any sharper," he said. "I'd have cut it right off." Then, apropos of nothing, he said, "Jimmers and his damned machine. I have half a mind . . ." he started to say, but then he fizzled out and simply sat there looking tired. He stared at his thumb again and then wiped the blood off onto the pumpkin-spattered newspaper.

"Why don't we head home?" Sylvia said, putting her hand on her father's arm. "Give it up for tonight. Let's eat some dinner."

"Only days to go before we open," Uncle Roy said, shaking his head. "There's no time for dinner. I'm generating my second wind." He forced a replica of a smile. "Here, Howard—take a gander at this. This one is a knockout. Stick your hand into this bag."

Howard obligingly shoved his hand into the paper sack, while Uncle Roy supported it on the bottom, which was soggy and ready to break through. "Wet spaghetti?" Howard said.

"Guts," said Uncle Roy. "Doesn't it feel like guts? I got the idea at dinner last night. You can buy tripe down at Safeway, but it doesn't feel like anything at all. Wet spaghetti, though . . . feels like guts, doesn't it? Had you going for a moment there. I saw it on your face." Spaghetti leaked out onto the plywood through a tear in the bag, and Uncle Roy shoveled it back in and twisted the bag shut. "That damned Jimmers," he said. "I'd hit the son of a bitch myself, if he was here. Sylvia, tell me this doesn't feel like spaghetti—I mean guts. It feels like guts, damn it. Gopher guts. How does that jingle go? Great big gobs of greemy grimy gopher guts . . . It can't be 'greemy,' can it? We'll fill a plastic trash bag with the stuff—shove people in up to their elbows." Then, cheering up abruptly, as if he'd just then remembered something, he said, "Hey, Howard, I've got a couple of cow brains over in the ice chest. The real McCoy, too. Take a gander at them. Bring me a beer while you're at it, will you?" He wiped his cut thumb on the newspaper again, then picked up his pumpkin and sliced out a triangular eye.

Howard stepped past the pumpkin pile and pulled the lid off the Styrofoam ice chest. Uncle Roy seemed agitated, unable to concentrate, as if he were bothered not only by the truck being stolen but by whatever conversation he had had with Jimmers. He was avoiding all of it, though, perhaps because Sylvia was there.

Just then there was the sound of a car pulling up outside the door. It was Bennet, driving the station wagon. The two brains lay inside the ice chest, wrapped loosely in a plastic bag. Howard hauled a can of beer out and wiped it off carefully on his sleeve. "Good-looking brains," Howard said. "Will they last?"

Uncle Roy flourished his knife. "No, we've got to leave them in the freezer over at the Cap'n England. We'll cold-storage these pumpkins, too, once I've got them carved. Bring 'em in here!" he shouted suddenly toward the door, and he took the open beer from Howard, nodding happily at it. Bennet appeared just then, grappling two naked mannequins around the middle, both of them androgynous-looking males. He set them down on the floor near the pumpkins and then went back out and returned with two chrome-plated supports, propping the dummies up and securing them so that they stood looking at each other.

"Any word about the truck?" Bennet asked.

"Not a lick. I've got feelers out, though. We'll get it back. The scum-sucking pigs. They'll regret this one." Uncle Roy looked at the dummies. "Watch this," he said. "Where's that Japanese saw?"

Bennet disappeared into a back room, and Uncle Roy picked up a felt-tipped pen and drew a dotted line around the dummies' craniums. "Saw the bastards up," he said to Bennet, who had returned with the saw. Uncle Roy looked at the dummies with an artist's eye. "Don't spare the horses."

Bennet slid the little saw past the edge of his thumb, skiving into the head of the first dummy and parting its skull so that the top of its bald head came off like a cap. Uncle Roy fetched the brains out of the ice chest himself while Bennet worked on the second dummy.

"Watch this," Uncle Roy said proudly, laying one of the brains into the trepanned head of the first dummy. The hiatus was too deep, though, and the brain nearly disappeared inside, down beneath the thing's nose and eyes. Undefeated, Uncle Roy crumpled up a page of newspaper, pushing pumpkin innards off onto the floor, and then, removing the brain, he pushed the paper into the dummy's neck and head, stuffing it full, then laying the brain back in. It rode too high now, perching there like a bird on a nest, so he plucked it out once again and slugged the newspaper a couple of times to smash it down, and then lay the brain back in. "There," he said, standing back and admiring his work. "What do you think?"

"That's—something," Sylvia said. "Are you going to put clothes on him?"

"Of *course* we're going to put clothes on him—dress both of them up in these silver-glitter shirts we got down at the thrift shop. It'll be a sort of 'men from the stars' display. 'The Brainiacs.'"

Bennet finished up with the second dummy, and then, as if in a hurry, said, "Adiós," and went back out toward the front, past the hanging skeleton. "Got to pick up those plaster-of-Paris cats," he said, before going out.

Uncle Roy waved at the back of his head, shouting, "Hit Yum Yum for a dozen sinkers!" Bennet disappeared without answering and drove away in the wagon.

Howard looked at the mannequins, trying to summon whatever emotion it was that they were meant to evoke—fear? mystery?

awe? Maybe when they were dressed and the lights were turned down . . . Truthfully the place needed something more, and lots of it.

As if Uncle Roy were thinking the same thing, he seemed to deflate suddenly. Tiredly he sat back down in his chair and studied the face of a pumpkin. "Alas," he said. Then he smelled his hands, grimaced, and wiped them on the bib of his overalls. "We need something big." He looked out toward the street, sighing deeply.

"How about the corpses?" Howard asked, thinking to cheer him up.

"In there." Uncle Roy gestured toward the back. "Ready to shoot marbles." He ran his hands through his hair. "You tell me," he said, looking at Howard. "What do we need here? What would *you* do? What is it that kids want to see in a haunted house? What kind of crap puts the fear into them? Jack-o'-lanterns? Skeletons? Back in my day a good skeleton would have sent them screaming. Now they want blood. Sex. Both together, for Christ's sake. Nothing less. Blood and gore and flesh. I won't have it, though. I won't. This damned world's rotten. Morality's on the slag heap. Cut a woman up with a chain saw—that'll fetch 'em in. But a skeleton? That went out with the trash." He looked up timidly at Sylvia suddenly, as if remembering there was company present, and said, "Sorry to talk dirty."

He buried his face in his hands, resting for a moment, composing himself. Howard stood silently, embarrassed for his uncle. In the morning, when Howard was fresh, he would put his mind to it. With a little imagination he and Sylvia could come up with something.

"I called down to Jimmers' place an hour ago," Uncle Roy said to Howard, sounding beat and resigned. "We're going to lose our shorts on this venture, me and Bennet both. It doesn't seem like that—a small show like this. But our shorts aren't worth much. They were worn pretty thin before we started out. What I did was I called Jimmers after Sylvia told me about the machine, and I flat out asked him for it. Told him it would bail me out. We could get away with any damned trash in here if we could crank that damned machine up as a sort of finale. They'd come in droves. We could give the press a sneak preview. The papers would be full of it, and we'd be rolling in cash. What the hell good is it doing him, rusting away out in that damned shed? Anyway, he wouldn't budge."

Sylvia laid her hand on his arm, trying to stop him from working himself up. "Maybe he'll come around," she said. "He's still remembering all those pranks you two used to play on each other. He's bound to be touchy when you call him out of the blue asking for a favor like that. Let him sleep on it. He'll see it different in the morning."

"Well, he owes me, doesn't he? Drove me right out of business with that damned cow. No man likes being a laughingstock. This would have made bygones bygones. But no, he's a man who holds a long grudge. I'm half tempted to go out there and steal the damned thing, or wreck it, one or the other—just shove it off the cliff along with the goddamned Studebaker. I told him so, too."

"You shouldn't have," Sylvia said. "Now he's mad at you."

"Mad at *me*! I'll give him something to be mad about! Look at this damned mutant!" He reached out then and gave the dummy a shove, toppling it over, the brain spilling out onto the dirty carpet. Howard scooped it up, surprised at how rubbery and firm it was. There were hairs and bits of debris and dirt clinging to it now. Uncle Roy sat there with his face in his hands again, nearly in a state of collapse.

Sylvia set the dummy up, and Howard shoved the brain into its plastic bag and put it back into the ice chest. After that he popped the top on another can of beer and handed it to his uncle. Sylvia put her arm around her father's shoulder and said, "You're anticipating things. You always anticipate the worst sort of defeats, and they wear you out. Just last week you were crazy with ideas for this place. Wait till tomorrow; they'll be there again."

He looked up at her, gripping her hand. "Just last week Halloween was about a year away, and there was hope. This is the end, though. I'm going to be living out of the back of the station wagon, down behind the Texaco station, just like Mrs. Lamey says. Hell. I guess . . . I guess I'm just tired out."

A sudden voice interrupted them. "Knockety-knock," it called playfully from the vicinity of the skeleton.

"Mrs. Deventer," Uncle Roy said, standing up and giving her a little half-bow. His remorseful face turned pleasant all of a sudden, as if he didn't want to burden the rest of the world with his troubles. Mrs. Deventer stood in the doorway holding a pitcher of lemonade. She was short and gray-haired and dressed in thrift-store-quality clothes that didn't quite match up. A gaudy lot of costume jewelry hung around her neck, weighting down a long red scarf. She had the air of a five-year-old playing dress-up. All of that, along with her wild hair, gave her a naturally batty look. She was cheerful-looking, though, and the red scarf was almost dashing, as if she were geared up for a night on the town.

"Made in the shade," she said, winking.

"By an old maid with a spade," Uncle Roy said, winking back.

She feigned horror. "*Mister* Barton!" she said, stepping forward to set the pitcher and a stack of paper cups on the table. She looked askance at the dummy.

"Mrs. Deventer," Uncle Roy said, "meet Brainiac, the man from Mars."

"Charmed," she said, reaching her hand out toward Howard. "Welcome to planet earth."

"Wait," Uncle Roy said, pretending to be confounded, and then both of them, Uncle Roy and Mrs. Deventer, laughed and laughed. "You've heard me talk about Mrs. Deventer, Howard."

"Yes indeed," Howard said, remembering. She was the one being squeezed by Mrs. Lamey. Somehow she didn't look like a very formidable opponent.

"I've brought these cookies for all of you." Mrs. Deventer produced a sandwich bag full of cookies from the purse around her shoulder. "Leave some for the children," she said to Roy, and nodded toward Howard and Sylvia. Then to Sylvia she said, "Is this one yours?"

Sylvia blushed just a little bit. "Stray cat," she said.

Mrs. Deventer cast Howard a coy smile. "Pleased." She shook his hand again.

It struck Howard that Mrs. Deventer wasn't anywhere near sober. She wasn't falling down, but she wasn't steady, either.

"My young man is taking me out," she said happily.

The statement had a freezing effect on Sylvia and Uncle Roy both.

"Now, don't start in," she said. "He's pretty nearly saved me from ruin." She directed this at Howard, as if to assure him that the opinions of Uncle Roy and Sylvia weren't worth very much. "They'd have the place by now if it weren't for him, and you know it." Her nearly giddy attitude had switched to something near anger. Howard was clearly the only disinterested party in the room. "He's a godsend," she said to him.

"Good for him," Howard said, humoring her.

"Paid my taxes."

"Good man," said Howard.

"He's wealthy, you know. Pays my mortgage, too, when I can't afford it. He's looking out for me."

Uncle Roy looked about to burst, but he kept quiet for another moment, for as long as he could, maybe, while he systematically chopped the latest pumpkin into cubes. "That would be our friend Mr. Stoat," he said to Howard, not looking up.

Howard nodded, dumbfounded. Mrs. Deventer was grinning again, though, at the mention of the name of her "young man." Here was trouble. Howard wondered if Uncle Roy knew just how much trouble. Paying her mortgage and taxes?

She turned to leave, slightly miffed, Howard thought, as if she had expected enthusiasm and gotten doubts instead. "I'll just be on my way, then."

Howard walked with her toward the door, wanting to be gallant, thinking it best to win her favor in some little way. "Thanks for the lemonade," he said. "It was a pleasure meeting you. Live near here?"

"Right up on Dawson," she said, bumping into the skeleton, which swayed back and forth like a tired pendulum. Outside stood an old two-tone Pontiac, pink and gray, looking as though it had just been waxed. It was gorgeous, not a scratch on it, except for the rear bumper, which was smashed in. "Roy Barton is a good man, but he gets the most amazing ideas sometimes."

"Well," said Howard diplomatically, "he wouldn't be Roy Barton otherwise, would he? He's pretty fond of you, you know. He's told me quite a bit about you."

"Has he?" she asked, sounding pleased.

"Beautiful car." Howard opened the door for her.

"My poor old Bob bought it back in fifty-six," she said, her voice growing instantly husky. "God rest his soul. I don't take it out much. Just once a month, up to Willits to visit my sister. There isn't even ten thousand miles on it."

"Wow." Howard ran his hand across the clean pink paint. "Take care of it." He was vaguely conscious of a telephone ringing nearby, over and over again. Mrs. Deventer nodded, telling Howard through the open window that he was a good boy and looking about half wistful. She made several efforts to shove the key into the ignition, banging it on either side of the keyhole before sliding it in finally and starting the car. It died almost at once and then wouldn't start. There was the smell of gasoline as she pumped the accelerator. The telephone rang off the hook and then suddenly stopped.

"It's flooded," Howard shouted. She had rolled her window up, though, and she smiled at him and said something that he couldn't hear. Mashing the accelerator to the floorboard, she twisted the key again, holding it on until the motor roared into life and a cloud of dark exhaust blew out of the tail pipe. She backed out quickly, swerving in the gravel, and then rocketed up the hill past a startled man in an apron just then coming out of the back of the Cap'n England.

Howard turned to walk back into the haunted house, working the Mrs. Deventer problem over in his mind. "Hey," shouted someone from behind, and Howard looked back to see the aproned man hurrying toward him. "Roy Barton inside?" he asked, out of breath.

"Sure is," said Howard. "What's wrong?"

"Phone call. Artemis Jimmers. There's been trouble; he's pretty well worked up."

"Thanks," Howard said over his shoulder. He was in through the door in a second, shouting for Uncle Roy, who was up and past him, hurrying out into the night. Howard and Sylvia followed along behind.

The pay phone hung on the rear of the restaurant, the empty black cover of a telephone directory dangling against the yellow stucco beneath it. A moth the size of a small bird fluttered wildly around the light overhead.

"Yeah," Uncle Roy said into the mouthpiece. "What the hell?" He listened for a moment, his eyes narrowing. "You're completely over the edge," he said, raising his voice. "You're just exactly the nut I always said you were. That's right. You, too. I wouldn't touch your goddamn shed with a dung fork. Oh, yeah, well . . ." He stopped talking suddenly and looked at the silent telephone. Then he listened again and hung up furiously.

"What on earth is it?" Sylvia asked. "What's happened?"

"Somebody's stole his shed."

"His tin shed?" Howard asked, finding it hard to believe. "*Stole* it?"

"The whole megillah, lock, stock, and barrel. Jacked it up, slid it onto a truck, and drove off with it. Jimmers got a phone call luring him down to Point Arena. He thinks I put someone up to it. Anyway, he figured out it was a fake call, turned around to

179

head back, and blew out a tire a quarter mile from home. When he pulled in they were just taking off down the highway. He followed them for a mile on the flat. Tore the tire to pieces, apparently. Turned the tube into a sausage, it got so hot. They left him in the dust, of course. Now he wants the shed back along with a new tire. He thinks it was me."

"Why would he think it was you?" Howard asked.

"Because they were driving Bennet's truck."

 18

GRAHAM didn't sleep much anymore. Sleep didn't come easy to him, and there didn't seem to be any great need of it, anyway. The hours of darkness dragged along. He couldn't fish at night. Getting down the hill to the pond was treacherous enough in daylight. A couple of times he had sat in his chair on the front porch in the middle of the night, watching the moon rise over the trees. But it was cold, and the cold tired him out these days. Sometimes at night he read—the Bible, mostly, a large-print edition he'd had to switch to a few years back.

How many years? He couldn't remember now. The years ran together like watercolor paints, and his memories surfaced in confused order, some days clear, some days dull. Most often at night he simply lay awake, letting his mind drift. In the morning either Edith or Sylvia would arrive with his breakfast and coffee. Midmorning he would work his garden, which, although it was new, seemed to be blighted somehow. He had his suspicions, but there was little he could do about it except work. There wasn't a lot of sun out in the forest there, especially not in the fall. But the cabin and garden were in a clearing, and he ought to have had some luck with leafy things, with lettuce and cabbage, even though there wasn't enough of the season left for the vegetables to mature. In a month it would be too cold.

But this trouble wasn't weather; it was some kind of rot that came up through the soil, which seemed always to be dry, no matter how often he watered it. Nothing at all had grown well for him for a couple of years now. He had expected most of this. He knew it would be so at the end—all the dust and the dying. It was the strange blight, the rot, the tainting and withering of the leaves that he wondered about. They had a bad smell to them, too, even while they were still mostly green.

This morning in particular he felt heavy and tired. He had awakened twice in the night with chest pains, but they'd subsided now. He had found himself awake a third time. He was out of doors, standing in the moonlit garden and wearing his long underwear and his hat. He couldn't remember having gotten out of bed. The dark woods stretched away on all sides, and in the clearing overhead the stars shined thick and bright like a thousand promises. He had his walking stick with him, and with it he was drawing wavy-edged circles in the dirt, like clouds in the sky.

He was filled with the vague notion that he had been dreaming the whole time he was sketching with the stick—a dream about salmon schooling in deep ocean water. And one of the fish, responding to some sort of deep and primitive calling, had turned landward, swimming lazily toward the river mouth where Graham had sat fishing with his pole and line. Someone had stood behind him in the dream, watching his back—a shadowy presence that had begun to fade, along with the dream itself, almost as soon as he hooked his fish.

IT was just after three A.M. The living room clock had tolled, and in another hour Uncle Roy would be in to wake him. It wasn't just the looming adventure of stealing back Mr. Jimmers' shed that kept Howard awake. He sometimes worried about small things in the early morning—unpaid bills, long-avoided errands, elusive rice paper sketches which were pretty clearly not what they appeared to be. At home he got around the problem of insomnia by moving out to the living room couch—the change alone was usually enough to put him back to sleep. But he couldn't do that here. It would imply that his bed wasn't comfortable, and Aunt Edith would worry herself ragged over it.

The bed wasn't worth a damn, though. It sagged in the middle, and if Howard slept on his stomach for more than two minutes, he woke up in the morning with a backache that threatened to keep him in a chair. He lay on the very edge now, where the rail of the bed frame stiffened the mattress a little, and thought of all the things that he ought to be doing with his time but wasn't. Tomorrow he would clean up the rest of that pile of barn lumber, maybe steal a half dozen slats to throw under his mattress.

He had meant to be on vacation here, to sort things out, to discover whether his feelings for Sylvia had changed any. Well, they hadn't. That much was clear. It had taken him exactly two days to go nuts over her. Meanwhile she pretty clearly had found in him another man who needed looking after, like Uncle Roy—a slightly daft brother who had appeared out of the south, unable to keep out of trouble. And if he did stay in Fort Bragg, if he didn't return to his job at the museum, what would he do? He could move in with Uncle Roy, of course, and be a burden. When his money was gone, he could hustle food stamps, maybe get a job at the mill and get laid off in the rainy season.

The thought of going home left him empty, though. There wasn't a single thing to entice him back down to southern California except a scattering of friends, who seemed to be more scattered with each succeeding year. His coming north had cut some sort of mooring line, and he was drifting. It was time to put on some sail, to break out the compass and the charts. He looked at the clock for the tenth time. It wasn't even three-fifteen. The big old house was cold, and he pulled the blankets up around his neck and listened to the wind.

He began counting backward from one hundred. Sheep were too complicated. After a while his troubles scurried off to the back of his mind, where they winked and waved at him, not quite out of sight. He could see them back there in the shadows, as dream images now, and his counting backward faltered at around forty-five. He started again, but soon slowed and then stopped, and he found himself dreaming about a ship that had gone aground on a rocky shore. He was on the beach, ankle-deep in the rising tide, thinking that there was something on board that he needed or that he wanted. He was a castaway, thinking to salvage rope and timber and live chickens from the staved-in ship. He turned and faced the shore, and above him on the cliff top was the stone house, dark but for a single light in the attic window.

He could see the silhouette of someone sitting in one of the Morris chairs, reading a book, and he knew all at once that it was him, at home there, whiling away a peaceful evening, impossibly content. A dream wind blew off the ocean, into the dark mouth of the passage beneath the cliffs, and when he turned around again to face the sea, there was no longer a ship on the rocks but the old Studebaker instead, a ruined hulk sitting just above the tide.

182

He clambered across the rocks toward it, his pant legs rolled to the knees, the ocean neither cold nor warm nor even particularly wet. The car's door hung open, its top hinge broken, the musty upholstery smelling of seaweed and barnacles. He climbed in behind the wheel, grasping the Lucite steering wheel knob and thinking that if only he had a chart he would pilot the car out through the scattered reefs and into the open sea.

Looking deep into the Lucite ball, he was convinced that something was drawn or written way down in there, floating in the depths like clouds in a fishbowl sky. He could make them out now—the constellation of images from the rice paper sketch. Then he perceived them to be words and not drawings at all—a message scrawled in the shaky handwriting of someone old and frail. "Look in the glove box," it read, and with a feeling of immense anticipation and reluctance both, he reached across and punched the button. The glove-box door banged open so heavily that the entire car tilted sideways, farther and farther until he began to slide toward the open passenger door, looking out and down toward the now-distant ocean, scrabbling to hold on to the rotten old upholstery and knowing that he couldn't, that he would fall.

Howard sat up in bed, having waked himself up with a cut-off scream. The gauzy remnant of an idea was fading at the back of his mind. He had the certainty that it was an important idea, and he trapped the tail end of it and fixed it there so that he could study it when he had a chance. There was something in his waking, as horrible as it was, that left him almost satisfied with things. Somehow the worries that had plagued him an hour ago had evaporated. He felt distinctly as if something were pending—that somehow, in some inconceivable way, his course was being partly charted for him. There was a knocking on the door just then, low and secretive. "Howard!" a voice called. It was Uncle Roy.

A half hour later the three of them, Howard, Bennet, and Uncle Roy, sat in the station wagon, eating doughnuts and drinking coffee out of Styrofoam cups. The night was dark and silent except for the crash of waves and the sounds of chewing and sipping. They were parked on Elm, on the ocean side of the highway, down near the far end of the Georgia-Pacific yard. Hundreds of acres of stacked lumber lay drying in the night wind, fenced off with chain link and barbed wire from Glass Beach and from the weedy bluffs above it that stretched all the way out to the highway.

Directly across from them sat a white, flat-roofed wooden warehouse that must have been forty yards long and without a window in the entire length of it. There was nothing around it but weeds and berry vines growing right up against the sides. Around behind was a door with a small transom window above. No light showed through it. A single car was parked beside the door, hidden from the street—the red Camaro that had been at Jimmers' house yesterday afternoon.

According to Uncle Roy, Mrs. Lamey owned the warehouse, which was empty, he was willing to bet, of everything except Bennet's truck with Mr. Jimmers' shed on it, which they were going to steal back before the sun rose or know the reason why. Howard realized that he was in the company of committed men. What did that mean? he wondered. Probably that he'd be committed himself before the sun rose—to a cell in the county jail.

So now his vacation had taken a serious turn. His adventures at Mr. Jimmers' place had been dangerous enough, but compared to this they hadn't been anything but play—guns or no guns. Here he was setting out to break into a warehouse, to steal back Mr. Jimmers' shed, to steal a car, for God's sake. And what for? For Sylvia? Well, hardly. For Uncle Roy? Not entirely. What he ought to have done was try to talk his uncle out of this venture. Aunt Edith would think he was a hero if he could squash it. This was called aiding and abetting. He was going to help Uncle Roy go to jail, too, and the whole haunted house caper would be in the trash can. Sylvia would kill him.

Uncle Roy patted him on the knee, as if he sensed that Howard was uneasy. "Want to wait it out down at Winchell's?" He said it matter-of-factly, as if there were no shame in it.

Howard shook his head. "It'll take both of you to get the truck out of there."

"That ain't got nothing to do with it," Bennet said, pitching half of a doughnut back into the white paper sack. "This ain't convenience we're talking about. Nobody owes anyone any favors. There won't be no turning back when you start up that car engine."

Howard was silent, but not because he was thinking of turning back. He couldn't "wait it out at Winchell's." He was either in or out. There wasn't any in between—no choosing not to choose. He couldn't be a fair-weather conspirator. And somehow, sitting out there in the old station wagon, getting set to strike a blow against the enemy, he felt for the first time in months, years maybe, that something mattered. It was as if one of his eyes had been shut for a long time, and now it was open, and things had dimension to them at last. He reached into his coat pocket, pulled out a pair of thin goatskin gloves, and put them on, flexing his fingers. Then he pulled his stocking cap down over his face, adjusting it and looking out through the eyeholes.

"God almighty," Uncle Roy said. "You look like an IRA assassin. If the cops come anywhere near you, ditch the mask and the gloves both. They'll shoot you on sight looking like that. You've got the name of the foreman up at the yard?"

"Jack MacDonald."

"That's it. He's a good man. You'll be safe there. He's ready with an alibi, but I don't want to make him lie if we don't have to. He'll say that he sent you down to the Gas 'n' Grub for a couple of boxes of crumb doughnuts. He gave you three dollars."

"In my front pocket," Howard said.

"You need to look at his picture again?"

"Nope."

"What is it you do at the mill?"

"Run a stroke sander."

Uncle Roy was silent for a moment. "In general, don't cross the highway if you don't have to. Leave the car at the other side of the train yard and look for us at the old library building. Make sure the bastard chases you, though. He won't think it's us making a move on the shed, not this quick, so it ought to be possible to draw him away for a couple of blocks or so. Farther if you can. Play hide-and-seek with him. We just need enough time to break in there and get the door open. My hunch is that he'll come back finally looking to call the old lady on the telephone. We'll have cut the wire, and he'll have to head down to Gas 'n' Grub to use the pay phone."

He fell silent again. The time to talk was past. They had gone through it a half dozen times, and all of them knew that the plan was full of optimism.

"Let's go," Howard said, opening the door and sliding out. He eased the door shut. Uncle Roy fired up the engine and backed away a half a block down Elm, where they would wait. Howard loped across into the weeds, patting the bulge in his coat pocket where two cherry bombs lay along with a throwaway lighter.

The streets were abandoned and the nearby houses dark. A car sailed past down the highway, bound for points north, but there was no one out and about except Howard, the night wind, and the two in the wagon. Aside from the cold, conditions were nearly perfect. He tucked his hands into his armpits to try to warm them through the gloves.

The Camaro was unlocked, which was a relief, since he wouldn't have to break a window. And thank heaven there wasn't any car alarm. That would have cooked his goose, although it would have made the whole theft more grand. It would have been wonderful if the keys were in the ignition, but they weren't. Trust to a thief to hold on to his keys. Howard would have to start it up without them, which was just fine.

He listened first at the closed back door of the warehouse and heard nothing. It was entirely possible that there was nobody at all inside, in which case the elaborate distraction was a noisy waste of time. But surely the car wouldn't be there if no one was guarding the place. He stepped out away from the building, checking the street for traffic one last time. There was nothing at all but nighttime silence—no pedestrians, no prowl cars. He waved once at the distant station wagon, and the headlights blinked the go-ahead signal.

Then he climbed into the car, leaving the door ajar. He found the ignition wires under the dash, and, with one last quick look around, yanked the wires out in a clump, mashing the bare ends together in order to jump out the ignition. The motor turned over and he pumped the gas lightly.

He let it idle for a moment, watching the door for signs of stirring inside the warehouse. Then he shifted down into reverse, checked the emergency brake, and backed away from the building, turning out again toward the street so as to have a straight run for it. He raced the engine a couple of times again, hoping that whoever was inside would simply hear it and come out. He considered honking the horn, but it was such an idiotically doubtful thing for a car thief to do that he gave the notion up at once.

The cherry bombs, though, would take his man by surprise. He would wake up and hear the car engine and think it was backfiring, and he would wonder who in the hell was fooling around out back. He would take a cautious look out the door and discover in horror that . . . Howard wound down the window, still watching the door, ready to roll out of there. He pulled out both cherry bombs and held them side by side in his left hand, bending the fuses away from each other. Then, holding them out the open window, he flipped the lighter on with his free hand, lit both fuses, and pitched them toward the door, rolling up the window furiously.

They exploded one right after the other, slamming out like gunshots. A second passed. A light flipped on inside and then off again, and the door opened. Howard raced the engine a couple of times before hurtling out toward Elm Street, throwing up a rooster tail of dust and gravel. He waited for an instant at the edge of the street, giving his man time to make sense of things. Howard could see him through the dust, outside now, hopping on one foot while he pulled a shoe on. Howard jammed his foot down on the brake and accelerator both, then eased off on the brake, spinning the tires as if stuck in a hole. The man ducked back in for as long as it took for him to snatch out a coat, and then he was out through the open door again, pulling it shut behind him and running fast across the weeds, trying to catch up with Howard before the car took off again.

Howard bit his lip, waiting for the last moment, watching him come. In the moonlight, the man's face was wild with loathing. It was the man who had worn the fright wig out at Jimmers'. He had the same black T-shirt on, and his build was right. He ran at a gallop, one leg working harder than the other, and he wrestled with the coat in his hands as if he were groping after something. Howard spun the tires once more, slammed the transmission into reverse, and backed up a wild ten feet, nearly running the man over before shifting back into drive, the car lunging down onto Elm Street.

He headed straight toward the ocean, bouncing up onto the dirt road that ran out to Glass Beach. The road went nowhere— dead-ended two hundred yards down. Howard counted on the man's knowing that and following along behind, thinking that Howard was a nitwit, that he knew nothing of the local streets. He had to draw the man away, down the block, around the corner, out onto the bluffs, anywhere.

In the side mirror Howard could see the station wagon moving without lights. It angled across and disappeared from view behind the front of the warehouse. His man was still following, running wildly after the fleeing Camaro, which rocked from side to side down the dirt road, throwing Howard back and forth on the seat. The man had dropped his coat, but he held something in his hand now—a gun.

Howard nearly choked, spinning the steering wheel hard to the right and sliding in a wide doughnut across the dirt parking lot above Glass Beach, clipping a fence post with the rear fender and fishtailing back out in the direction of the highway, fifty yards down from his startled pursuer, who stopped dead at the corner of Stewart Street, leaped up onto the curb, dropped down into a crouch, and pointed the gun at the windshield, straight at Howard's head, tracking the Camaro as it hurtled toward him.

Howard stomped on the accelerator, angling straight toward the curb and smashing himself down onto the seat, almost hidden by the dashboard. Fear of being shot pounded through him. To hell with the man's car. If he started shooting, there would be lights on all over the neighborhood and telephones ringing down at the station house. Howard's career as a felon would be assured.

The Camaro slammed into the curb, up and over it with two wheels, as Howard pulled it hard to the left now, back onto the street, when his man lunged backward against the fence and out of the way, and then at once was up and aiming the gun again, training it on the car as Howard slewed around the corner onto Stewart, heading south now toward the train station.

He sat up in the seat again and slowed down, watching in the mirror. There was too much stuff in the way—telephone poles and parked cars—for the man to get off anything but a wild shot, and Howard was confident that he wouldn't risk any such thing. "Follow me," Howard said out loud. "C'mon. Chase me."

He didn't, though. The man wasn't going anywhere, but stood looking back at the warehouse. He clearly couldn't see anything of the station wagon, but he seemed to be thinking hard. If he gave up on Howard now, then stealing the car would become suddenly pointless. Howard had to draw the man away. Right now.

He punched the accelerator and shot forward again, tires squealing. Then he slammed on the brakes, locking them up and yanking the steering wheel hard, the car drifting sideways and forward in a slow spin. Howard threw himself down onto the passenger seat, covering his head with his hands. Almost instantly the car smashed into a curb tree, tearing out a length of grape-stake fence that catapulted across the hood. The crash threw Howard forward, nearly onto the floorboard, his knee cracking hard against the steering column. The horn honked one desperate blast, and then all was silent except for the clank of something falling onto the street.

Howard groped for the door handle, throwing the door open and pulling himself out upside down. He rolled to his feet and loped away down Stewart, not looking back but pulling wildly at his ski mask, which had been yanked around so that he was nearly blind. His knee hurt like a bastard where he'd knocked it against the steering wheel, and he limped and hopped in a zigzag course, waiting for the sound of gunfire or for the hammering of feet on pavement.

He was in trouble if the man caught him—the whole enterprise was in trouble. But it was in worse trouble if the man had gotten suspicious and gone back to the warehouse. For another few minutes at least, this had to look like a car theft, not a break-in. Howard rounded the corner onto Bush, past someone's fenced-in back lawn. He stopped short, looking back now, past the corner of the fence, both relieved and horrified to see his man sprinting up the block, not twenty yards behind. There were people at the curb, too, wearing their nightclothes, gathering around the smashed car.

Howard ran toward the ocean, his knee shooting a fiery pain up and down his leg every time he hammered his foot against the sidewalk. It was run or fight, though, and the farther he could lure the man away . . . He cut across the street, up onto a lawn and down a gravel alley, running south again, toward the lumberyard. The gate was a solid three blocks away. He could hide, maybe. But where? The fences along the alley were old and rickety and high, and even if he had time to pull himself over one, he'd be trapped in someone's backyard.

He looked back and immediately threw himself sideways. The man was at the mouth of the alley now, down on one knee, taking aim. He was sixty feet back, maybe—too close. Howard zigzagged again, hobbling and nearly pitching forward when his knee buckled. There was the sound of a shot, and a metal trash can ahead and to the right was punched backward, its lid jumping and clanking.

Like a heavy wind the sound of gunfire propelled Howard forward. He was out in the street again, running up the center of a pair of railroad tracks toward the Georgia-Pacific yard. Everything was fenced with chain link and barbed wire, and there was a confusion of tracks running down toward the train depot and another up toward vast warehouses and stacked lumber.

Somewhere back in there was the gate. It was after five. Men would be going in and out. What would they make of him in his ski mask and gloves? He couldn't pull the mask off, though, not yet. Not while the man who chased him could get a good look at him. He vaulted over a waist-high cinder-block fence, sliding on gravel. His feet flew out from under him and he landed hard, his breath whumping out of him. A shot pinged off the top of the wall, showering him with rock, and he jumped up and ran again in a crouch, trying to keep low behind the wall. Nearly winded, he ran in a half-stagger, half-trot, fueled only by momentum and fear.

The cars of the Skunk Train sat in parallel lines on the several tracks between the depot and the machine clutter of the lumberyard, and he ran in among the cars, past the comical skunks painted on the sides. He couldn't outrun his assailant. He would have to lose him among the silent trains, maybe work his way back around toward the old library, where his uncle would be waiting.

He listened hard for the sound of feet scrunching on gravel, but there was only silence. Had the man given up? Howard tried to calculate how long they'd been chasing around. Not long enough if Uncle Roy and Bennet had run into any trouble breaking into the warehouse. Maybe the man hadn't given up. Maybe he was sneaking around into position. Maybe he didn't give any kind of damn about the car, but was simply hunting for Howard, just to take it out of his hide.

Dropping to his hands and knees, Howard looked beneath the cars. A pair of feet were walking cautiously along the outside track. The man hadn't given up. The feet stopped and suddenly there was a face peering back at him, and then, quick as a snake, the hand with the gun.

Howard was up and moving, and he heard the shot ricochet off heavy steel as he clambered between two cars, trying to get around beyond the trains. He ran straight back along the chain link, north now, toward Fir Street. He needed company, people around. They could grab him and lock him up if they wanted to, but unless there were bystanders, witnesses, the man would shoot him dead. He was certain of that, and the certainty gave him a second wind.

He rounded the corner, slamming away up Fir, across a set of tracks and past an old rusted crane and a water tower. There was the gate ahead of him and a half dozen men in flannel shirts and jackets, standing around. Howard ran straight toward them. "Hey! Help!" he shouted through his ski mask. He couldn't think of anything else. The whole crowd of them turned toward him, looking serious, and a man stepped out of a little glassed-in guardhouse and stood there with his arms folded.

Howard felt as if he were running toward his doom and with more doom following along behind. He risked a glance over his shoulder. His pursuer was coming along confidently and easily, like a man who had just hit a home run and was circling the bases as a matter of form. He had pocketed the gun, and was now just an innocent citizen chasing down a vicious car thief.

For a wild instant Howard nearly stopped. He was trapped, fore and aft. Everything depended on the mythical Jack MacDonald, a man he had never seen. He wished he had paid more attention to Uncle Roy's description of the man, but somehow he hadn't meant things to go this bad. There was no place else to run now except up another alley, across another vacant lot, and that was so obviously futile that it wasn't worth a second thought. His job was done, and done thoroughly—thoroughly enough to account for the next couple of years, during which he would learn to make license plates, maybe stamp one out to replace the one on the wrecked Camaro that he had stolen.

He limped through the gate, exhausted, horrified to see a forklift bearing down on him fast, carrying a short, knee-level stack of plywood. The men around the gate closed in on him, between him and his pursuer, and the one who had come out of the guardhouse said, "Did you get the goddamn doughnuts?" Then the forklift slid to a stop in front of him. Someone said, "Hop on," and at the same time pushed Howard forward so that he fell onto the plywood, sprawling on his stomach. He flailed for a grip on the edge of the wood, nearly sliding off as the forklift hummed away again.

Howard looked back in time to see the mill workers approaching his pursuer, who slowed down, looking puzzled. "He's got a gun!" someone warned, although there still wasn't any gun visible. The man stopped, holding up his hands as if in surrender as they surged in around him. A fist lashed out in a wild haymaker to the man's belly as someone pushed him hard from behind, and he went down with a look of profound amazement on his face, the men surging in around him. The one who must have been Jack MacDonald walked placidly back to his guardhouse and lifted the receiver on a telephone, and for the moment Howard was safe, borne away on the forklift deeper into the yard, back among loaded pallets and stacked lumber and idle equipment.

WITH a scream, Heloise Lamey awakened from a dream involving fish. She had stood on an almost deserted pier, where an old man was fishing with a pole made out of a stick and a bit of string. The end of his pole wavered in little circles as he sat there, leaving a misty afterimage behind, like chalk drawings on the sky.

In the dream she had looked over the railing into the clear salt water, seeing nothing at first, but with the understanding that something was pending, that something under the surface of the ocean had shifted and was drawing near. There were shadows beneath the surface, too deep and dark to identify, but she knew abruptly that beneath the pier there was a great shoal of fish, and that the old man had hooked one and was pulling it in.

His line tightened and his pole bent, and the entire pier shifted with it, as if his fish were so vast that it would pull them, pier and all, into the sea. Mrs. Lamey held on to the iron railing as the pier tilted. Her feet slid across the wooden floorboards. Her hands were torn loose from the railing, and she slid wildly past the old man, who still sat there placidly and steadily, holding the bent pole, playing the fish.

She screamed as she plummeted toward the shadowy green ocean, and the scream woke her up. She sat for a second, breathing hard, pulling herself together, reminding herself that it was simply a dream. She was shivering beneath her nightclothes. After a moment, when she could think, she reminded herself that it was the same dream she had had last night, too, and the night before, only this time the old man had caught his fish.

She climbed out of bed and switched on the light. It was four-thirty in the morning—early, but there'd be no more sleeping for her tonight, anyway.

She dressed and went downstairs to put on water for instant coffee. Then she stepped out into the predawn morning and found her pruning shears. She hurried around the dark garden, clipping off a bouquet of discolored flowers, wide enough awake now to make a joke in her mind about never going to visit someone without taking him a little gift.

 19

THERE was a knock on the door. It was too early to be Edith bringing around the breakfast. It might be Roy Barton, smelling trouble and dishing up plots, but it didn't sound like his knock. Graham got slowly off his bed and pulled his pants on over his long underwear. Then he put on his hat and slippers, found his cane, and made his way to the door. It was just dawn, and the morning was gray and dim. He could see who it was, through the window glass, and he knew for certain what was wrong with the garden.

It had come to this at last, his showdown with Heloise Lamey. He knew what she wanted to take from him, but such a thing was impossible. It was out of his hands now. The die was cast, his successor chosen. The man had come north of his own free will, had asked to come. He was caught in the turning of things. Heloise Lamey, Michael Graham's half sister, was too late.

Together they walked down to the pond in the half-light of early morning. Graham leaned heavily on his cane, moving slowly on the hill, taking a step, setting his cane and his feet, and then taking another. She was impatient with him for being slow, so he stopped entirely to give her blood time to boil. He pulled a clasp knife out of his pocket and began to scrape his fingernails, working methodically.

"What are you doing?" she asked, exasperation in her voice.

"What?" He blinked at her, as if he only half recognized her.

"You wanted to fish. We were going down to the pond so that you could fish. Do you remember?"

He looked at her curiously. "I moved up here in 1910," he said slowly, gazing into the dark woods across the pond. "Worked on the railroad. Built me a house down on the bluffs. One thing was that there was whales going up and down, twice a year. Like clockwork. Jimmers had a telescope. He could watch for hours."

He shook his head slowly, watching the look on her face. Her eye twitched and the side of her mouth rose toward her ear every time it did.

"You were going to *fish*, Michael. Try to grasp that. Forget about the past. It's the future we care about."

He shook his head. "Nothing but a mud hole," he said. "Used to be trout in it as long as your arm. Trout everywhere."

She took him by the elbow, urging him down the hill. He let her lead him along, as if he didn't know quite where he was bound anymore, but would trust her to take him there, anyway. He stopped for a moment, though, when a knife edge of pain shot across under his ribs and down his left arm. Closing his eyes and breathing evenly, he wondered if this was it, if he would die without hearing what she had to say. He half hoped so.

The pain dwindled, though, and he forced himself to go on. Irritating her was easy, but tiring. What he wanted suddenly, more than anything else in the world, was to sit peacefully on the bank and watch the water striders play across the surface of the water. There was a duck on the pond, too. That was good, almost an omen. He stepped over the side of the beached rowboat, finally, and sat down heavily on the middle thwart, pulling his fishing pole out from underneath.

He hadn't ever caught anything at all in the pond, although there supposedly had been a time when it was full of fish. He remembered when that was generally true, when you could pluck abalone off the rocks of any cove along the north coast and the fishing boats hauled in tuna fish as big as milk cows. Salmon ran thick and huge in the river mouths and in the longshore currents in those days, and the lakes and rivers were full of native trout.

That was always the way, wasn't it? The seasons changed. Time passed. Things lived and died, and as you got older, there seemed to be more dying than living. Nothing was the same anymore, and you regretted the passing away of bits and pieces of the world.

He baited his hook slowly while she yammered at him, perched on the edge of the bow. He only partly understood her complaints and her desires. Her greed was lost on him. He couldn't believe in it like she did, because he didn't share it. He reached up and pretended to adjust the brim of his hat, while actually turning down his hearing aid. The morning was suddenly nearly silent, and her voice blathered along distantly, in a garble now, like the voice of a dissatisfied spirit. He could hear the blood rushing in his veins. He tossed the salmon eggs out into the pond, and they sank to the bottom, dragged down by a couple of small split shot.

194

She was suddenly yelling something. He nodded, jerking awake. The duck on the pond flew off in a rush of beating wings. He had dozed off and infuriated his half sister. There was no time in her day for his dozing off. "What?" he asked, smiling. "You what?" He turned his hearing aid back up, conspicuously this time, and she glared at him, her mouth set in a line. She seemed to be counting to ten, trying to keep an even temper. He could probably goad her until her heart burst, but he wouldn't. She might kill him then and there. She had it in her.

"I said that I'm prepared to take it. I've readied myself.'

"Take what?" he asked, trying to look puzzled.

She said something, but he didn't hear her because his throat suddenly was full of stuff, and he hacked up a clot of phlegm and spit it onto the grass, shaking his head tiredly and catching his breath. After a minute he could talk again. "What?" he asked, pretending to be confused.

She stared at him, clearly horrified, either at all the coughing and spitting or at his seeming failure to understand her. "I said that I've prepared myself," she said slowly, enunciating each syllable roundly and loudly, like a person trying to force English into the head of a foreigner.

"How? For what?"

"I've had an operation. I'm infertile now. There was a secondary infection that affected my hip joint. It won't heal. I know what you know, Michael, and I've cultivated certain powers. I'm a vessel now, waiting to be filled."

"The garden," he said. "I don't know why you bothered to blight it. It's part of the process, anyway, all the drought and the dying. Why do you try so hard to help it along? Why don't you simply let it alone to run its course?"

"There's no profit in letting things run their course. That's what I mean. That's what I'm talking about here. I'm prepared to take up the burden, to relieve you of it. You're dying. You know that, don't you? And when you die, there will have to be someone else. The Grail is rightfully mine. We're of the same flesh and blood. You have no more right to it than I have, and you know it. It was selfishness, your keeping it hidden all these years when it might have been put to use."

Explaining things to her was futile. She heard what she wanted to hear, what her mind was long ago made up to. He would try, anyway, briefly. "The Grail, is it? Don't be so confounded specific. It's not meant to be 'put to use.' The world is full of things that aren't *useful*, Heloise."

"I'll be the judge of that."

He looked at her. Talking to her was like shouting into a hole. Your words evaporated. "I'm not sure what it is, and neither are you. There's danger in that. It's meant to be *kept*, not used. It's . . . what? A scrap of paper that someone folded into a cup and caught some blood in. If I had it my way, he never would have brought it back from the East. It's a Pandora's box, and all you can think about is to tear the lid off it."

He began to wheeze. Long speeches took it out of him. He closed his eyes and stayed as still as he could, trying to relax so that he could catch his breath. It came finally, along with another jab of pain which he tried to keep from showing on his face. After a time he opened his eyes and saw the growing impatience on her face. She had been listening hard, waiting for some scrap of information that she could bank on. There must be something in this old man that I can *use*, her face seemed to say, that I can profit from.

"Was it the reason for John Ruskin's impotence?" she asked.

He shrugged and gave his fishing pole a tug. His hook was stuck in something, as usual. People had thrown junk into the pond for years. Trees had fallen across it. There was no telling what was down there, except that it wasn't a fish. He pulled harder, managing only to set the hook tighter.

"And you. You've had no children. Why? You've lived like a monk."

"I was never suited to be a family man."

She looked at him skeptically, implying that he wasn't being honest with her, that she saw right through him. "What I believe," she said, "is that it was Ruskin's impotence that made him a Fisher King. The Grail fell into his hands, and—"

"What *Grail*? You're literal-minded to the point of insanity, Heloise. You've driven yourself crazy, finally, with all your grasping and clutching. There's only a sheet of paper . . ."

"I don't care what it is. Hear me out. Ruskin had all the necessary tools. He was a natural, and the task simply fell to him." She looked out over the water, thinking hard, animated by her ideas.

"You're a born fool, Heloise. You can't see the forest."

"It's you that can't see."

"It doesn't matter what I see. I've spent my time building up my house. That's what the Scriptures advise."

"The Scriptures! To you it doesn't matter. You've wasted everything. You have no future. I do, though. I have the whole world within my reach, and I'm warning you right now—"

"Wait," he said, finally tired of her talk. He pulled on his fishing pole again. Whatever the hook had caught on was moving. Slowly he reeled it in, the trout pole bending almost double. It might just conceivably be an immense catfish—a lazy beast that had lain on the bottom of the pond for years. Heloise Lamey watched, her face expressionless, humoring him, waiting him out. A dark shadow rose toward the surface, and a cloud of mud and waterweeds churned up around it. It was a rubber boot, a knee-high sort of Wellington, rotted and covered with black mud and slime. He hauled it dripping onto the bank.

He turned toward her, blinking as if mystified. "It's a boot," he said. "A rubber boot." He chuckled at the idea.

"I can see that it's a *boot*," she hissed, going pale with exasperation and urgency. "Listen, old man. What I'm telling you is this. The world and the future are mine. You can stand in my way as long as you're alive, but your paltry little army of so-called friends cannot. When you're dead, there'll be a very brief and nasty conflict, I can promise you, and your friends will suffer needlessly. I don't give a tinker's damn what it is—a piece of paper or a golden cup. I'm destined to have it, I tell you. And it's your own obstinacy and foolishness that prevents it . . . for the moment. If you would do your friends a favor, give it to me now."

He wasn't indifferent to what she said. She might even be right. But it changed nothing. By way of answering, he unhooked his hearing aid entirely and threw it into the pond. Then, laboriously and without looking at her again, he wiggled the hook out of the toe of the boot, dropping the boot over the bow of the rowboat. He unscrewed the lid from the jar of salmon eggs and fiddled a couple out, baiting the hook again. He took his time about it. There was no rush. He was certain he wasn't going anywhere, ever again.

He sat for a moment watching the water striders scurry back and forth across the water like ballerinas. There was a quacking overhead. The duck that had flown off had returned along with three friends, and they landed on the pond, paddling toward him curiously.

Graham poured a quarter of the jar of salmon eggs out onto his hand and scattered them on the water, the ducks scooping them up enthusiastically. He noticed then that there were rabbits on the grass of the hillside, and a pair of gray squirrels chattering in a fir tree overhead. He could see a doe and her fawn coming along through the trees. A mole waddled down the hill past the rabbits.

Slowly, fighting the pain in his chest, he got up off the hard thwart and stepped over the side of the boat, onto the grass. He stumbled, falling forward and rolling over onto his back in order to look up through the trees at the sky. The forest was full of the sound of the world, ancient and wobbly and creaking toward the morning.

He remembered then that he had been talking to someone, but it seemed a long, long time ago, and the hillside was empty except for the mole and the rabbits. Whatever had been said meant nothing to him anymore. It was just wind now, sighing in the fir trees.

"SHE'LL pay for the damned thing," Uncle Roy said. "Let your conscience take a rest."

"Well, I still didn't want to smash his car up. I didn't see any other way, though. He just quit at the corner there. He knew he couldn't chase me on foot, and it wouldn't have made any sense for me to pretend to get stuck in another hole or something. What else could I do? I had to run it into the tree."

"Hell, we were probably out of there by then. The whole job didn't take a minute. We clipped the padlock off with the bolt cutters, fired up the truck, and got the hell out, shed and all. Nothing to it. It would have been a dead bore if you hadn't wrecked the bastard's car. There's only one thing would have improved it—him being in it at the time, or in front of it, the dirty little creep."

"Well . . ." Howard said.

"He starts shooting up the damned neighborhood! I didn't expect that. That was bad news. Secrecy is paramount in this business, paramount. He nearly tore the lid off the whole thing. The boys down at the mill worked him over pretty good, though. When the cops came, they said they thought *he* was the bad ass, waving his gun like that. Gave them a bogus description of you, and the cops tore around the yard for a half hour and then figured that you got out over the fence and headed down toward the airstrip. Fellow name of Dunbar who works out there saw you climb over. He swore to it. Somehow he gave out the same description of you that MacDonald and his boys did— short, overweight, baggy pants, and work boots. Two or three of them noticed you were missing two fingers on your right hand."

Uncle Roy grinned, obviously happy with himself. If ever there was a campaign run successfully, this had been it, all except the shooting and Howard's getting hurt. Uncle Roy had a sort of underground army of loyalists around Fort Bragg. Howard had clearly seen only the tip of the iceberg that morning, and the respect he had for his uncle had increased. Jimmers' tin shed was safe down by the harbor, locked in the back of the old icehouse.

Apart from Mrs. Lamey and her confederates, the only person who would suspect it was there was Jimmers himself, probably, and Howard had already found out that he wasn't the sort to call in the police. There could be no doubt that he would make his move to fetch it back, but it would come from some unguessable direction. And the harbor was a sort of enclave of Uncle Roy's people. The dilapidated house trailers and shacks down there were tenanted largely by poor fishermen and cannery workers and welfare unemployed, many of them living on land owned by Mrs. Lamey and her associates. Coming in after the shed would be tricky even for Jimmers but would be doubly tricky for the enemy. Howard was half surprised that he had come to think of them as that—that he had fallen so completely under Uncle Roy's sway.

After a moment's silence Howard asked, "What was she doing here this morning, anyway? That was weird, her driving away just now when we were pulling up."

Uncle Roy shrugged. "Watching the house. Harassment. Whatever. We've put a bee under her bonnet, or you have. This whole bottle of juice has started to ferment."

"I figured she knew about us stealing back the shed, that she was waiting for us."

"I don't see how she could have. She probably came around looking for money, saw that the car was gone, and took off again. We just happened to be getting home at the same time, and when she saw us, the two of us together, she got cold feet and just kept on going. These landlord types are like that. They come round in the early morning, hoping to catch you in your pajamas when you're naturally one down. They knock on windows and shout loud enough for the neighbors to hear, thinking they'll shame you. All you can do is ignore them."

Howard nodded. That seemed reasonable enough. Something in him had been startled by the sight of Mrs. Lamey driving off at that hour of the morning, though, just when they were driving in. She hadn't even glanced at them or slowed down.

Uncle Roy's explanation of it didn't quite wash. "If I had it to do over again," Howard started to say as Uncle Roy stood up and moved off toward the kitchen, "I'd—"

"For now you could sit still," Sylvia said, cutting him off. She pulled the Ace bandage tight around his knee and wrapped it half a dozen times. "I think this whole escapade was a lot of stupid nonsense, all over that damned machine."

Uncle Roy had disappeared, out clanking coffee mugs around in the kitchen. Outside, the sun was barely up, still hiding behind the trees. In a half hour it would be another beautiful, dry autumn day. Howard watched Sylvia happily as she clipped the bandage in place. She wore a woolly sort of bathrobe with big pink flowers on it, and her hair was a sleepy mess, falling half in front of her face. She had pretended to be exasperated with both of them, but she had clearly been more frightened than mad when Uncle Roy waked her up, asking about the bandage.

Howard felt like a knight, having gone out to slay the dragon, or something like that, and then come home to the fair Sylvia, who was tending his wounds. This whole north coast adventure was developing a Knights of the Round Table feel to it, and Howard realized that as stupidly romantic as such notions were, he was happily letting himself be swept up in it all. Sylvia pushed a low ottoman across and propped his leg up on it. "It's a little swollen," she said. "Keep it elevated."

She leaned against his thigh for a moment before pushing herself up off the floor and looked straight into his face. There wasn't anything flippant in her eyes, just worry, he thought—for him. He was filled suddenly with the urge to put his arms around her, to pull her closer and say something equally serious. In her loosely tied robe and wild hair she seemed to be still warm from her bed, and if ever there was a more perfect, custom-built moment to say what it was he meant to say . . .

She spoke first, though. "You don't really believe in this nonsense about Mr. Jimmers' machine, do you? About it manufacturing ghosts?"

Howard shrugged. "*Something* pretty weird happened in that shed. I don't know what. I thought *you* were the spiritualist type, though. Now you all of a sudden don't believe in ghosts?"

"I believe that Mr. Jimmers would go a long way to put one over on Father."

"Really?" Howard said, surprised. "Would he go *that* far? How about the wild phone call down at the harbor last night? And look who stole the damned thing. It wasn't us. Do you think he set

200

up the theft with Mrs. Lamey and her crowd just to confound your father? I don't follow this whole line of reasoning."

Sylvia shrugged. "I don't think he's got anything to do with Mrs. Lamey anymore. My guess is that Jimmers outright hates her. He doesn't have anything to do with anyone but himself, and Graham, of course. But now that Graham's not living in the house, Jimmers is a loose cannon on the deck, and I have the feeling that this machine of his is going to roll all over the place smashing things up. I think he was mad, all right, when he called last night, because he thinks that Father stole the shed out from under his nose, and he can't stomach the idea. Secretly, though, he might be happy as a clam. Now Father's got Jimmers' loony machine and is proud of himself for having it. Father's guard is down. Do you see what I mean?"

"I see it," Howard said, "but I'm not buying it."

"I've been thinking. Yesterday, when you unlocked the shed— I'm thinking that Jimmers knew you were in there all along. His surprise seems faked to me now, like he was hoping that you'd break in there, see something strange, and come away convinced."

"Convinced of what? I came away convinced that I don't know what the hell to think."

"That's just his style, isn't it? That's Mr. Jimmers in a nutshell. Maybe he saw you as an easy mark, and you swallowed the whole ghost-out-of-a-machine notion and came home and got Father all fired up about it."

"He didn't need any firing up. You know that."

"Mr. Jimmers couldn't have known that, though, could he? They hadn't spoken to each other in a year—probably haven't even seen each other."

Howard thought for a moment. Mr. Jimmers' emotions *always* seemed fake. You couldn't tell with Jimmers, which admittedly gave him an edge over you. But somehow the idea of Jimmers merely fooling them all didn't satisfy him. There had to be more to it than that. The idea of it all was comical, though. Here was Sylvia talking sense, and he himself talking mysticism. Go figure it, he told himself.

Uncle Roy came back in just then, carrying three cups of coffee, and Sylvia stood up to take one of the cups from him. She pulled her bathrobe tighter and tied it securely, the action reminding Howard of the opportunity that had come and gone. If the morning had accomplished nothing else, at least Sylvia was worrying about him now. He was an actor, finally, in this strange play, which, if Mr. Jimmers had his way, would maybe turn into a farce.

"Tell me about Jimmers' machine," Howard said to Uncle Roy. "What are we going to do with it?"

His uncle sat there for a moment, sipping his coffee and gathering things in his mind, either because he was weighing how much he could safely say to Howard or, more likely, because what he had to say wasn't entirely credible. "It's complicated," was what he said finally.

Howard raised his eyebrows. "I was thinking that it might be. What is it, though?"

"I believe it to be a machine that transports spirits through time and from one place to another."

"I've been through this before," Sylvia said, heading toward the stairs. "You men thrash this out. I've got to get ready for work."

"The ghosts of dead men?" Howard asked, waving haphazardly at Sylvia. They were getting down to it now.

Uncle Roy shook his head. "Nope. The spiritual essences of live men—the men who built the machine for that very purpose. It's a device that could transport you and me across astral planes. Don't laugh when I ask you this, but have you read Burroughs' Martian novels?"

"John Carter? Thuvia?"

"That's the ones. They're a lot of colorful nonsense, of course, but the notion of out-of-body travel isn't. It's simple as that. You're a rationalist, and scoff at it, but since you asked me, I'm telling you the simple truth. Believe it or don't."

"You know," Howard said after pausing for a moment, "I could have sworn that the ghost in the shed yesterday afternoon was John Ruskin—that portrait of him that you see with side-whiskers and with his hair white and ragged and his eyes all rheumy."

"It was. I believe I can say that with some authority. What do you know about the Pre-Raphaelite Brotherhood, besides the fact that they were a lot of Victorian artists collected around Ruskin?"

"A bit," Howard said. "I know there were a couple of generations of them and that there were as many photographers among them as there were painters."

"Lewis Carroll was one."

Howard nodded.

"And Dean Liddell, Alice's father."

"I saw the photograph on the wall down at the museum—the visage that appeared on the wall of Christ Church Cathedral. That was pretty intriguing. Did they figure out how it was done?"

"Done? Do you mean did they discover that it was a hoax? No, they didn't. It wasn't *done* at all. It was the real thing, and no mistaking it—the result of an experiment with the machine." Uncle Roy paused heavily then, letting this sink in.

"I thought all the Pre-Raphaelites were artists of one sort or another. What did Liddell have to do with them?"

"He was a sort of soldier, actually. Carroll was living with George MacDonald at the time. Have you read MacDonald?"

"A couple of fantasies. I don't know much about him aside from figuring out that he was a Christian writer."

"First of the great Christian fantasists. Back then there wasn't anyone writing in the fantastic vein who could touch MacDonald, unless it was Carroll. They got caught up in Ruskin's web, specifically in the dealings of the Guild of St. George—Ruskin's efforts to destroy industrial society, which he saw as the Dragon, so to speak."

"I've read a little about them. Didn't they build a few workers' cottages or something? It wasn't a crafts guild so much as a political action group—failed efforts, mostly. That's what I remember, anyway."

"Well, that's right, mainly. They never destroyed industrial society, and they didn't produce much that was worth a damn when it came to art or furniture or any other typical crafts guild stuff. But then, as you say, the Guild of St. George wasn't any typical crafts guild, and they did manage to skewer a dragon or two while they were at it. What do you know about James Graham?"

"Only what I found out after I looked into this sketch business. He was a photographer, mostly. Michael Graham's . . . what? Grandfather?"

"That's it. He's the *connection*. He was a member of Ruskin's crowd, very pious and dissipated both. He spent a long time in the Holy Land, taking photographs in the name of God. Lived in a tower overlooking Jerusalem. Holman Hunt lived there off and on, too, along with a couple of other Pre-Raphaelites who had gone native. Now, what were they looking for? What sort of pilgrimage were they on? It was Ruskin that sent them, and it was a long damned way into a desolate country. They were all engaged in a search, a quest. What were they looking for, though, really? The answer to that question is the key."

Howard shrugged. He didn't have the answer. "History has it that they were painting and taking photographs, that it was an artistic expedition."

"History," Uncle Roy snorted. "You can have history. Don't pay more than a dime for it, though, or you've been cheated. This Holy Land quest was *passed off* as an artistic expedition, but what it really was, was a modern-day crusade, and nothing less. And I'm not talking metaphor here. I mean what I say."

"What?" Howard said. "A crusade? In what sense? They were looking for the Grail?"

Uncle Roy widened his eyes and blinked, laying his hands out in front of him, palms up, as if to say that he couldn't be blamed for their pursuits; he was only relating what he had heard.

"Did they find it?"

"They found something, and brought it back, too. And let me clarify a few things. It wasn't just industrialization that the Guild of St. George wanted to annihilate. They weren't pitted against a generality or an abstraction. History has seen these lads as political and social failures—Ruskin and Morris and all the rest of them—and it'll see us as failures just as surely. The work we do will have to be its own reward."

"I'd be surprised to find that history can see us at all," Howard said.

"Who can say? Anyway, and more to the point, half of their story has never been told. It's too fantastic, too many high mucky-mucks brought low. Most of it was suppressed by people in power, who stayed in power, and later mapped out history in their own invented images."

"What did they find, then, Graham and Hunt and all of these people who went East? The machine?" Howard was anxious to drag the conversation back down to earth. He thought he knew the answer to the question, but he wanted to hear it from Uncle Roy himself.

"The piece of paper. The sketch."

"The Hoku-sai?"

Uncle Roy gestured. "There's some that guessed it was a Hoku-sai. I don't think so." He squinted at Howard, like a man who had secret knowledge, smiling just slightly, like a moon man with a Mona Lisa grin.

"You don't think it's a Hoku-sai? That's what I understood it to be. It's pretty clearly one of his sketches of the Takara-mono, the luck charms. And that's what Graham told me nearly fifteen years ago, too, when I was staying up at his place. That's what the hell I came up here for, to bring back a Hoku-sai sketch. Now you're telling me it's not a Hoku-sai at all? What is it, then? An imitation? A piece by someone nobody's ever heard of?"

"That's a good way to put it. Exactly that. Someone nobody's heard of, just like you and me. Although the one who made the sketch wasn't the imitator, he was the originator. And if Hoku-sai was influenced by it, well . . . what great artists aren't influenced in one way or another? As for why Graham lied about it, he'll have to tell you that much himself. That's not my duty."

"Is it valuable, then?"

"To a museum? How do I know? You're the expert. It's old—predates Hoku-sai by a long damned time. So it has a certain value as an antiquity. Now, you wouldn't guess it to look at him, but Bennet is something of a scholar, in his way. He's looked into this, gone to . . . *sources*. Bennet says this piece of paper was folded into the shape of a cup. Legend has it that it was inked with blood—not painted on, mind you, but splashed on. At Golgotha. It was smashed flat and smuggled out in someone's robe, probably. Later when it was unfolded, it was found to have been . . . sketched, so to speak, with fundamental shapes. It could be folded again to derive other shapes, other pictures—a changeable pictograph, if you follow me. A sort of paper kaleidoscope inked with blood, entirely randomly. And yet the images that fall together are perfect representations of essential order."

Howard sat in silence, trying to process this notion, but it was bothersomely schizophrenic to him. Suddenly he understood that there were patterns, whereas before there had seemed to be none—patterns, perhaps, in the random wash of gravel on a roadside, in the placement of leaves on a tree and stars in the night sky. Messages spelled out in hieroglyphics by a flock of birds passing overhead, by the ice fragments in the tail of a comet.

What was most puzzling and troubling was that Howard seemed to have been *sent* for. Finding the paper lily—had that been just a happy blunder, or had it been a mystically contrived step in a centuries-old process? And the dreams, the sketchy clouds full of suggestion, of travel, of compulsion. Even the signifying pelican . . .

Uncle Roy stood up and peered out through the curtains at the street, as if checking just for safety's sake before drawing them open. "Let me say that you can no more avoid all this, now that you've thrown in your hand with us, than a meteor can avoid the gravity of a nearby planet. And I won't mince words. I won't lead you down the garden. Men have died in this struggle. Those were real bullets this morning. Lamey and her crowd aren't just a real estate cartel or something. What I'm telling you here is that you're the innocent pedestrian stumbling into the territory of a feud. You think you're selling encyclopedias door-to-door, and then there you are one day with a gun in your hand and a bunch of hillbillies spitting tobacco past your shoulder and calling you Brother Howard. Do you follow me?"

"I think so. Maybe you shouldn't tell me any more. If the sketch isn't what I thought it is, then there's nothing holding me here. I could drive back south."

"Nothing holding you here but a car theft and a gimp knee . . . and Sylvia, I suppose."

Howard's face got hot immediately, and he nearly denied it. There was no point in denying it, though. Silence was better. There was too much going on right now, and no room for complications. Uncle Roy looked monumentally grave all at once, and said, "I'm going to ask you once more, nephew. Think everything through before you answer. Are you in or out? You could have sat it out down at Winchell's this morning, eating glazed doughnuts and thinking about that goddamn museum job of yours. Maybe you still can. Maybe we can rig it to get you out of here. There's sides drawn up, and when that happens a man's either in or he's out. There's nobody left on the fence except the stupid man when the hurricane blows. What do you say?"

Sylvia came in just then, along with Aunt Edith, both of them heading for the kitchen. Sylvia was dressed for work, wearing a sweater and jeans, her hair combed out and lipstick on. When she caught Howard's eye, she smiled, glancing down at his knee and shaking her head, as if his shenanigans confounded her. There was a rattling of cups out in the kitchen, and then a moment later the back door opened and closed.

"I'm in," Howard said, after taking a look at Sylvia's face. "Of course I'm in." He felt at once relieved and at the same time like some sort of Secret Service agent heading out into the cold with only bits and pieces of information, because he couldn't be trusted with the whole business. "So the sketch fell into Michael Graham's hands, and Jimmers, we guess, is keeping it safe. I understand that. But how about the machine?"

"Built by the Guild of St. George hand in glove with Morris and Company. It was invented by a Morris acolyte named William Keeble, who later became a noted London toymaker. The man had very exotic notions. That was a few years after these sojourns in the Holy Land, when the battle was heating up. The sketch had been hidden at Red House, Morris' place at Upton, in Kent, which was built for no other reason than to hide it, although that's something that the historians won't tell you, probably because they don't know it. There was a well in the front yard, a slate-roofed brick well, very pretty. That's where they put it—down the well, in a bucket. Philip Webb, the architect, designed the whole shebang. Anyway, it's my belief that the machine finally was used to transport certain . . . valuable objects out of the reach of the enemy at the time of Ruskin's death.

"That was in 1900, of course. The man had been stone crazy for ten years. There was a crowd that tried to stop them from burying him in Westminster Abbey. You can figure out why. He was laid out, finally, at Coniston, in the Lake District, but just between me and you, he didn't stay there."

"He left?"

"There's some question about where his bones ended up. There was more than one attempt to get at them—a couple just recently. But they haven't been in Coniston for years. Never were, for my money."

Uncle Roy studied his fingernails for a moment, then said, "I got most of this from Jimmers, of course. And we both know what that's worth. Could be end-to-end nonsense."

"Do we *want* the sketch, you and I?" Howard asked.

"Best not to think in terms of ourselves."

"Fine. Practically speaking, though—do we want it? Do we need it?"

"Not me, certainly. I wouldn't touch it with a pole."

"How about me? I seem to have been invited up here to find it or take it or help protect it or something. I don't know what."

Uncle Roy shrugged. "The old man might know. He's probably fishing in the pond right now, trying to hook a salmon."

Just as he said this, Howard became aware that his chair was moving. The air seemed full of a vague rumbling, and for an instant Howard thought that a truck was passing outside. Then there was the sound of the house creaking and of objects rattling in cupboards. The curtains tossed and coffee sloshed in a wave out of Howard's still-full cup.

"Earthquake!" Uncle Roy shouted, and he was up and out of his chair, weaving toward the nearest doorway as plaster dust rained down onto his head.

20

HOWARD stood up, testing his knee, and at that instant there was a second jolt, as if something huge had struck the earth. Howard sat down hard, holding on to the arms of the chair and expecting the roof to cave in. He staggered to his feet and tottered into a doorway, bracing himself against the frame. The old house swayed and creaked, crack lines shooting ominously across the ceiling plaster. Glasses clinked together furiously in the kitchen cupboards, and there was the sound of a cupboard door banging open and of something shattering on the countertop.

Then it was over, and there was a dreadful, still sort of silence during which neither he nor Uncle Roy dared move. But the earth was solid. The morning had started up again. Outside, there was the sound of birds calling. A dog began to bark down the street. Howard stood up again and limped across to steady the chandelier, which was still swaying back and forth, dropping plaster dust from around the ceiling fixture.

The dog quit barking. Howard and Uncle Roy stood still for a few moments, waiting for it to start up again, but there was nothing. Together they went into the kitchen. Lying on the countertop, having fallen out of the thrown-open cupboard, was Aunt Edith's porcelain Humpty Dumpty, broken to pieces.

"Hell," Uncle Roy said softly, picking up the top of the thing's head.

"Super Glue?" Howard asked.

"Could be useless in this case. Let's keep the pieces, though, just in case Sylvia wants to have a go at it." Silently they put all the pieces in a paper sack. "That was a good one," Uncle Roy said, referring to the earthquake. "I bet it was a five or six. Epicenter was close, too. You can tell when they're sharp like that. A real jolt." They walked back out into the living room and sat down again, both of them edgy. For the space of a minute neither one of them spoke, then Uncle Roy said, "What the hell were we talking about?"

"Fishing," Howard said. "You told me that Graham spends his time fishing for salmon. How can there be any salmon in that little mud hole?"

"There's not now. In wetter years the pond connects by a tributary to Pudding Creek. Used to run the year round, and the odd trout could find its way back there. That was before all this drought. Anyway, that's what he's doing, whether there's any salmon in there or not. He's got used to fishing off the rocks below his place. Plenty of salmon out there in the ocean, or used to be. Fishing industry's slow now, and going to get slower if all this offshore-oil nonsense starts up. That's Lamey, too, and your man Stoat. She's a hell of a squid, like I said—got a finger in every pie conceivable." He shook his head, getting mad at the idea of Mrs. Lamey. "Anyway, used to be that the creeks were full of fish, back when they were full of water. Things change, though. Graham's the man to answer your questions. He asked me just yesterday whether you were a man who liked to fish. Ain't that something? Same question *I* asked you."

"Quite a coincidence," Howard said.

"Well, he seemed to guess that, about you being a fisherman. I'll warn you, though, that talking with him is rough. He's in and out, you know. Sometimes the light's on and sometimes there's nothing inside but a little flashlight bulb, sometimes outright darkness."

"In the cabin?"

"Not in the cabin. In his head. He's been going downhill pretty quick. He's frail, like old cobweb. That's one of the reasons he moved back into the woods, out of the house on the bluffs. His days had begun to look numbered. He was tired, worn out. The struggle had got too much for him. Just getting up and pulling on his boots had got too much for him. There was nothing left for him but fishing. Could be he caught something when he wrote that letter back to you. It took a while, but he's finally reeled you in. He's set the hook." Uncle Roy winked at him.

"Anyway, he's been living in the cabin off and on for more than a year, although we tried to make it look like he was still in his house, out on the bluffs. They caught on that there was something up, and so Jimmers pulled the suicide gag. It wasn't worth much. I would have done it different. Graham just wants some rest, and he deserves it, too."

Uncle Roy yawned and stretched. "I'm going to put in a couple of hours sleep," he said, standing up and heading for the stairs. "Later on I'm going down to the harbor. Probably be there all day. Now that you've, ah . . . come to all these decisions, maybe you ought to mosey out to the cabin and have a confab with old Graham. You might get some answers. Then again, you might not." With that he shuffled away up the stairs, but had gotten just out of sight when the back door slammed open, banging into the clothes dryer.

"Father!" It was Sylvia, shouting. She ran into the living room, breathing hard.

Howard jumped up, thinking of the stolen car, the police, gunfire. He flexed his game knee. He could walk on it fine—a little stiff-legged, maybe, but . . .

Uncle Roy appeared at the bottom of the stairs, ready for action. "What is it?" he asked, breathing hard. "What's wrong?"

Sylvia caught her breath. There was fear and grief in her eyes. "Graham's dead."

Howard stood paralyzed, struck with the notion that the world had stopped spinning, that time stood still. He knew that on the instant everything had changed. A door had shut. Another had opened.

"How?" Uncle Roy said, breaking the spell. "Foul play?" He pulled on his coat while striding toward the back door. Howard followed along behind. "Graham's dead"—the words played through Howard's mind like a closed-loop tape. He had heard the words more than once over the last few days, but now they signified—not only because this time it was true but because the truth had changed things.

"No. I don't think so," Sylvia said. "We found him on the grass, sort of trying to sit up. He'd been fishing. We called to him, and he just . . . went. There was an earthquake; did you feel it? It might have been that, I guess. Maybe he was frightened by it. Except that he looked like he was in trouble before the earthquake, faint or something. I think he was dying when we saw him. That's what it looked like. We tried to revive him—everything we could think of—but it wasn't any good."

They hurried down the path, into the woods. The sun was up, but still below the tree line, and the woods were dark and dense. At least there was no fog. Within minutes they were there, at the clearing in front of the cabin. Howard must have gone far off course the other morning to have wandered for so long in the woods. The old man lay now at the base of the grassy hill, down by the pond. Aunt Edith knelt beside him as if guarding the body.

"The king is dead," Uncle Roy said quietly, standing over him. Clearly there was nothing anyone could do for him. His face was relaxed, as if he'd died in his sleep and was finally truly at rest. It was deeply lined, the face of a man who had spent his life on a sea cliff. Howard hadn't realized that Graham was so old. He remembered him at something near eighty, still hale and hearty, sawing out rough planks with his chain-saw mill, running wheelbarrows full of cliff rock across the meadow. He looked frail now, and thin, although the lines cut into his face gave him a craggy sort of chiseled-out look, the face of a man sculpted by wind and ocean.

Uncle Roy nodded grimly at Howard. "Let's get him up to the cabin." He bent over and latched on to the old man's feet. Howard picked him up beneath his arms, surprised at how light he was. Gravity seemed to have given up on him already.

They moved off, Howard walking backward and Uncle Roy redfaced and breathing hard with the exertion of it. Beneath where the body had lain there was an unseasonable scattering of white daisies, growing up through the stiff grass of the hillside as if a little fragment of spring had risen to the surface of the land where the old man had died. It smelled briefly like spring, too— like wildflowers on a breezy, sunlit meadow in April.

Aunt Edith carried Graham's cane, a gnarled piece of manzanita, polished to a deep bloodred and wet with dew from where it had lain in the grass.

Slipping and sliding on the damp hillside, they finally reached the rear of the house and got onto level ground. The old man was heavier than Howard had thought. "Hold it," he said. His knee felt like rubber, throbbing with pain beneath the Ace bandage.

Sylvia stepped in and supported Graham's shoulders.

The three of them carried him around and onto the porch, setting him down carefully. Howard waited, wondering what was next. Old Graham looked so peaceful that there was nothing very different in it than if he had been merely asleep. Except that Howard felt a weird sort of affinity to him that he couldn't explain, as if this were his father lying dead at his feet. He could remember almost nothing about his own father aside from what he had gleaned from photographs—strange images of a man who was forever distant, lost to him.

He was struck suddenly with the uncanny feeling that he had been there before. He had stood just like that on a wooden front porch, looking down at a dead man. Then it was himself in his memory, lying on his own back, dead, looking up into faces of people who lived in a world that no longer contained him, a make-believe landscape on a movie screen. For one jolting moment he didn't know who he was, the living Howard Barton or the dead Michael Graham. He shook his head, nearly falling over. Uncle Roy clutched him under the arm in order to steady him, but Howard was already himself again, his confusion gone. He was dizzy, probably from the exertion.

"Couple of spades around back," Uncle Roy said, collapsing into an armchair. Aunt Edith composed the old man's clothes, pulling his jacket straight and buttoning it up and then combing his hair with her fingers. With Sylvia alongside, Howard limped around after the shovels, and together they began to dig the grave in the center of the garden, careful not to disturb the few rows of lettuce and onions, even though they were discolored and blighted-looking.

After a few minutes, Uncle Roy offered to dig for a spell. Howard gave him the shovel gratefully. His knee was stiff as heavy cardboard, and he hobbled across to sit down by Aunt Edith on the porch again. His senses were strangely acute, as if every sound and smell were picture-framed, separate from every other. Something had happened to him. And it wasn't simply that a man had died.

Somehow the notion of burying Graham at once struck him as right and natural. Whether it was legal didn't matter. There wasn't any practical reason to wait. In fact, there was a sense of urgency in the air, as if the land were hungry for the body— not in any horrific sense, but in a dust-to-dust sense.

Dreamily, feeling vague and removed, he looked again at the resting corpse, and in that moment it looked to him to be made of dark loam, of forest debris and mulch, sprouting with oxalis and moss and weaved into shape with tiny roots. The porch floor around him was littered with acorns and oak leaves. Tendrils of berry vine grew up between the wood slats, winding across Graham's arms and chest like fibrous muscle.

Howard stood up, shaking the image out of his eyes. He was acutely aware of the sound of the forest around him, of the wind in the treetops and the stirring of undergrowth, as if the woods suddenly were full of life—of crawling things, of creatures slipping up out of hidey-holes and thickets. The sun edged into view through a sort of avenue in the trees that led off toward the eastern horizon. The garden was stippled with sunlight, and the heat of it fell on his face, angling beneath the porch roof, bathing old Graham in golden rays. There wasn't any moss on the body, not really—no berry vines—just an old man who was dead, lying on the scuffed floorboards of the porch.

It was time to have another turn at the shovel. Exercise would help—physical exertion. Uncle Roy wasn't built for it, and was sweating freely despite the morning chill. He had taken off his coat and thrown it over the back of the wheelbarrow. Sylvia worked steadily, standing in the grave now, shoveling out loose dirt while Uncle Roy skived away at the side, widening it out. Howard found that he was suddenly too faint to dig, and he tried to pull himself together. Graham's death coming on top of the earthquake must have unnerved him.

"Come inside," Aunt Edith said to Howard. "You don't look well." She opened the front door of the shack and stepped in, Howard following. On the table in the center of the room lay a bouquet of lilies, brownish green and bruised purple. A sickening odor rose from them. Edith swept them up angrily. She pushed past Howard through the front door again and flung them off the porch with so much force that the heavy, moist flowers flew to pieces in the air, scattering into the weeds. She came back in and pulled the windows open to air the place out.

"She was here, then," Howard said. "She killed him, didn't she?"

"She isn't strong enough to have killed him, although she wishes she were. Here," she said to Howard, "take his cane." She looked old herself in that moment, and tired. She had an even-keeled air about her, though, as she handed Howard the stick, looking him full in the face. Her eyes were as green and deep as well water, as if she had endured great suffering in her time, and it had made her wise. "He won't be needing it anymore."

Howard looked down at the cane. He could use it, certainly, lame as he was. It looked old, polished from long years of use, and it occurred to him that if he were to take it out to the garden and thrust the tip of it down into the dirt, green tendrils would sprout from the old dry wood. He knocked it against the floorboards. It was stout enough to trust, and he leaned on it gratefully as they walked outside and clumped down the porch steps.

The sky was full of crows now, circling high above them, waiting and watching. There must have been thousands, tens of thousands. He could see them through the trees in every direction. Sylvia had laid her shovel down alongside the grave and was watching Howard intently, a little fearfully maybe, as if she saw something in his face that suggested his own mortality.

He shifted the cane in his hand, feeling a little dizzy. There was something sticky on it—sap? He looked at it more closely.

Was it blood, leaking out of the cane as if out of a wound? The notion was crazy. He shook his head to clear it and leaned heavily against the cane with both hands, steadying himself and wondering suddenly if he was sick. He was certain that he didn't have any sort of fever, but his mind refused to focus. It was drifting at the whim of some vast tide, almost as if his normal concentration had come unstuck, and something else—the forest itself, or nature, or something even more boundless than that—was peering in at him from outside, assessing him.

He remembered the dream he had had for months now, the dream about the fireplace, the hot coal. And the dream suddenly was more real to him than the forest and the people round about. He stood staring into the fire again, the dark mill around him, the sound of the millwheel turning, and his knee throbbing with pain where he'd burned it. Only this time the mill didn't have walls or a roof except the dark tree line and a sky black with crows, and he was aware that even though people stood silently just a few yards away, just on the edge of the firelight, he felt alien and alone, with the sea wind blowing and the night sky turning overhead. He put his hand to his mouth and touched his tongue to the sticky residue on his fingers, the sap that had flowed from the stick. It was coppery-tasting, salty, like blood, and the taste of it made him feel faint. He sat down hard on the ground and closed his eyes, and the cawing of the crows fell down around him like raindrops.

HOWARD spent the day cleaning the rest of the barn lumber. What had happened to him in the woods was nothing but hyperventilation. He had told himself that a dozen times. He had been at a seance once, years ago, where a college friend of his had gotten excited and hyperventilated, making everyone think for a moment that a ghost had gotten into her. Someone had made her breathe into a paper sack, and she was all right again. This business up at the cabin was no doubt the same sort of thing—lack of sleep, a dead man, the strange conversation he'd had with Uncle Roy, the earthquake, the hurt knee. There were a thousand reasons for him to have gone temporarily off the deep end. Certainly there was no need to get mystical over it.

He was convinced that work was the antidote. After breakfast, Uncle Roy had gone off to meet Bennet, leaving the lumber to Howard. By two o'clock Howard had a big clean pile of it, all stacked and stickered alongside the house. There was nothing left of the pile on the grass but junk—firewood, boards too cracked and twisted to work with. He felt good for a half dozen reasons, although he was growing nervous as the afternoon wore on. It was Monday, and that meant that Mrs. Lamey's "little circle" was meeting tomorrow night.

Since he had last talked to Mrs. Lamey, things had gotten vastly more complicated. They couldn't know anything certain about him, though. Not really. As far as Mrs. Lamey knew, Howard was a free agent, or else represented the museum, and so was in a position to be lured away, into the enemy camp. He was a potential new recruit. Certainly the man who had chased him through the streets that morning hadn't identified him, although he would know by now that it had been no simple car theft.

The man was still in a holding cell at the police station, and might stay there for a while. He wouldn't be at Mrs. Lamey's place tomorrow. The police weren't fond of his shooting up the neighborhood, and MacDonald down at the mill had testified that he had threatened the yard hands, waving his gun like a murderer, clearly out of his head. Of course it was his own car that had been stolen, so there were mitigating circumstances. Mrs. Lamey, or more likely one of her paid acquaintances, would come to his rescue eventually. Palms would be greased, doors opened.

Certainly it would be dangerous for Howard to show up at her house, but not all that dangerous. They had nothing to gain from assaulting him. But maybe there was a potential gain from winning his favor. Of course there was. There was time enough to worry about it later, maybe lose a little sleep over it tonight. In an hour and a half, though, he was meeting Sylvia for dinner and then they were taking in a movie, whatever the hell was playing. Howard didn't care.

Whistling, he looped the extension cord and rolled the radial arm saw back into the shed. Then he pitched a coffee can full of bent nails into the trash and put away the hammer and pry bar. The stack of lumber sat there solid and clear, a thing of value now and not a pile of trash. It would be a tonic for Uncle Roy, money in the bank. The afternoon was fine—almost hot—and the ground around the house was hard and dry. He could hear the cawing of crows still, out over the woods. His knee felt pretty good. It had started to improve when he got the walking stick that morning. Howard picked the stick up from where it was leaning against the house and inspected it one last time. There was no sap on it, no blood. It was smooth and tight-grained. Shrugging, he knocked the dust off his shoes with it and then went in to change clothes.

21

ALMOST two hundred dollars in Roy Barton's pocket, and the sun was barely over the yardarm. The lumber that Howard had so kindly cleaned up yesterday had only fetched eighty bucks—not even twenty cents a foot. Still, it was all profit, and only Tuesday, to boot. No sense in even thinking about labor. What difference did it make to a retired man like himself? A dollar an hour, a nickel an hour—time wasn't money anymore and hadn't been for years.

He slapped his shirt pocket and started to whistle, but then he remembered his conversation with Jimmers that morning, and he quit whistling. News of the old man's death had nearly bowled Jimmers over. "Shit," Uncle Roy said out loud, wishing that it hadn't been him who had to tell Jimmers. Jimmers was fragile. Graham had been his only real friend, and now Jimmers was left alone . . . Uncle Roy shook his head. Things fell apart; there was no denying it.

He thought about the morning again in order to cheer himself up. He had driven around the city after selling the barn lumber, and had found a garage sale up at the end of Perkins Way that was hustling a lot of old construction debris, including a dozen French windows that the owner had torn out of his house. Roy had bought four wooden planes from the man, too, the irons all rusty and the wood gummy and dark.

The lot of it had cost him forty-eight dollars of his barn lumber money. It took him a half hour to pull the hardware off the doors—brass hinges and sliding bolts and glass doorknobs. He spent another hour on the planes, buffing out and sharpening the irons and cleaning the junk off the wood, then rubbing the wood and steel both with mineral oil. He sold the doors for sixty dollars to a man he knew of on Oak Street who was building a greenhouse, and the door hardware and planes to an antique store in town for another eighty.

It had been luck, though. The man was a fool to dump the

doors for that kind of money. If Roy had taken some time with it—stripped the old paint off and refinished them, replaced a couple of panes of broken glass—he might easily have doubled his profit, tripled it. But, hell, who was he kidding? The truth was that if he had gotten fancy, the doors would have spent the winter stacked in the weeds, just like the barn lumber had done. They would have come to nothing. A quick turnover—that was paramount. Don't overreach yourself. Get in and get out.

He wondered idly whether there wasn't a book in it: *One Hundred Ways to Make One Hundred Dollars. Overnight*. What did Xerox cost, a nickel a page? You could have the copier bind the thing, too, inside colored boards, and then distribute them yourself out of the back of the station wagon. Half the north coast was out of a job, it seemed. People would snap them up. You could leave half a dozen on a liquor store counter—forty percent for the owner on consignment, sixty percent if he bought them outright.

That would be best, selling them outright would be. To hell with consignment; there was no profit in that. People would steal them or else the store owner would say they did. He calculated profits in his head as he pulled into a parking place in front of Sylvia's shop. What were there? Fifty thousand people out of work along the coast? Twice that? He could buy an address list, maybe, of all the poor bastards on food stamps, and send them a mailer. They could afford a fiver easy enough when they knew they could parlay it into something big. The sky was the limit, wasn't it? The whole damned country was going broke. The future lay in a man's doing for himself, outside the stinking system. Barter, co-ops, labor trading, neighborhood day care, backyard gardens, chickens in pens, goat cheese.

He pulled the wad of money out of his pocket, amazed at how a little bit of dough set a man thinking. The horizon wasn't any kind of limit for an onward-looking man. He hesitated out on the sidewalk, not going straight into the shop.

Sylvia would only be happy to see him for a moment. She would know he was up to something. She was too serious sometimes, though. What she wanted was a longer view. Easy come, easy go; that was the nature of the wicked world. It was better to be philosophical about it. If he himself was a responsible man, he would give the money to Heloise Lamey; or rather, he would give it to Edith and let her parse it out according to her budget.

He hated budgets. There was something small and mean about them that killed a man's gumption and imagination. Spend it when you get it; that was his motto. A man couldn't be running across town to save a nickel on a bottle of ketchup or to put his few miserable pennies in the savings bank. By God if you wanted a drink in the afternoon, because you were thirsty and because that's what the Good Book advised—he couldn't recall the chapter and verse, but he knew it was in there—then you either had a drink or you shut the hell up forever after. Did you want to be happy, or work up a reputation for being thrifty?

He walked into the boutique, and there was Sylvia, behind the counter, folding up some sort of oriental swan out of paper. There was one other customer in the store—a woman trying on a felt hat. Roy waved at Sylvia and then looked around at the merchandise, taking it all in. He nodded expansively. There was plenty to spend his money on.

In truth, he hardly ever came in. He didn't give a damn for women's clothes, and he didn't want to seem to be meddling in Sylvia's business affairs. This was her shop, after all. And, if they could keep out from under the thumb of the landlord class, the boutique would succeed where his enterprises had failed. If she made it through the winter, she'd be in the black. Come the spring, tourist money would start to flow, just like sap. Then all of them would rest easy. He was proud of her, and today he would do his best to help out.

He found a bulky, knitted sweater for a hundred dollars, Scottish wool dyed with berries—custom-built for the north coast climate. It was expensive, but nothing to a pocket-lined man like him, who had a daughter who was worth every penny. The sweater would do for Sylvia. Next he found a blouse for Edith, a dark green rayon blouse with a green and white scarf. It was youthful, and she would complain about that. But he wouldn't listen. The blouse and scarf would cost him another fifty dollars, which would leave fifty for dinner—sixty if you counted the secret tenner in his wallet. Altogether that would just about make the nut. Edith would murder him, if Sylvia didn't get him first. He nearly laughed out loud. This was rich. It had been too long since he'd lavished money on his family.

"What's that for?" Sylvia asked suspiciously when he laid the stuff on the counter.

"Wearing apparel," he said. Then, noticing the felt-hat woman standing behind him, he said, "Take the lady first, perhaps." He backed away and nodded at the woman, who smiled and said he didn't have to do that, that she could wait.

He bowed gallantly. "I anticipate trouble," he said to her. "This could get nasty." She shrugged and stepped in front of him, chatting amiably with Sylvia and paying her thirty dollars for the hat before going out.

"What's the story?" Sylvia asked. "What's this?"

"Sweater, blouse, and scarf. Nice, aren't they?"

"Very. What are they doing on the counter?" She narrowed her eyes at him. He thought she looked a little tired, not up to a contest of wills. He would walk all over her. She clearly knew very well what he was up to, though, and was going to try to humor him into submission.

"I did a spot of business this morning," he said. "Not much, mind you, given that it took me nearly three hours, but for once I'm a little flush. Where, I asked myself, does a man go to spend a little mad money? And the answer jumped into my head like a trout—why, down at the boutique!"

"Will you put the stuff back, or will I? What money? Did you do something illegal?"

"Illegal! Of course not. Ring these up, Sylvia. Don't argue with your old man. You can't refuse to do business with me just because I'm a senior citizen. That's pretty clearly ageist. There's laws disallowing that."

"*Ageist*? Where on earth did you hear that?"

"Program on the television. I'm insisting on my rights here. Just because I'm an old man and your father doesn't mean . . ."

Sylvia smiled at him suddenly and shrugged. "How much money?" she asked. "I keep a strict accounting."

"A heap of it. I'm spending it here to keep it in the family. Think about that. How do you think all these big-money families keep the coffers topped off? They buy and sell to themselves—keep the profits in the family and the goods, too. It's simple capitalism."

"Sounds like inbreeding. Eventually they'd end up with mutations."

"Mutations! Have you *seen* some of those people? There's not one of those Fortune 500 crowd that has a chin left. Fins, tails, spare toes—they keep the plastic surgeons hopping. The trick is that the surgeon is their second cousin. It's all in the family. What with kickbacks and tax write-offs, the whole thing's free. Money's just electricity for that crowd."

"I can't argue with that kind of logic," Sylvia said, having suddenly given up the fight. She put the clothes into a bag and took his money.

"I'm going to show your mother a night on the town," he said.

219

"Not Cap'n England's," she said. "Not the fish restaurant."

"What's wrong with the Cap'n's?"

"There's nothing wrong with it, if what you want is fried oysters and a slab of grilled swordfish. But if you want something more romantic . . . there's that new place out over the water, by the bridge—the Silver Salmon. All glass. There'll be a nice moon tonight. The woman who owns it comes in here a lot. I'll give her a call and reserve a table along the window."

"Your mother will flip. It'll be hard enough to get her down to Cap'n England's."

"We'll gang up on her."

"That's just what we'll do," Roy said happily. Together, he and Sylvia could accomplish about anything. He was tempted to tell her about his book idea, to lay the statistics out on the counter and watch her eyes shoot open. But he had learned long ago that you don't whisper that sort of thing around prematurely unless you wanted to bleed the magic off. He pulled out his pocket knife, took the sweater out of the bag, and cut through the plastic string that held the tag on. Then he shook the sweater out and held it up. "This is for you," he said. "For your birthday."

"My birthday's not till January."

"I know. Today I'm rich. In January I'm a pauper. Or maybe not. The future's full of . . . something. Go ahead, try it on."

Slowly Sylvia took it from him and slipped it over her head, standing in front of the mirror and pulling it straight. She took her hair out from the back and shook it down over her shoulders.

"Just your color, isn't it?"

She looked at him, saying nothing, her mouth set in an even line.

He waited for a moment and then realized that she wasn't going to say anything, not for the moment, anyway. "What on earth are you crying for, daughter? What a little fool I've raised."

She threw herself on him and hugged him, and then kissed him on the cheek and pushed him toward the door. "You're impossible," she said. "I love this sweater. I've tried it on a dozen times. I've wanted it for weeks. How did you know?"

"I have impeccable taste." He gestured at his own clothes—the worn-out tweed coat, the baggy trousers, the penny loafers. "You'd do worse than to hire me as a fashion consultant."

"Yes," she said. "I could do worse than that. Dinner at seven, then, for you and Mom. I'm making the reservations. Leave Mother to me."

"She's yours until seven." He went out into the afternoon sunlight whistling. There was Howard, coming along up the sidewalk, looking reasonably cheerful himself. Roy waited for him. "I've just now left her, my boy. I've softened her up. It's not my fault if you can't accomplish anything now. My advice is to compliment her new sweater." He slapped Howard on the shoulder, climbed into the station wagon, and sped off, carrying his package home to Edith and working out in his mind how he would force her to take it. He loved a challenge, especially when it came to women. When he set his mind to it, he was irresistible.

IT was dark and the wind was blowing when Sylvia dropped him off that night in Mendocino, in front of the store. He would walk around the corner and up to Mrs. Lamey's, while Sylvia went off to a New Age gathering up at the top of Pine Street. A Mrs. Moynihan was scheduled to channel the spirit of her dead companion—a traveler along the astral planes whom she called Chet, but whose true name was secret. She consulted him on important issues because he had a more spacious view of things. He spoke a Celtic tongue, but the words were filtered through Mrs. Moynihan's cranium and were uttered as modern English.

Last week Howard would have made fun of the whole business, but he held his tongue tonight. Last week was worlds away now. And in the lonesome darkness of the north coast night nothing seemed very funny to him. He agreed to meet Sylvia back at the store at eleven, and he walked west down Main, carrying his cane, although aside from the occasional twinge, he could get along well enough without it. Wasn't that typical? When he had it, he didn't need it; when he didn't have it, he limped around like Amos McCoy.

Mrs. Lamey's house was lit up, and coarse, self-conscious laughter sounded inside, as if someone were laughing at his own vulgar joke. There was music in the air—some sort of electronically spawned, almost atonal melody that sounded as if it were being torn to pieces by the wind. Through the window, Howard could see three men sitting in the living room, and another man and woman holding champagne glasses in their hands and standing in what must have been the kitchen. Bennet's house sat cold and dark across the street, and would probably stay that way, since Bennet was up in Fort Bragg working late on the haunted house. Howard wished that Bennet were home, and Uncle Roy with him. It would have been nice to have an ally or two nearby. Things might very easily turn bad—maybe quickly.

There was a gust of sea wind, and the plywood Humpty Dumpty on Bennet's roof waved solemnly at him, as if in reassurance. Howard waved back, then turned around and walked up the street, back toward Main, paying attention this time to the dark neighborhood. Forty yards down he stopped in the shadow of a cypress tree. There was only one house beyond Bennet's, a wooden shack with a tiny front porch and patchwork roof. The place was dark.

On the other side of the shack lay the bluffs—hundreds of acres of grassy meadow that made up Mendocino Headlands. There were rocky islands offshore and dozens of little coves along the deserted shoreline. Howard wasn't in the mood to do any more swimming, though, and there was something in him that didn't like the idea of being pursued out onto the deserted bluffs, especially not with a game knee and with nothing to hide behind but dead, knee-high grass.

Somehow he was certain that it would come to something like that. He was full of the premonition that he wasn't here to spend a pleasant, chatty evening. There was something in the cold air that made him edgy—a brittle atmosphere that was tensed and ready to break like a sheet of thin glass. He could feel it in the jerky music on the wind and see it in the moonlit face of the grimacing egg man on the roof. In fact, he had felt it all afternoon, but had worked hard to convince himself that it was merely his imagination, that he was still reacting to whatever it was that had caused him to hallucinate yesterday morning out in the woods.

There weren't any houses right adjacent to Mrs. Lamey's, only weedy lots that backed up onto an alley, which was half blocked by a partly torn-down Volkswagen bus settled onto a couple of four-by-fours. Its side door was missing and the old curtains around the windows were ragged and drooping. Fifty yards down lay a half dozen houses running down Kelly Street, which dead-ended into berry vines and grass. He heard laughter from Mrs. Lamey's house again, followed by a woman's curse.

There was nothing more to be gained by studying the street, so he stepped out of the shadows and strolled across to Mrs. Lamey's door, past the discolored roses and the pot of fish blood. He rang the bell twice so as to be heard over the noise. No use being timid.

Mrs. Lamey answered the door, dressed in her red kimono and a necklace made, apparently, of dried flowers tied together with thinly braided hair. Her face was almost hideous in the light of the porch lamp, which betrayed a crust of ghostly powder and rouge and penciled-in eyebrows. Under her kimono she wore a turtleneck sweater that covered her wattle but didn't, somehow, mask her resemblance to some species of exotic turkey. "Well!" she cried, clapping her hands. "It's our Howard!"

Talk died in the living room, and the man and woman in the kitchen looked out toward the door. Even at that distance Howard could see the woman roll her eyes at the man beside her. She might have been a year or two over thirty and she had the face of a lean divorcée who smoked too much and whose life had become a running complaint. The man had a pale sort of dog's face with a sparse, adolescent mustache, although he must have been in his mid-thirties. He grinned back at her and raised his eyebrows, too, and they both walked out into the living room with the pretend expressions of people who wanted nothing more than to make Howard's acquaintance. Howard stepped in through the door and waited for Mrs. Lamey to undertake introductions.

Stoat stood up from where he sat on the couch. He had the pale-looking skin of a person from an icy climate with more night than day, and he smiled at Howard with perfect teeth. "You two have met," Mrs. Lamey stated, waving her hand back and forth between Howard and Stoat, who nodded very pleasantly and sat back down, resuming his conversation in a low voice. Howard thought that there was something nervous in him, though. He looked like a man who expected a fire alarm to go off at any second but was pretending to act perfectly naturally.

Mr. Jimmers' burglar, the man in the wig, wasn't there, thank God. That would have made for a bad moment. Probably he was still in jail. Either that or Mrs. Lamey couldn't afford to have him around, given his new reputation. The other two men in the room were strangers to him. One had a shock of wild gray hair and a black businessman's suit and wore a red patent-leather belt and shoes. Everything about him was gaudy and vulgar.

The other—the one who was talking to Stoat—was a thin, ascetic-looking man in his twenties, maybe, who didn't look up when Howard was introduced. He wore a sweater tied casually over his shoulders and smoked a cigarette in a silver holder, his pinky finger waving in front of his face as if he were thumbing his nose at the wall.

So this is a "salon," Howard thought, shifting his cane from one hand to the other and shaking hands very heartily with the man in the suit.

"This is Reverend White," Mrs. Lamey said. "The Reverend is on television in the Bay Area. Quite a ministry. Started out fifteen years ago preaching on a street corner in the Market District, and now he owns half the renovated mansions along Haight Street."

"Glad to meet you," Howard lied, wanting to wipe his hands on his pants and trying to work out the broken-backed logic of the introduction, to make the jump from street-corner preacher to landlord.

"His is the Ministry of the Profiting Christian," Mrs. Lamey said. "And I'll warn you that he's a powerful debater. He'll win you over, Mr. Barton, just like he's won me over."

The man looked Howard up and down, clearly taking his measure. "Gimp leg, Mr. Barton?"

"Football injury. Nothing much. It acts up in a cold climate."

"Carry a cane, though. Are you a Christian?"

"I'm more often a sinner," Howard said evasively.

"Wrong answer. You'll have to work on that. Don't bother with the truth *all* the time. You'll develop a low opinion of yourself. Say 'Yes, I am!' and you'll feel better about yourself. I can do something about that leg of yours if you want, but it'll mean a real commitment on your part. No more of this half-ass crap you're used to. I'm a man who says what he means and gets things done. That's quite a cane." He bent over just a little bit, studying Graham's cane, then looked hard at Howard.

Mrs. Lamey put her hand on the Reverend White's elbow and said, "Be a dear, Lawrence, and pour Mr. Barton a glass of champagne, will you? That's what needs to be done first. You can lay your hands on him later." She favored the minister with a quick smile meant to dismiss him, and the man with the cigarette holder giggled. Mrs. Lamey turned to the two who'd been dallying in the kitchen, introducing the man as a literary critic and reviewer named Glenwood Touchey, also from the Bay Area, who favored deconstruction and didn't hold with frivolous views about books. Howard knew only vaguely what that meant. The woman turned out to be a writer with an unmeasurably high IQ.

"Show him your Mensa card, Gwen," the thin man with the cigarette holder said. And then to Howard he said, "She's had it laminated."

224

Howard smiled at the man, not knowing whether he was being funny or nasty. Probably nasty. "Where can I buy your work?" he asked the woman, anticipating the answer. "I'd like to read some of it."

"Ms. Bundy is largely self-published," Mrs. Lamey said for her, as if saving her embarrassment. She put her hand on the woman's arm and gave her a squeeze as if in encouragement, and then let her hand trail away down her forearm until their fingers touched for a moment.

"City Lights carries three volumes of my poetry," the woman said resolutely to Howard. She wore khaki clothes with a sort of political air, and had the long, straight hair of a practicing political activist. There was something in her eyes that said she despised Howard, along with all the other men in the room. "You wouldn't find them very entertaining, I'm afraid—no sex, no fistfights."

"Her poetry is very erudite," Mrs. Lamey said. "Very avant-garde. An utter disregard for traditional poetic contrivances. She was among the vanguard of nonsense-syllable verse and what has been called flat meter. An investigation of the theme of the existential woman that common publishers can't begin to fathom."

"Nor men, either," the Reverend White said, sticking his head out of the kitchen and winking broadly. "There's a number of us that can't fathom the existential woman, I'm afraid. I've probed the subject more than once in my time, and they're still a goddamn mystery." He guffawed, hiccuped loudly, and disappeared back into the kitchen, still chasing Howard's champagne.

The man with the cigarette holder snorted just then, as if he had tried to laugh but the laughter had come entirely out of his nose.

"He's got money," Stoat whispered loudly at Howard, jerking his head toward the kitchen. "That's enough to recommend him."

"And this is our artist." Mrs. Lamey extended her hand toward the man with the cigarette holder. "Jason, be a good boy and say hello to Howard Barton. He's the curator of a very large museum in Los Angeles, aren't you, Mr. Barton?"

"Not actually," Howard said. "I'm afraid it's a very small museum in Santa Ana, specializing in local history more than anything else. A lot of Indian bones and pot shards. It's got pretensions of becoming more grand someday."

"I welcome a humble man," the artist said, standing up and bowing at the waist. "The world is full of poseurs. It's uncommon

225

to run across someone who sees clearly what he amounts to and has the courage to admit it."

Howard bowed back at him, swallowing the insult as the Reverend White handed him a champagne flute, which Howard passed in front of his nose as if to better appreciate it. He thanked the man, thinking that he wouldn't bother to drink it but would pour it into a potted plant when he had the opportunity. There was no profit in being either drunk or poisoned. He had pretty clearly fallen into a nest of snakes. The entire company seemed to be prepared for him. The introductions being made were for his benefit only; he had clearly been discussed, and the idea of it put him on guard.

Ms. Bundy, the poet, cast Reverend White a disparaging glance just then and wandered off toward the kitchen again with Mr. Touchey . . . Howard realized that he didn't like these people at all, except maybe Stoat, ironically, who was the only one among them who wasn't playing any sort of complicated game. Howard realized that he was in danger of becoming flippant, along with all the rest of them, and that wouldn't do. Not only was he outnumbered, but what he needed was to project the notion of being enthusiastic about the company and their no-doubt-formidable talents. Things had changed since his adventures at Jimmers'. He was there with a purpose now, although he had no idea what that was.

He sat on the couch and leaned his cane up against the arm of it, resting his hand along the back and feigning interest in the conversation that had sprung up again between Stoat and the artist, who Howard still knew only as Jason. He couldn't address the man as that, though, because it was too familiar, and he couldn't address Stoat as Stoat, either, any more than he could have addressed him as Elephant or Wildebeest. So he listened to the two of them carry on about performance art, and about a Bay Area artist whose name seemed to be Heliarc and who had, apparently, developed a way to plug himself into an electrical socket in order to shoot light beams out of his eyes and elbows.

"Really?" Howard asked. "Light beams?" He meant it to sound sincere, but the artist gave him a sharp glance and then ignored him, lighting another cigarette off the end of the last one. Mrs. Lamey had disappeared, but came out just then with a tray full of tiny sandwiches made of goat cheese, nasturtiums, and dill weed.

"Nouveau California," she said. "The cheese is from a farm up near Caspar and the nasturtiums are out of my own garden.

You'll notice that they're green instead of orange. That wasn't easy, and I won't tell you how I accomplished it, but I will say that the flavor of these canapés is unique."

"Just ate," Howard said, as if he regretted it vastly but couldn't do anything about it beyond that. He patted his stomach and tried to imagine what gruesome liquids Mrs. Lamey had stained the nasturtiums with—pulverized tomato worms, probably.

Just then there was a squeal, like a piglet with its foot caught in a gopher hole, followed by the sound of a champagne glass smashing down onto the kitchen floor, a burst of shrill laughter, and someone being slapped. Mrs. Lamey looked up sharply, along with the two men, and in that instant, when their eyes were on the kitchen, Howard poured his champagne out into a potted plant and then set his glass down decisively on the coffee table as if he had drained the glass at a single gulp.

Ms. Bundy stepped out of the kitchen and into the living room, looking back over her shoulder, her face livid. "You'd screw a chicken," she said, "if you could get close enough to it without making it blind or sick."

Stoat bent over in Howard's direction and said, "Gwen is very witty. That's the key to the success of her poetry." He winked cheerfully. "She doesn't like men touching her, though, even if it's Glenwood Touchey. They're a pair, Glenwood and Gwen, but she's afraid he might heat up untapped passions. Her verses couldn't stand it. They'd have to be written on asbestos."

Mr. Touchey came out looking sour-faced, and the artist, taking his cigarette holder out of his mouth, said, "Don't touch me, Touchey," in an effeminate voice, which drew an intake of breath from Mrs. Lamey, who asked very sincerely whether Ms. Bundy was all right.

"You old whore," the poetess said to her, and stalked off down the hallway in the direction taken ten minutes earlier by Reverend White. Mrs. Lamey looked sincerely hurt and then a little puzzled, like a mother insulted by her daughter. Moments later there sounded a titter of laughter from a distant corner of the house, which seemed to infuriate Mr. Touchey and Mrs. Lamey about equally. The artist winked at Stoat, and Howard stood up and moved off toward the kitchen, carrying his cane.

"Champagne out here?" he asked Mrs. Lamey, nodding in that direction.

"In the ice bucket. Be liberal with it."

There was the ice bucket on the kitchen counter. Howard poured himself a glass but didn't taste it, looking around at the furnishings and the layout of the kitchen. Through a glass door at the back lay a service porch, and beyond that a door, which, if he had things laid out clearly in his mind, must lead out to the backyard and the alley. Left down the alley would be Ukiah Street and Little Lake and the bluffs beyond; right would lead past the blocked-up Volkswagen bus, back toward Main Street. In a pinch, he could head up Little Lake toward the highway and reach Pine Street, where Sylvia was hustling crystals and herb teas.

No one had followed him into the kitchen, and he could hear conversation rattling away in the living room. So he poked his head around the door and into the ill-lit service porch, which was immense, with a couple of big pantry cupboards, a washer and dryer, and a service-porch sink. It was carefully organized, with a big metal-boxed first-aid kit hung on the wall alongside a fire extinguisher. The linoleum floor was waxed like glass. After glancing over his shoulder he stepped across and unlocked the back door, both a chain lock and a dead bolt, and then went back out into the kitchen, where he pretended to study a row of hanging pots and pans made of polished copper.

"Do you cook, Mr. Barton?" asked Mrs. Lamey from the doorway. She regarded him almost happily, as if something had happened to restore her.

"Can of Spam now and then," Howard said. "I'd love to have a set of copper pans, although they'd probably be wasted on me."

"Well, truthfully," she said, "they're rather wasted on me, aren't they? I buy most of my food at the deli. I'm too busy for domestic chores. The kitchen was designed by one of the foremost decorators on the West Coast, though, a man from Palo Alto. Do you like it?"

"It's beautiful," Howard said truthfully. "I love the mossy color of the counter tile. It's perfect with this white linoleum. How do you keep it spotless like this? Is there some kind of trick to it?"

"Yes. Never cook in your kitchen, and avoid walking on the floor whenever you can. My decorator insisted on it, though. He drove up here personally to study the climate and landscape. He spent a week in town before he laid a hand on my kitchen. It was a matter of studying my personal space, vis-à-vis the concrete units of my existence. It was very complicated, I assure you, but I think he succeeded admirably. I learned a great deal from him—modes of perception."

She paused for a moment as if summoning the right words, and then said, "I've paid attention to *your* space, Howard, over the last few days, and the place you occupy in the local—what?—universe, you might say. I've become a shrewd judge of people, of human frailty. You're a puzzler, though, aren't you?" She took a good look at the cane right then, seeming to see it for the first time. There was something like surprise in her face, which disappeared at once. She turned toward the sink with a distracted air, cranking on the water and rinsing the already clean porcelain.

Howard shrugged, trying to think of something to say about his "space" but unable, really, to catch her drift. "It's a strange world you all seem to inhabit up here," he said. "I felt a little like an outsider, a tourist, when I got up here a few days ago. I guess that's partly why I'm here, you know. To strike up a few new acquaintances, get to know a couple of people. Don't want to be the only living boy in New York and all that." He smiled at her.

"New York?" she said, a little puzzled.

"Just a saying from a popular song." What would Uncle Roy do in my shoes? he wondered, raising his still full champagne glass at Mrs. Lamey. Then he asked, "What on earth is that?" and squinted out toward the window of the living room.

Mrs. Lamey spun around to look, expecting heaven knew what, and Howard dumped half his champagne down the sink. Outside, the moon was higher and the night had lightened. Bennet's Humpty Dumpty waved frantically at them from across the street, driven by the wind. Howard hadn't meant to call attention to it, specifically, but Mrs. Lamey apparently thought he had. "That's a nuisance," she said. "An eyesore and an insult."

"This is first-rate champagne," Howard said, grinning loopily at her and topping off his glass again. "I'm drinking too much of it."

"Nonsense," she said, brightening up. "That's an interesting sort of walking stick you have there. Is it decoration, mostly?"

"Not really. I'm sort of lame these days. Minor knee injury."

"Do you mind if I have a look at it? It quite fascinates me."

"Sure," Howard said. "I don't mind." He handed Mrs. Lamey the cane, knowing that he shouldn't but not really seeing how to avoid it. Still it was obvious that letting her examine the thing wouldn't cause him any real trouble.

Ms. Bundy came up just then and slipped a hand through the crook of Mrs. Lamey's arm. Her face was flushed and her hair disheveled.

"Glenwood has come up with a first-class idea," the poetess said, and she whispered it into Mrs. Lamey's ear, giggling just a little.

"Oh, that's naughty!" Mrs. Lamey said.

Ms. Bundy let go of the old woman and took Howard's arm now. "*He's* not any kind of wallflower," she said. Her khaki blouse was unbuttoned halfway to her navel and she was clearly braless underneath. She rubbed against Howard's arm seductively, and she tossed her hair out of her face and cocked her head at him, giving him a sort of come-hither look. He knew that he ought to be repelled by it; the more pleasant the company became, the more dangerous it was.

The fingers of her left hand snaked around his waist, vaguely tickling him, and he grinned crookedly.

"He's not the daring sort," Mrs. Lamey said, smiling at the two of them and unconsciously licking her lips.

"Stoat has his video camera with him," Ms. Bundy said. "We can film it, all of it." She adjusted her blouse, pushing it open indecently, as if by mistake.

"I don't know," Howard said, horrified now. He thought about the back door. Thank God he'd unlocked it. He could turn and bolt. Right now . . .

"Oh, I see what *you* thought I meant," Ms. Bundy said, tittering through her fingers. "He *is* a naughty boy!"

"Let's go!" shouted someone from the living room, and Touchey strode into view, waving the video camera that must have belonged to Stoat. Ms. Bundy opened her blouse for the camera, kissed Howard on the cheek, and curtsied. The Reverend White appeared just then behind Howard, carrying a ball-peen hammer, his face flushed with drink.

Howard very nearly ran for it. It was the hammer that did it. But Ms. Bundy shouted "We're off!" just then, and hauled Howard into the living room.

"Where?" Howard shouted back at her, determined not to show his fear. This was what he had come for, wasn't it? Of course it was.

"To kill the Humpty Dumpty!" Ms. Bundy yelled, and led Howard and the rest of them out into the night.

22

"Not going along, Stoat?" Touchey asked in a sneery voice. He stopped on the front porch, talking back into the house. Stoat stood up and headed toward them, shaking his head. Reverend White trained the video camera on Jason the artist, who looped his arm around Touchey's shoulder and struck a pose, turning to profile and drawing on his cigarette holder.

"Malicious mischief isn't in my line," Stoat said. "This sort of prank leaves me rather cold, I'm afraid. And it accomplishes nothing at all. It's frivolous. I don't *brawl*." There was a pettish tone to his voice, as if he thought he was being picked on.

"Howard's going to pound it," Gwendolyn Bundy said.

"*Pound* it!" Reverend White laughed out loud. "I dare say he will if you don't keep your hand out of his pants." He pinched Ms. Bundy on the flank, and she turned and slapped playfully at him.

"Come *on*, Stoatie," she said. "Don't you want to see Howard get tough? He's the spitting image of one of those quiet detectives with steel fists, isn't he? My kind of man. Drinks Scotch out of an office bottle and calls women dames. He's going to wax manly with Humpty Dumpty—show it no mercy at all. Isn't that right, Howard?" She grinned into his face and moistened her lips, flicking her tongue at him. Her breath smelled of champagne.

"That's right," Howard said. "No mercy at all." He hesitated, though, on the porch, remembering Graham's cane—his cane—and he turned to look back through the window, into the well-lit living room where Stoat had sat back down in a sulk. Mrs. Lamey had evidently put it down somewhere. She waved at him happily, like somebody's mother sending a pack of children out on a scavenger hunt.

The idea of losing the cane panicked him. He was a fool to have brought it here in the first place—although he couldn't quite say why—and he was a double fool for letting it out of his sight. "My cane," he said, slapping his forehead. "I'd better get it."

"Later," Ms. Bundy said decisively. "We're only going across the street. We're not going to make an evening of it. This is a sort of guerrilla raid. Slash and burn. We'll come back and play with your cane later."

Howard was doubtful, but he let himself be led away through Mrs. Lamey's front-yard garden. He had no idea what sort of high jinks they were up to, but it was true, apparently, that they were only going across the street. The sea wind was cold; there was no way they'd be out long.

"It's a battle in the art wars," Glenwood Touchey said. "All that cut-out crap in that front yard makes me sick."

"Throw up for us, Glen," Ms. Bundy said. "Get sick. I love performance art."

"I'll show you performance art," Touchey said, skipping across the street toward Bennet's house and kicking a wooden pansy into the air.

"Hey!" Howard shouted, taken utterly by surprise, but his shout was lost when Reverend White howled out a drunken whoop and followed along behind Touchey, chasing him with the camera. Ms. Bundy pulled up a pair of long wooden tulips and tossed one to Jason. The two of them began to fence with the tulip stems, trampling back and forth across the lawn and through the flower beds.

All of them were kept quiet now, giggling and challenging each other in hushed tones. Howard stood watching. He had to do something to stop it, but, like Stoat, he didn't like the idea of brawling, and he didn't want to lose his cane, either. Their antics reminded Howard of when he and his friends had toilet-papered lawns when he was a teenager, except that this was malicious and somehow deadly serious. They were making a hash of Bennet's flower garden for some ulterior purpose that he only barely understood, unless it was just pure, idiot meanness.

"Come on," Ms. Bundy said to him, lunging toward him with a tulip and jabbing him in the crotch with it. "Don't be a jerk. Have some fun for a change." Her blouse was half untucked and pushed all askew by now, another button having been lost in the tulip skirmish. It was clear that she was just warming up. Her eyes blazed, and there was a sadistic look in them that propelled Howard a step backward toward the curb.

It occurred to him abruptly that there were worse things waiting, that this smashing-up-the-Humpty-Dumpty prank was nothing more than a prelude for grander, more depraved things later in the evening—things involving him.

Mrs. Lamey stood on her front porch now, watching. Her red kimono flapped in the sea wind, and her hair blew straight out away from her head so that skinny and painted and powdered in the light of the porch lamp, she looked like something that had crept up out of a subterranean bordello. She waved at Howard, as if to encourage him, and then stepped back into the house and shut the door, having nothing more to do with the nighttime frolic.

He shrugged submissively as Ms. Bundy grabbed his arm and wrestled him toward the Humpty Dumpty. She gouged him in the ribs and then thrust her hand into his pants pocket, pushing up against him and shoving her tongue into his ear, biting him hard on the lobe.

"Hey!" he shouted, pulling away and very nearly losing a piece of flesh. The Reverend White stood panting next to a wooden, man-milking-a-cow whirligig, bathed in light from the video camera. One of his eyes jumped with a massive twitch, and there was a runnel of drool along his mouth. He handed the camera to Jason and then grabbed the cow with both hands, yanking it off its stake, throwing it over the house, end over end like a Frisbee. "Raise a little hell," he said to Howard, winking broadly.

Glenwood Touchey surged past just then with the hammer upraised, leaping up and swinging it at the Humpty Dumpty. The thing was too high for him, though, and the blow was a feeble one. He cursed, taking another ineffective shot at it. "Damn it," he said. "Reverend!"

"At your service," Reverend White said, bending over. Touchey climbed onto his shoulders, and his horse stood up shakily, staggering and nearly pitching over. Touchey yelped, holding on, and then when they were nearly steady he grasped the Reverend's collar like reins, and the two of them rushed at the Humpty Dumpty, which regarded them out of faintly Asiatic eyes, waving one last morbid goodbye at Howard, as if it knew it was about to undertake the fateful fall, had perhaps been waiting for it all evening.

Ms. Bundy grasped Howard's hand, pulling him forward. She had the look in her eye of a lecher at a pornographic film. He dug his heels in, though, looking around, and then shrugged out of her grasp and stepped across to the post that had held up the whirligig cow, just as Touchey slammed away futilely at the egg man with his hammer again.

Touchey cursed out loud, furious with the painted sheet of vibrating plywood. He had his left hand curled into Reverend White's hair now, and the preacher bucked and lunged, trying to shake him loose and yelling "Ow! Ow!" so that half of Touchey's blows hit nothing at all, but swung wide, the force of them nearly throwing him from the Reverend White's shoulders.

Howard wiggled the stake out of the ground—a length of two-by-two fir painted white and some four feet long. Gripping it like a baseball bat a foot from the bottom end, he steeled himself, drew in a deep breath, and then shouted at Touchey, "No! Like this!" Jason moved in, flooding all of them in electric light, camera whirring as Howard set his feet. Reverend White backed away gratefully, wheezing, anxious to give Howard a chance.

"Swing away!" he said. "One for the Gipper!" He bent into a shaky crouch in order to tumble Touchey off onto the ground.

"Hey!" Touchey yelled, holding on like a rodeo rider, clearly nowhere near finished with the smirking Humpty Dumpty, and at that moment Howard said, "Sorry, Reverend," and whipped the stake around, slamming the preacher across the stomach.

The preacher crumpled at the waist, his breath shooting out of him like wind from a rusty machine. Touchey shrieked and flew forward, face-first into the dirt, scattering wooden flowers and helplessly trying to throw his hammer at Howard, who side-stepped, turned at the same time, and smashed the heavy stake across the top of Jason's video camera. There was a satisfying crack of something breaking, and a large black chunk flew off and skittered away down the sidewalk. Howard took a half-step back and swung again, smashing out the lamp in a spray of glass.

Ms. Bundy lunged in furiously, clawing at Howard, raking her fingernails across his neck. He spun around, swinging the stake deliberately high so that she was forced to fall to her knees as the club whizzed past overhead. Then, after aiming one last blow at Jason, who swung the ruined camera wildly at his head, Howard loped across the street, up Kelly toward town, flinging his club into the weeds of a vacant lot.

He was around the corner and into the darkness before they were after him, and without looking back he cut hard to the left, crawling into a row of bushes along Mrs. Lamey's back fence. Footsteps approached, passed him, and pounded away down the block. He thought he could hear more going off in some other direction. They'd gotten clever and split up, maybe, thinking to surround him. Taking the time to do it had cost them. He looked out carefully. There was no one around. He heard one of them shout from a good distance away. Apparently they were scouring the bluffs for him.

He hoisted himself up and over the wooden fence, dropping heavily to the ground beyond and wincing at the pain that shot up through his ankle and knee. He was surprised to find how much he had come to depend upon Graham's cane. Since he had given it up a bare half hour ago, the pain in his leg seemed to have tripled.

Without waiting another instant he limped in through the unlocked back door, shutting it noiselessly, and climbed straightaway into one of the big service-porch pantries. It turned out to be the hot water heater closet, and had a vent in the door that he could just barely see through. He steeled himself for a long wait, running through his mind the layout of the rest of the house. Somewhere in there lay his cane, and he wasn't leaving without it.

He might have taken the chance of going right in after the cane, except that Stoat still sat in the living room, talking to Mrs. Lamey. Howard could hear their voices. He wasn't keen on the idea of fighting any more, not if he didn't have to. He discovered that his knees were shaking from the last battle. It was necessary to get the cane out of there without anyone getting hurt, especially himself.

Howard resigned himself to waiting it out. There was still an hour to go before eleven. If nothing at all could be done, he could easily slip out the back door and be gone, having made an utter hash of the evening. So much for convincing the enemy that he had the soul of a mercenary.

Gwendolyn Bundy was the first one home. Howard could hear her nagging at Mrs. Lamey with news of Howard's treachery. Stoat laughed out loud, pretending to be confounded that this came as any surprise. He and Mrs. Lamey had watched the whole escapade through the window. The lot of them had got nothing more than they deserved. He wasn't in the business of pulling wings off flies, he said. He favored crushing them outright— quickly. That's why God had invented fly swatters.

Then Ms. Bundy asked, "Now who will we use?" Mrs. Lamey was silent.

Use, Howard wondered. What the hell did that mean? Only that his instincts had probably been correct. They had been toying with him, tenderizing him in some foul way. Gwendolyn Bundy came into the kitchen. Through one of the vent slats he could see her haul the bottle out of the bucket and tilt it back, sucking the champagne out in long gasping drafts.

"You're hurt!" she said to someone. It turned out to be Touchey, whose face was covered with garden dirt.

"He's a dead man," the critic said, slamming his fist down onto the counter and then turning on the faucet. He filled his palms with water and splashed his face.

"What a sad thing he's not a novelist," Gwendolyn Bundy said, petting the back of his neck. "You could work him over in the *Chronicle*."

"Go to hell." Touchey strode back out as the woman opened the refrigerator door, pulling out and uncorking another bottle. The voices of Stoat and Reverend White could be heard then, arguing, and for the space of five minutes everyone was talking at once.

Someone mentioned the "staff," which Howard understood to mean the cane, and suddenly the voices dropped and for another five minutes there was nothing but murmuring. Then there was silence, and Howard could hear footfalls echoing away up the stairs as the lot of them shuffled away.

The cane was upstairs, then, or so it seemed. There was no way on earth to get it, either, short of a massive sort of diversion—and quickly, too. Stealing a car wouldn't work this time. An explosion would be better. If only he had three or four of the cherry bombs left over. He could light them and then throw them into the downstairs toilet and shut the lid.

It was closing in on eleven o'clock. He couldn't wait all night to act. It was possible that Sylvia, finding him missing, might come around to investigate. The very thought of it got him down to business. Who would they *use*? That's what Gwendolyn Bundy had asked Mrs. Lamey. Howard looked around wildly. What would *he* use? He could unscrew the gas line, climb out of the closet, and toss a match in. That was insane, though. The old wooden house would go up like tinder along with half the people in it. And the cane, for that matter. It would divert the hell out of them, though, and would add murder and arson to his rap sheet.

He'd have to get out of the closet. That was first. He peeked through the vent, and seeing no one in the kitchen, he stepped out into the service porch and straight off saw the first-aid chest hanging there on the wall. He opened it, hauling out a pile of gauze bandages and compresses and a bottle of iodine. Then he opened the next pantry, pushing around bottles of rug shampoo

236

and detergent and boxes of Brillo pads. Shoved in among the clutter was a plastic half gallon of bleach, which he pulled out, listening for a moment. There was the sound of talking from upstairs, but it was nothing but a mutter. They would hear him if he started scraping around.

He decided that the moment had come to act. There was no time for a debate between the devil and the angel that sat on either shoulder. Providence had seen to it that Mrs. Lamey had a well-stocked service porch, and it was clearly bad luck not to make use of providential gifts. That's what Uncle Roy would say, anyway.

He opened the bleach bottle and carefully drained the iodine into it, putting the top back on and swirling it around. Then he set the bottle into the service-porch sink and counted to sixty while he pulled out his pocket knife and opened it, shoving the blade into the plastic bottle a half inch from the bottom. Bleach dribbled out around the blade as he wiggled it back and forth, widening the hole until the bleach ran out in a rivulet down the drain. After a moment the flowing stopped, and Howard worked the knife lower, draining off most of the rest of the bleach. Then he twisted the knife sideways, cutting the whole top of the bottle off.

Left in the bottom was a chalky precipitate beneath a thin pool of bleach. He made a big wad of the gauze bandage and poured everything through it and down the sink, catching the precipitate and shaking as much of the moisture out of it as he could. What should he do with it? He wanted something sensational. Heat would do it.

Stepping hurriedly into the kitchen, he opened the drawers one after another until he found one that was full of ladles and spatulas and corncob skewers. The stuff inside clanked around when he searched through it, and he had to slow himself down and work carefully and quietly. There it was—a wire-mesh tea strainer. He stuffed the saturated gauze into the strainer and then closed and latched it, stepping across to turn on the gas stove.

In order to dry it out, he dangled the strainer over the heat, careful not to jostle it, and turning his face away so that if it blew up then and there, at least he wouldn't be blinded by it. He'd only done this once before, just a small one in a high school chemistry class, and the bomb had blown his desk open. He needed more than that now—something to send them running, to put the fear into them.

The stuff was nearly dry, and the whole business hadn't taken him six minutes. The rest was a matter of luck. Either it would work or it wouldn't. He shoved it into a sock from the clothes hamper, just to keep it from clanking too much, and laid the sock gently into the clothes dryer before turning it on.

They might hear it bouncing around in there, but that was a necessary risk. A couple of minutes on high heat ought to produce spectacular results. He slipped quickly to the kitchen door, and, seeing no one in the living room, went out through the front and crouched in the shadows of the porch to wait and think things through.

There wasn't any time for thinking. Almost at once there was a hellish explosion on the service porch. Howard had thought that the dryer would muffle it, but the sound was almost cataclysmic, like a dynamite blast, and there was the clamor of stuff crashing to the floor when something—the dryer door, probably—blew off and slammed against the opposite wall. The echo of it reverberated down the kitchen, and in the heavy silence that followed there sounded the clatter of footsteps on the stairs.

The entire crowd of them appeared in a rush. Crouching on the front porch, Howard watched them surge into the kitchen. Then he stood up and slipped in through the front-porch door, running for the second floor.

Someone shouted "Shit! Look!" and someone else shrieked, probably Mrs. Lamey, and then hollered something about the fire extinguisher. Howard heard it from halfway up the stairs. At the top, he pushed into the first room he came to.

It was big, wallpapered in a bloodred Victorian floral, and there was a circular bed very nearly in the center of the room. His cane lay on it. On the floor were a little propane torch, a saw, and Touchey's ball-peen hammer. They had been working at the cane—sawing pieces of it off. There was wood dust on the bedspread, and the tip of the cane was cut flat. The room was heavy with a resiny, sappy smell. The bits that had been cut off were gone.

Howard grabbed the cane and went out into the hall again, stopping at the top of the stairs to listen and catch his breath. He could just barely hear people talking down in the kitchen. Then there was the sound of the back door shutting. They would think he exploded the dryer and then went out the back. Maybe they would go out, too, thinking to follow . . . He tiptoed down the stairs, hugging the wall.

The front door still stood open, a long six yards from the base of the stairs. He stopped, hunkering down to take one quick look toward the kitchen door before running for the street, and in that moment Glenwood Touchey and Jason the artist stepped out of the kitchen, laughing between themselves, as if they thought that the blowing up of the dryer had been a wonderful trick. Then a look of doubt and suspicion crossed Touchey's face, and he stared at the open front door.

Howard jumped for it. There was nothing at all to be gained from waiting. He leaped off the bottom stair, waving the cane and landing on his bad leg, stumbling, and nearly going down. The two men regarded him momentarily with a look of wonder, as if they weren't sure what he meant by any of it. Then Touchey shouted, picked up a heavy glass ashtray, and threw it at Howard, missing him by three feet. The ashtray smashed through the front window in a shower of breaking glass, and Howard took a vicious swipe at Jason with the cane when the artist moved to cut him off.

Howard banged right into the screen door, knocking it open. He ran straight up the sidewalk and around into the alley. There was shouting in the house—Touchey and Jason hollering for help, not wanting to go out into the night alone. Howard climbed into the Volkswagen bus and crouched in the darkness between the two rear seats.

He could smell old vinyl and grease and upholstery stuffing as he waited there, thinking that this was either a good idea or a dead-bad one. They wouldn't expect him to stick around, now that he'd got his cane back. If they checked the bus, though . .

He heard them running off, up and down the street. After a moment Stoat's car started up, its bad starter whirring for a moment before catching. Howard waited until there was silence and then peeked up over the top of the seat. The alley was dark and empty. The night was wearing on. Sylvia might already have finished hobnobbing with the spirit world and gone back to the shop. Climbing out of the bus, Howard headed that way, down the alley toward Main, sticking to the shadows and watching over his shoulder.

The store was dark. Sylvia was still up at Mrs. Moynihan's. Howard set out in that direction, suddenly wanting to be there, too. Who could say what Mrs. Lamey's little circle would attempt next? Listening for approaching cars and footfalls, he hurried up Main, all the way to Evergreen before turning up toward Pine. The village was dark and silent and the moon was high, lighting up the street. Abruptly he started to run, full of premonition, and just then a car turned up from Main, cruising slowly. Its headlights caught him, and the car sped up.

Vaulting a picket fence, Howard ran across the shabby front lawn of an old house. He rounded the corner into the backyard, bowling through a covey of metal trash cans and heading straight into the adjacent yard. He heard a door open and someone shout. A dog began to bark and then another joined it as Howard jogged on, past the backs of dark houses. Looking between two of them, he could see Stoat's car out on the street, keeping pace with him. There were three men in it—Stoat, Touchey, and Jason.

Howard leaned heavily on his cane as he jogged. There was a fence in front of him, blocking off the next backyard. He stopped, looking out again toward the street. A light came on in the top story of the house behind him, and he realized that there was nothing to be gained by trying to escape over fences. He headed for the sidewalk again and found himself fifty feet from the corner of Pine Street.

Stoat pulled up beside Howard as he panted along toward Pine, looking hard at street addresses. Howard had run himself out. That had to be clear to the three in the car, who shouted encouragement at him through the rolled-down windows, merely following along now, enjoying themselves, but none of them seeming willing to confront him on the sidewalk.

There was Sylvia's car parked in the drive of a rambling white house. Lights shined through the front window. Howard turned and jogged up the walk, knocking hard on the door. He could hear voices inside. Stoat's car stopped abruptly and backed crazily into the curb. The three piled out, heading up the walk after him as he whacked on the door again. It opened, and, as if in a cartoon, he nearly knocked on the face of a matronly-looking woman in a sack dress, who stared back at him half suspiciously.

Sylvia stood behind her, though, and at once said, "Howard!" as if she were happy as anything to see him.

The woman smiled a little then, looking past him at the other three on the walk. Howard panted for breath, almost unable to speak. "Won't you come in?" the woman said pleasantly.

"We'd love to," Stoat told her, stepping up onto the porch. "We're friends of Sylvia. We're visiting in the area, and Sylvia was nice enough to invite us around. We can't stay but a moment, though. I hope we're not too late."

Howard stepped in through the door, past Mrs. Moynihan, and drew his finger across his throat so that Sylvia could see it. Sylvia shrugged. What could she do?

A blond-haired woman sat on a sofa in a big room beyond, along with a man in a flannel shirt, with a beard and a large nose. He wore a half dozen big pieces of gaudy Navajo jewelry and had the flushed and broken-veined face of a heavy drinker. On a low coffee table lay a scattering of crystals, copper and silver jewelry, and a stack of paperback books and tracts.

"We've interrupted something!" Stoat said, as if he regretted being impolite. "I was afraid of this, Howard."

Sylvia had disappeared. Howard looked around wildly, hoping that she would appear to rescue him, but she was gone. "Yes," Howard said, trying to look apologetic. "Are you a fancier of New Age philosophy, Mrs. Moynihan?" He picked up one of the paperbacks. On the cover were three out-of-focus butterflies and the title "Who You Are."

She looked at him skeptically as he smoothed out his hair.

"Mrs. Moynihan is not a 'fancier' of philosophies," the man with the beard said.

"Of course." Howard smiled at him, wondering where the hell Sylvia was. She appeared just then from down the hall, and winked at Howard, who had no idea on earth what the wink meant. "I met Rodia Davis at Esalen last year," he continued, pulling the name out of a hat, talking wildly.

Mrs. Moynihan widened her eyes. "I'm sorry . . ." she said.

"The woman who channels the spirit of the Carpathian slave. Wonderful book that she's written, out in paperback from Amethyst Imprints. Do you have a copy, hon?"

"No," Sylvia said, looking doubtful. "I might have one at the shop, though . . ."

"Let's just go round and find it, shall we?" Stoat asked, putting his hand on Howard's shoulder. "Seriously, we're interrupting things here. Coming along, Sylvia? Or should we pick you up in—what? A half hour, say?"

"A Carpathian slave?" Mrs. Moynihan asked. "That's fascinating."

"I could have sworn that the Carpathians were a mountain system," Touchey said cheerfully. "Are you sure you mean Carpathian?"

Mrs. Moynihan gestured at the couch. "Do sit down," she said. "We were just finishing up, actually. Most of the guests have gone. This is Susan MacIntyre."

The blond-haired woman on the couch smiled and nodded. There was a hammered-copper comb in her hair and she wore a quartzite ring as big as a goose egg. "I've got to be going myself," she said, standing up, and after a few parting pleasantries she hurried through the door and was gone.

"Glass of wine?" Mrs. Moynihan asked.

The bearded man scowled and checked a wristwatch that was hidden beneath the sleeve of his flannel shirt. "Coming onto eleven," he said.

Sylvia gestured at him. "This is *Mister* Moynihan."

"Glad to meet you." Howard leaned over and shook hands with the man, who looked more doubtful than ever. "You know," Howard said, "you have an uncanny resemblance to Abraham Maslow," which was a lie, or probably was. Howard couldn't recall ever having seen a picture of Maslow.

"Do you think so?" Mrs. Moynihan said, looking sideways at her husband, maybe a little skeptically.

"Right on the money." Howard sat down on the couch, settling in comfortably. "A glass of wine would be spectacular, actually— as long as we're not keeping you folks up."

"Of *course* we're keeping them up, Howard." Stoat shook his head at him, as if he were a naughty boy.

"Jason here is an artist," Howard said, nodding at the scowling Jason, who still hadn't sat down.

"A painter," Mrs. Moynihan said. "How lovely. I paint myself. *Please* sit down." Jason sat, dusting off the chair cushion first.

"Don't tell me that's your work on the wall there?" Howard asked, gesturing at two massive, unframed seascapes sitting side by side on the wall opposite. Together they composed a single scene of a rocky cove with waves the color and texture of cheesecake breaking on the rocks. A fishing boat stood out to sea, blocked in heavily with what must have been a rope end— the sort of picture that might easily have hung on the wall of a suburban bank.

Howard heard Touchey mutter something under his breath, and Jason seemed about to explode. "That reminds me of Bigler," Howard said, "only the work here is much finer—far keener eye for detail."

"Bigler?" Jason asked, accepting a glass of white wine. "Who on earth . . . ?"

"Howard is the curator of a very upscale museum in Los Angeles," Sylvia interrupted, talking to Mrs. Moynihan. "Getty money."

"*Really*!" Mrs. Moynihan said.

"Well," said Howard. "I can tell you this much: the oils on the wall there are very nice, no matter who painted them. Superb rendering of detail. Don't you agree, Jason?"

The artist said nothing.

"Mrs. Moynihan painted those herself," Mr. Moynihan said. "She's been hung in several galleries in town."

"I'm certain of it," Touchey said. "Bigler, though. I haven't heard of him, either. Was he a Carpathian slave, too?"

Howard looked sharply at him, as if he had insulted Mrs. Moynihan's paintings.

"I'm interested in hearing about that," the woman said, too modest, perhaps, to carry on about her own paintings. Howard found that he liked her. There was something big and round and generous about her. "What was the woman's name again?" she asked. "I'd like to read her book."

Howard searched his mind. He couldn't remember it, having pulled it out of the air in the first place.

"Rodia Davis," Sylvia said helpfully. "I think that's what you said, isn't it, Howard? Maybe you could search out a copy for Mrs. Moynihan tomorrow." She smiled broadly at him. Then to Mrs. Moynihan she said, "Howard is my father's nephew. He's a Barton."

"*Is* he? Your uncle is a gravely misunderstood man," she said to Howard. "His spirit museum was a fascinating place. Men of real vision suffer in a culture that runs on greed and cynicism."

"Isn't *that* the truth?" Stoat said, shaking his head sadly.

Mr. Moynihan drained his glass. "Mrs. Moynihan is a channeler herself."

"Are you?" Stoat asked, seeming genuinely enthused. Touchey and Jason sat silently, as if not trusting themselves to speak.

"She's in touch with an entity that is known only as 'Chet,' " the bearded man said gravely, then looked around as if he expected one of them to challenge him. "He was here tonight, in this room. It was not his corporeal self, of course. It was his astral projection."

"Does he know Howard's Carpathian?" Touchey asked.

"He spoke to us for nearly twenty minutes tonight," Sylvia said, ignoring him.

Touchey snorted under his breath. "Any tips on the market?"

"Glenwood!" Howard said, scowling faintly. Then, aside to the old man, he made the quick gesture of someone tippling, then winked and shook his head in a rapid little negative.

"Oh," the man said flatly, shaking his own head.

Stoat checked his watch. "Well, I'll be damned. Coming up on eleven-thirty. We've really got to be going. Thank you both so much for the wine." He stood up, and so did Jason and Touchey.

"Well, that *is* a shame," Mrs. Moynihan said. "Thank you for saying such nice things about my paintings." Her husband stood up and collected the wineglasses from the table, as if disposing of the glasses would also get rid of his unwanted guests. He wiped a water ring off the tabletop with the sleeve of his shirt, scowling tiredly.

Howard worked hard to think of something to stall things. He had to *act*, to do something to save them. It was too late for more conversation. He could hardly call the police; he had put in far too active a day for that. Sylvia looked at him suddenly as if puzzled. "I think I've lost one of my stones," she said.

"Oh, no!" Mrs. Moynihan lamented. "Sure it wasn't one of the ones that Susan bought?"

"No," Sylvia said. "It was a pyrite orb, about the size of a golf ball. I bet it's rolled under the couch or something."

"Perhaps we can all have a look around," Howard said to his three adversaries. "It can't have gone far. Glenwood, crawl behind the chair, would you?"

"For the love of . . ." Touchey started to say, but Stoat cut him off with a gesture.

"Have a look under the chair, Glen."

Howard peered under the couch, pretending to search for the mythical ball of pyrite.

"We'll turn the place upside down in the morning," Mr. Moynihan said. "No need to be crawling around the room now. Not at this time of night."

Just then the doorbell rang, and Mrs. Moynihan said, "Isn't that a surprise? It's a regular party," and she stepped across to open it.

"Christ on a bicycle," Mr. Moynihan said. He strode off toward the kitchen, muttering and carrying the wineglasses.

Howard hefted Graham's cane and moved in behind Jason and Touchey and Stoat, standing between them and the rest of the house. He was afraid it would be Ms. Bundy and Mrs. Lamey and the Reverend White, having tracked down Stoat's car. This would be bad business. He shouldn't have come here at all. Now Sylvia was involved, along with the innocent Moynihans.

But when the door swung open, there stood Uncle Roy and old Bennet and the man from the restaurant in the harbor, who looked like a hod carrier and wore a stained butcher's apron smeared with what must have been blood. Behind them, half in shadow, were two men wearing the patchwork clothes of gluers. The one on the left could have passed for Moses in an illustration out of Exodus, except that in his right hand he held a tire iron that he slapped against his leg.

23

"FATHER!" Sylvia cried happily.

Touchey backed up a step, as if getting set to sprint for the back door. Even Stoat seemed to pale visibly, and Jason the artist was shifty-eyed and scared, like a nasty sort of petty criminal collared at last by the law. Howard jabbed Touchey in the back with the tip of his cane, and the man turned on him furiously. Howard widened his eyes and tipped his head toward the door as if inviting him out onto the front lawn.

"Hello, Mrs. Moynihan!" Uncle Roy said happily.

"Good evening, Mr. Barton," Mrs. Moynihan said.

"We've come to collect Sylvia and Howard." Uncle Roy had a big, cheesy smile on his face, as if he'd just found out that the world was his oyster.

"What a wonderful young man her Howard is," Mrs. Moynihan said, looking dubiously now at Roy's friends. "He's astonishingly knowledgeable. I believe he has some of his uncle's genetic material."

"He's a peach," Uncle Roy said.

"Where's my car?" Stoat asked suspiciously, looking past them toward the street.

Uncle Roy looked baffled. He shrugged and made a long face, as if he couldn't be blamed for whatever had happened to Stoat's car. Then he smiled broadly again and bowed like Mr. Pickwick, gesturing toward the lawn. "Come on out," he said. "We'll have a look around. I think maybe it was stolen by that damned Arab crowd that runs the deli up in Caspar. What was their name? Mohammed something or other. Same bunch that beat up Jimmers, I bet, and then came back and stole his shed."

They filed out of the house then, waving goodbye to Mrs. Moynihan, who closed the door behind them. "Run these boys down the road apiece, will you?" Uncle Roy asked one of the gluers. "Put them through the usual paces."

"What?" Touchey said. "Wait. I'm not going anywhere."

Uncle Roy smiled at them. "Little ride. Night air will do you good."

At the curb sat a gluer vehicle, the Day of the Dead Chevy that had been parked up at Sammy's three days ago. The plaster-of-Paris skulls glowed ghostly white in the moonlight. Miniature skeletons wearing top hats and carrying canes sprawled across the hood in a heap as if they'd been shoveled out of a mass grave with a skip loader.

Glenwood Touchey began to back away, and then turned to run, pushing Uncle Roy aside and bowling past the two gluers. Old Bennet shoved out his foot and tripped him, though, and Touchey sprawled onto his hands and knees in the grass, grunting softly. The aproned man pulled Touchey to his feet again, obligingly dusting a few grass clippings off Touchey's clothes and then wiping his own hands on his bloody apron. Then he pointed toward the Chevy, explaining something to Touchey in a low voice, as if Touchey were a child being told about the terrible dangers of playing in the street. One of the gluers, his face set like concrete, latched on to Touchey's arm and hustled him toward the waiting car.

Stoat followed almost willingly, as if he would just as soon get it over with and not lose his dignity in the process, and Jason made a show of doing the same, although his face betrayed him and he looked dispirited, like a wet dog, and he glanced around nervously as if looking for a chance to run for it. It was too late, though, and he climbed into the car along with his two friends, the three of them sitting there wooden-faced, like mannequins. Touchey's hands fumbled on his knees, drumming out a nervous rhythm, and he bit at his upper lip, looking to the left and right and fidgeting around, staring hard at the door panels. Then, as if someone had poked him with a cattle prod, he crawled across Jason to hammer at the window, a look of terror on his face. Jason shoved him back into his seat, but immediately he was up again, trying to climb over into the front seat now.

"He's just discovered that there's no backseat door or window handles," Uncle Roy said cheerfully to Howard, like a sportscaster delivering a play-by-play.

"Father!" Sylvia cried, putting her hand over her mouth. The gluers climbed silently into the front seat, rolling Touchey back over onto the laps of his companions.

Then Uncle Roy leaned down to speak through the passenger window, talking to the three in back. "You boys are going on a little retreat," he said, "up to the hills. Diet of sprouts and berries. Fresh air. New outlook."

"You'll wish you were dead!" Touchey shouted at him from the backseat, his face twisted by hatred and fear.

Uncle Roy looked at him for a moment, as if Touchey were a cockroach on a sidewalk. "Put the *machine* on that one if he acts up," Roy said to the two in front. "But keep the electrodes away from his salivary glands. And for Christ's sake, don't turn it up above twelve volts this time. It isn't a goddamn hot-dog cooker."

The Chevy rolled away up the street then, carrying the three stricken prisoners and their strange jailers. It turned south toward the highway.

Uncle Roy looked as if he'd just eaten a bad snail. He heaved a long sigh and rubbed his forehead tiredly. "Poor bastards," he said, watching them motor away. "I hope they deserve all this." He widened his eyes at Howard. "Strike that. I *know* they do. One of them does, anyway. That one in the middle—his face was an advertisement."

"That's him, all right," Bennet said. "I'll bet you a shiny new dime. Either him or the other one, name of—what was it? Marmot? What the hell kind of a name is that?" Bennet stood on the lawn with the man in the apron, who shrugged at the question. Both of them had their arms folded across their chests, like bodyguards waiting for a signal.

"What'll happen to them?" Howard asked. "I'm not sure what they deserve, but—"

"Deserve?" Uncle Roy said. "Lord knows what they deserve. The Sunberries are just going to give them a thrill. Silent bunch of guys, gluers. They won't say a word. That'll drive your men nearly nuts. They'll take them up into the hills above Albion, push them out of the car, and let them walk back down—not more than three or four miles. Call it six. They'll be snug in bed by three in the morning."

He pulled a wad of bills out of his pocket and thumbed

247

through them tiredly, sorting out the hundreds and straightening the wrinkles out of them.

"Could have got a sight more for it," the man in the bloody apron said.

Uncle Roy grunted. "Maybe. Say, Howard, you haven't met Lou Gibb, have you? Not officially?" He gestured at his friend, who shoved out his hand. Howard shook it.

"We ran past each other last night down at the harbor," Howard said, "but there wasn't any time for introductions."

"Me and your uncle go way back," Gibb said.

Uncle Roy nodded, managing to smile again. "Gibb here owns the Cap'n England. Chief cook and bottle washer, too. Answers the phone out back for us. Nobody rings up a pay phone, mostly. So when it does ring it's probably for us, and Lou grabs it. When he got Sylvia's call tonight, he was doing a spot of business with those three gluers, trading for a few cases of hooch."

"Two gluers," Howard said.

"Well, there was the one that took Stoat's car. You didn't see him. We delivered the car out of bondage. Liberated it. Money for the cause. Next time Stoat sees the car he won't know it from Adam. The Sunberries were talking about turning it into a motorized flower bed. Here you go, Lou." Uncle Roy counted out a few bills, pocketing the rest.

"Give it to Mrs. Deventer," Lou said, waving the money away. "I don't need it."

Uncle Roy nodded, not arguing with him. "Eight hundred bucks, cash on the barrelhead. What do you figure is blue-book on a car like that?"

"Five thousand easy," Bennet said.

"Yeah, but those Sunberries did us a hell of a favor, didn't they? They'll be ready to do us another one now, *quid pro quo*."

Sylvia was pretty clearly seething. "What the hell is going on?" she asked. "Stoat didn't hit Mr. Jimmers on the head. He wasn't even there. Howard said so."

"That's right," Howard said. "None of them were."

"You two shouldn't fret," Uncle Roy said to Sylvia. "Let me worry about it. Lou here wanted to beat them to a pulp right out here on the lawn. They got Mrs. Deventer this evening, coming back down from Willits."

"What?" Howard asked, shocked. Somehow he hadn't anticipated anything like that.

"What do you mean?" Sylvia said. "Is she . . . ?"

"No, she's not dead. Dead drunk, actually. That's what saved her. Crash tossed her around the floorboards like a rag doll. If she'd have been sober, and tensed up, there's no telling what would have happened. They took her up to the hospital and set her arm and then drove her back down to her house not a half hour before you called."

"How do you know it was them?" Howard asked.

"Someone loosened the lug nuts on the right front wheel," Bennet said. "Must have done it while she was in at her sister's, up in Willits. Road up that way is nothing but curves." He ran his hand through his hair and then shook his head darkly. "I put new pads on the brakes a week ago, and I tightened them lugs down. I know I did. Now the blame falls to me. I'd be in it deep if she was hurt bad. They towed the car back down to her house."

"There was trouble over at your place tonight, too," Howard said to Bennet. "They kicked your flower beds apart and tried to break down the Humpty Dumpty. I did what I could to stop it."

"The creeps," Uncle Roy said, heading for the station wagon. "Let's get over there."

Bennet shrugged. "Not much lost if all they did was kick wooden flowers around. Nothing that can't be patched up."

"If you boys don't need me," Lou Gibb said, "I'm out of here. I got three or four hours' work left."

"Take some of this dough, damn it," Uncle Roy said to him, turning around and pulling out the money again. "Enough to pay for that Sunberry whiskey, anyway."

Gibb hesitated, then took what Uncle Roy offered him, shoving it down into his pocket. "Give the rest to Mrs. Deventer, though."

"Sure I will." Uncle Roy nodded a goodbye to him as Gibb climbed into his own car and started it up. "Hell of a good man, isn't he?" Roy asked. They watched Gibb pull away from the curb. "There was a book I read once: one guy kept asking people what was the most surprising thing—that people could treat each other so good or so damned nasty. I think about that a lot. Then I run into people like Gibb, or Mrs. Moynihan here, and I see that they treat people square and friendly and it doesn't take any kind of effort at all. It's like breathing to them. Nothing to it. What does that mean?"

"That some of us have a long way to go," Howard said, yawning. "It doesn't answer your man's question, though."

"I guess not," Uncle Roy said. "Let's roll." He and Bennet climbed into Roy's station wagon and drove off up Pine, swinging around toward Main.

Howard and Sylvia followed in Sylvia's car. It was midnight, and the streets and houses were dark. Trees swayed in the sea wind, and there was a winter chill in the air that made Howard think of the three men who would very shortly be walking home up the Coast Highway in their fashionable sweaters and shoes. For a moment he half hoped that they'd catch a ride with some late-night traveler, but then he thought of Mrs. Deventer and her smashed-up Pontiac and the moment passed. Before they'd driven the four or five blocks to Bennet's house Howard was asleep.

The sound of a car door slamming woke him up, but he decided not to get out. There hadn't been all that much damage done, except to the whirligig cow. The others could deal with it. Howard felt as if he hadn't gotten any sleep in about six weeks. Tomorrow morning—*this* morning, that is—he would sleep till noon. He watched groggily as they moved around on the lawn. Uncle Roy was fired up, letting loose the energy now that he'd kept bottled up back at Mrs. Moynihan's house. Howard heard him shout something, and then saw him stride toward the street, in the direction of Mrs. Lamey's. Sylvia and Bennet chased him down, pushing him back toward the station wagon, but he broke away from them and hurried across to pound on her door.

Wearily Howard tried to climb out of the car. His knee joint felt packed with sand, and his leg was so stiff that he had to pick it up with his hands in order to shift it. It wouldn't do for Uncle Roy to start harassing Mrs. Lamey at midnight. There were probably laws to protect landlords from wild tenants. He stood up in the weedy gutter, nearly falling down, and hung on to the car roof for support. He pulled the cane out and leaned on it. At once he felt lighter, and some of the pain and stiffness seemed to leak away into the vegetation beneath his feet.

Uncle Roy beat on Mrs. Lamey's door again, kicking it finally with the toe of his boot. "Wake the hell up, you old pig!" he shouted, cupping his hands and yelling toward the second story. The banging reverberated through the darkness. Sylvia and Bennet both pulled him away again, but it was like trying to shift a piano. Uncle Roy leaned past Sylvia and kicked furiously at the already broken front window. What was left of the pane shattered to pieces, tinkling to the floor inside.

"I know that's you, Roy Barton!" Mrs. Lamey's voice called down from upstairs. Howard could see her face outlined in the dark, half-open window. "The whole street knows it's you! I'll have you jailed for assault!"

"Try me!" Uncle Roy shouted back. "Come down here and I'll shove your damned rent money down your throat!" Wrenching furiously loose again, he picked up the bowl still half full of fish blood and splashed it over the front door as if to mark the house in some grisly, Old Testament manner. He allowed himself to be pulled away toward the street then, still cursing, as Mrs. Lamey slammed the upstairs window. Lights blinked on then.

"She's calling the cops," Bennet said.

Uncle Roy breathed hard, nearly flattened by the exertion. "Shit," he said, hauling the wad of bills out of his pocket again. "Ditch this in your house."

"Sit down somewhere," Sylvia said to Howard when she saw him limping across toward them.

Bennet nodded at him. "Come up on my porch and sit in the rocker."

The four of them stepped onto Bennet's lawn, and it was then that Howard saw that the Humpty Dumpty had been wrecked. It lay crazily in the flower bed, smashing down wooden tulips. Someone had pried its arms and legs off and thrown them here and there around the yard, and its spring mechanism had been wrenched back and forth until it hung from half-torn-out screws, twisted and bent. The plywood head and body of the thing were cracked in half, and long splinters of fragmented plywood had torn away so that the painted face was mostly obliterated by what looked like jagged, grass-blade shadows.

"It's a wreck," Bennet said. "There's no fixing it, not busted in half like that."

"Dirty, rotten sons of bitches . . . Did you see them do this, Howard?" Uncle Roy looked at him, not angrily now, but as if suddenly worried.

"Not this, no. They kicked the flowers around a little when I was here. That's all. I broke it up and then sneaked back into Mrs. Lamey's house and blew up her clothes dryer."

"Did you!" Uncle Roy said, as if hearing good news at last. "Why?"

"Well, they'd stolen Graham's cane, and I decided to get it back. So I blew up the dryer and when they all ran downstairs, I went up and got it. Then they chased me down to Mrs. Moynihan's."

"You were here, though, for some of this?" Uncle Roy gestured at the lawn.

"At first, yes."

"How about the old lady? Was Mrs. Lamey out here, too, raising hell?"

"No," Howard said. "She stayed home."

"Of course she did. When you were gone she and whoever was left over came back out here and finished the job." Uncle Roy stood thinking for a moment. "Sylvia," he said, "get Howard out of here. Quick. We'll handle this. If Howard sticks around, she'll finger him, too—say she saw him with the other hooligans out breaking up Bennet's stuff. She'll get us all if we don't look sharp. We'll skin through, though, as long as that damned Stoat doesn't make it back down the hill while the cops are here." He thought for a moment, squinting his eyes. "Yes, that's it. You and Howard vamoose. Get home and put Howard to bed. He's earned his pay."

Bennet stepped back out of the house just then. "Coffee's on," he said.

"Did you ditch the money?" Uncle Roy asked him.

"Under the floor."

"Get four hundred back out, will you?"

"*Now* you tell me," Bennet said. "You aren't going to give me change, are you?"

Uncle Roy shook his head. "There isn't going to be any change." He waved decisively at Howard and Sylvia, gesturing toward the road. "Get going," he said.

Howard climbed gratefully back into Sylvia's Toyota, and together they drove down to Main Street and swung left toward the highway, cruising past Sylvia's darkened store. In his mind he didn't want to abandon his uncle. The rest of him, though—his muscles and joints and bones—was happy to. Anyway, Uncle Roy was good at this sort of thing. Howard couldn't teach him any tricks. And there was no doubt at all that Mrs. Lamey *would* implicate Howard in something if she had half a chance to—the clothes dryer atrocity at the very least. She had invited him over with the most friendly and hospitable intentions, and he had blown her service porch up with a homemade bomb . . .

"Go to sleep," Sylvia said. "He'll be all right. Here." She pulled a parka out of the back and handed it to him, and he stuffed it against the seat and door as a pillow, settling himself against it. "What the heck happened to your neck?" She touched him on the spot where Ms. Bundy had raked him with her fingernails, and he winced at the raw streak of pain.

"I had a little fracas with another woman tonight," he said sleepily.

"Another woman?"

"I'm afraid so. She was a feisty one, too."

"*Another* woman? Who's the first one? You can't have another one without having one to start with."

She was being playful, but Howard was too tired to carry on in that vein. "Maybe you are," he said, watching her face out of half-shut eyes.

She smirked at him, as if to say that she knew he was being silly, as usual. At least she hadn't denied it. But was she being agreeable or putting him off? This was no time to work through it. She looked worried and doubtful and tired, Howard realized She was single-handedly keeping the whole family afloat, working overtime to sell her strange wares to the Mrs. Moynihans of the world and trying to save Howard and Uncle Roy from themselves with what little time she had left over.

"You're a brick," he said to her. "Will you help me break into Jimmers' place tomorrow afternoon?"

"Enough!" she said. "Give it a rest."

"No time for that now. The merry-go-round's spinning too fast. We can't crawl off anymore." She sighed, shrugging her shoulders as if she didn't trust herself to say anything. Howard squeezed her arm again. "He *will* be all right, you know. It would be better for you to believe it." She cast him a little smile and then winked, as if recalling just what sort of a man her father was.

Up on the highway they passed a patrol car turning down onto Lansing Street.

THE whine of the power saw woke him next morning. It was eleven o'clock, and sunlight streamed through the window. Uncle Roy hadn't spent the night in jail, then. Howard had slept dreamlessly through the night and morning, and he could easily turn over now and drift off again.

There was too much to do, though. He bent his lame knee, and it was stiff and sore, although far better than it had been last night. He wrapped the bandage around it again, then grabbed the cane and hobbled to the window. Uncle Roy was bent over the saw, cutting up the rest of the lumber. He tossed a couple of pieces of scrap into the weeds and laid a clean piece on the pile, then stopped to drink from a coffee mug.

Fueled by the idea of coffee, Howard dressed and went out into the kitchen, taking the cane with him. He was determined not to let it out of his sight again, although he didn't know quite why. His knee loosened up when he moved, and he felt like the Tin Man, creaking back to life after rusting stiff in the rain.

Aunt Edith appeared, carrying a feather duster. She had the look on her face of someone longing for past, simpler times. "Good morning," she said. "Coffee's probably cold by now."

"Hot enough," Howard said, pouring milk and sugar into the cup she handed him. She was looking steadily at him, as if taking his measure. He wondered what she knew about yesterday's she-nanigans, and suddenly he felt as if he were twelve or thirteen and had been caught throwing eggs at houses. "Uncle Roy all right?"

"He'll always be all right. He doesn't know how to doubt himself. He just rides along on his enthusiasms."

"He got home late last night."

"After two. He said that Bennet and him closed down the Tip Top Lounge, but he hadn't been drinking."

"No," Howard said. "It wasn't that. There was a little bit of trouble down in Mendocino, and he bailed me out."

"I know what kind of trouble, or can imagine it." She brushed her hair out of her eyes, pinning it up so that half of it fell back down again. There was no hint of a smile on her face. "He's one of the lilies of the field," she said. "He's blessed, I think. I'm worried about you, though. You haven't been here a week, and you're in trouble. I can feel it. It's deep, too. I know it's nothing of your doing. It was waiting for you up here, in the weather. You drove into it like a boat into a storm. You could probably leave—sail right back out of it."

Howard was silenced by the abrupt finality of this last statement. He knew she wasn't being rude, that she wasn't ordering him out of the house.

"Talk Sylvia into going back down south with you. This is no place for her. She could make a go of it down there. I've thought about it, and if she opened a little store, in one of those big malls, there's nothing she couldn't accomplish. She could establish a chain of them. I was reading about someone who did that, a woman who sold cookies and made her fortune at it. It's too small for her up here. She hasn't got a chance. She's staying for us. We'd get by, though."

"Maybe she thinks you're worth staying for."

"Maybe she thinks you're worth leaving with."

It was another statement that struck Howard silent. And it was a strange statement, too, coming from his aunt. But Aunt Edith, he was finding, often said just what she meant. He shrugged. "I can't leave yet," he said. "There's something that's only half done."

"What is it?"

"I'm not sure what it is, but I can feel it. You know—this thing with old Graham . . ."

"What *thing*, Howard? Can you tell me? You don't know what you're talking about, do you?"

He shook his head. The saw started up outside again, and Howard could hear his uncle tossing boards around.

"Maybe that's good," she said. "Maybe that's some kind of charm. Take care of my daughter, though. She's not as tough as she thinks she is. We all lean on her." Aunt Edith smiled proudly then, and in that moment her face softened and she looked like Sylvia. Then the saw blade shrieked outside and the saw abruptly stopped.

"*Chingatha!*" Uncle Roy shouted, and the lines of worry and care and work reappeared in Aunt Edith's face. They both looked out the back window, where Uncle Roy wrenched at a board that was cocked up into the jammed saw blade.

"I don't see any blood," Aunt Edith said, pushing the window open. "What happened?"

"Nothing," Uncle Roy said, hammering at the piece of wood with his fist now.

"Turn the saw off, then. Watch out it doesn't come on while you're working with it."

"Overload switch shut down. It *can't* come on. Damn *it*," he shouted, looking around for something to hit it with and picking up a short length of two-by-four. His eyes were wide, as if he were going to show the jammed board a thing or two, and he smashed the two-by-four against the board, driving it down and out of the saw blade, denting and splitting the wood in the process. Once out of the blade, the board tumbled off the saw table onto the ground, and Uncle Roy slammed away at it another three or four times for good measure, splintering the board into rubbish. He stood over it, legs spread, his stomach heaving with exertion. Then he straightened up and yanked on his suspenders, kicking the pieces of board out of the way.

Aunt Edith still stared out of the open window, her hand over her mouth.

Uncle Roy gaped back in at her. "Had to kill the patient," he said. Then he felt around under the saw motor until he found the overload button. The saw whined and took off, and he reached up and shut it down with the on-off switch. "Sometimes you have to beat the bastards up," he said.

Aunt Edith stayed silent, but she gave Howard a look. He realized that he hadn't talked half enough to her. It was a shame that they couldn't have sat down over coffee and really chewed things over, gotten to know each other. There were a hundred questions he would have liked to ask her, about her and Mr. Jimmers, about Sylvia's father, about the spirit museum and their lives on the north coast. Uncle Roy was just then coming in at the door, though, and it was too late. It would have to wait.

On the back corner of the kitchen cabinet sat a ceramic Humpty Dumpty—exactly like the one that had fallen and broken in the earthquake. "Hey," Howard said. "Another one." He pointed at it, and Aunt Edith picked it up.

"Same one," she said. "Sylvia went to work on it with a tube of glue. She's good with her hands—good at fine work. You can hardly see the cracks."

Howard inspected it. "Just looks like cracks in the glaze, doesn't it? I like that, actually—like old china in an antique shop. I like a bit of age in his face. He doesn't look so smug."

Aunt Edith smiled at him. "That's our Sylvia. She has that effect on people sometimes."

"She got that from her mother," Uncle Roy said, kissing his wife on the cheek. Then he shrugged, threw his arms around her, bent her back clumsily, and kissed her on the lips. "Hah!" he said, straightening them both up. "Wonderful dinner last night, wasn't it? Sylvia hit the nail on the head with that place."

Aunt Edith smiled at Howard. "It was," she said. "We don't go out very often. When was the last time, Roy?"

"Back in eighty-three, wasn't it? Remember, we went to that polka dive. I could dance back then." He winked at Edith. "Dirty shame I had to go out last night, after we were through with dinner. Poor Bennet, he—"

"No need to lie," Edith said. "Howard's told me why you went out. There'll be other nights."

"By golly, you're right." Uncle Roy lit up, as if a momentous thought had just struck him. "There's one later today, isn't there?" He kissed Edith again. "Call me insatiable," he said.

"Call you an old fool," Edith told him, dusting the wood chips off the front of his shirt with her feather duster. She headed toward the door then. "I'll just let you men talk shop. I've got cleaning to do while you two live the life of Riley."

Uncle Roy watched her go. There was a look of longing in

his face. He sighed deeply. "Never underestimate the value of a wife," he said. Recovering, he asked, "How's the knee?" and poured the last of the cold coffee into his empty cup.

"Better, I think."

"Sandwich?"

"Sure." Howard realized that he was half starved.

Uncle Roy hauled out mustard and mayonnaise and lettuce and packages of bologna and American cheese. "Well," he said, "we skinned out of it last night." He went to the door and stuck his head out into the living room as if to see whether Aunt Edith was still around.

"What did you want the four hundred for?" Howard asked.

"Payola. I gave it to Mrs. Lamey." He stopped squirting mustard onto his bread slice and looked steadily at Howard, who widened his eyes in bewilderment.

"I told the cop that Bennet and I had just come up from Petaluma, where we'd got a load of chicken manure for old Cal down in Albion. You remember Cal. I said he'd paid us off, along with money he owed us for six more loads. And then when I dropped Bennet off, I figured that even though it was late, I'd knock on Mrs. Lamey's door and wake her up, in order to pay her overdue rent money. That way she could get the money into the bank tomorrow, which is today, of course. Anyway, I said that I couldn't wake her up at first so I knocked harder, and she must have waked up out of a dream or something and thought there was a nut at the door." Uncle Roy chuckled, layering meat and cheese onto the bread and smashing it all down with an inch of lettuce.

"So you gave *her* the four hundred?"

"Right there in front of the cop. Just handed it to her. Pissed her off, too."

"Did they check the story, the chicken manure story?"

"Damned right they did. These hick cops aren't stupid. They called Cal up and grilled him, right then and there. Used Mrs. Lamey's phone. We'd got to him first, of course, right after you left. Iron-clad story."

"How about the window? Did she accuse you of breaking the window?"

"Of course she did. But what was lying in the bushes outside? An ashtray. Someone had pretty clearly thrown it through earlier. Why? That's the question I asked, right there on the spot. It was obvious that I hadn't broken the window at all. Someone else had done it, *from inside the house.* When I knocked on the door a piece had fallen out. She didn't deny it. Not for a moment. She didn't want cops snooping around there, getting suspicious. You should have seen her. Looked like something out of a nightmare. I'm pretty sure the cop wanted to lock her up on general principles. They don't like being called out at midnight to deal with a batshit old woman when nothing's wrong except she's been offered four hundred dollars.

"Then of course there was the fish blood all over everything. I pointed that out before she had a chance to. 'What the hell's all this?' I said, stepping back. The cop looked hard at it. Stunk like a cannery. He thought it was some kind of creep joint. You could see it in his face. I reasoned with him, though—said she was an eccentric old woman but not dangerous. Luckily he didn't know who she really was. She probably owns the mortgage to his house. Anyway, it blew over and he left without any trouble. Between her place and Bennet's place, though, he was a confused man."

Uncle Roy was smiling now, wolfing down big bites of sandwich and talking around them. He had won through again, pulled himself out of another scrape. His army of irregulars stretched down the coast, into Albion. The day had been full of victories, although it was unclear to Howard whether any of the battles had been decisive. "How about the three that walked home?" Howard asked.

"To hell with them. Maybe they got run over by a lumber truck. And say, that reminds me, thanks again for getting a jump on that barn lumber. I made out all right on it. Bought a little something for Edith and Sylvia and took Edith out to dinner with what was left over. Squandered the hell out of it."

"Good for you. Sylvia showed me the sweater. She's nuts about it."

"She's a good girl. Sees things clearly. She gets her good looks from her mother, but I've had a little bit of influence on the way she thinks. I've worked hard to knock some of the practicality out of her. What I've been doing out back is trying to clean up the scrap that's left over. I figured to rip out another few feet of one-by-two, but it's so warped it keeps binding the blade up. It's firewood, I think."

"That was my conclusion. We ought to chop it into lengths and stack it."

Uncle Roy changed the subject, as if he'd gotten all the mileage out of the barn lumber he cared about. The practical business of turning it into firewood didn't interest him. "I hated like hell to give Mrs. Deventer's money to old Lamey last night, but what could I do?" He shrugged, to show that he'd had no other option. "Anyway, I owe it to Mrs. Deventer now, especially after what I told Lou Gibb."

Howard didn't bother to question his logic, to ask what it was Uncle Roy owed himself and Aunt Edith.

Uncle Roy shoved down the rest of his sandwich and then washed his hands at the sink. "Time to meet Bennet down to the harbor. What are you up to?"

"I thought I'd pay a visit to Jimmers'," Howard said.

"He won't be there. It's his town day."

Howard nodded. "I know."

Uncle Roy shrugged. "Do what you have to."

 **24**

"WE'RE certain he's not home, then?" Howard watched the ocean out the window as they drove south. The swell had come up considerably since last night, and the tide was higher than he would have liked. It looked as if he'd be getting wet again if they dawdled.

"Trust me. He comes up to town, up to the Safeway, once a week to buy supplies, and then he'll eat a late lunch down at the harbor. You can set your watch by it. He won't be home until dark. It's now or wait till next week, though, because if we show up while he's home, he won't let you anywhere near that passage. He'll thank you for bringing his clothes back and try to interest you in UFO sightings or disappearing rabbits or something. He'll be on his guard now, especially since the shed was stolen."

The day was beautiful—sunny and dry, almost warm. Howard wished they were simply going down to the beach for a picnic. There wasn't time for that sort of pleasure, though—maybe. Mr. Jimmers would be home before dark, carrying his bags of groceries. It wouldn't do to be confronted in the living room or to be trapped down on the beach and have to swim around the point again, especially if they were carrying the sketch.

They passed the driveway slowly, not turning off. Howard craned his neck to look back down toward the house, trying to catch a glimpse of Jimmers' car, just in case he hadn't made the usual Wednesday trip. He couldn't see anything at all, the car included. A quarter mile south, Sylvia pulled off at a turnout and cut the engine, and without waiting another moment they were out and walking back up the road just as fast as Howard could manage it. He felt almost spry, but he carried his cane in case he'd need it in the steep passage—and partly, he had to admit, out of superstition. He still didn't want to be without it. At the mouth of the driveway they held up, making sure there was no one out and about, and then slipped across and started down in the shadow of the woods.

For once, Howard thought, they could have used a little fog, if only to cover up all this breaking and entering. Abruptly he felt a twinge of doubt, but he shooed it out of his head like a pigeon out of the rafters. What he was going to steal didn't belong to Mr. Jimmers, and neither did the house he and Sylvia were about to break into. Both of them belonged to a dead man who had summoned Howard north, it seemed, to accomplish just such feats as this.

Jimmers' car was indeed gone, and the place was deserted. Where the shed used to be, out on the meadow, there was a rectangle of moldery-looking dead grass and dirt with a few stalky tendrils of Bermuda grass growing up through it. The ground was broken where the comers of the wooden skids had been yanked around, and there were four rusty old bottle jacks left behind that were still lying there in the dirt. It looked as if someone had been surprised in the middle of the theft and had to run for it. They had probably jacked up the comers enough to back the lift gate under the skids, then winched it forward onto the truck bed while they were rolling back up the highway.

Sylvia wandered off, back to the house, where she was methodically checking the doors and windows. Before joining her, Howard took a quick look over the edge of the cliff, to where the Studebaker sat rusting on the rocks. A pelican stood placidly on the car's roof, watching the waves break. Howard wondered whether it was his pelican, and just then the bird looked up at him. Howard waved and then headed for the house.

"How convenient," Sylvia said when Howard limped up, and she threw open one of the French doors that looked out onto the sea. The wind caught it and slammed it open against the edge of a table. She stepped back and gestured at the open door.

It turned out that simply walking in wasn't easy for Howard. Mr. Jimmers' presence seemed to fill the place, even if he himself was in town, shopping at the Safeway. "How can he be so sloppy?" Howard asked. "We could be anybody. And after he got beat over the head, too."

"We *are* anybody, aren't we?" Sylvia asked, pushing him through the doorway and into the interior. "You're looking a gift horse in the mouth. What did you want to do, break something, kick the door in?"

"Well . . ." Howard said. "You know what I mean." The house was cold and musty and dim, lit only by sunlight through the dirty windows.

"Should we check beneath the rock in the fireplace?" Sylvia asked.

"It's not there."

"You *know* that? What if it is there? We could be on the road in five minutes."

"It's not there. I had a dream that revealed where it's hidden. I told you that."

Sylvia grinned at him. "I love that kind of dream," she said. "I had one once where this enormous brass baby's head advised me to call a particular telephone number in order to establish contacts. That's what it said, 'contacts.' It was a UFO dream, you know, like I used to get." She took his elbow as she followed him up the dark stairs.

"Did you call the number? You must have. You couldn't bear not to."

"Of course I called the number."

Howard waited, but Sylvia said nothing more. "Well? Who was it?"

"I don't know. It sounded like a Chinese man, at a laundry, I think, so I hung up."

He waited again. "That's it? That's the whole story?"

"Uh-huh. I got busy with something and forgot all about it. I think I had to wash the dishes."

Mr. Jimmers had made a small effort to straighten up the attic, or at least to get the closet door closed. Half the stuff Howard had hauled out still sat on the floor, though, and the cut-up quilt lay heaped by the Morris chair. The desk, which Howard had tried to bar the door with, was shoved sideways into the middle of the room, and more of the closet debris lay on top of it. He pulled the closet door open, revealing the arched hole torn into the wall and the dim antechamber beyond.

"This is it, then?" Sylvia asked in a hesitant voice.

"The secret passage."

"What if Mr. Jimmers didn't go into town? What if he's down in there somewhere, waiting for us?"

"Why on earth would he be waiting for us?" Howard asked, alarmed at the notion of Jimmers lurking below them in the darkness. "Don't say that sort of thing."

She shined her flashlight into the interior, and the light glowed dimly down the stairwell. "Maybe he's got an axe down there."

"Would you shut up?"

"Did you read about those severed heads they found perched on guardrail posts? That wasn't two miles south of here. They never found the bodies. It's my guess that Jimmers ate them."

"Shine that light in here," he said, "and drop that sort of talk."

"I bet it's sharp enough to split a hair with, like in the cartoons. *Your* head goes first." She pushed him forward, handing him the flashlight.

"Shut that closet door, then," he said. "No use advertising that we're here."

Carrying his cane, he bent hesitantly into the passage, playing the light around on the walls. In the yellow glow, Howard could see that the stairwell was paneled and roofed with wooden car siding, painted white, with a raised framework of sticks forming a pattern of circles and crosses on the walls. The wood was scuffed and dented and dirty as if furniture or equipment of some sort had been hauled up and down for fifty years. It had been a well-used passage, not just the scrimshaw of an eccentric architect.

The corners were hung with cobweb and there were rat droppings and stains along the edges of the stair treads, which were worn in the centers from use. The passage, apparently, had been a regular thoroughfare. Howard almost preferred the utter darkness he had found there two days ago, which had hidden the evidence of spiders and rats.

When the stairs ended, they followed the tunnel down through the cliff itself. Root tendrils grew through the ceiling, and for a distance of three or four yards after the last stair tread, the walls of the tunnel had evidently been cut away with picks and then had been shored up with timbers. The dirt gave way to stone, though, and the rest of the tunnel seemed to Howard to be a natural cave—wet and dark and cold. Here and there the walls were streaked with veins of whitish crystal, smooth and shiny, almost like heavy snail tracks. They could hear the muffled crash

262

of waves now, and in minutes there was a sea wind in their faces and the smell of the ocean as they wound down around the last curving slope, skirting a pool of dark water left from the high tide, and stepping into the sunlight that poured into the tunnel mouth.

"I don't see any Studebaker," Sylvia said.

"Not so damned loud," Howard told her.

"Who's going to hear, the sea gulls?" She took his arm, leaning against him and gazing out into the empty sea. A foghorn sounded somewhere to the north, the faint sound of it carried on the wind. "You're really tensed up, aren't you?"

He said nothing, but then nodded. In truth he felt just a little like he had in his dreams—just when they were beginning and the pieces of the dreams were still misty and disconnected and yet he knew, even in sleep, that something was waiting. In contrast. Sylvia seemed fresh and exuberant with her face rouged by the wind and her hair wild.

"Romantic, isn't it?" she said. "I love deserted beaches."

He nodded, feeling it, too. There seemed always to be such an infernal hurry—four days of it now, always with desperate destinations and the hands of the clock spinning and spinning. They had a good three hours yet before Mr. Jimmers' return, though—time enough.

"We should have brought a blanket and a picnic lunch," Sylvia said.

"That's just what I was thinking not a half hour ago. Why didn't we?"

The world was utterly empty of anybody but the two of them. There was nothing but the rocky cove and their little corner of beach, mostly sheltered from the wind and from the eyes of people above. The cliffs rose sheer and stark behind them, faintly echoing the sound of lonesome gulls and of breaking waves. The sun shined down on the moving ocean, illuminating the pale green waves that quartered across the reefs, throwing themselves into the air in long sheets of spindrift foam.

Sylvia stood silently, holding on to his arm, watching the ocean, waiting, maybe, for him to speak or move. There was nothing to prevent him from kissing her, right then and there, except that suddenly he felt like a teenager, his heart fluttering and his mind troubled by what might lie within the glove box of the wrecked car. The dream anxiousness returned, and he looked nervously toward the rock shelf that separated them from the Studebaker.

"First things first," she said, and he wondered what she meant, what came first in her own mind just then.

He stepped up onto the rocks, though, and she followed, the two of them picking their way easily over the top. There sat the Studebaker, as ever, the front end crumpled, sun-dried kelp tangled around the tires. The doors hung open on broken hinges, the window glass shattered, and the hood was torn loose, hanging over the fender and crusted with sea salt. The windshield was a spiderweb of cracks.

The back windows were unbroken, and the radiant heat of the sun through the glass had warmed the interior. Sylvia clambered over the front seat, which was thrown forward into the dashboard, and settled herself into the back. Howard set his cane across the exposed engine, then pulled the front seat roughly back into place and climbed in behind the steering wheel.

There was a steering knob on the wheel, just as his dream had predicted. It was an oval of pale Lucite with an ivory ground. There was nothing in it—no symbols, no messages. The sight of it, though, made him hesitate, his hand on the button of the glove compartment. Again the unreality, the dream-likeness of the whole business washed over him. There was something mythological about it, as if at any moment some symbolic animal, a lamb or a kid or a centaur, would descend the rocky cliff above. There was something timeless about the moment, and he turned to look at Sylvia, who lounged on the seat, regarding him silently.

He opened the glove box. Inside lay a hammered-cooper rectangle about a half inch thick. He lifted it out and examined it. There were two rectangles, actually, pressed together, like a book without a spine. They were old-looking and etched with verdigris, and were sandwiched very tightly over a rubber flange. Four silver clips, cut into the shapes of tiny swords, were thrust through each of the corners, somehow fastening the two halves of the case. Cut deeply into the top plate was a rampant dragon with a knight on horseback before it, burying a lance into its heart. Below were the words "The Guild of St. George."

Howard hesitated half a moment, wondering how the sword clips were meant to work. They appeared to be corroded into place, almost fused to the metal plates. When he pulled at them, they slipped out impossibly easily, though—so easily that they might have fallen out if he had turned the case over.

The two halves parted just as easily, revealing the rubber flange laid into a channel inside as a seal. The sketch lay loosely on the bottom plate. It was almost translucent, the paper was so thin, and it showed a thousand creases, as if the paper were of such quality that it could be folded infinitely without any single crease being muddled by the rest. Sketched onto it were the figures that Howard remembered from Mr. Jimmers' copy.

"It's an unfolded piece of origami," Sylvia said suddenly into Howard's ear, startling him so that he nearly dropped it. "I wonder what this discoloration is," Sylvia said, leaning forward and looking over his shoulder. He could feel her breath on his neck. "Looks like coffee stains."

"Blood. That's what your father thinks."

"Remember those *Mad* magazine covers?" Sylvia asked. "Where you fold part of it over another part? Try to fold it the way Mr. Jimmers folded it."

On impulse Howard folded it lengthwise so that half the sketch disappeared. Lines joined, forming a picture.

"What is that?" Sylvia asked. "A tower or something?"

Something blocked the sun just then, throwing the car into shadow. Howard leaned forward and looked through the cracked front windshield, surprised to see what looked like a raincloud, and perhaps more on the horizon. "Or something," he said. A rush of embarrassment colored his face. It was a domed turret, unmistakably phallic-looking.

Sylvia reached up and pinched his ear, running her hand down the front of his shirt, and he realized that the heat that he felt wasn't embarrassment at all. "I think it's the Castle Perilous," she said, slumping back into the seat and untying her shoes.

"I think we're *in* the Castle Perilous."

"Or somewhere. Who cares?" She kicked her shoes off onto the floor and then shrugged out of her jacket. "Warm in here," she said, tossing the jacket down onto the shoes and pulling her sweater smooth.

He unfolded the sketch and centered it in its aperture. Then he laid the top plate back over the bottom, carefully sliding the tiny swords back into place with a faint click. He set the case on the dashboard. Sunlight shined onto it through the spiderwebbed window like lamplight through an aquarium full of diamonds, and the hammered copper glowed warmly.

Howard was filled with the inescapable knowledge that the sketch was his. It had belonged to Michael Graham, and to others before him, but now it was his, Howard's, for reasons he felt but didn't understand. The reasons didn't matter, though. His curiosity was beside the point.

Something vast—the energy of growing things, of the seasons, of the turning of the earth and of the stars themselves—flowed through him, filling him up like a goblet full of red wine.

He climbed hastily into the backseat with Sylvia, and she lay in his arms, the two of them sprawled together in the warmth of the autumn sun. She pulled his jacket off and pushed it onto the floor opposite her own and then began to unbutton his shirt. "What do you need," she whispered, "a written invitation?"

He put his finger to her lips to quiet her. If he had needed an invitation before, he didn't now. He was surprised at how easily he slipped her sweater off, how roomy the backseat of the old Studebaker seemed to be. They might as easily have been in a palace. "Remember that dead-end street?" he asked, recalling a shared moment of passion nearly twenty years past. "Near the cornfield? Not as much room in the back of a Dodge."

"You can't talk if I can't," she whispered to him, and put one hand gently over his mouth while the other hand worked deftly at his belt. There was no sound after that except breathing and the swish of fabric on skin and of the rising and falling of the ocean. The world around them, outside of the wrecked car, ceased to exist, and the whole notion of time disappeared with it.

He lay beneath her finally, gazing through the rear window at the afternoon sky. They didn't need to hurry. There was still time. And even if there wasn't, even if Mr. Jimmers was right then descending the coast road with his groceries, so what? The world had changed in the last hour, and couldn't be changed back.

He wondered if Sylvia was asleep now. She was breathing softly and regularly, like a contented cat. He had found her and the sketch both, in one languorous afternoon. The museum and his life down south were fast becoming little more than foggy memories, like the hazy recollection of a past life.

Puffy little clouds drifted slowly through the deep sky. Still half drugged with the smell of her hair and skin, he watched the clouds curiously through the rear window. There was something about them, about their shapes, that was deeply mysterious, like the five sketches on the paper in the copper case, like the suggestive pattern of a constellation in the night sky.

Two of the clouds floated above the three, all of them slipping slowly together until, for the space of a long moment, they formed the exact pattern of the clouds in his dream.

Startled, he half sat up, nearly tumbling Sylvia off onto the floor.

"Hey," she said. "You're pretty romantic."

"Sorry. I must have fallen asleep." He watched the clouds drift apart, his heart hammering.

"What's wrong?" she asked, brushing back her hair and looking at his face.

"Nothing. I thought for a moment that I was dreaming, that I dreamed this whole thing . . ."

"What *thing*, exactly?" She grinned at him, hooking her hands over his shoulders and pulling herself up along him so that her breasts brushed his chest. "This thing? You're not dreaming," she said. "I guarantee it."

He moved toward the edge of the seat so that they could lie side by side, and she kissed him on the lips and cheeks, running her left hand up and down his chest, kissing his neck, shutting his lips before he could say something about Mr. Jimmers' return, about the hour. And suddenly once again there was nothing to say, and time disappeared as they shifted positions, kneeling on their clothes, their body heat warming the car as the sun descended the sky.

"Time to be practical, maybe," Sylvia said later, as they lay quietly together again at last. "How come you wear two pairs of socks?"

"My feet get cold in the winter, especially when I'm in the same house as Artemis Jimmers." He took his socks from her and pulled them on, one inside the other. Now that they had decided to go, to get on with their lives, he was impatient to dress and be out of there. He felt both conspicuous and late. "What time is it?"

"Only four," she said. "No rush. I told you he probably wouldn't be home until after dark."

"Famous last words." He poked his head out of the car and surveyed the top of the surrounding cliffs. There was no one. He stepped out onto the rocks and pulled on his pants, holding the cuffs up out of the water in the shallow pools and watching the ocean. A wave surged up out of nowhere, rushing toward him, and he sat back down on the car seat, lifting his legs so that his feet rested on the floorboard. The tide had risen farther, and the ocean washed across the undercarriage of the car now, lapping at the open door. It swirled out again. "Better hurry. Either that or leave your shoes off. You'll be wading."

"Get out of the way, then," she said. "You're the slowpoke. I'd have been on the beach by now."

He pulled his own shoes on, and then his jacket. Then he reached in and picked up the sketch, checked to see that it was tightly sealed, and waited once more for the ocean to recede. "Bye," he said, stepping down onto the rock, grabbing his cane off the engine, and loping toward the shelf that ran out along the tunnel mouth. He clambered atop it and waited for her, giving her a hand up, and then they climbed down the other side and stood for a moment on the little slice of beach that was left dry, shaded entirely now from the sun. He kissed her one last time, and they stepped into the darkness of the tunnel.

 25

THEY walked along through the musty darkness, neither of them speaking, listening to the scraping of their shoes on the rocky floor of the tunnel. The flush of comfortable optimism that had filled the sun-warmed Studebaker had disappeared utterly, flown off like a wonderful bird in the few yards of their ascent back into the old house. As he wearily climbed the stairs, Howard's mind was full of a confusion of memories and rationalizations, excuses and half-built plans.

He leaned on his cane tiredly now and carried the copper plates with the sketch while Sylvia played the flashlight onto the stairs ahead of them. He imagined himself explaining to Uncle Roy and Aunt Edith that he and Sylvia . . . What did it mean? He would move out of the house; that was the first thing—maybe take a room at a bed-and-breakfast for the time being.

The closet door wouldn't open. Sylvia shined the light on it while Howard turned the doorknob, which twisted uselessly in his hand, clearly a dummy. Unbelieving, he pushed in on it and pulled out on it, turning it left and right, thinking that it was simply worn out, that something would catch and the door would open.

"It's useless," he said at last. "The knob just spins. We're trapped down here. Why the hell did I close the closet door?"

"Because we found it closed and you thought you could open it again."

"Do I break it down?"

268

"I don't see why you should."

"Do you want to swim, or pound like hell on the door and hope that Jimmers will hear us and let us out?"

She looked at him steadily. "There has to be another way out. You're the one who broke this hole in the wall. What did people do before that?"

"It was only recently walled up—maybe just a week or two ago—after the car went over the cliff, I'd bet. Before that there was probably a door in the back of the closet, but Mr. Jimmers wanted to make it all less obvious, so he took out the door and walled it up."

"Did you look for another way out?" Sylvia asked.

"No."

"Think about it—Mr. Jimmers has lived here for years, most of the time invisibly. You're the one who said that you didn't know he was here back when you came up in seventy-five. That's why I called him a mole man. He was living in secret rooms, probably beneath the house. It wasn't any big secret."

"How did he get in and out?"

"That's what I'm saying, isn't it?"

"The stairs outside," Howard said, suddenly remembering. "That door's locked, too, and the stairs are broken off. No use trying to find our way to it."

"That can't be it. If Mr. Jimmers had come and gone through that door, you would have seen him, wouldn't you?"

Howard shrugged. "Maybe, unless he hardly ever used it. Maybe he avoided coming and going when there was company in the house."

"There was always company in the house—at least a few locals helping Graham build things. Father was out here himself half the time, along with Mr. Bennet."

They turned around and Howard followed Sylvia back down the dark stairs. What she said made perfect sense. Of course there must be another exit, what with all this tunneling, all the excavation. The place was riddled with secret passages, and apparently with secret rooms, too, if this had been Mr. Jimmers' hideaway for so many years. He knocked on the paneling with his knuckles, hoping for some sort of telltale hollow sound. Sylvia shined the flashlight methodically, up and down the panels.

"Here it is," she said suddenly. They were halfway down, on the top landing of the final flight, where the stairs doubled back at the level of the second floor. There were handprints on the dirty white paint, visible in the flashlight beam. Above the handprints, recessed into the wall so as to be invisible unless seen from straight on, was a light switch. Howard pushed it and light glowed down from overhead, shining through a muslin shade hidden in the design of the ceiling panel and lighting the stairs all the way down to the mouth of the underground tunnel.

He pushed at the paneling tentatively, and when nothing happened he rapped on it with his knuckles again. It thumped hollowly. "This has got to be it," he said, pressing again. "Probably some sort of spring latch."

Sylvia stood studying the design of the paneling for a moment while Howard tapped and pushed. Then she reached out and pulled on one of the circles of wood laid on over the top of the panel. It rotated beneath her hand. There was a click, and the panel swung open an inch or so, revealing a head-high opening into a small dark room. Howard pushed the panel open gently, standing back out of the way, half expecting something to leap out at them.

Half a dozen wooden stairs led down into the room. Sylvia shined her flashlight down them, playing it onto the floor. A rat scurried away, out of the light, disappearing behind a tumble of cardboard boxes. The room smelled of damp wood and moldering paper. Howard leaned in and felt around on the wall, opposite where the passageway light switch was recessed into the panel. There was another switch. He pushed it and a bare bulb blinked on, hanging from a cord in the center of the ceiling.

"Storage room of some sort," Howard whispered, pointing out the obvious. There were dusty shelves of old books and piles of wooden crates and cardboard cartons. The room was windowless. They could hear the rat scratching in the corner near an old mimeograph machine that sat on a banged-up desk alongside an almost empty bottle of printing chemicals and a half dozen books. Pinned above it on the wall were dozens of star maps, overlapping each other and yellowed and drooping with age.

The pine floor was covered with a heavy layer of dust disturbed only by the footprints of rats, except for a clean, scuffed trail leading across toward a door surrounded by bookcases.

"This must be where he put together his publications," Sylvia said, pushing past Howard to the desk and picking up one of the scattered books. "Look, it's all flying saucer stuff. *Flying Saucers on the Attack, Aboard a Flying Saucer, Flying Saucers Uncensored, The Saucers of December. Saucer on a Hot Tin Roof.*"

"Let me see!"

"So what if I'm a liar? Hey, look. Here's Mr. Jimmers' own book, *The Night of the Saucer People*."

"You *are* a liar!"

"I swear. Here it is. Look at it."

Howard stepped across and took the book from her. "You didn't tell me he'd written a book. What a great title. What is it, fact or fiction?"

"Fiction, sort of. It's a novel about something that happened to him back in the forties. He worked on it forever, apparently, and finally had it self-published. It's dedicated to my mother even though it didn't come out until years after they parted—when he was out of the hospital for good, in 1958. I think."

"Really? Let me see it." He flipped through the first few pages, looking for a moment at the frontispiece illustration—a sleeping neighborhood beneath a night sky full of stars and with three lit-up saucers spinning in out of deep space. It was published, it said, in an edition of two hundred, in 1952 from the Phoenix Restaurant Press in San Francisco, priced at two dollars.

"You're way off on the date."

"It might have been fifty-seven. I can remember it, though—I was in Mrs. Webostad's class at that school in Lakewood we went to. That would have been second grade. It was my birthday and Mother had brought cupcakes to school. That's how I remember. Anyway, Mother found a copy of his book in the mail after school that day and started telling me all about this man named Mr. Jimmers, whom she'd known before she married Father. It was the first time she'd said anything about him. We've still got the book at home. When I was a kid I used to look at it all the time because of the pictures in it."

"Sorry," Howard said. "What about the pictures?"

"Nothing. I didn't say anything about the pictures. You weren't listening." She turned toward the door in the bookcases. "C'mon," she said.

He stared at the dedication page, which said simply, "For Edith," and then below that, "And for Sylvia." His thoughts leaped ahead, too quickly to keep up with. "Why," he started to ask, but then stopped himself and flipped back to the title page to check the publication date again. Mystified, he slipped the book beneath his coat, into an inside pocket.

"Look at this," Sylvia said, already gone on into an adjacent room.

Howard followed, down another flight of a half dozen stairs and into a room larger than the last. Along one wall was a heavy, scarred workbench with tools hung above it. On the floor sat an arc welder and drill press and grinder and heaps of brass and copper pipe and sheet metal. Rolled-up blueprints stood in a deep wooden box, crammed in together.

On the floor along the opposite wall, in an area otherwise clear of debris, crouched what was either an automobile or a vehicle from the stars. It appeared to be built around the chassis and body of an old Buick, with the top chopped and lowered to streamline it and the interior gutted and replaced with a single reclining, leather-covered seat. The whole car rested on a circular plate, with vents cut through the running boards and bent pipes running into and out of the sides of the vehicle.

It was old and dusty, most of the steel rusted and the chrome corroded. It looked like a nearly finished project that had been abandoned and then had sat in place for twenty or thirty years. The exterior of the vehicle was the weirdest part of the thing. It was covered with a profusion of tin toys, gaudily painted in bright primary colors—hundreds of toys, cemented on randomly like a confused army.

There were great-headed babies riding wind-up tricycles past lunatic birds with whirligig hats. There were cross-eyed elephants driving automobiles alongside ape-driven zeppelins, train engines, biplanes, and hot-air balloons carrying entire tin families. Tiny tin soldiers and zoo animals, circus acrobats and strolling couples dressed in wedding clothes were glued among the windup toys as if wandering between giants. In the center of the crowd, towering above them, sat a big-eyed Humpty Dumpty with a crown on his head. His arms apparently rotated and he held a baton as if he were leading an orchestra. At the side of the car, as if it were an immense wind-up toy, was a square brass key.

"He's a gluer," Howard said. "That's what I said, remember?"

"Yeah. I never knew anything about *this*, though. I knew he went into the hospital that first time because he suffered from some kind of gluer compulsion that had got out of hand, but I didn't know he'd kept at it."

"That's weirdly common around here, isn't it?"

"Ask Dad. He has a car of his own somewhere that he works on, or used to—I don't know where. He doesn't talk about it. It's like alcohol, I think. Some people get the habit worse than others. Some people glue in public; some of them are closet gluers."

"Uncle Roy is a closet gluer?"

"I think it has something to do with knowing Graham."

"With *this*, I think," Howard said, waving the copper case.

"Father refers to it as the Humpty Dumpty complex, the desire to always be putting things back together."

"Say," Howard said, "speaking of that—it was you who glued Aunt Edith's Humpty Dumpty back together again."

"Uh-huh. Better to keep things whole."

"You don't have a gluer vehicle stashed somewhere, do you? Covered up with origami fish or something?"

"A fleet of them, up in Willits. I sneak up there on weekends with Mrs. Deventer. What happens if we turn this crank?"

"The thing flies?"

"Where to? Do you realize that he's built this intricate contraption in a cellar? If it did fly, or drive or something, he couldn't get it out of here."

"He doesn't want to," Howard said. "What's important is the gluing. Go ahead and twist the crank."

"You do it."

"Remember that phone call you made, after the dream? Down to the Chinese laundry? The one where you hung up before you knew what the dream meant? This is a second chance for you. You can make up for that now, play out your destiny."

Sylvia considered this for a moment, then shrugged, widened her eyes at him, and twisted the crank twice. The works were stiff, and it took both hands to do it. There was an instant clanging of dozens of tiny bells and the whirling of tin propellers. The creatures on bicycles pedaled furiously, the front wheels rotating while the back wheels stayed in place, cemented to the body of the car. Trains tooted and spun their wheels, circus animals beat on drums and banged cymbals, and the Humpty Dumpty waved his baton, orchestrating the whole seething mass of toys. There was a sound like a fan starting up, and the entire plate with the car on top lifted off the ground three or four inches. A gust of air blew out from underneath, ruffling their hair for the space of thirty seconds, until the toys finally wound down and fell still and the ship bumped to the floor.

"That's something," said Howard. "Isn't it? A wind-up flying saucer car. Jimmers is a genius."

"It's indescribable. How long do you think it took him to build it?"

"Lord knows. There was a man who cut a chain out of a single toothpick. I saw it at Knott's Berry Farm once, in a display of miniatures. Took him years, and he went blind carving it, too."

"What does that have to do with this?"

"Nothing," Howard said. "I admire that sort of attention to worthless projects, though—doing things for the sheer sake of doing them."

Sylvia nodded. "I think it ought to be in a museum. Kids would go nuts over it."

"Imagine riding in it," Howard said. "Cranking it up and driving it into Fort Bragg at eight in the morning, dressed in a foil hat. What's the rest of this stuff in here?" Howard gestured around the room, at the heaped pipe and sheet metal. He stood up and moved across to lay his cane and the copper case on the benchtop, and then pulled out one of the blueprints in the box, half expecting to find the plans for a flying saucer. What he found was a diagram of the ghost machine, drawn to scale, covered with symbols and illegibly written notes that he didn't understand. "Oh-oh," he said, holding it up for Sylvia to see.

She stared at it until she understood what it was. Then she shrugged. "It doesn't change anything, really. Who cares where the damned thing came from? Somebody had to build it. Did you really expect it to generate ghosts?"

"I don't know," Howard said. "I guess I did, finally. If you had asked me three days ago, I would have laughed at the idea. Now I'm not laughing."

"Good. Don't laugh. Think of the one human being on earth who might build a machine that generates ghosts. It's Mr. Jimmers, isn't it? You're only skeptical because he built it in a basement on the coast. When you thought it was a hundred years old, you were half convinced. I don't think that anything's changed. Besides, how do you know who drew those plans? They look old to me."

He shrugged. "I don't. I wonder what else is in here."

"I think we should leave Mr. Jimmers' stuff alone. It's nearly six. If we were smart we'd find our way out of here. I don't feel right meddling with all of this. It's all private, hidden away down here like this. It's the last thirty years of Mr. Jimmers' life that we're pawing through. I shouldn't have wound up the flying saucer."

"No harm done, apparently. And if you hadn't wound it up, I would have."

"Let's go," she said, standing up. Howard rolled the drawing and shoved it back down into the box, then picked up his cane and the copper box. Together they went out through the next door and down more steps into yet another room, the flashlight illuminating a bed chamber with a single chair against one wall. There was a table with a lamp and hot plate and with open shelves above it lined with books and with cans of Spam and hash and hominy and Postum. A single faucet was piped straight out through the concrete wall. There was a small doorway leading into a toilet and yet another heavy, closed door like the one leading into the attic closet.

"That's it," Howard said, stepping across to open it up. Darkness lay beyond. There was no knob at all on the outside of the door. It led out, not in. "We need something to wedge it open," he said. "No telling where this goes. It can't go far, though. Shine the light through here."

It was a tunnel like in a mine, shored up with old railroad ties. The floor of the tunnel seemed to run gradually uphill. "Hold it for a moment," Howard said, "and throw some light on the shelves there." He stepped back into the room, grabbed a can of Spam, and set it onto the threshold, letting the door close against it. Then they set out down the passage, through two hundred feet of darkness, until once again they came to a door, this one barred with a heavy piece of wood slotted into the timber of the door frame. An immense garage-door spring hooked the center of the door to the post it was hinged to.

Howard pulled the bar out of its niche and hooked it back into a tremulous sort of clip, like the hold-down of a rat trap. Carefully he leaned all his weight into the door, pushing it open a couple of inches before it jammed against something that sounded like dead leaves and brushwood. Fresh air whirled in around them, smelling of the ocean and evergreen trees and eucalyptus.

"Hold on," Howard said, handing Sylvia the copper case and taking the flashlight from her. He loped back up the tunnel, put the Spam can back onto the shelf, and closed the door that the can had propped open. He hurried back toward the door into the woods again, anxious to get out.

In the woodsy darkness outside, tree branches swished together in the sea wind. There were no lights visible through the partly open door, no sign of the highway or the house, just the shadow of the woods in moonlight. Sylvia helped him shove the door farther open, skidding it through forest debris, the springs creaking and straining. They slid out, ducking beneath overhanging ferns and brush and letting the door pull shut behind them. The bar slammed down into place.

The door itself was set in the side of a hill, mostly hidden by vegetation and elaborately painted with depictions of twigs and leaves and ferns, most of the paint having been scoured off by weather and the wood beneath discolored to a granite shade of gray.

Up the hill above them a car roared past. They trudged along a tiny, disused trail, up onto the highway, and walked the quarter mile back up to their car. The sun was low in the sky, and the afternoon was dim with pending evening. They could see the house now, out on the bluffs. A light glowed downstairs and another upstairs. Smoke tumbled up out of the chimney. Mr. Jimmers was clearly home and had been home long enough to get a good fire going. He had probably been strolling around above them when they wound up the device in the cellar; perhaps he had been there for hours, knowing exactly what Howard was doing downstairs and no longer interested in stopping him.

"Maybe we can just sit here for a moment," Sylvia said, looking out over the ocean. The sky was clear and the distant edge of the ocean sparkled and danced in the dying sunlight. Howard put his arm around her shoulder, wishing that the Toyota didn't have bucket seats. "Not just now," she said, still looking out the window. She turned and smiled at him briefly, then went back to looking out the window.

The copper case sat on the dashboard. Howard picked it up. It was warm, maybe because he'd been carrying it. Its warmth felt like something else, though—as if it were alive in some strange way or charged with barely contained energy. He pulled the plates apart and lifted out the sketch, holding it up in the sunlight so that the paper was translucent. Clearly it had been pressed from a mixture containing leaves and flower petals. A stem of wheat lay outlined like a watermark within the paper, striated by the hundreds of creases.

"Let me see it," Sylvia said.

For a moment Howard hesitated. He was filled with the notion that the sketch was his in some fundamental, mystical sense and that he shouldn't be passing it around to satisfy idle curiosity. "Sure," he said, feeling foolish. "This paper seems so delicate, I can't imagine how it's held together through so many foldings. You'd think it would fall to pieces like an old road map."

"I think it was meant to be folded," Sylvia said. "It's like a puzzle. I can see the start of a few different shapes here. I think I can follow these two folds and get the start of a simple balloon."

"An egg, maybe?"

"I don't see an egg."

"What else?"

"Maybe a fish. I don't know. I'd have to start on one of them in order to see steps farther along. Like following a map again or working your way through a maze. It's impossible to see connections unless you take them one at a time."

"Go ahead and fold it."

She looked at him and shook her head.

"Why not?"

"It's like Mr. Jimmers' car in the basement," she said. "I felt like I was meddling when I wound it up."

"This doesn't belong to Mr. Jimmers, does it? It belongs to me."

"It does?"

"Who else?"

She shrugged. "I'd feel like I was . . . *intruding* or something."

"That's a strange word," Howard said. "Intruding on what? What do you mean intruding?"

"I don't know. What do you think this *is*, anyway?"

"Your father seems to think it's the Grail."

"Then *you* fold the damned thing up. I won't have anything to do with folding it up." She gave it back to him, but kept looking at it, as if she were studying it with something like longing. "It has some sort of effect on you, doesn't it?"

"Like out on the beach there, in the Studebaker," Howard said.

"We shouldn't have done that. We've known for years that we couldn't, or shouldn't."

"Now we did. Simple as that. It was nice, wasn't it?"

"Nice, yes," she said, "but maybe not good."

"Maybe it *was* good. What happens if I fold it lengthwise, like this?" Howard folded it down the center. There was no need to run his thumb and forefinger along the crease. It folded flat by itself, as if the fold were part of its natural state. The car shook in the wind just then and Sylvia jumped.

"God," she said. "I thought someone had stood on the bumper. That thing makes me nervous as hell."

"So what have I started? I could fold it into the shape of a diamond, I guess. I can't see past that."

"Might be anything. You've got to picture it three-dimensionally. Haven't you ever taken those tests where you have to guess

277

what an unfolded box will look like when it's folded up?"

"I always failed that sort of test," Howard said. "To me they always look like crossword puzzles for morons."

Sylvia pointed out the passenger-side window. The sun was just then disappearing into the sea. "Look at the sun now," she said. "The sky around it is hazy. The sun's almost red."

"Sailor's delight," Howard said. "How did that rhyme go? 'Midget at morning, sailor take warning. Midget at night, sailor's delight.' "

She stared at the folded paper, concentrating on it.

"Pretty funny, eh?"

"Sure. What did you say? Fold it again, in half. Turn it into a small square. I think I see a cup in it."

Howard folded it just as the wind shook the car again, sailing up and over the bluffs, bending the dead grasses almost flat and howling around the door frames. Sylvia pulled her coat out of the back and jammed it between the seats, sliding over beside Howard, snuggling up to him. "Now open it up and tuck the two top corners in, diagonally."

Darkness fell across the car now as if a vast shadow had blotted out any light left over from the now-departed sun. There was the sound of distant thunder, and Howard and Sylvia looked out through the windshield to find that great black clouds were roiling in double time over the water, soaring along madly in the wind, driving toward land. Lightning forked down toward the ocean, which leaped now with whitecaps. Long, black swells drove in to smash against the rocks with a concussion the two of them could hear even above the wind.

For the moment they ignored the partly folded sketch that Howard held in his hands, and they watched the storm sweep toward them, seeming almost to be pulling water upward out of the Pacific and into the clouds. Way out over the ocean a waterspout rose momentarily and then fell, and within seconds rain flailed against the car, obscuring the ocean entirely.

There were headlights on the highway suddenly, and a car swerved toward them, half on the wrong side of the road. It swung wildly back into its own lane, running up onto the right shoulder and glancing off the rock face of the cliff, the driver honking uselessly as he drove past, disappearing through the deluge.

Rain beat down now in vast waves, sluicing sideways into the car. It forced its way past the weather stripping around the doors and windows and ran in rivulets down the inside of the passenger door to pool up on the mat. Sylvia tried to crank the window shut, but it was already tight.

"It won't last long," Howard half shouted, squinting to see through the murk and trying to be heard above the roar of rain drumming against the roof. He could see nothing in the sky now, only a black, low canopy. Water poured down the inside edge of the highway in a muddy torrent, wrapping around the cliffside and rushing beneath the car and over the cliff in a cataract. Howard switched on the headlights, but most of the light was thrown back at them, reflected off the heavy curtain of rain. A shower of fist-sized rocks tumbled down the cliff, scattering across the highway in front of them before being swept up in the torrent.

"We can't stay here," Sylvia said. "There'll be slides in weather like this. A few years ago fifty yards of road just fell into the ocean. It was a month before it was open to travel again. You had to drive inland nearly to Philo and then back out to Elk."

"Fine," Howard said. "We *can't* go anywhere. We can't see ten feet." He turned the radio on but there was nothing but static. Three rapid flashes of lightning lit the dark landscape like noonday, and Sylvia screamed, jamming herself back into Howard so that he was crushed against the door handle. An explosion of thunder masked her scream, and in the silence that followed there was a furious knocking at the window on the passenger side and a face peering in at them, its mouth working as if it were shouting something.

Howard lunged for the ignition, instantly remembering every apocryphal story about cult murders and escaped lunatics with hook arms. He twisted the key, wondering how the hell he was going to turn around on the flooded highway. Forget turning around. He threw the car into gear and edged forward, looking wildly at the face in the window. Sylvia was shouting at him, slugging him on the arm.

"It's Jimmers!" she shouted. "Wait! It's just Jimmers!"

Howard stepped on the brake, his hand on the key again. She was right. It was Jimmers, his hair wild in the wind. Rain poured off his yellow rain slicker, beating against his back as he held on to both door handles for balance. Howard cut the engine and Sylvia unlocked the rear door, letting Jimmers pull it open as he fought against the gale. Rain hammered in around his shoulders as he crammed himself into the backseat, and the door smashed shut behind him, driven by the wind.

"Unfold the paper," he gasped.

26

HOWARD looked at him, not understanding what he meant. "The sketch. Unfold it." He pointed at Howard's hand, which was still closed over the folded paper. Howard opened the paper up so that it lay flat again. Almost at once the storm began to abate. There was a flash or two of distant lightning but only the vague echo of thunder now. The wind fell off and the rain lessened to a sprinkle. Out over the ocean the starry sky shone through torn-apart clouds that seemed to sail away in all directions at once, leaving the windswept sky clear again.

"Perhaps you'd better quit fiddling with it and put it away," Mr. Jimmers said slowly, as if he were talking to a man with a loaded gun.

Howard laid it back into its case, clipping the thing shut and setting it onto the dashboard again. "What did I do?" he asked.

"Very simply, you called up a storm. Or started to at any rate."

"*Started* to?"

"It was nothing alongside what it might have been. It was the lemon next to the pie."

"The pie?" Howard said.

"It was my fault," Sylvia said. "I was the one who wanted to fold it."

"Fault doesn't enter in." Mr. Jimmers wiped his hair back, wringing water down his raincoat.

"How did you know?" Howard asked. "I'm just curious. Were you home all afternoon?"

"I went up to town to buy groceries and got back about a half hour ago. I spotted your car through the attic telescope and so knew it was you two banging around down below. And then when the storm rose out of nowhere like that, I went upstairs again, and there you were, sitting in your car on the roadside, meddling with the . . . sketch, oblivious to the danger."

"And you let us have the sketch, then, when you knew it was us in the cellars."

"You knew where it was," Jimmers said.

"What difference does that make?"

Mr. Jimmers stared out of the window. Suddenly he began shivering, and Sylvia said, "Start up the heater."

"That's the stuff," Mr. Jimmers said. "A cup of Postum would be nice, wouldn't it? I'm going to pop back up to the house and brew one, but you won't want to come along. There was trouble down at the harbor. I saw it from the road on the way back down here. You'll want to have a look. Fire department was there. It looked like a fire in among the trailers, maybe. A couple of eucalyptus trees were burning like torches."

He paused for a moment to contemplate before going on, and then said tiredly, "A week ago it wouldn't have mattered what you wanted. It wasn't mine to give, was it? But now poor old Graham is dead and someone's got to carry on. I believe that's you. It certainly isn't me."

"Why isn't it you?" Howard asked softly.

"Because I'm a pawn," Mr. Jimmers said sadly. "You're the king, aren't you? Promise me you'll remember something that I once forgot. Heloise Lamey is a dangerous adversary. The people who surround her are thugs and morons. She uses them as easily as she once used me. I thought I loved her once, years ago, and betrayed poor Graham by giving the sketch, as you call it, to her. I simply gave it away. I did it out of love, mind you. No one can say that I didn't. I had good intentions in some ways, but as they say, the road to hell is paved with that sort of brick. She threw me out when she thought she had what she wanted, and I knew I had betrayed my friend for nothing. Then it turned out that Graham had manipulated all of us by manufacturing a spurious sketch, and she had got nothing, after all.

"I was furious with him. He had seen the truth all along, seen straight through both of us, and yet had allowed me to betray him, and because of it I lost everything. I moved north and was living in the old Vance Hotel, on Second Street up in Eureka, when he found me at last and brought me back, saying that he was sorry to have used me to fight a battle in a war that I hadn't signed up for. He *hadn't* used me, though. I was sharp enough to see that. I had used him, and for purely selfish reasons. It's been my perpetual shame. I'm . . . unworthy. I won't be the man to pretend to protect the thing I once betrayed."

"That's the worst sort of rubbish," Sylvia said. "Tell it to the prodigal son."

Mr. Jimmers looked vaguely startled, as if he hadn't expected her to disagree. It had sounded like he was reciting an apology that he had worked out over and over for twenty-odd years. "Pardon me?" he said.

"That's all nonsense," Sylvia said. "It's true, maybe. The facts are. I'm not saying you're lying about what happened. But all these years of locking yourself away, living in your cellar—that's more a matter of feeling sorry for yourself, isn't it?"

"Well, yes, I suppose it is. How transparent I've become." He smiled at her, putting on his old theatrical face but making a bad show of it. He looked hard at her for a few seconds before putting his hand on the door handle. For a moment Howard thought of pulling out the book that he had in his pocket, of asking Mr. Jimmers about it outright. But he had already presumed too much, involved himself in other people's business.

"We ought to get down to the harbor," he said to Sylvia.

"Yes, you should," Mr. Jimmers said.

"You'll be all right?" Sylvia asked him.

"Right as rain." He stepped out onto the muddy roadside and half closed the door before pulling it back open. "Remember what I said about Heloise Lamey. There's trouble on the boil. She'll see through this storm, too," he said to Howard, looking grave now. "They'll know you've got it, and they'll know you've used it."

MUCK-COLORED lilies, soft-throated and with curved, heavy-headed stamens, lay scattered across the bed, which had been partly covered with a sheet dyed red. A thick, milky-pink fluid leaked slowly out onto the sheet. The color of the flowers was nearly indescribable, as was their odor, which reminded Stoat of a pig farm. Their throats were almost black, fading to the brown-ocher of old blood at the outer rim of the petal.

A small earthen pot half full of muddy, grassy water sat on a little table beside the bed, as did a ceramic tray on which sat a slice of the cane that they had begun to cut up last night, before Howard Barton exploded the clothes dryer and stole the cane back.

"Those lilies have to be your most startling creation," Stoat told her, not particularly happily. He sat in a chair near the window, peering out through the curtain at the street now and then. He yawned and rubbed his face blearily. "You get used to the smell, I suppose."

She said nothing, and after a moment he said, "Maybe it's a necessary hazard to the occupation of power broker—living in the middle of bad smells."

Still she said nothing, but went about her business humming. He seemed determined to make her speak, to make her acknowledge his existence. "Curious thing about the water, too. I don't see why we can't bottle it. Make a fortune."

She took a step back and surveyed the bed, looking satisfied with what she had accomplished so far. "Because it's already stopped flowing," she said to him. "I found a half dozen indentations altogether—all of them in the backyard of that little hovel halfway down the block. I assume that he ran through the backyard in an effort to elude the three of you, although I can't for the life of me determine why he bothered at all. Collectively you don't amount to much of a threat. The other boys sleeping the afternoon away, I suppose?"

Now it was Stoat who didn't respond, but looked out the window again instead. After a minute of silence he said, "He'll be full of regrets before the night is through. You'll have some satisfaction out of it."

"He who?"

"The fat man. The other one—Howard—what will he be full of? You tell me. Silver or lead?"

Mrs. Lamey began to hum again as she worked away at one of the lilies, pressing the liquid out of it with her fingers so that it dribbled into the convex hollow of a tautened patch of silk cloth. "Too late for silver," she said. Then, after a pause, "Pity the water dried up so quickly. The earth behind the house was soft, or the cane wouldn't have left any indentation at all. It was like six little fairyland springs—artesian water bubbling up through wells the size of a nickel and no deeper than your knuckle, flowing out into the grass. A cat was actually drinking at one of them when I came along and found them. It was a very satisfied-looking creature, quite clearly drunk, too. Dreams of springtime in its eyes. Within ten minutes of my coming all six were dry."

"I don't believe that for a moment," Stoat said facetiously, letting the curtain drop. "Surely your coming had nothing to do with it . . ." He fell silent. There was a look on her face that suggested she was in no mood to put up with him. "What interest do you have in—what did you call it? Inglenook Fen? Why not some gesture more grand than that? Why not Lake Tahoe? Why can't you dry up Lake Tahoe?"

She shrugged. "I rather like Lake Tahoe. I own considerable interest in a casino at Lake Tahoe. I don't require grand gestures, anyway. They're inartistic and they call attention to one, don't they? If we succeed this afternoon, though, I'd like to see what I can do with some rather large and useful reservoir. Hetch Hetchy, I think."

"Why *my* neighborhood?"

"The East Bay is so utterly dependent on that one source, isn't it? Imagine what two years of absolute drought would do to them? They would begin to *think* differently, and that's appealing to me. I would love to have been in Los Angeles in the thirties and forties and had a hand in draining the Owens Valley. For today, though, I'll concentrate on Inglenook Fen. It's always been one of my very favorite places—a remnant of the ice age. Did you know that?"

"Fascinating," he said. "Kill it as quick as you can."

"I used to go out there to walk on the dunes. I've come to think of it as my own, I guess. I'm just a nostalgic old fool." For a moment her face was overcome with a wistful, faraway look, as if she were remembering a distant, more pleasant time—days, maybe, when she could see some point in walking on the dunes, or perhaps when she had gone out walking with someone else, before that had all been spoiled for her. Just as suddenly as the wistful look had appeared, it was gone, and she applied herself to her work.

She finished with the lilies, having pressed all the juices out of them onto the silk, and she picked up a knife and swept it back and forth across the surface of the cloth, forcing the heavy juices through it, collecting the sieved liquid drop by drop on a circular mirror. "Water is everything, you know. Money is nothing. Would you own north Africa, or would you own the Nile? And imagine the billions of gallons of water flowing south through this state right now, through the California Aqueduct alone, irrigating tens of millions of acres of orchards and vineyards and cotton and rice fields. What if one could shut off the flow, like water out of a sink? Imagine two or three snowless years in the Sierra Nevada. No ice pack. No rain at all across the Northwest. Water is power. It's more than that. It's life and death."

Stoat had fallen silent again. There was no arguing with her about that. She wasn't talking to him, anyway. She was talking to hear her head rattle. He wondered uneasily just how badly she needed him. An organization was necessary, perhaps, when you were in the real estate business, bleeding small animals like

Mrs. Deventer or Roy Barton, or when stalking bigger game—meddling with oil drilling rights offshore, lobbying the Coastal Commission. But this talk about water was something else. He had no intrinsic stake in that. In a moment she would simply dismiss him. There were secrets that she wouldn't reveal to him, and that was dangerous and tiresome. He hadn't bought in to that.

"Well," she said. "It's nearly time for me to be about my business. I'll see you at the motel later this evening?"

He nodded, putting on a smile. He was being invited to leave. There was no answering her, really—just obedience.

HE closed the door after himself, and she waited, listening to his footsteps on the stairs. Through the gap in the curtains she watched him drive off. Then she dialed the phone. "Glenwood," she said into the receiver. "It's time." She listened for a moment and then said, "Good. We want it all, this time—Jimmers' device, all of it. We want to put an end to all their shenanigans Do you understand me? Be thorough, but don't be foolish."

HOWARD and Sylvia had to park up the hill and walk down to the harbor, past Mrs. Deventer's house, where the half-wrecked Pontiac sat in the driveway. The road was cluttered with cars full of people who had come down to watch the fire and who were maneuvering now to get back out. Down below, fire trucks and equipment had blocked Harbor Drive, and firemen were spraying the burned-down remains of the old icehouse with hoses. A crowd of people milled around talking and speculating.

Sylvia started running, and Howard followed her, carrying his cane. There was no ambulance, no evidence that anyone was hurt. The haunted house had been burned pretty much out of existence, though. The walls were nothing but blackened studs and the roof had caved in right through the first-floor ceiling. The stairs were still there, leading nowhere, and with tendrils of white smoke curling up through them from where a fireman mopped up the last live embers with a fine spray. The wind off the ocean was full of the smell of wet, charred wood.

A squad car was parked behind Lou Gibb's fish restaurant, where old Bennet sat on an upturned plastic crate, pressing a bloodstained handkerchief across the back of his head. His hands and arms were smeared with ash, and his khaki pants were nearly black with it. He nodded in response to something a policeman asked him, and the man jotted notes in a spiral binder. Sylvia headed straight for them.

Howard saw Mrs. Deventer herself just then, standing at the edge of a group of onlookers. Her right arm was in a sling and in her left hand she carried a closed umbrella. She wore an apron, too, as if she'd been baking cookies and the fire had interrupted her.

"Howard!" Bennet said when Howard and Sylvia strode up. Then to the policeman he said, "This is Howard Barton, Roy Barton's nephew."

"Where's Father?" Sylvia asked.

"He's fine. Went down to Caspar before this all started."

The policeman stroked his mustache and sized Howard up suspiciously. Then he seemed to recognize Sylvia and brightened a little, growing chatty. "You work at the boutique down in Mendo, don't you?"

"That's right," she said. "I'm the owner, actually. I'm Roy Barton's daughter, Sylvia."

"I bought my wife a shawl in there about a month ago. Bright green . . ."

"With big red paisleys. I remember it. Very Christmasy. Weren't you in with a little boy who wanted an ice cream?"

"That's it! That was me. I'll be damned," he said, then turned to Howard, less suspicious now. "And you're Barton's nephew?"

"Howard Barton. I'm visiting from down south. What's happened?"

Mrs. Deventer's voice answered from behind him. "There's been a fire," she said.

Howard turned and nodded politely. "Hello, Mrs. Deventer," he said. "You must be freezing, out in this kind of weather without a coat." He took his jacket off and held it out to her. Without protesting she slipped one arm into it, and pulled the opposite shoulder around, clutching it shut across the plaster cast on her left forearm.

"Young men are so attentive," she said to Sylvia.

The policeman looked suddenly irritated, as if he had work to do and it wasn't being done. He ignored Mrs. Deventer's remark about the fire and said to Howard, "Looks to me like the old icehouse has burned down. It and a couple of trees. Mr. Bennet here claims that he and Mr. Barton were putting together some sort of fun house for Halloween."

"We pulled a temporary license," Bennet said. "Didn't we, Syl?"

286

"That's right," Sylvia said. "I turned in the application myself."

"Mr. Barton was particularly proud of his store window mannequins," Mrs. Deventer said. "He had some notion of filling their heads with noodles. I'm the one who cooked the noodles for him, aren't I?" She addressed the question to Sylvia, but clearly in order to set the policeman straight.

"Fine," said the cop. "The license isn't the issue. The license doesn't figure into the picture anymore, does it?" He waved at the smoking building. "Mr. Barton along with Mr. Bennet here were involved in a little imbroglio late last night down in Mendocino. Don't know anything about that, do you?" He looked as Sylvia.

"Not a thing," she said. "Father sometimes has a little too much fun, I guess. He's harmless, though." She cast the policeman a winning smile and he smiled back.

"We'd had a couple of drinks on the way back up from Albion," Bennet said. "Roy got a little loud with his landlady, that's all."

"And today someone burns him out." The cop's smile vanished.

"*Where* is he?" Sylvia asked, looking at Bennet.

The policeman spoke first. "That's it, isn't it? We don't know where he is. Down in Caspar is what Mr. Bennet says. We'd like to ask him a thing or two when he surfaces."

"*Surfaces*?" Howard asked. "What's he suspected of? What's he done?"

"Clear case of arson," the cop said.

"You think he burned his own place down, his own haunted house? He's been working on this for weeks. Why in the hell would he do something like that?"

"Lou Gibb owns the place," Bennet put in. "They figure that he *hired* Roy to burn it down. Worth more burned to a cinder than turned into a haunted house. That's the logic. But who gave me this sock on the head? That's what I want to know. It wasn't Roy Barton. Thieves, that's what I think. I described the man that did it. Sneaked right up behind me. I stood up and saw him clear enough before he hit me, and it wasn't Roy Barton, not unless he was wearing a skinny-man costume. Unless of course Lou Gibb hired Roy to hire this man to hit me. If I'd have been thinking, I'd have hired him to hire me to hit myself, and we could have all kept our money and went home."

The cop frowned. "There's no call to get worked up, Mr. Bennet."

"I don't like all this hitting," Mrs. Deventer said. "Why does everyone have to be hitting each other all the time? The television is full of it."

"That's the truth," Bennet said.

Mrs. Deventer smiled suddenly. "It was my young man who pulled Mr. Bennet from the flames."

"Stoat," Bennet said.

"Was it?" Howard asked, not knowing exactly what this meant.

"Yes, it was," Mrs. Deventer said. "He ran straight in and hauled Mr. Bennet out of there. And very grateful for it Mr. Bennet was, too."

Bennet gave Howard a look. "The boy ought to get an award," he said.

The cop squinted at Bennet. "You know," he said, "I can't figure your *tone* here. Your *attitude*. Man pulls you out of a burning building and you get hostile about it. That doesn't make any sense, does it?"

"No," said Mr. Bennet. "I don't guess it does." He looked sheepish for a moment. "It's this knock on the head. It's been a rough night. Where'd that young man of yours go?" he asked Mrs. Deventer. "I'd like to thank him personally, give him a little gift."

"He's not the sort to bask in glory," she said proudly. "It's not in his nature. He did what he could and went on his way. He's so thoughtful."

"He's a prince," Howard said.

The policeman waited Mrs. Deventer out, smiling widely and nodding his head. "Thank you for your insights," he said to her. "I'll see what I can do to get the boy a written commendation of some sort." Then to Sylvia and Howard he said, "You've got to admit that there isn't much motive for robbery here, regardless of what Mr. Bennet says." He gestured toward the wall of the restaurant, back into the shadows. "No thief in his right mind wants this kind of trash." There in a charred heap lay the remains of the two Brainiacs alongside the partly melted ice chest, which stood open now, the cow brains inside cooked white and standing in a half inch of milky water. Pieces of blackened skeleton lay in a pile, too, along with a half dozen jack-o'-lanterns that somehow had survived the blaze.

"My God," said Mrs. Deventer, covering her mouth with her hands. "It's the dummies. And Mr. Barton was so proud of them, too."

"That's all that's left," Bennet said sadly. "Just the stuff that was sitting in the front room. I managed to get that much out. Rest of it's charcoal. The bastards pretty much wiped us out. Thank God Roy hadn't brought the eyeballs down yet or the equipment for the ghost woman on the stairs. If it hadn't been for that freak storm, the fire would have torn through the whole damned harbor in a wind like this. Rain put it right out, though. It was an act of God."

Mrs. Deventer nodded.

"That's true enough," the cop said. "First rain we've had, too, in months." Just then there was a blast of static on the patrol car radio followed by someone chattering. He nodded at the three of them and hurried across to the car, climbing in and talking back to the radio. He slid entirely in and fired up the engine, then shouted through the open window on the passenger side, "Tell Mr. Barton to come downtown when you see him. Either that, or we'll be around to pick him up. Thanks a lot, folks." With that, he drove off up the hill.

"They don't believe that nonsense about Uncle Roy and the insurance," Sylvia said flatly.

Bennet touched his forehead gingerly. "Of course they don't. Icehouse wasn't even insured. Gibb put up the money for liability insurance for a month, just until after Halloween. Then the place was coming down. A phone call or two would blow a hole in the whole theory. What they probably think is that we were up to something else here—hustling dope, maybe—and a deal went bad. That would make more sense, except that there's people swarming through here all the time—tourists, locals. Door stands open all day. We haven't kept any secrets here. What I think is that they'll end up writing the whole thing off to a nut. Come on inside."

"I'll just be walking back up the hill," Mrs. Deventer said, starting out in that direction.

Bennet waved at her and then stood up and opened the back door of the fish restaurant, leading Howard and Sylvia into the kitchen, where Lou Gibb filleted fish at a long steel counter. A busboy sloshed a mop around the floor. Through the dining room door Howard could see that the restaurant was empty of customers. "My doggone coat," he said to Sylvia.

"Go get it," she told him.

He shook his head. "It'll give me an excuse to drop past her house. Let her wear it home. She needs it on a night like this."

"Still waiting for the phone call," Gibb said to Bennet, and then pulled three beers out of a refrigerator, handing one to each of them. "I've locked up for the day. Sent everyone home. Sit down." He pulled a stool away from the wall, nodding Sylvia toward it. "You take off, Jack," he said to the busboy, who put the mop back into the bucket, untied his apron, and stepped out the back door.

"So what's Father doing down in Caspar?" she asked.

"She don't know?" Gibb looked up suddenly at Bennet, who shook his head.

"He's not down in Caspar," Bennet said. "We're not sure where he is. We think he's all right. No reason that he shouldn't be all right."

"What do you mean?" she asked, standing back up.

"They've got him. I couldn't say anything in front of the cop."

"*Who's* got him?"

"We all know who's got him, don't we? It's her. The old woman. They knocked me on the head, grabbed him, and burned the icehouse. Out of spite, I guess. After last night."

"Did they get the machine?" Howard asked.

Bennet shook his head. "I drove it up to the Georgia-Pacific yard this morning. Turned out to be a good thing. MacDonald's looking out for it. He's moved it across town by now. No one knows where but him."

"We don't *know* it's them," Lou Gibb said to Sylvia. "Might have been Jimmers. He was down here this afternoon, snooping around. He ate lunch and then went round back and had it out with Roy. They got pretty hot under the collar. Regular shouting match. Jimmers went off mad as hell. He might have come back and torched the place just as easy as anyone else. Maybe he finally went off the deep end."

"We just left him," Howard said. "He didn't have anything to do with anything. Last thing he'd do is kidnap Uncle Roy or burn down the haunted house. Take my word for it. It doesn't matter how mad he might have been this afternoon."

Gibb shrugged. "I guess I know that. But it would have made things easier if it *was* Jimmers, wouldn't it?"

Sylvia moved toward the door. "We've got to go," she said to Howard as soon as Gibb had finished talking. "At least I do. We can't leave Mother alone. They might have gone there, too."

"She's safe," Bennet said. "I talked to her fifteen minutes ago."

"I'm more help there," Sylvia said resolutely.

"Call us first thing you hear anything," Howard said, following Sylvia out into the evening.

Most of the crowd had dispersed by then. Harbor Drive was empty of parked cars and the only people milling around the burned icehouse were local children from the house trailers, throwing rocks at each other and dodging in and out behind buildings and fences and trees. Two firemen rolled up hoses while a couple more poked through the ashes along with a policeman and a city official of some sort wearing a suit and a pair of knee-high rubber boots.

Howard looked back at the old icehouse as they trudged silently up the hill. Burned buildings had always seemed lonesome and horrifying to him in some way all their own. There was something final and deadening and dark about them that suggested the worst kind of tragedy, even if, as was true of the icehouse, they were going to be torn down, anyway. It occurred to him that at least now Uncle Roy wouldn't have to face the failure of another doomed business venture. Except, of course, that the venture might have worked. Or at least if it hadn't, Uncle Roy ought to have been able to take a stab at it. Perhaps that's what made the burned icehouse such a sad thing—that one of his uncle's dreams had gone up with it, and it was dreams, largely, that kept Uncle Roy afloat.

They were almost to the car when they heard the phone ring, back down on the outside wall of the restaurant. They turned and ran without saying a word, watching Gibb come out of the back door to answer it, followed by Bennet, who cocked his head by the receiver, listening to the call. Gibb had already hung up by the time Howard and Sylvia got there. He stood scowling, deep in thought, and Bennet had sat down tiredly again on the plastic crate. "It's them," he said to Sylvia. "They contacted your mother. She just hung up. They want the sketch in a swap for Roy."

"We don't have the goddamn sketch," Bennet said.

"Yes, we do," Howard said, closing his eyes. "And they know we do."

HELOISE Lamey drove north up the coast highway, through Fort Bragg. She smelled the tips of her fingers. Soap and water hadn't begun to eradicate the odor of the lilies. There was the smell of charred wood on them, too, separate and distinct from the lilies, like the smell of pruning fires on the wind. She wondered if the smells would ever entirely go away. She drove through Cleone, pulling off onto Ward Avenue and parking at the beach. From there she walked north on the old logging road until it disappeared beneath the sand. She set off across the empty dunes then, scuffing along through the gray sand.

The rotten lily smell hovered on the sea wind along with the smell of ashes, as if it had blown that afternoon through the second-story window of her house, drifted out across the bluffs and north along the coast, reaching long and smoky fingers toward Inglenook Fen. Could everyone smell it? Were people remarking on it right then, back in Fort Bragg, wondering what it was, what it meant? There was something satisfactory in the idea of people turning their heads, wondering, sniffing the air. Still, it was vanity that made her think so, and what she lived for was of vastly more importance than any momentary evidence of her power.

She topped a tall dune, looking for the distant, telltale stand of willows that ran down into the fen. The tiny lake itself was hidden by hills of sand, fed only by rainwater, as it had been since the ice age. Supposedly there were ice age microorganisms still in the fen, too, as well as water lilies and cattails. That was rather nice—the notion of reaching out a hand and brushing away not just any body of water, but this wild little isolated fen that was connected by rainwater to antiquity.

The dunes were empty of human footprints. Few people wandered out into the miles of rolling dunes, and the sea wind sculpted the sand continually, obliterating the evidence of life. Rodent prints and the splayed tracks of sea gulls stippled the sand in sheltered spots, and occasional clumps of horsetail ran down into the valleys. Here and there lay the scattered, bleached bones of small animals and the dried, white husks of dead plants. In the valleys the wide world round about disappeared utterly. There was only the sky and the sound of seabirds, and she was connected to her past and future only by the odor lingering in the air, more potent now, it seemed to her, as if it were hanging in an invisible cloud over the depression that contained the fen.

From one comparatively high ridge she could see the willows again, and she corrected her course, starting down into another valley and up the other side. She walked for twenty minutes, topping a little rise no different from all the others, except that below her now, walled in by dunes, lay the fen, protected from the wind and the sea.

Already the willows lined an empty stream bed in which the mud was drying and cracking. There was no longer any water emptying into the fen. Even as she watched, the cattails in the tiny lake seemed to rise up out of the water along the shoreline, as if they were growing. The smell of lilies and ashes was heavy in the air despite the sea wind. The water receded, emptying away into the surrounding sands, giving the illusion of a speeded-up motion picture. There was a tangle of roots and rotted vegetation around the cattails now, and the broad green leaves of the water lilies lay limp on the drying bed.

She sat in the sand and watched the fen evaporate, thinking of the central valleys, of the San Joaquin River, the Sacramento River, the Feather River. She pictured their dry beds, white stones hot in the afternoon sun. Farther north lay the Eel and the Trinity rivers and to the east flowed the Colorado, straight through the desolation of the great Southwest deserts. She sat picturing what it would be like merely to wiggle one's finger at this lake, say, or at that river or reservoir, and to see it begin to evaporate like water off a hot sidewalk, just like that into the air. And then she imagined rain in the desert, irrigating the Mojave. She would turn the Coachella Valley to dry dust, wither the grapefruit trees and the date orchards. She would grow ice in Death Valley. They could play golf in Boron and sift sand in an abandoned Palm Springs. Coyotes could have the resort hotels with their broken windows and cobwebby cinder block and empty swimming pools.

It was an ambitious afternoon, all in all—this small beginning out in the dunes. It made her hunger to possess the Grail, to have the power in full, to make these dreams as clear and solid as ice.

She realized she was cold suddenly, and the cold brought her up out of her dreaming about water. The fen was empty now. The wind scoured along the top of the dunes, blowing sand down into the forest of willows surrounding the bed of the dry fen. Slowly the sand began to cover the roots of the cattails and water lilies. She wondered how much time would have to pass before there was no evidence of water at all below the broken tops of scattered cattails.

It would be a long walk back to the car, success or no success, and there was a busy evening ahead. From her aerie atop the dune she could see black smoke rising over Fort Bragg—over the harbor, more exactly. That struck her as entirely satisfactory. Things were coming along. Her minions were going about their humble duties. She sniffed the wind, hoping to catch a hint of burning. That was asking for too much, perhaps. The odor of lilies and ash was faint, as if it had been a sort of magical catalyst that had finally been transmuted into something else, the remnants of it muffled by shifting sand.

She walked crab-legged down the edge of the steep dune, her shoes filling with sand. At the bottom she stopped and sniffed the air suspiciously. There was the smell of ozone on the wind now, of impending rain. She hurried up the next slope in order to get a view. Miles to the south, out over the ocean and driving in toward land, were heavy, black storm clouds—a clump of them, like someone's private hurricane. She could hear distant thunder.

The lily and ash magic had faded entirely from the sea wind now, and the sudden rainwater smell that had taken its place struck her unpleasantly as being its utter opposite, a sort of magical counterpoint. Overwhelmed with the sudden fear that the fen had somehow restored itself, she turned around and trudged back down into the valley, then up again to have one last look at it, to make sure of her work. It was empty—scummed over with a half inch of dry sand. With a growing smile, she watched the storm clouds suspiciously for a moment before starting out once again for the car.

Surrounded by sand and with the storm invisible beyond the dunes, she was suddenly greedy for dry things, for bringing another body of water into nonexistence—something that would matter next time, that would make people uncomfortable, change the way they perceived the world around them. The fen was gone, erased. It had no further value. The past was of no consequence to her.

She cursed Howard Barton out loud and cursed Stoat, too, for having been so damned slow about slicing up the cane. And then all of them running downstairs like fools at the sound of the explosion . . . If only she had more of it, more of the little disks of wood, she could return home now and start to work again, drying the standing and moving water out of the north coast like so many rain puddles.

27

"THAT'S Jimmers' car," Sylvia said when they turned the corner and drove toward the house. "Jimmers is here with Mother."

"Good," Howard said happily, realizing that he was filled with immense relief but not, strangely, with surprise. Mr. Jimmers had come through, out of nowhere. He would help them. Suddenly it seemed to Howard that they had a chance, after all. Although he couldn't have explained it easily, Mr. Jimmers had become like a giant to him—an unpredictable force, one of the kings of the night, who watched the weather and stars through his tower window and navigated secret tunnels in the earth.

Sylvia pulled in at the curb, cut the engine, and jumped out of the car, heading for the house without waiting for Howard. Mr. Jimmers met them at the door. He looked haggard and upset. His hair was wild, and he worked his hands together, forcing air through his fingers and making a sort of squeaking noise while he apologized for being there at all, for having come in uninvited. His clothes were rumpled and damp. Clearly he hadn't changed since going out into the storm.

"Where's Mother?" Sylvia asked, pushing past him into the house.

"Gone," Jimmers said at once. "She went after him." He handed Sylvia a note, hastily written on the back of an envelope.

"Gone to get your father," it read, and below that was the address and telephone number of the Sea Spray Motel.

"Damn it!" Sylvia said, sitting down on a chair and then standing up again. "*Why* did she go?"

"Because she loves him," Jimmers said.

Sylvia shook her head. "Of course she does. But she can't *do* anything at all. Can she?"

"She couldn't just sit here, either. Not your mother. She can at least try to be with him. I couldn't stay away, either. Not after our little discussion in the car tonight. I know what Edith's thinking, what she's feeling. She and I, well . . ." Mr. Jimmers sat down shakily on the couch and stared for a moment before going on. "She called thirty minutes ago and told me what they'd done, where they'd taken him and what they wanted. I rushed straight up here, and when no one answered the door, I let myself in and found this note. Should have waited for you, I guess."

"No," Sylvia said. "Thanks for doing it. There was no telling what sort of trouble . . ."

"Exactly."

Abruptly Sylvia began to cry, slumping in the chair again. Howard perched himself on the chair arm and put his hand on her shoulder, awkwardly trying to do some good. Edith's having gone after Uncle Roy made the whole thing about twice as hard, not just because now she was in trouble, too, but because she had set a standard for them to follow. Aunt Edith had gone straight to the heart of danger and was right then confronting the enemy at the Sea Spray Motel, while Howard was lounging around the living room, unable to reason any of it out.

"Where's this motel?" Howard asked.

"Right up the street," Sylvia said. "It's on the ocean side of the highway, right above Pudding Creek. It's empty—being renovated, I think. There's new owners, or something."

"I bet I know who." Howard stood looking out the window, chewing his lip. His mind spun. What was called for here? A show of force? Trickery?

"How serious is Mrs. Lamey?" he asked Jimmers.

"Deadly. I warned you." He glanced at Sylvia, who wiped her eyes with the back of her hand. "No use mincing words."

"They'll kill him," Sylvia said.

"Surely not both of them." Howard appealed to Mr. Jimmers. It was impossible to believe that things had gotten so desperate so quickly. "They can't get away with murder. It's one thing to knock apart Mr. Bennet's Humpty Dumpty, even to burn down the icehouse, but murder . . ."

"Mr. Bennet might easily be dead now if Stoat hadn't pulled him out of the fire," Sylvia said.

"That's what I mean. *Stoat* pulled him out. They were anxious not to murder anyone, just to burn us down—and probably steal the truck back if Bennet hadn't been one step ahead of them."

Sylvia shook her head. "What if Stoat didn't burn the icehouse? What if Mrs. Deventer is right?"

"You can't believe that," Howard said.

"I *do* believe it. You can't, because you're jealous of him, and—"

"Wait a minute," Howard said, interrupting her. Mr. Jimmers studied his fingernails, keeping silent. "I'm *not* jealous. That's not the problem. Let's not confuse the issue here."

Sylvia looked at him steadily.

"All right. Maybe a little. Of course I am. Why shouldn't I be? That doesn't prove anything in any direction, does it? That doesn't make him innocent of any crimes. Who do you think loosened the lug nuts on Mrs. Deventer's car? Stoat's the one who's always hanging around there. Maybe I *am* a little jealous, but that doesn't alter anything."

"I just wanted to make you admit it," Sylvia said, almost smiling for a moment. "And I didn't say he was innocent of any crimes. I only said that I don't think he'd stoop to arson and murder. I don't think he had anything to do with screwing up Mrs. Deventer's car. I saw him next morning downtown. He'd just heard about her accident. He was pretty shaken up."

"Easy to fake," Howard said sulkily.

"That's true, too. Anyway, what I'm saying is that they *would* be murderers, and that they almost murdered Bennet. Your being jealous of Stoat makes you underestimate them. That kind of thinking is dangerous here."

No one spoke for a moment while Howard grappled with this notion. Finally Mr. Jimmers said, "She's right, you know."

Howard shrugged. It was possible. Hell, she probably *was* right.

"I'm familiar with this jealousy business," Jimmers said. "It's a potent thing. It'll fill you up with false regrets. Take it from a man well seasoned in it."

Howard nodded. "I'll try to keep things straight," he said. He smiled at Sylvia, though, rolling his eyes, and got a smile in return. Maybe there hadn't been any harm in clearing the decks. He could get on with it now. "So what are we talking about here? What's the stakes?"

"Higher than you can imagine," Jimmers said. Then, after a pause, he added, "It was your coming here that brought it to a head. You were bound to come. There's no blame involved. But all of us knew something was coming, Roy included. Graham was fishing for someone, and out of the blue you called up and volunteered for the post. You were a natural. You can bet it didn't surprise Roy Barton any when they made their move. He was primed for it. I'm afraid that of all of us, you're the one who knows the least. So I'll be blunt. Right now the stakes are high and simple: they want you and the print."

"That's the deal?" Howard asked.

"That's it in a nutshell."

Howard shrugged. "Then let's get on with it." There seemed to be no option. He was moderately certain now what it was he had inherited, and he was equally sure that he didn't want it. What he wanted, he had come to understand, was Sylvia and a change in the way he lived his life. As unsettling and strange as the north coast air seemed to be, in the few days he'd been there he had come to like it. It suited him. Southern California had grown gray and hazy for him. "Let's give the damned thing up, right now. We'll go up to the motel and deliver it like a pizza, trade it straight across for Uncle Roy. Then we'll all go out for dinner. Maybe we can squeak a couple of months' free rent out of the deal."

Mr. Jimmers sighed. "She doesn't just want the *object*. She wants to *use* it. She wants its power. If she can't use it, it's worthless to her."

"Let her go to town on it. She can use it like crazy. We need a little rain."

"She couldn't even begin to get the pizza out of the box," Jimmers said. "She would need you for that. And you can bet she won't be satisfied with a little rain. She sees herself as the queen of the weather, and right now, she's too close to being right. If there's any going out to dinner tonight, you wouldn't be along for it, I'm afraid. She'll put you to some sort of . . . use."

"To hell with dinner," Howard said, although doubtfully now. "I'll grab a bite at the Gas 'n' Grub."

"Father's been fighting this war for years," Sylvia said. "We can't just go up there and chuck it all in. He wouldn't want that."

"No, he wouldn't," Jimmers said. "Nice of you to offer, though, Howard. It's exactly what I'd expect you to do. And more importantly, it's exactly what *they* expect you to do by now, or rather, what *she* expects you to do. 'How serious is Howard Barton?' she's been asking herself. 'What does he *want*?' As soon as she discovers that you don't *want* anything, not like she wants things, then she'll think you're easy to read. There's nothing particularly complicated about a hero. A hero will take another man's bullet without thinking it out first. And when he does have time to think it out, he'll take the bullet, anyway."

Howard waved the notion away. "That's somebody else you're

talking about. I'm not big on bullets. But what do we do? How long do we have?"

"They've given us a deadline, actually. Very melodramatic. We come through by midnight tonight if we want to see Roy Barton alive."

THE Sea Spray Motel sat above the ocean, cheerfully painted in yellow and white and blue, with scalloped bargeboard trim along the length of the single-story row of rooms. Edith parked the station wagon in the deserted lot and surveyed the motel, not letting herself think, but simply keeping on. Roy was in one of the rooms, and she meant to find out which one. And then join him there. It was simple as that.

The night was lit by moonlight and neon, and she could see Pudding Creek just to the south of the motel, running out through a drain under the highway and then looping around toward the ocean. It was very nearly dry and it pooled up into a little slough between big sand dunes. A railroad trestle some thirty or forty feet high spanned the water and dunes at the mouth of the creek, and beyond the trestle the sandy beach was heaped with big clumps of brown kelp, looking like low, creeping shrubs in the moonlight. There was the smell of the ocean and of diesel exhaust from trucks on the highway.

Seeing a movement of drapes in a nearby lighted room, Edith stepped along up the concrete walk and knocked squarely on the door, holding her purse.

There was nothing for a moment except the sound of gulls and traffic. Then there was a swish of quiet movement inside and hushed talk, followed by a muffled shout—just the word "Hey!" very loud and cut off by the sound of a hand slap and a grunt. Edith knocked again, hard this time. More silence followed.

"I have it!" she shouted, knocking once more. "Heloise Lamey, I have what you want!" The light in the room blinked out, and there was the sound of a chain lock sliding and rattling. The door swung halfway open. The room inside was dark, and Edith squinted to see.

"Come in," a woman's voice said.

And then immediately there was another shout, the word "Don't!" followed by the sound of another hand slap and voice hissing out a warning.

Edith steeled herself and walked into the room. The door shut behind her and a man stepped out from behind it and switched on the light. Heloise Lamey sat in a chair by a wood-grain Formica table. There was a crossword puzzle and pencil in front of her, along with a couple of Styrofoam cups empty except for coffee dregs and lipstick stains.

"Timothy!" Edith said, surprised to see the man who had stepped out from behind the door.

He nodded at her, looking half ashamed of himself. Mrs. Lamey glanced at him sharply, as if suddenly unhappy and doubtful. "I didn't know that you and Edith Barton were on such familiar terms, Mr. Stoat."

"Years ago," he mumbled. "Knew each other briefly."

"It *was* brief, wasn't it?" Edith said. "I seem to remember, though, you having eaten at our table more than once. You must have forgotten that."

He shrugged and moved away, sitting across from Mrs. Lamey, his usual cool and haughty demeanor gone from his face and replaced now by something like the look of an embarrassed teenager. "Lock the damned door," Mrs. Lamey said to him in a disgusted tone.

"It *is* locked," Stoat replied. "It locks automatically."

"The chain lock, too."

Edith turned around and slipped the chain lock into place.

"Thanks," Stoat said politely, cutting it off sharp when Mrs. Lamey gave him a vicious look. He shrugged, narrowing his eyes, and then started to pick at the rim of one of the coffee cups, tearing off little fragments of Styrofoam and avoiding the gaze of either woman.

"Well?" Mrs. Lamey asked.

"I don't have it," Edith said. "That was a lie to get you to open the door."

Mrs. Lamey nodded slowly and wide-eyed, as if Edith were a first grader at share time. "Then what do you want?" she said.

"I want my husband."

"Well, you can't have him." Mrs. Lamey's voice drifted up an octave. "Except in trade. That's what I told you over the phone. Things haven't changed any, have they? I expect I'll have to dispose of both of you now. You can't leave, you know, after walking in here like this. That was your second great mistake. Your first was to marry Roy Barton. What an unhappy and unfathomable thing. I can't say I understand it at all."

"Of course you can't. You don't understand anything, not really. If you did, you'd know that I don't *want* to leave, not without Roy. Didn't I just tell you I wanted my husband? That meant nothing at all to you."

300

Mrs. Lamey stared at Edith for a moment, as if she were going to contradict her. Haughtily Mrs. Lamey said, "You know *nothing* about me. Nothing. How *dare* you judge me. I am . . . I'm a . . . *victim*, Mrs. Barton." She smoothed her hair, straining to keep her face composed.

"Aren't we all?" Edith said softly.

"Some of us more than others, I assure you," Mrs. Lamey said. "There's no time for philosophy now, though. What you do or do not understand is of no concern to me. I told you that you can't *have* your husband, although why on earth you'd want a bloated old hulk like that I can't say." Mrs. Lamey was blinking hard now, staring at the tabletop, her lips pursed with tension. "He was young and fit once, I suppose, which might explain something. But now . . . I'm afraid he's become a commodity now. Something to be bought and sold."

"That's all there is to you, isn't it?" Edith said. "Buying and selling. You're as simple as a wrinkled old dollar bill."

Mrs. Lamey gave Stoat a sudden furious look. "What are you grinning at, Cheshire Cat?" she asked him, and abruptly he went back to picking at his Styrofoam cup, dropping the pieces onto a little heap inside. "It's *you* that knows nothing and never has," she said to Edith. "You've lived an empty, wasted life. You've accumulated *nothing*. You've come to *nothing*, except perhaps the end, finally." With an air of furious dismissal she picked up the crossword puzzle book, asking Stoat, "What's a five-letter word for a confounding problem?"

"Bitch," Stoat said flatly, standing up and heading for the door. "I'm going down the road for another cup of coffee." As he passed Edith he widened his eyes briefly, meeting her own and then looking hard at the door and throwing his head back a barely perceptible half inch.

"Try 'poser,' " Edith said to Mrs. Lamey, ignoring Stoat entirely. Stoat went out into the evening, shutting the door after himself. Then Edith asked, "Where is he?"

Mrs. Lamey nodded toward a connecting door to an adjacent room. Without asking anything more, Edith strode across to it, opened it, and stepped through. Beyond was a room identical to the first, except that Uncle Roy sat tied to one of the two chairs at the Formica table. In front of him was a Coke can and an ice bucket half full of melting ice. Lying on the bed was an oily-looking man in his twenties, smartly but casually dressed and with small, close-set eyes. He jotted notes in a spiral binder and didn't look up.

Edith ignored him just as thoroughly. A line of blood trickled from the corner of her husband's mouth and the side of his face near his right eye was puffy and bruised. She forced herself to smile at him, and he smiled back, wiggling his ears and then wincing. "You shouldn't be here," he said.

"I couldn't stay away. I missed you too much. This isn't one of your little business ventures, you know. You need me here."

"That's a fact," he said simply.

"And there's a lot we haven't said to each other," she said. "There's a lot we haven't done." She sat in the chair across from him and put a hand on his knee, giving him a squeeze.

His chest heaved and he grinned lopsidedly, tried to speak, and couldn't. She reached up and wiped the corner of his eye, starting to cry herself, and then, suddenly angry, she began to untie the rope that held him in the chair.

The man on the bed looked up tiredly, as if the whole business were a bore. "Would you *please* give that up?" he asked.

Roy nodded at her, and she sat up. "We'll wait, then," she said. "Shouldn't be long."

"Something happening?" Roy asked aloud.

"Jack MacDonald and thirty or forty mill workers are coming down here with something—what was it? Iron pipes, I think he said."

She looked up at the man on the bed, who was very casually rubbing an automatic pistol with a rag now, buffing out finger-prints. He sighted down along the barrel, swinging it from the swag lamp to the ice bucket to Roy's head. Edith gasped and half stood up, as if she would push Roy's chair over backward. "Bang," the man said quietly, and then laid the pistol down on the nightstand next to the bed.

"This is Glendale Flounder," Roy said to Edith. "Something unfortunate like that. I misremember his exact name. He's a hoser of the first water, though. A literary critic out of San Francisco, who's got this thing about pistol barrels that would make Freud sick. Nearly shot his foot off a half hour ago. I had to show him how to release the damned safety. With her money you'd think she could afford pros, and instead she hires a bunch of goddamn artists and poets. It's enough to make you wonder. He's writing his novel right now. As we speak. I bet it's good. A laugh a minute. Excuse me. Glendale. What's the title again? I forgot."

The man said nothing. His pencil scratched across the page.

"Don't antagonize him," Edith whispered.

Roy shrugged. "Say!" he said, brightening up. "I've come up with a great notion, speaking of business."

"Good," she said cheerfully. "What's your idea?"

"A sort of miniature golf course and amusement park, out between the airport and the azalea gardens."

"Really?" Edith said in an encouraging tone of voice.

"A sure bet, too. Almost no risk. Limited capital outlay. There's a whole lot of Georgia-Pacific acreage lying fallow out there. Hasn't been used in thirty years. I figure that Bennet and me can build a stucco castle—big and gaudy but just a cheap façade, something you can see from the highway—and fill it full of video games. We'll lay out a pissant little golf course along the bluffs, indoor-outdoor carpeting and that sort of thing. A bunch of Bennet's whirligigs. That'll draw the families, you know. Families are paramount, even though financially speaking they aren't worth anything to you. It's the video games that pay, but we don't want this just to be some kind of teenage hangout."

"Of course not," Edith said.

"Anyway, picture a driving range out into the ocean. Maybe buoys out there as yardage markers. Turns out you can buy worthless old balls from courses all over the country for next to nothing, as well as seconds from the golf ball factory. The way I figure it, people will pay plenty for a bucket of balls if they can just knock them to hell and gone into the Pacific."

Edith smiled happily. "Yes," she said. "That would be nice, wouldn't it? A golf course on the ocean, like Pebble Beach. Remember when we took the Seventeen-mile Drive down around Carmel and stayed at that Spanish-style hotel? We had the worst food in the world at that Mexican restaurant."

"Tasted like dog food," Roy said. "All that black, shredded meat. It wasn't beef; I know that much. Anyway, we'd paint them, the golf balls—dip them by the basketful and then pick out the worst of them for the driving range. We'll buy secondhand putters and drivers. You see them all the time at garage sales. That's where you and Sylvia come into the picture."

Roy stared off into space as if he were picturing the whole thing in his mind—a seaside kingdom above the ocean, built of stucco and electronics and wooden whirlibobs. "Like I said," he continued, "the video games would draw the kids more than the golf would. You don't even have to buy the video machines— just pay a percentage. A man comes around once a week to service them and haul away gunnysacks full of quarters. They're doing this sort of thing all over the place down south. There was a big article in *Forbes* . . ."

The phone rang just then in the next room, and Glenwood Touchey jumped up from the bed, slipped his pistol into his pocket, and pushed open the connecting door in order to listen in on the call.

"Who?" they heard Mrs. Lamey ask. There was a moment's silence.

"Not *the* Artemis Jimmers," she said, affecting astonishment. "Well, yes, we *are* here at the motel. We're beating poor Mr. Barton to within an inch, aren't we? You can have the inch, though, if you hurry. And please don't send any more emissaries unless you want to lose them, too. I believe I made it clear that I'm most anxious to consult with Howard Barton, not with his extended family. Listen very carefully now. When I hang up, I'm sending the Bartons away in a car, in very capable hands. If anyone shows up on my doorstep, anyone at all, except Howard Barton, I'm going to place a single phone call to the awful place that they've taken the poor Bartons. I'm going to let the phone ring exactly once, and then hang up. That ring will be the last thing that either one of them hears this side of hell. Tell that to the daughter, please. None of us can afford secrets."

After this speech there was another silence. Through the door Edith could see Mrs. Lamey's eyes narrow. Then she turned away to face the opposite wall as she listened. The door opened and Stoat came in, chain-locking it behind him and carrying a cup of coffee. He stood silently and expectantly, waiting for Mrs. Lamey to speak.

"It's *what?*" she asked finally. "A machine that conjures up ghosts? Built by John Ruskin? It only conjures up *his* ghost? Ah! It's because his bones are in it? That's rather cheap, isn't it?" She broke into a theatrical titter, turning around to look into the second room. There was no laughter in her face. "Mr. Barton has been telling me that your tin shed contains the Ark of the Covenant. He had me half convinced. I've never seen such a pack of liars as you two silly men. Really, you're both quite amusing. This whole situation is just as entertaining as it can be, isn't it?"

After another moment's listening, she held her hand over the receiver and said toward the second door, "Mr. Jimmers insists that you made up this nonsense about the Ark of the Covenant, Mr. Barton. He claims you were lying to protect him, to keep the *real* identity of the machine a secret. He claims that we can

304

use it to call John Ruskin up from the spirit world."

"That's entirely correct," Roy said, nodding broadly. "I was lying about it all along."

Into the receiver Mrs. Lamey said, "Mr. Barton admits to having lied. We'll have to punish him for that." She listened again and then said, "But it's so very enjoyable, isn't it? No, I'm not interested in trading anyone for your machine. Yes, I've read your pamphlet about phone-calling the dead. When did you publish that, by the way? Back around 1961, wasn't it? And I'm just as familiar as I can be with the work that Mr. Edison was doing on the spirit telephone when he died. He was a lunatic, too. They come in all shapes and sizes, Artemis, genius notwithstanding. I'll tell you what I'll do, though. I'll allow Howard Barton to bring the machine along, as a sort of gift. That's right. I'll take it into the bargain, since you've been gracious enough to offer."

She hung up right then and sat looking at the phone. "The fool's going to bring the machine back around, too," she said to Stoat. "Lord knows what it *really* is." To Touchey she said, "Get them out of here now. Gwendolyn is waiting for you. You two behave yourselves. Pay no attention to what I told that idiot over the phone. If I don't call by two A.M. do what I've asked you to do."

"THE machine angle was a dead loss," Mr. Jimmers said unhappily as he hung up the phone. "It was worth a try, though. One more quick phone call. What's the number of the pay phone down at the harbor? We've got to get someone down to watch the motel, to follow anyone who tries to move them out of there."

Sylvia recited the number. "I'll stay here for now," she said after Jimmers made the call. "Someone ought to be near the phone. Mother . . . I don't know . . . Maybe she'll come back. I'd want to be here. Why don't you two pick me up on your way back down?"

"Good enough," Jimmers said. "But watch out. Don't answer the door without knowing who it is."

"They won't bother me," she said. "There's no reason for it." Then she ushered them out the door as if she wanted to be alone, and Howard very nearly suggested that Jimmers drive back down to the stone house by himself. The night was windy, clear, and cold, and what Howard wanted to do was to spend the next forty minutes alone with Sylvia, just the two of them, before he had to confront Mrs. Lamey at the Sea Spray Motel.

"We'll take your car," Jimmers said, heading for the street. "If they see my car parked out front here, they won't get up to any tricks. They know me."

Howard was swept along by Jimmers' haste, and the two of them piled into Howard's truck, driving out to Main Street and turning south. There would be plenty of time to spend with Sylvia later, Howard told himself optimistically. Before the sun rose in the morning he and Sylvia would thrash things out. It was either that, or Howard would go home. There was no staying on the north coast unless his staying involved Sylvia.

"So Mr. Bennet's truck is parked downtown now, behind the Tip Top Lounge," Jimmers said. "We'll pick it up on the way back. Key's under the mat."

"Mrs. Lamey won't fall for the fake sketch," Howard said, pulling his mind back around to a more immediate problem. "Not a second time."

"Of course she won't. I'm betting on that. She'll make you *use* the thing, is what she'll do, and that can't be done indoors. She'll take you somewhere—not far, because she'll be in a sweat to get this business done. My guess is that the two of you will go down to the beach, and she'll insist that you demonstrate its authenticity right there. You can bet your eyeteeth that she's aware of your little storm this afternoon. If I'm right, it'll be a dangerous moment on the beach there, which is where you've got to take her. You'll insist on it. You've got to seem desperate to free Roy and Edith. She'll expect the thing to be a fake, of course, and if you don't come through with something—a rain squall or whatever . . ."

After a moment's silence he went on. "I'm tolerably certain she won't kill *you*, though. Not yet, anyway. It's Roy and Edith that we're worried about. She's *utterly* capable of any sort of atrocity. Remember that. She's terribly hungry, though, for what she's been chasing all these years. Graham's passing puts everything within her reach, and I'm thinking that she'll be nearly insane with all her nasty passions. That'll be to our advantage. You'll make use of it. She's got to be convinced that she's got the real article, though, which is where Sylvia and I play our part."

"Do you think she'll move them out of there," Howard asked, "like she says?"

Jimmers thought for a moment before answering. "No, she just wants to scare us away from calling in the authorities. We'll have to let our friend Bennet watch that angle. We can't worry

306

about that now. We've got to pick up the fraudulent copy and get back up here."

Howard accelerated to sixty, checking the rearview mirror.

"Damn it!" Mr. Jimmers said. "*Why* didn't I think to bring it in the first place? I don't like all this rushing up and down. It propagates confusion."

"There wasn't time to think," Howard said, watching Caspar hurtle past on their right. "How do you manufacture these fakes? They look awfully good, don't they?"

"They look good enough to fool almost anyone. It won't fool Heloise Lamey, though, not once she gets a chance to study it out. We're depending on haste and disorder. It's an easy trick, forgery is. You use a photographic negative to expose a light-sensitive zinc plate, then etch it with nitric acid. Simple printing plate, really. The paper was authentically old. I bought it years ago in San Francisco from a dealer in oriental antiquities. You can fake up old-seeming ink out of common iron gall ink treated with chemicals—hydrogen peroxide, mainly. The process is absurdly simple and cheap for a man with time on his hands. Many a successful forger has used it. The trouble in this case, of course, is that an accurate forgery isn't enough. She'll want to see *results* from it, when what you have to offer her is a scrap of trash."

His mind clouded by thoughts of Sylvia again, Howard only half listened to Jimmers' discussion of the art of forgery. He realized, though, that Jimmers was looking at him with a serious face, as if he expected a response of some sort.

"Sylvia's your daughter, isn't she?" Howard asked him, the question leaping out of him before he had time to temper it.

Mr. Jimmers said nothing at all, but sat staring at Howard with a stricken face.

"I found a copy of your book this afternoon," Howard said, rushing to explain. "I'm sorry we were fooling around down there. We'd locked ourselves into the passage, though, and were trying to find a way back out. Anyway, I found what must be a first printing of the book, and the dedication is different from what Sylvia remembered it to be. You changed the dedication when Edith married Uncle Roy."

Picket fences and moonlit hillsides flew past as they sat in awkward silence, and the silence made Howard realize that Jimmers was struggling to say something, but couldn't say it. Suddenly Howard hated himself. What an insensitive clod he had been just to blurt all this out. Why couldn't he have been a little bit subtle? He wasn't the only person on earth who had an interest in Sylvia. "Sorry," he said then. "I shouldn't have thrown you like that, I . . ."

"You need to know the truth," Jimmers said shakily, "and so does Sylvia."

Howard slowed the truck, turning off the highway and into the shadow of the cypress trees, bumping along up the driveway toward the stone house.

"I . . . Back then, I wasn't well," Mr. Jimmers said, staring out through the windshield. "I told you about some of it. Sylvia is my daughter, but obviously I couldn't bring her up. That was clear. Roy Barton could. He was happy to. Roy Barton has a heart like a whale. And I'm not being facetious, either. We've had our differences, but I won't say anything against the man now. He succeeded where I would have failed. There was no reason, back then, to saddle Sylvia with the stigma of having a father who . . ."

Howard shut off the ignition, happy for himself but not very happy for Mr. Jimmers, who had apparently finished talking. "It must have been hard for you," Howard said, the two of them sitting in the quiet truck.

"Yes," Jimmers said, and then he opened the truck door and climbed heavily out onto the ground, walking away toward the front door. In the light of the porch lamp, he stooped to untie his shoes, his hands fumbling clumsily with the laces.

 28

JIMMERS and Sylvia, driving Sylvia's Toyota, dropped Howard off at the Tip Top Lounge, and from there he drove back up to the Sea Spray Motel in Bennet's flatbed truck. Leaving the keys in the ignition, he parked so that the truck faced the highway. He climbed out into the night and looked south toward the lights of town. The Toyota was parked near the Gas 'n' Grub, its front end just visible in the glow of the parking lot lamp. He scanned the dunes along Pudding Creek. There they were, Sylvia and Jimmers, waiting in the darkness beneath the railway trestle.

Mr. Jimmers waved slowly at him, and then the two of them vanished back into the shadows.

The tin shed sat on the truck bed behind Howard, full of garden tools, empty flowerpots, sacks of fertilizer, folded-up aluminum lawn chairs, and Mr. Jimmers' oddball machine. Holding the fake sketch beneath his coat, Howard walked straight to room 18 and knocked on the door. The light went out inside. The curtain shifted momentarily, and the door opened partway.

Howard slid through, ducking toward the bed as a man stepped out from behind the door. The light blinked on suddenly. It was Stoat, looking tired and haggard. Mrs. Lamey sat at a table, her hair pulled back in a tight bun that made her head seem unnaturally small and skeletal. "Produce it," she said.

He pulled out the print, still in its case, and laid the case on the table, one by one pulling out the clips and opening it up to reveal the sketch. He hadn't wanted to bring the case, but Jimmers had insisted. It would lend the fake sketch a certain credibility.

"There it is," Howard said. "It's yours, and you're welcome to it."

Mrs. Lamey picked up the copper case and examined it carefully, running her fingers over the cut-in picture and the words beneath it. Her hands shook, and she seemed to forget entirely that Howard was standing there.

"Where are they?" he said finally, losing patience with her. "I want to see them now, this instant. I have friends on the beach. You can see them out the back window if you look. They're timing this whole thing. I'll call them off when I see Roy and Edith together, here and now."

She blinked at him, almost in confusion, as if she were pulling her mind back from some distant place. "They aren't here, are they?" she said. "I told our friend Jimmers that over the phone. And if the friends you refer to are the two men in false beards pretending to surf-fish on the beach above the trestle, then we'll go out together to confront them. I *thought* one of them looked a bit like our Mr. Bennet. *Very* artistic. I love the idea of your confederates masquerading as bearded fishermen. There's nothing like a touch of the dramatic to make death seem idiotic rather than tragic. Come along, then." She stood up and removed the sketch from its case, squinting hard at it. "If this is a false copy . . ." she said.

"It's authentic," Howard said. "I've . . . made use of it once already. If we're going out, anyway, I'll demonstrate it."

"Wait here," Mrs. Lamey said to Stoat. "And leave the television alone. Keep your ears open and watch out the window

309

for foul play. You can't trust men in false beards." Then to Howard she said, "If there's treachery, remember that your aunt and uncle will die. Their lives depend on my making a phone call and uttering a certain phrase that you can't hope to guess. So you can't compel me. Violence is useless to you. I'm going to appeal to your common sense here, and say that if this works smoothly, when the sun rises in the morning Heloise Lamey will be gone from your pitiful lives."

"I understand," Howard said. "Let's get to it."

She nodded, picking up a leather satchel from the floor beneath her chair. A bad odor wafted up from it, as if it contained a dead animal. She hung the strap around her neck and shoulders, unlocked the door, and stepped out into the parking lot. Howard followed, hearing the sound of the door catching behind them and then of neon buzzing from the overhead lights. A truck roared past, fouling the air with diesel exhaust. "Fetch the stick," Mrs. Lamey said. "Mr. Jimmers assured me that you wouldn't be so foolish as to arrive without it."

Howard opened the truck door and pulled out Graham's walking stick. "Let me get the feel of it," Mrs. Lamey said, taking it from Howard and hefting it. He was tempted to snatch it back, but there was no use pushing her, no use taking chances—not yet. She set out through a stucco breezeway, carrying the cane and with the leather satchel pushed around behind her back. Howard followed along like an obedient servant, the path being too narrow for them to walk side by side. Whacking the ground now and then with the cane, she angled across a weedy sort of back lot and down a sandy path toward the beach, walking hurriedly. The dark trestle loomed overhead to the left of them.

Howard could hear the breakers now, and could see Lou Gibb and Mr. Bennet fifty yards north, their fishing poles thrusting up from holders jammed into the sand. The two men stood still, watching the ocean. Pretending to meddle with his fishing pole, Mr. Bennet turned to look at Howard and Mrs. Lamey. "Wave the fool down this way," she said.

Howard waved. Bennet stood still, waiting, pretending not to understand, then waved back, as if merely being cheerful. Howard waved again, gesturing him down the beach. The two men talked back and forth, and then Bennet trudged down toward them, wearing an Amish-looking beard not connected by a mustache. It made his face look like a hair-fringed egg, disguising him thoroughly. "Stop!" Mrs. Lamey commanded when he was ten feet away. "Howard wants to tell you to go home. Reel in your lines and go. Be quick about it, because Howard and I have a bit of an experiment to perform, and you're inconvenient. Isn't that so, Howard?"

Howard nodded at Bennet. It was clear that Mrs. Lamey was serious. She was talking in a brittle, forced-facetious tone that seemed about to crack. Howard was pretty sure she was on the edge, running cold and sharp, but with all her margin used up. She didn't have time to waste. Her whole twisted life had come to a focus on this moonlit beach, and everything about her seemed to suggest that this was no time for false talk or false beards. "We've got to trust her," Howard called, knowing that the word "trust" wasn't what he wanted, really.

"Like hell we trust her," Bennet shouted back. He scowled, standing solidly, his boots sinking in the wet sand. Mrs. Lamey said nothing, but stared at him like a desert lizard until, with a dismissing wave of his hand, he turned and headed back up the beach, apparently having made up his mind. Mrs. Lamey waited in silence until the two men had reeled their lines in, picked up their buckets and tackle boxes, and started up the rise that led to the highway. She stood watching them go, until a wave broke high up on shore, and the ocean swirled in around their feet, sending Mrs. Lamey high-stepping toward dry sand.

The night was clear and starry and cold, and the wind off the ocean whipped beach sand across Howard's pant legs as he followed Mrs. Lamey farther down toward where Pudding Creek trickled into the ocean, nothing but a few little rills a couple of inches deep. She seemed to be using the cane now, as if she were truly tired, and she headed straight toward a big driftwood log, where she could sit down and let Howard work.

The trestle stretched far overhead and threw an immense crosshatch moon shadow across the beach. Somewhere back in that shadow Jimmers and Sylvia stood ready to play their part. Howard wanted to search the shadows with his eyes, to find a familiar and friendly face even if it was hidden in darkness, but he didn't dare.

Right now they would be trying simply to keep him in sight, to forecast his movements. All Howard had to do was make a show of folding the sketch up. Sylvia would work over the real sketch in secret, hidden back under the trestle.

Mrs. Lamey tiptoed across Pudding Creek, where they would be partly sheltered from the wind. She stopped at the far side of the trestle, sitting down on a big driftwood log. She looked out over the ocean, listening to the night wind. Behind her, the cliffs rose forty feet or so, nearly vertically, the trestle connecting them with the smaller, sandy bluffs at the opposite side of the creek bed, behind the motel. Howard looked hard at the rocky cliff face, cut out of dark sandstone and hung with tough shrubs. A fringe of ice plant grew down from the top. It wouldn't be hard to climb the side of the cliffs if it came down to it . . .

"Convince me," Mrs. Lamey said, startling him and settling herself on the log.

Howard nodded. "You want a storm."

"I want two inches of rainfall in the next three hours."

"I can't . . ." Howard began.

Mrs. Lamey interrupted him. "I know you can't. You can't do anything at all. You're an ignorant, passive instrument, is what you are. Just do *something*. You called up a storm this afternoon, probably by mistake. Do it again."

"I'm warning you that I can't control it very well." The truth of this statement occurred suddenly to Howard, and for the first time he began to doubt Mr. Jimmers' plan. The storm that afternoon had nearly washed out the road, and in the space of only a few minutes. What would it have become if Howard hadn't stopped it?

"Of course you can't control it," Mrs. Lamey said, abruptly losing patience with him. "It takes a stronger hand than yours. Use the sketch—whatever it is you did to it this afternoon. You didn't follow me out here to argue about it, did you? Think of your uncle, your aunt."

Howard shrugged. "All right." He turned to face the trestle, his back to the ocean, trying to look as if he were summoning some sort of mystical power. "Here we go," he said to himself, and then kneeled in the sand, laying the sketch out on his thighs. Carefully, as if he were following some sort of method, he folded the paper from corner to corner, making a triangle. Then he folded it again, joining the opposite corner, cutting the size of the thing in half. He waited, squinting at it with an artist's eye.

Out over the sea the sky remained clear. There wasn't even the hint of a fog. Rain was impossible on a night like this. He folded it again, turning each of the corners into the middle, and then cocked one corner across and down to make a little tab of it, which he tucked into the opposite corner, creating a sort of circular pointy-fronted crown that might have fit a chicken. Still there was nothing. Mrs. Lamey watched him dubiously. The look on her face suggested that they didn't have all night, that her temper was wearing thin.

"All part of the process," Howard said. He looked up just then, having seen movement at the very top of his vision. There was Jimmers and Sylvia. They weren't under the trestle at all. They were edging along the cliffside, picking their way through the shrubbery, from rock to rock, and hidden from Mrs. Lamey only because her back was turned. Howard lowered his eyes casually, wondering what in the hell they were up to. He studied the ridiculous hat. Then, laboriously, considering every crease, he unfolded it, opening it up to a full square before folding it in half again, lengthwise this time.

He risked a look toward the cliffs. Why on earth had the two of them come out of hiding like that? He couldn't see them now, but he knew they were crouched like cats behind the only bush big enough to hide them both. What did they intend to do. leap out and grab her? They couldn't be that stupid. Howard was struck with the notion that Sylvia had failed, that her folding of the print hadn't done anything at all, and he wondered how much power lay in the sketch and how much in himself.

"What are you up to?" Mrs. Lamey asked ominously. And then, seeing something in his face, she turned suddenly around, scanning the hillside and then peering into the shadows beneath the trestle. The night was silent and empty, and the only thing that moved was the wind and the ocean. "You have thirty seconds," she said, looking at her watch. Her voice was pitched too high, as if she were about to come unhinged. to start shrieking.

"I've got it now." Howard opened the rectangle into a square again and then folded it perpendicular to the first fold. He tucked the corners in, working as accurately as he could to make one of those finger-manipulated Chinese fortune-telling devices, remembering back to the fourth grade. He didn't dare look at the cliffside again, but he listened hard for telltale sounds. Mrs. Lamey watched his face rather than his hands. He met her eyes once, and her face was filled with suspicion. The corner of her mouth twitched badly, as if it were being yanked by an invisible thread. She looked as if she knew she had been taken, that Jimmers had slipped her another fake, the old fool . . .

Howard barely breathed. The paper, delicate from age anyway, had been so overfolded that it was beginning to come apart. A crease line tore along the edge, and quickly he folded it at the tear in order to hide it, folding it over again on top of itself, and then again, abandoning the Chinese fortune-teller. The thing rapidly became a lump of paper, too thick to fold again without turning it into a mere wad. There was nothing to do but unfold it once more and start over, try to brass it out, maybe utter some mumbo jumbo. One way or another, though, the charade was about over.

The paper tore again as he was unfolding it, through three creases at once this time, leaving it webbed with two-inch-long slits. Quickly, before she saw that it was shredding, he folded it back in half, following no pattern at all, but merely covering up the sad fact that soon it would be worth nothing outside of a hamster cage.

She looked at her watch. "Seven seconds," she croaked. She was breathing heavily, as if hyperventilating, her eyes nearly shut with rage, and she pounded his cane into the sand between her feet, thumping out the seconds one after another. This will be it, Howard thought. Better to throw it in her face right now and run. Better to grab the cane and hit her with it, tie her to the trestle, then sneak back up to the motel and beat the truth out of Stoat, find out where Roy and Edith were being held. Bennet was right. They had been fools to play along with Mrs. Lamey this far. She wasn't going to let them get away with anything.

"Well!" she said, as if she had just that moment been insulted. She stood up, making her pickle face at him, looking like a withered corpse in the ivory moonlight.

And just then the air was full of the smell of ozone, and a bolt of lightning and nearly simultaneous crash of thunder slammed out of the sky, illuminating the ocean in a yellow-blue flash. Mrs. Lamey staggered against the driftwood log, going down onto one knee in the sand, and then pushing herself upright, her face stretched in an amazed mask of greed, satisfaction, and surprise.

"Give it to me!" she shrieked, pulling the still-folded paper out of his hands and shoving him pointlessly on the chest with the cane, as if to get the first blow in just in case he tried to fight her for it.

"Better unfold it!" Howard shouted, although it didn't matter a bit what she did with it. It was best to play the fraud out to the end, though. Raising the storm was only the beginning. Roy and Edith were still held prisoner somewhere, and it would have to be Mrs. Lamey who released them.

She stood gaping at the stars now, ignoring him as if he were an insect that she had already destroyed. Stopping the storm wasn't conceivable to her. She *wanted* a storm—a storm to end all storms, a sky full of rainwater that would illustrate her newfound power. That afternoon she had dried out Inglenook Fen; now she would fill it again.

She still thumped the ground with the cane, as if counting out the seconds, her eyes narrowed, focused on the sky over the ocean. Mindlessly she licked her lips and then pushed out the side of her mouth as if to stop its twitching. Howard could hear her breathe, an almost frantic mewling sound, like a person in the grip of nearly terminal excitement.

Clouds dropped out of the empty night as if the darkness itself were congealing, and the air between the clouds and the ocean went black with falling rain. The storm clouds tumbled toward land, moving like a roiling black avalanche and seeming to suck ocean water straight up into the air in a hundred spinning twisters. Lightning tore through them, forking down into the electrified ocean as the night was shattered by the sound of peal after peal of thunder.

Then the ocean flattened and the wind fell off to nothing. The sound of the waves diminished so that between thunder cracks the night was weirdly silent except for the distant hiss of rain that washed across the surface of the sea. The rain was a black wall that surged toward them, obliterating the horizon.

Mrs. Lamey remained motionless, gripping the worthless sketch in her fist as if it were a treasure map that the wind would tear out of her hands. Howard realized that she thought she was watching a manifestation of her power, seeing it materialize right there in the sky after she had plotted and schemed and dreamed about it for years. She was entranced, hypnotized, and it wasn't until the ocean began to recede and the first flurry of wind and rain hit them that she regained her senses and started to unfold the paper.

The tide ran outward in a visible rush of moving water and with a weird sucking sound punctuated by thunder. Submerged rocks seemed almost to leap up out of the ocean, sitting like dark little islands covered in kelp and eelgrass and barnacles with the sea swirling around them, its level falling like water in a draining bathtub.

Mrs. Lamey tore at the sketch now, trying to flatten it out as the rain engulfed them, the wind tearing at her hair as she turned around and hunkered down against it, a vague look of fear visible on her face. The driving rain hammered at them, achingly cold in the grip of the furious wind. She turned and staggered back toward the log, huddling over like a beached seabird to deflect the wind and rain with her back and clutching her leather satchel in front of her now to protect it.

Howard shielded his face with his hand, watching the ominous ocean for one last moment before being driven back by the rain and wind. The clouds flew overhead now, lashing rain across the highway and forest, and the wind spun in a vortex, coming from all directions at once. The night was black, and the cliff beyond them was nothing but a sloping shadow. Two figures moved across it, clambering upward, slipping and crawling in an effort to gain the top.

At first Howard couldn't tell them apart in the darkness. He didn't care about that, though, as long as both of them were safe. One of the figures stopped right then, standing straight up and waving furiously down toward him with both arms. It was Jimmers, urging him to follow and gesturing wildly at the ocean.

Mrs. Lamey was oblivious to everything but the sketch. She wasn't going anywhere, and clearly didn't want to. Howard grabbed her with his free hand, towing her by the elbow. She screeched straight into his ear, leaning forward and trying to bite it, twisting away at the same time and swinging the cane at him.

He grabbed the cane in the air and held on tight, hauling her forward with it. She kicked him hard on his bad knee, flailing away with her pointed-toed shoes like a machine, hitting at his face with her fist, which was closed around the sketch.

"I'll kill them!" she screamed. "Leave me! Get out! It's mine!" She released her grip on the cane, tearing away from him, clearly convinced that it was the sketch he wanted, that he was trying to take it away from her. Clumsily she pawed at her leather satchel, casting him a look that seemed to suggest she could do him serious harm, that she had something inside the satchel she would destroy him with.

He backed off a step, gesturing at her that he was giving up. He had to calm her down, somehow, if he was going to get her out of there—which he was determined to do, since he still had no idea where his uncle and aunt were being held.

He looked up the hill just then, and in the glow of a lightning flash saw that Jimmers had Sylvia by the arm, endeavoring to pull her to safety. But in the moment that Howard looked, Sylvia yanked herself free, sliding downward across the ice plant on the seat of her pants until she jammed herself to a stop against a rock. She pushed herself to her feet, but then slipped on the wet ice plant and went down again as Jimmers crept back toward her, climbing carefully, holding on to roots and branches and rocks.

Howard saw Jimmers cup his hands to his mouth to holler at Sylvia, but the rain lashed down in a deafening tumult, and there was no hope of making her hear.

The wind blew just then in a gust that staggered Howard, as if it were compelling him to move, to act. The force of it spun him half around so that he faced the ocean again. The sandy seabed was visible as far as he could see through the rain-shrouded darkness. The rain drove into his eyes, though, half veiling the strange sight of the empty ocean bottom. He stepped backward, full of sudden fear, abandoning Mrs. Lamey and making for the cliff. He couldn't have Sylvia coming to his rescue—not now, with the ocean going mad.

Mrs. Lamey collapsed on her knees on the other side of the driftwood, where she bent down to shelter herself from the wind-driven rain. She was oblivious to Howard, and to Sylvia, too, who wasn't ten feet behind her now, nearly at the bottom of the cliff. Using the cane to support himself, Howard fought his way up to where Sylvia slipped and hopped down onto the sand, grabbing Howard's arm and hauling on it, helping to tug him to higher ground. Jimmers joined them, unwilling to abandon them even though it was everything he could do now just to save himself.

They set out up the cliff, climbing as fast as they could, slipping on the wet rock, hanging on to shrubs and giving each other a hand up. Rocks broke loose and skittered down the hillside behind them, raining down around where Mrs. Lamey still crouched next to the log, the edge of which was partly submerged in the rising floodwaters of the creek.

Halfway up the hill, Howard turned to look. She was a shadow beyond the curtain of rain, and was straddling the driftwood log now, the leather satchel lying across her back. In the almost continual glow of the lightning, he saw that she was holding the fraudulent sketch in the air as if she were showing it to the storm. "Look," she seemed to be saying, "I've unfolded it. Enough is enough. I'm satisfied."

The wind took the fragile paper, though, and tore it to pieces in an instant, so that she was holding two rain-soaked banners that flailed themselves to soggy shreds.

Far out to sea loomed a shadow even blacker than the darkened sky—a tremendous wall of seawater rushing across the open ocean toward a half mile of empty seabed. Mrs. Lamey saw the wave then, too, and stood up slowly, unbelieving, still clutching little handfuls of worthless rice paper. Turning again toward shore, she hunched forward against the wind, clearly intending to cross Pudding Creek in order to make her way to the path that led back to the motel.

Shouting at her pointlessly, Howard took a step back down the cliff. She wouldn't make it to the motel. He watched as she plunged into the deepening water of the creek, nearly up to her waist. As the floodwaters swept her off her feet, she struck out swimming, her hands still balled into fists, but the creek tumbled her forward and she disappeared beneath the surface.

Mr. Jimmers caught Howard around the waist, hollering in his ear to let Mrs. Lamey go. They had to get to higher ground. They couldn't save the old woman, not now. Howard knew that Jimmers was right. It was too late for Mrs. Lamey. The fake-sketch idea would accomplish little beyond the old woman's death.

Then he saw Mrs. Lamey lurch to the surface, and for a brief moment he thought she might make it. She staggered forward, slogging her way free of the creek at last, but bent over and coughing up water.

Howard turned around and started back up, pushing Jimmers ahead of him now toward where Sylvia waited, holding out her hand for Jimmers to grab. The slope lessened, and Howard found himself scuttling upward like a crab, clutching handfuls of ice plant to steady himself. Then the slope leveled altogether, and the ice plant ended at a verge of rough gravel. They lunged forward, up onto the train tracks, where they stopped. There was no higher ground.

The wind dropped then, the rain falling off with it, and in the sudden silence a distant roar filled the night air—not the deluge now, but the wave feeling the ocean bottom, pushing itself skyward, still hundreds of yards out. It rose vertically, a long, glassy, upended plane, the top of it lost in the night.

Then there was the far-off sound of water pounding into water, heavy and powerful in a long, ceaseless roar as the wave broke in a mountain of white foam, seeming to mirror the clouds overhead, which tore themselves to pieces now and vanished like steam into the sky. Clumps of shooting stars appeared and disappeared past the holes in the clouds, and for a moment it looked to Howard as if the entire universe were revolving overhead like a mill wheel.

Mrs. Lamey turned at the sound of the wave breaking. She took two steps back toward the creek, then stopped, unsure of herself like a small animal on a highway. She seemed to see her mistake for the first time. The motel was too far away. And as the house-high wall of churning foam drove shoreward, it was clear that the motel was doomed, anyway. The wave would smash right through it.

Cramming the fragments of the sketch down the front of her dress, she made a wild dash for the log again, running up the edge of the creek toward where it was wide and comparatively shallow. She waded into it, looking back out to sea as the wave rushed shoreward, turning over and over on itself, flattening out in a wide, surging river.

Wildly she flung herself onto the log, up among the branches, hugging it to herself. The churning wave slammed across the beach, funneling into the creek and smashing thunderously across the face of the cliff. It picked up the big driftwood log as if it were a stick, and went booming beneath the trestle, swirling around the S-curve of the creek bed and blasting up and over the empty highway. In the dwindling lightning flashes they could see the log riding high on the top of the foam in a quickly revolving eddy, driving toward the dark forest. Mrs. Lamey still clung to it as if crucified to its broken-off branches.

Suddenly the ocean was calm again, and moonlight shone through the scattered clouds. A little flurry of raindrops pelted down, and then there was one last timid lightning bolt that lit up the surface of the sea. In that instant Howard saw what he thought at first was cloud shadow on the ocean. But it was moving too quickly, swarming up toward the creek mouth—schools of fish moving just under the surface. They crowded up and across the inundated beach in the wake of the wave, leaping and splashing in the shallow water.

"Where are they!" Sylvia shouted.

"What?" Howard asked, half hypnotized by the sight of the wave and the fish.

"Are they in the motel?"

"No!" Howard understood her now. "She moved them out."

"How do you *know*?" Jimmers asked, looking suddenly panicked. "That wave would have knocked the motel to pieces."

"I don't," Howard said, already moving down the railroad tracks, toward the distant motel. Carefully he stepped from tie to tie, out across the top of the trestle, which seemed to him suddenly to be as narrow as the top of a brick wall. With the road gone and the creek flooded, though, there was no other route. The ocean boiled and churned forty feet below them, and the trestle vibrated at its foundations, the water booming past the pilings.

A surge of vertigo washed through Howard when he looked down at the moving, moonlit water, and he had to look back up quick, fixing his eyes on what was left of the roofline of the Sea Spray Motel. He tried the trick of imagining that on the other side lay a warm room with a fire and a cup of hot coffee, but he couldn't manage it. The night was too wild, and it would be impossible for him to cross the trestle without focusing on each dizzying step, balancing himself with his stick.

He turned his head slowly to look at Sylvia, who followed two ties behind him. Mr. Jimmers was behind her, farther back, though, and crawling on his hands and knees from tie to tie. His face was a mask of fear and concentration. Howard wanted to help, but it would mean having to shift past Sylvia, which was out of the question; they would both go over the side. And what could he do, anyway, to steady the man? Mr. Jimmers would make it right enough—if a train didn't materialize.

They waited to let him catch up, and Mr. Jimmers, seeing that he was slowing them down, stood up bravely, waving his arms in front of him in little spirals to keep his balance. He stepped along in a halting crouch, looking down fearfully. Then he stopped and wavered, trying to keep steady, and both Howard and Sylvia turned back to help him.

"Go back!" Howard shouted past Sylvia, who was busy making Jimmers get down on his hands and knees again. She turned Jimmers around slowly and ponderously, as if he were an elephant in a closet, and without saying anything he set out south again, desperate to get off the trestle and back on solid ground now that his mind was made up. "Go with him," Howard said to Sylvia. "Take the car and get help."

"No!" she shouted back in a tone that was utterly final.

The two of them waited, watching Jimmers struggle across the final twenty feet of trestle to where it merged with the hill. He stood up solidly and waved them on, then turned and set out along the tracks. Howard set out again, keeping his mind clear, taking it one step at a time.

Minutes later they stepped off onto firm ground themselves. Howard felt the cold now, exposed to the wind and with his clothes soaked with rain. He wore two shirts and a heavy sweater, but the wind blew straight through them. Sylvia, at least, wore her parka, which would do something to cut the wind. There was nothing to do but ignore the cold, though. With a little hurrying they could be back at Sylvia's Toyota in twenty minutes, cranking up the heater.

Below them the water was already flowing back into the ocean, and Pudding Creek was falling toward its banks. They could see a gaping hole in the highway nearly fifty feet across. Big chunks of asphalt lay on the mud. The ridge that the railroad tracks ran along had sheltered the coast to the south, and the lights of the Gas 'n' Grub shined as ever. There were sirens in the night, though, from fire trucks and police cars approaching along the highway.

"Where's the sketch?" Howard asked her suddenly.

"Mr. Jimmers has it."

He nodded doubtfully.

"It'll be all right," she said, and then set out at a run for the motel, Howard limping along behind. The authorities would be stopped at the flood, and it was just possible that the two of them could search the place and get out again before help arrived that they didn't need.

In another moment they saw the motel from end to end. It was half swept away. Sheets of stucco hung from torn-away chicken wire, windows gaped empty. A single bed, still draped in its bedspread, angled out one broken window, driven through it like a boat. The broken wave had battered the motel to pieces, and only two or three rooms at the upper end appeared to be whole. Debris from the wrecked building littered the highway and parking lot, where the Sea Spray Motel sign lay heavily across the top of a piece of roof. Bennet's truck was gone, swept away, maybe, along with Mr. Jimmers' tin shed.

At a glance they could see that the wrecked rooms were empty, mattresses and tables and chairs lying in puddles of seawater and smashed against walls. Half a dozen rooms had no furniture in them at all, evidently in the process of being restored. The doors of the final few, unwrecked rooms were locked.

Howard and Sylvia banged on the windows and shouted until banging and shouting began to seem pointless. If Roy and Edith were safe in one of the rooms, surely they would have thrown a chair through a window and gotten out long ago. Probably they *had* been moved, just like Mrs. Lamey had said—a development that was either good news or bad; it was impossible to say. It was equally likely that Stoat had taken them off in Bennet's truck, deserting the sinking ship.

They could see red lights revolving down the highway, where police and firemen tried to negotiate the flood, which was still deep enough, due to the steep walls of the creek bed, to prevent their simply wading across. Several rescuers were halfway down the little road to the dunes, though, just above the trestle, looking for a crossing. In minutes they would be at the motel, wondering what Howard and Sylvia were up to, asking questions, taking up time.

"What do we do?" Howard asked. Roy and Edith were Sylvia's parents, after all. He couldn't insist that they abandon the search.

She shook her head.

"Break the windows out? We'd better be quick about it."

"No," she said. "They aren't here. The place is empty. I can feel it. We're wasting time, and we can't afford to. We've got to figure out where they've been taken."

They set out around the far side of the motel, heading down toward the beach so as to be hidden from the view of anyone on the highway. The sand was covered with debris, with kelp and rocks and seashells and dying fish, and they had to pick their way through it, watching the top of the trestle for a sign of anyone crossing that way. From the shadows of the trestle itself they watched the men wade through knee-deep water, not thirty feet off, making for the destroyed motel.

Howard recognized one of them as the cop that had grilled them down at the harbor. Would he find Bennet's wrecked truck and trace it back to them? Would he conclude that some heavy sort of mysterious crimes were being committed up and down the coast? And what if he did? The authorities could hardly blame Bennet or Uncle Roy for the storm and tidal wave.

There were more sirens suddenly on the highway, and a paramedic unit wheeled up, lurching to a stop, the doors sailing open. "Someone's hurt, after all," Howard said, feeling wretched all of a sudden. For the first time this whole fiasco had injured an innocent person, maybe killed someone. Howard felt as if he himself had been swept along on a tide this last week, except that somehow, just in the past couple of days, he had *become* that tide in some unfathomable and not very pleasant way. That, partly, was what Mrs. Lamey had wanted for herself.

They crouched there another moment, in order to wait until the men had forded the creek and were entirely out of sight. Then they slogged out into the current themselves, angling downstream with the flow so that when they got to the opposite shore they were near the edge of the ocean. They hiked along past weed-covered rock for some fifty yards, nearly to Glass

Beach, before they cut inland, toward the little rise behind the Gas 'n' Grub.

"Why did you and Jimmers creep down the damned cliff like that?" Howard asked when they were safe on the beach and the going was easy. "You scared the hell out of me. I thought you were under the trestle, and then there you were, sneaking around behind Mrs. Lamey."

"The sketch wouldn't work," Sylvia said. "We were back under the trestle, something like thirty feet away. I was folding it up like crazy even before you started in on the fake. Mr. Jimmers said that we ought to get a jump on you, that Mrs. Lamey wasn't in a mood to wait, and that he wasn't entirely certain of the way to fold it. Anyway, nothing was happening, and suddenly Jimmers decided we were too far away from you, that you had to be right there, like in the car this afternoon. We couldn't just walk out into the moonlight, though, where she would see us, so we came around from behind her in order to get as close as we could."

"She never knew she didn't have the sketch," Howard said.

"That was the point, wasn't it?"

"I tried to save her. You saw that."

"She was beyond saving, I think—wave or no wave."

Howard shrugged. "Maybe that's true. There was something about her, though, that wasn't as bad as all that Something about the way she liked to putter around that house of hers, sit out on the front porch."

"She should have stayed on the front porch," Sylvia said.

Howard put his arm around her. "You came back down the cliff to help me, didn't you?" he asked.

"Well, it did occur to me that you were doing a damned poor job of helping yourself, fencing with Mrs. Lamey down on the beach like that when the ocean was going nuts."

"Thanks," Howard said. "I needed the help. My knee wasn't worth a damn."

"Seems better now. You're not limping as badly."

"Walking in the sand is murder. It helps that it's wet, though. She kicked the hell out of me. And there's something in that sort of storm, I think. Wet weather's murder on it."

They topped the hill and walked down the other side. Howard kept making small talk, secretly worried about Uncle Roy and Aunt Edith. There was no way to tell where they had been taken. Mrs. Lamey seemed to own half the coast. She could have hidden them anywhere. Howard couldn't bring himself to believe that anyone would have killed them without word from Mrs. Lamey, regardless of what she had threatened.

"Isn't that Mr. Bennet's truck?" Sylvia asked suddenly.

For a moment Howard was filled with the happy notion that somehow if Bennet's truck were recovered, Roy and Edith would be, too.

But it wasn't Roy and Edith, or Bennet either, who stood talking to Mr. Jimmers alongside Sylvia's car; it was Stoat.

29

HOWARD was suddenly tired. He shut his eyes and stood for a moment. Somehow he hadn't bargained for this, and he admitted to himself for the first time that Stoat scared the hell out of him. Stoat was too sure of himself, too fit, too unfathomable, and Howard wondered how much of this, along with the jealousy angle, had made him misread the man. As awful and dangerous as she was, Mrs. Lamey was easier to confront.

But it was apparently time, finally, to find out what it was that Stoat wanted. Howard hoped it wasn't trouble, because Howard wasn't up to it. If it came to that, though, Howard would oblige him, up to it or not. Stoat didn't have a pistol or any other sort of weapon, not in his hands, anyway. If Howard could get around behind him without being seen, maybe he could give Jimmers a sign and the two of them could work this out together. They had made the mistake of playing along with Mrs. Lamey, completely at her mercy and letting her order them up and down—something that had very nearly ended in disaster for all of them. They wouldn't make the same mistake with Stoat.

Stoat couldn't know what had happened to the sketch, or that Mrs. Lamey was dead. Jimmers could tell him anything at all—that Mrs. Lamey had taken it, say, and driven away north, up the highway. What on earth would Stoat demand from them? Money? It was blood out of a turnip. The man would have to be a living idiot. More likely he was confronting Jimmers out of pure nastiness, thinking to cut a last-minute deal in order to glean some little trifle out of his wrecked plans. Maybe it was the machine he wanted, although apparently he already *had* that. Whatever his game was, it was time that Howard found out.

He gestured at Sylvia to stay put. They were in the shadow of the building that housed the Mendo Machine Shop, and he would have to slip across fifteen yards of lighted parking lot unseen in order to sneak up behind Stoat. He moved as quickly as he could, ready to break into a full run if Stoat turned his head and saw him. Stoat was busy talking to Jimmers, though, pointing down the highway, one hand in his pocket now. Howard ducked in behind a battered old Cadillac that was nosed almost up to the rear wall of the Gas 'n' Grub.

If Jimmers had seen Howard and Sylvia coming up over the hill from the beach, he didn't let on. He revealed nothing, but stood listening to Stoat talk, nodding broadly, as if the man's speech fascinated him. Howard looked out from behind the Cadillac's fender, then looked back at Sylvia, who stood ten yards behind him with her arms folded in front of her. Her face was doubtful, but she seemed to be determined to let Howard have his way this time. She couldn't take the chance of interfering and then finding out that Stoat was the villain that Howard said he was all along. Her parents were at risk, and it was no time to exercise her natural generosity.

Howard waited another moment, steeling himself. He found that it wasn't easy, though, just stepping out into the clear and—what?—hammering Stoat senseless on the sidewalk? Throwing some sort of hammerlock on him? Putting up his dukes? It wasn't cowardice that held him up; it was that it was so visibly idiotic. And there wasn't any obvious *reason* to hit him in the head or clip him across the back of his knees. Stoat and Jimmers almost seemed to be pals. Howard stood up slowly, stepping out into the light and keeping a good grip on his cane just in case. He was ready if it came to it, but he would let Stoat make the first move—reach into his coat or something.

"My Lord, it's Howard!" Mr. Jimmers shouted, throwing his hand to his mouth and grabbing Stoat by the shoulders, pulling the man toward the car and out of harm's way, clearly thinking that Howard was going to bean him with the cane.

What kind of behavior was that? Howard wondered. Had Jimmers and Stoat struck some sort of deal? Suddenly he remembered that Jimmers had the sketch again. He had taken it back with him from the train trestle. Was he selling them out to Stoat? Had he knuckled under?

"What's this?" Howard said to Stoat, watching him carefully. He heard the sound of Sylvia's footsteps, running up behind him. Stoat made no move to attack him or to run or anything else, but stood instead with a resigned look in his eyes. Puzzled, Howard waited him out, leaning against the stick now, a world of fatigue sweeping over him in a wave. Sylvia slumped against the fender of the Toyota. She looked wet, cold, and tired.

Without hesitation, Stoat took his coat off and handed it to her. Somehow the act of kindness irritated Howard, clearly because he hadn't been able to do it himself, and because coming from Stoat, it seemed to Howard not to be kindness at all, but a smarmy sort of pseudo-gallantry. He fumed for ten seconds before telling himself to quit being a fool—or to quit with the jealousy, just as Sylvia had told him. She had been right about that. He had to stop defining Stoat's actions from such a dangerously off-kilter perspective.

"I'm sorry," Stoat said, speaking to all of them at once. He looked confused and strained, as if saying such a thing took an effort that he hadn't been trained for. His leading-man air was gone along with the starch in his trousers, and he looked rumpled and despairing and worn out, like a man just out of the jungle and wanting to rest up in some safe haven. Stoat turned around then and walked the several steps to Bennet's truck, opening the door and pulling out the jacket that Howard had given to Mrs. Deventer down at the harbor—when was it? Months ago, it seemed. On the instant, Howard's fear and distrust of Stoat evaporated.

"Thanks," Howard said, pulling on the jacket and realizing that his fingers were too cold to work the zipper.

"I was at Mrs. Deventer's house when you two were down at the harbor talking to Mr. Bennet and the police. She told me she'd forgot to give you this back, and so I took it, knowing I'd see you tonight."

"She said it was you that saved Bennet at the icehouse," Howard said.

Stoat shrugged. "I guess I did. I should have done more. I didn't know it would come to that until it was too late to stop it. That was Glenwood Touchey's business. Heloise wanted the truck, and when she discovered that it had been seen in the back of the icehouse, and that the shed was still on it, she sent Touchey after it. I didn't know anything about it, or about setting the place on fire, either. She didn't trust me that far. She knew I'd balk finally. She was working to take Mrs. Deventer's house away, too. That . . . that was something I *did* know about."

"I figured that," Howard said. "By adverse possession. With you making payments for her and paying property taxes and seeming to live there off and on."

"Yes," Stoat said. "The money came out of consortium funds belonging to White and her and myself and a couple of others. Touchey and Gwendolyn Bundy work for shares, although Heloise pretends that she's a patron and is supporting the arts, or some damned thing. She's lost touch. There's no telling what she believes anymore. Anyway, it's a long process. At best, adverse possession takes five years. And in this case it wasn't working worth a damn.

"Mrs. Deventer was too decent to let me do anything consistent about making payments. Heloise thought she was just an addle-brained old woman who wouldn't recognize fraud when it was waved in her face, but that turned out to be wrong, and when it did, that changed Heloise's mind about the whole thing. We'd already determined that Mrs. Deventer had no will and no living relatives except her sister, who's as old as Methusaleh."

"And so Mrs. Lamey decided to kill her," Sylvia said, with a look of anger on her face, as if she were making her own nasty reevaluation of Stoat now, and didn't much like the result

Stoat nodded, looking unhappy. "I think Mrs. Deventer knew all along that there was something going on. And yet that didn't seem to have any bearing at all on what she felt toward me. That's the worst of it. It was me that convinced Heloise we couldn't prevail, that we couldn't take the place legally. I was trying to help Mrs. Deventer, but it turned out to be a mistake. I suggested we give it up. Mrs. Deventer was seventy-odd years old. She wouldn't live forever. When the time came we could quietly buy the place from the state. Why all the rush? Heloise seemed resigned to it. I had no idea she'd hurt the old lady, let alone that she would have Touchey work the car over in order to try to kill her. He followed her up to her sister's house in Willits. The highway back is treacherous. It's all cliffs along the right shoulder. Heloise thought it was a good joke on old Bennet that he had worked on her brakes so recently. If there was any blame, it would be him who got it, and there'd be no way on earth for him to prove otherwise. The first I knew of it was the morning after the trouble in Mendocino."

Howard believed him. There was no reason not to. Here he was, admitting all sorts of nasty guilt when he might just as easily have been halfway down Highway 128, running toward San Francisco. Stoat was sweeping away a lot of dust and cobweb, pitching out skeletons, and Howard wished that there were a table they could sit down at, with a pitcher of beer on it.

"So where are they?" Sylvia asked, interrupting his apology and sounding almost as if she were tired of hearing it. Her tone surprised Howard for a moment, but it didn't disappoint him. She seemed to have been right about Stoat. But, Howard was happy to find, that didn't make his activities in any way attractive to her. Nor did it guarantee that Stoat wasn't making up a grand lie here.

"I'm thinking they're not two hundred yards from us right now, right across there at the warehouse," Howard said, pointing back toward Glass Beach.

Stoat shook his head. "They're at Roy Barton's ghost museum. Touchey is there along with Gwendolyn Bundy."

"How about White and the artist?"

"White's too smart for this kind of thing. He prefers safer investments. Heloise Lamey was caught up in spiritualism and magic. The Reverend White's a flesh-and-money man. Jason's just another artist she's carrying at the moment. She'll tire of him when she finds a new boy. He doesn't have any real interest in her plots."

"She's dead." Howard watched Stoat's face for a reaction. There was nothing on it except a vague relief.

"Then the world's a better place," Stoat said. "And things are easier for us."

On the beach, an hour earlier, Bennet and Lou Gibb had watched Howard walk south toward the cliffs with Heloise Lamey. It was nearly impossible for Bennet to obey Lamey's order and leave, but he had to trust Howard. They were all taking orders from Howard now, although the boy didn't know it yet. The two men had trudged up toward the motel, carrying their poles and buckets. The parking lot was empty and the motel was dark. Bennet's truck should have been there, at least according to Jimmers, but it wasn't.

They had stood under the neon sign debating what to do, both of them filled with the certainty that there was no one left inside the motel, that Roy and Edith were long gone by then, along with the truck. Somewhere their friend was held prisoner. His life was threatened, and there was damn-all that they could do about it.

"Let's see who's home," Bennet said, and the two of them beat on each and every motel door in turn until they had convinced themselves twice over that the place was empty. The action had moved south. Unless it had moved north.

Feeling empty and helpless, they climbed back into Lou's car, throwing in the fishing gear and pulling off the false beards they'd gotten out of Roy Barton's box of dummy makeup. They drove back into town, past the warehouse at Glass Beach, which was locked tight, apparently deserted. They circled around past Roy and Edith's house, but it was dark and empty, too. At the harbor everything was equally quiet except for the sound of thunder from the storm to the north of them and a few scattered lights still on in the trailers at the Sportsman's RV. There was no sign of life at Mrs. Lamey's house or anywhere else in Mendocino, where almost everything had closed for the night. They drove back into Fort Bragg and stopped at the Tip Top Lounge for a late beer, then went tiredly back out to the street to keep looking.

Sirens wailed north up Main just then, and the two followed along behind, running out of highway within half a mile. The place was a mess of fallen trees and torn-up roadway. The mouth of Pudding Creek was inundated, and the Sea Spray Motel wrecked. Even at that late hour motorists were gathering to watch, and Bennet and Gibb pretended merely to be rubbernecking, and stayed in the car.

Bennet saw the cop from the harbor talking on his car radio, and reached into the backseat to retrieve his beard. There was no use being recognized now. Firemen seemed to have found someone— a body. Where had it come from? Had it just staggered out of the woods? It was lying in the wet grass. Bennet couldn't tell if it was dead or alive. He had to know, suddenly, who it was—or barring that, simply that it wasn't Howard Barton. Roy wouldn't be able to stand that. Heloise Lamey was treacherous, more than a match for the boy.

Moments later they heard the approaching siren of a paramedic unit. Cars began backing out of the way to let it in, and the crowd along the edge of the collapsed highway pushed back toward the shoulder. The paramedics went to work on whoever it was, the crowd closing in around them, people murmuring. More cars pulled up, spilling out people in pajamas and robes, who stood on the highway looking at the flooded creek and at the salmon flopping and dying on the edges of the washed-over dunes.

The cop from the harbor was long gone along with three other men, down the dirt road toward the trestle where they had waded through the shallows toward the motel. Bennet could see them poking around the wreckage now with flashlights. There was the sound of glass shattering as they bashed out a window with a broken-off wall stud and climbed into one of the remaining rooms, probably looking for victims.

Bennet watched the motel carefully, waiting for the panicked rush that would inevitably come if they found someone, if Roy and Edith *had* been there. There was no excitement at all, though, and after a couple of minutes the cop appeared from one of the open doors and set out toward the creek again, apparently in no hurry, leaving the firemen to work the place over more thoroughly.

Bennet turned his attention back to the highway. The paramedics weren't in any hurry, either. What did that mean, a corpse? The crowd parted momentarily, and Bennet got a quick glimpse of a leg and a foot. "It's a woman," Bennet said. "Someone wearing a dress, anyway. I can't tell—"

"Hey!" Gibb shouted, nearly into his ear.

"What!"

"The truck!"

"Where?" Bennet shouted, looking back down the highway. There it went, pulling out from behind the Gas 'n' Grub, heading south. "Let's go," Bennet said. "Step on it!"

Gibb backed the car around, honking his way past a dozen people. A child climbed up onto the highway right in front of them, happily carrying a three-foot-long salmon by the tail and mouth. Gibb braked hard, and the kid smiled into the windshield cheerfully, holding the fish up for them to see it. Three more children appeared, carrying fish of their own, and Gibb had to wait them out, too. Bennet drummed his fingers hard on the dashboard.

"Damn it!" Gibb said. "The damn thing wasn't two blocks down."

"What the hell was it doing at the Gas 'n' Grub?" Bennet asked.

"Search me," Lou said. He eased past the last of the children, pushing the pedal down into overdrive. The car shot forward toward town. It was late, after one in the morning, and Fort Bragg was mostly asleep. A half dozen cars headed north toward the excitement, but almost no one was southbound now. The highway was clear and straight. A pair of taillights shined about a mile down the road, and even at that distance they could see that it was Bennet's truck, with the tin shed shoving out a foot over either side of the bed.

"Give the bastards room," Bennet said. "Don't let them know it's us."

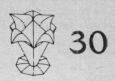

30

IT was pitch-dark as Howard and Sylvia bounced along down the highway, riding in their Trojan horse, the shed creaking and moaning as it sawed back and forth with the truck's movement. Jimmers rode up front with Stoat, who would have to make up some excuse for Jimmers being along with him. There wasn't enough room in the shed, though, for three people and the machine, too, unless they threw out all the garden supplies, and Jimmers couldn't see the point of that.

Howard sat on a pile of plastic nursery bags full of mulch, bracing himself with his shoulder against the cold, swaying wall. He would never have believed that a night could last as long as this one had. And it wasn't over yet. He was caught up in the rhythm of it, though, like a long-distance swimmer, and would be all right if he didn't think about the remaining miles. The truck swerved around an uphill curve, Stoat throttling down into second gear, and Howard tried to guess where they were on the highway, but it was useless.

Every now and then slivers of moonlight filtered through cracks, faintly illuminating the interior of the shed. In those moments he could see Sylvia sitting across from him on the aluminum lawn chair that she had managed to wedge open crookedly in the cramped space. Her eyes were closed but Howard didn't think she was asleep.

Perhaps it was darkness, or fatigue, or the lateness of the hour, but Howard's emotional guard was down, and he knew it and welcomed it. Suddenly he wanted to talk. It was time to clarify things, to cast a light on elements of the mystery that were still in shadow. They had ten or fifteen minutes entirely to themselves, and he determined not to waste it, although he was equally determined not to be as clumsy and abrupt with Sylvia as he had been with Mr. Jimmers earlier.

"What else do you know about Jimmers?" he asked her finally, breaking a long silence.

"I don't see all that much of him," she said after a moment.

"He seems to be pretty fond of you, though."

"He's always treated me like a daughter. Because of him and Mother, I suppose."

"Is that it?" Howard asked.

Sylvia was quiet for a time. "What else would it be?"

Then Howard told her about finding Mr. Jimmers' book, with the altered—or unaltered—dedication and the screwy, too-early date. "I knew that didn't *prove* anything at all," Howard said to Sylvia. "Not absolutely. But obviously I had to find out more. So last night, when we went back down to Jimmers' place after the fake sketch, I asked him outright about it. I told him that I had found the book, read the dedication, and figured out who you really are."

"What did he say?" Sylvia asked, her voice hoarse.

"He wasn't surprised at all that I knew. I think he was relieved. On the way back up to Fort Bragg he seemed almost *happy* about it. Maybe you didn't notice it when we picked you up and headed down to the Tip Top Lounge, but he was about ready to pop with it. He didn't say anything to you while you were hiding out under the trestle?"

"No."

"Well . . ." Howard shrugged. "There's the truth, though, if you want it. You're the only daughter of Artemis Jimmers."

There was silence then. After a moment he heard her sniff. She was crying in the darkness. It was dark now, and he couldn't even see her face. He leaned over, reaching out to stroke her hair, but he couldn't judge the distance and poked her ear by mistake. She laughed then. "Clod," she said, sniffing again. "At least now I don't have to claim you for a cousin."

Howard didn't comment on this. "And you didn't know?" he asked her. "Honestly?"

"Of course I didn't know. If I had known . . ."

"What?"

"If I had known . . . I don't know. Maybe I would never have come back up north all those years ago. None of this would have happened. Where would we be now? Married? Living in an awful house in the suburbs somewhere, in Inglewood or Garden Grove or Pacoima. You'd be working at Delco Battery or Tubbs Cordage, supervising the night shift. I'd be barefoot and pregnant."

"And now I'm not working at all," Howard said. "I'm a bum."

"Not going back to the museum?"

"Nope."

She was silent again.

"How does that strike you?" Howard asked. "Are you excited at the prospect of me lurking around up here, getting in the way?"

"I'll have to ask my therapist," she said. "I could use some help around the boutique, I guess—sweeping up and all. Minimum wage until you learn the trade, though."

"Could I talk to what's-his-name? Chet? I want to fly on his astral plane."

"Mrs. Moynihan would like that. She's another of your admirers, you know." After a moment she said, "It's not bad having two fathers, is it?"

"I don't know," Howard said. "I can barely remember what it's like to have one. Uncle Roy was pretty much my father, too. I feel a little shabby because of that. It isn't really my place to tell you all this. Uncle Roy and your mother kept it a secret all these years, and now I've torn the lid off it."

Sylvia started crying again at the mention of Uncle Roy. Howard waited for a moment and then went on. "They've been on the edge of revealing it, though. They keep hinting about me and you . . . you know . . ."

She sniffed again. "I know," she said finally. "They think you'd make a fine husband. Mom told me that. I thought it was pretty weird at the time. Still sounds a little weird. Why didn't you tell me all this yesterday, when you found the dedication in the book?"

"Because of what happened on the beach. I didn't want to sound like I was rationalizing things, like I was making up reasons to justify our . . . failing in love."

"Our *what*?" Sylvia said. "Is that the kind of thing you said to Jeanelle Shelly in the garage that time? Now you're saying it to me in a tin shed."

"All right," Howard said. "When we were down in Jimmers' basement, you weren't paying any attention to me, anyway. All you wanted to do was play with Jimmers' tin toys. Why *should* I have told you? I wanted to keep it for *ammunition*, to be one up on you. I was going to hold it over your head if you ever started in on Jeanelle Shelly or the ice planetoids again. I should have guessed all of it from the first, anyway. You and Jimmers. You're peas in a pod. How could anyone think you *weren't* his daughter?"

"You just wait," she said. He heard her yawn sleepily. "My memory is long. We'll see who one-ups who."

The truck bumped over a rut in the road just then, slamming from side to side and throwing Howard off his plastic sacks. He sat down hard on the plywood floor of the shed, hearing Sylvia's chair collapse at the same moment, and suddenly she sprawled across him in a tangle of arms and legs, clutching at him to avoid rolling into the closed shed door.

The truck slowed down then to turn off the highway. Sylvia lay against Howard, breathing softly against his ear, her hair in his face and her arms around his chest. She kissed him, and then said, "Why didn't we think of this fifteen minutes ago? A tin shed is nearly as romantic as a wrecked Studebaker."

With that, she kissed him again, long and hard, and he slid his hands up under her parka, along the small of her back. Her shirt was still damp with rainwater, but she was warm beneath the jacket. He held on to her as the truck crept across the gravel parking lot of Uncle Roy's Museum of Modern Mysteries and braked to a stop.

They quietly disentangled themselves then. Howard listened hard, full of sudden tension. One of the truck doors opened. There were footsteps, and then someone knocking against the door of the museum. Then came Stoat's voice speaking to someone. There was laughter, then the word "What?" followed by "Why?" They were asking about Mr. Jimmers. More talking followed, too low to understand, except that it obviously wasn't happy talk. Touchey's voice rang out clearly then, sounding irate.

Howard knew they would never get out of the shed without making God's own screeching racket, so he waited. But he would have to move fast when the time came—tear the doors open and vault right off the side of the truck. Stoat would let them know if it was safe—if Stoat could be trusted . . .

There was more talk and shuffling feet on the gravel now, but still no signal from Stoat. Howard heard Gwendolyn Bundy laugh and then ask, "So where is he?"

"Back at the Sea Spray," Stoat said. "He's tied into a chair."

"I'm going up there. He needs a playmate. You say he's *tied up?*" She giggled in what sounded like the voice of a tin can.

Glenwood Touchey said, "Perhaps I'll go along, darling. We can—"

"Nyah, nyah," Ms. Bundy yapped at him, interrupting. "You can have him when I'm done. You're such a bloodthirsty little man! You can practice on the two you've got. Do you know,

Stoatie, Glenwood wanted to take me in the woods just five minutes ago. And I mean *in*, not into. Do you want to know what he suggested?"

"Where is Heloise?" Touchey asked in a hollow voice, interrupting her.

"At home," Stoat said, sounding relieved. "The whole thing was a success. She's packing a bag and will meet us here."

"Packing a bag?"

"A little vacation. She's worked hard, and there's a lot of planning to do. You know how big this thing is."

"She owes me *money*," Touchey said, his voice rising. "She sure as hell *better* show up. She told me she'd be here a half hour ago. We've got people tied up in chairs and she's home packing a bag!"

"Settle down, Glen," Gwendolyn Bundy said. "Be a little soldier. It's late now to be full of suspicions, isn't it? I *told* you something was wrong when she didn't show up, but you were too damned stupid to . . ."

There was the sound of someone being slapped, and Gwendolyn Bundy let out a yelp.

"My ass I'm going to settle down," Touchey yelled. "She said you'd have the money, Stoat. *You're* her goddamn business partner. What's going on? She's got this precious sketch of hers and I'm getting stiffed, is that it? Or is it something else?"

There was a brief silence then, followed by a gasp and a shriek from Ms. Bundy and then the sound of Jimmers' door opening. In a rage, Touchey said, "I've had my eye on you for the last week, you phony prick, and—"

"Put the damned gun away!" Stoat yelled.

Gwendolyn Bundy screamed, and there was the noise of a scuffle. "You seedy little pervert!" she shouted. "That's *just* what we need, your damned penis substitute."

"Shut up!" Touchey shrieked, and there was the sound of another hand slap, and then of someone hitting the ground, followed by a single gunshot that echoed through the open night.

Howard tore the shed doors open, cursing himself for having waited. He threw himself over the edge of the truck bed, trying to take his weight on his good leg and expecting either to be shot by Touchey or attacked by Gwendolyn Bundy.

Mr. Jimmers was just then coming around the front of the truck, waving his hands as if to settle everyone down. Stoat and Touchey wrestled on the ground, and Gwendolyn Bundy kicked furiously at them, not seeming to care who she kicked. A look of

335

vast surprise and anger crossed her face when she looked up and saw Howard. For a moment he thought she would throw herself on him in a rage, and he put his arms out to ward her off.

She turned and ran around the corner of the building instead, out toward the highway. Howard let her go. Stoat and Touchey still rolled on the gravel, their feet kicking. Touchey's face was shriveled with insane anger, and he screamed nonsense into Stoat's ear.

Sylvia ran straight past Howard, heading for the door of the museum. Right at that moment Touchey fired the pistol again, wildly, into the eucalyptus branches overhead. Sylvia flinched, slamming herself against the wood siding of the museum and then dashing up onto the little porch and throwing herself through the open door, disappearing inside.

Touchey waved the pistol in his right hand, which Stoat held by the wrist, jacking the gun back and forth now and slamming Touchey's arm against the ground. Touchey gouged at Stoat's eyes and hit him futilely on the back with his free hand, gasping and mewling, his mouth biting air. Circling around them, Howard reached down and grabbed the gun barrel as if it were the head of a poisonous snake. With his other hand he pried Touchey's fingers off the grip.

Touchey went suddenly slack then, as if he had lost all his stuffing along with the gun. His mouth was pouty and sullen, like the mouth of a spoiled little boy set to cry. He sat up in the dirt and gravel, looking around. "Gwendolyn!" he shrieked. "Gwendolyn! Damn it! You damn bitch!" But she was gone, out into the night.

"She ditched you," Howard said. "Ran straight down the road."

"Go to *hell*!" Touchey croaked at him, burying his face in his hands as he hooted out a long sob. "You can't hold me here!" he shouted. "You're *all* guilty of something."

Stoat stood up, dusting at his pants.

"Hello," a voice said. It was Uncle Roy, standing now in the doorway, Sylvia no doubt having untied him. He looked a mess, his hair riled and the side of his face black and blue. "Where's the landlady?" he asked.

"Dead," Howard said. "Drowned."

"I *knew* it!" Touchey shouted at Stoat, so full of fury that he could barely speak. "Traitor! Stinking . . . pig!" He picked up a handful of gravel then and threw it at Stoat, cocking his arm back as if he were swatting flies on a tabletop. The gravel sprayed across Stoat's chest, and Stoat, suddenly furious, stepped in and clutched Touchey by the front of his shirt.

"That's enough!" Uncle Roy hollered. "There's no point in holding on to him. He's old news now. Let the bastard go. We won't see him again."

Stoat immediately pushed Touchey away, and the man sprawled back into the shadows of the eucalyptus trees. He stood there sputtering, looking hard at Stoat, as if he would gladly thrash Stoat then and there except for some very damned good reason. They waited for him to speak, but instead he stomped away, following in the wake of Gwendolyn Bundy, walking straight past his car toward the highway and looking back at them over his shoulder. At the corner of the building he turned briefly and, with almost lunatic intensity, made an obscene gesture so violent and wild it must nearly have broken his wrist.

"That's right," Roy said to him, waving.

"He deserves more," Howard said in a low voice, watching Touchey disappear beyond the edge of the building. He felt relief, though, at seeing him go, as if he were watching the departure of an irate door-to-door magazine salesman.

"All of us deserve more," Uncle Roy said. He flexed his hands and worked his shoulders back and forth. "I deserve a drink." He took a step forward, out onto the little stoop, but nearly fell over and had to catch himself on the railing. "My damned rear end is asleep from sitting on that bench for three hours. What the hell took you?"

Right then, though, before anyone could answer, there came the sound of pounding feet from the direction Touchey had taken. A man shouted. Then, weirdly, the voice of Gwendolyn Bundy piped up in a high-pitched hen's cackle. "That's him!" she yelled. "He's the one who shot the fat man! He tried to kill the old Dutch lady, too!"

Howard sprinted across the back parking lot, followed by Jimmers, Stoat, and Uncle Roy. There, coming along past the picket fence and the vigilant cow skulls, Bennet and Lou Gibb swarmed toward Glenwood Touchey. Ms. Bundy stood behind them, her hands over her mouth, watching excitedly. Touchey ran right into them, as if confident that his righteous fury would bowl them down.

It was Bennet who hit Touchey first, a roundhouse punch that caught him in the chest. Almost simultaneously Lou Gibb hit him in the stomach, and for a moment Touchey seemed to levitate there in a sort of airborne somersault crouch, before flopping to the ground, the two men closing in on either side.

"Hit him again!" Ms. Bundy yelled, dancing on the shoulder of the road next to Gibb's car. Howard sprinted toward them along with Stoat, shouting, "No one's been shot! No one's been shot!" Howard pulled Bennet away, shaking his head wildly to make him understand. Uncle Roy limped up then, yelling things himself, but it wasn't until Mr. Jimmers honked Lou Gibb's car horn three times that the two men stepped back, shrugging their shoulders and looking as if they would happily hit Touchey again and not ask overtime pay for it.

Touchey lay curled up on the ground, with his knees tucked up and his hands over his head, sobbing and shouting unrelated and purposeless obscenities.

"Roy!" Bennet said, grabbing his friend's shoulder. "You ain't dead!"

"Not a bit," Uncle Roy said.

"Then why are we beating this man up?" Bennet backed off another step, huffing and puffing, and Gwendolyn Bundy pushed past him, sinking to her knees next to Touchey. Tenderly she petted him on the back of his head.

"It's over," she cooed softly. "I'm so sorry. I thought . . . I thought . . . I was mad at you. I didn't think they'd . . . They won't hit my baby boy any more." She helped him to sit up, pushing his face into her chest and hugging him, rocking him back and forth gently.

"Cripes," Gibb said, a look of repulsion on his face. "This kind of crap ain't natural."

Gwendolyn Bundy turned on him furiously, her eyes pinched up. "You're *brutal*!" she said, pulling Touchey to his feet. A thin stream of blood ran out of his nose. He gave everyone what was meant to be a hard look, his mouth a quivering slit, but then Ms. Bundy touched his cheek with her hand, and he howled and swatted at her. Together they walked off across the gravel, back toward their car. Ms. Bundy stroked Touchey's back as he leaned heavily against her, whimpering like a small animal, his hand stroking her thigh. They could hear her talking a sort of baby talk to him, and he yelped once more, as if she had touched his cheek again.

"I didn't mean to be beating on the man," Bennet said apologetically. "The woman said . . ."

Uncle Roy gestured at him. "What that woman says would make you sick. It was him that burned the icehouse and worked over Mrs. Deventer's car."

"Maybe we ought to hit him some more, then," Lou Gibb said.

But it was too late. Touchey and Gwendolyn Bundy roared past just then, Ms. Bundy driving, their car kicking up dust and gravel as she slewed around south onto Highway One. Then Mr. Jimmers held out his hand to Uncle Roy, who pumped it heartily, clapping Jimmers on the back. Jimmers looked at Roy's face and shook his head. "Did they beat you?"

"Beat me? Certainly they beat me."

"The same lot as usual?" Jimmers asked, breaking into a grin.

"How does that go?" Uncle Roy asked. " 'Jesus, they beat me stupid.' "

"That must be from a different book," Jimmers said. "You never could keep that sort of thing straight."

"No, I couldn't. But it's tolerably good to see you. I've got that much straight."

Aunt Edith and Sylvia appeared from around the side of the museum then. The moon shone over the treetops, lighting the road and the parking lot and illuminating Edith's face, which was full of relief. It was apparently over. No one was hurt. The crisis was past. She regarded Stoat, who stood a few feet off, leaning against the side of the museum.

"Timothy," she said. "Welcome back. Sylvia's been telling me about things."

"I'm sorry," Stoat said. He looked haggard and worn out, not particularly happy. Howard wondered what it was he regretted the most.

Uncle Roy stepped across and shook Stoat's hand. "Who's not sorry for something?" he asked. Then, to Edith, he said, "Stoat here wrestled the gun away from Glenwood Flounder, right out back in the gravel. Saved everyone's life probably."

"Well," Edith said. "It's over, isn't it? Everyone is saved. The night is full of heroes."

Bennet began to jabber at Uncle Roy just then, telling him about the road being washed away, and Mr. Jimmers hugged Edith, talking very earnestly. Howard looked at Sylvia and smiled with pride. Her jeans were streaked with crushed ice plant and her hair was windblown and wild. He wanted to grab her right there on the spot and kiss her, sweep her right off her feet—the perfect end of a not-very-perfect day.

But the whine of an engine and the squeal of tires shut everyone up. Down the highway, from the direction of town, came a paramedics' van, weaving insanely from lane to lane but without any lights or siren. It drove straight toward them, the driver's face hidden in shadow, like the faces of the men in Uncle Roy's ghost car.

Howard stood there stupefied, unable to comprehend the meaning of the van's sudden appearance. Had someone innocently driven past and seen the commotion and called for help?

The van braked in a hard stutter, a half dozen jerks, as if someone were stamping the brake pedal into rubbish. It swerved into the lot, nearly clipping Bennet, who leaped out of the way when he saw who it was that was driving.

"God almighty," Uncle Roy said softly.

The van door opened and Heloise Lamey very nearly fell out onto her face.

Uncle Roy and Mr. Jimmers both stepped across to help her, Jimmers gaping in disbelief. She recovered before they got to her, though, sitting up very straight and fastening the two of them with a cold and wintry gaze. Slowly she opened her clenched fists, as if she had asked them to guess which hand held the colored bean, and with a triumphant laugh she displayed two water-soaked fragments of the fraudulent sketch.

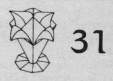

31

THE night was tremendously quiet, as if nature had been struck dumb. Even the wind had been stilled by Mrs. Lamey's unlikely appearance. The only sound was the ocean muttering faintly in the distance, like a great, sighing ghost. The headlights of the paramedics' van lit up the woods behind the museum, and Howard half expected the luminous cow to wander out of the trees, chewing its phantom cud. It was Mrs. Lamey who spoke first.

"Artemis Jimmers," she said in a voice meant to be commanding, but which was shaking, and was too highly pitched. "I've come for the machine and for John Ruskin's bones."

She breathed hard, as if she had been running from something, or else was so agitated that she was hyperventilating. The leather satchel still hung around her neck, and she hunched forward as she stood there, as if weighed down by it. Her hair was startling—full of twigs and leaves—and her face and hands were smeared with muck from her pilgrimage up Pudding Creek. She turned and pulled a dry, clean, hospital-issue blanket out of the open door of the van and wrapped herself in it, clutching the blanket shut with the same hand in which she held the shredded fragments of the sketch. Her eyes glowed with light that was the result of a private, newly discovered wavelength.

"I have swum with the salmon," she said, and then fumbled beneath the blanket, reaching her fingers into the satchel and pulling out her magical divining rod, which she waved in Jimmers' direction.

There was dead silence again as everyone stared mystified at the tied-together forearm bones—in stupefaction now rather than fear or wonder, since the bones didn't command the same respect that they might have earlier in the evening. Most of the debris that knotted them together had washed away, and aside from a few threads of bird feather hanging from a bit of adhesive tape, they might have been something scavenged from a garbage heap. Their terrible odor and their power to repulse people seemed to have been lost along with their nasty trimmings. She shook them in the air, though, back and forth in the manner of someone carefully salting a pot of stew.

"Of course," Mr. Jimmers said to her, watching the bones doubtfully. "The machine. Yes. I'm not sure that you're any longer in a position to—"

"*Position?*" she gasped, her voice cracking. She took a step toward him, pointing the bones at him specifically. He flinched just a little, not liking the look of them suddenly, even in their declined state. But he held his ground, ready to parley with her like he would parley with a creature from the stars. She had come to menace them with her mere presence, which was very nearly enough.

"I was told by this man that the bones of John Ruskin were entombed within your device," she said, cocking her head with great dignity and gesturing at Uncle Roy, who smiled, nodding at Jimmers.

"That's right," Roy said. "Ruskin's bones. All except for the fingers of his right hand. Those were ground up and used to seed clouds out in Iowa. That's what the machine is—a rain-making device built on the spiritual principle."

She nodded slowly, as if this were reasonable.

"She's off her chump," Uncle Roy whispered to Jimmers. "Swum with the salmon?"

"I was promised the device in the tin shed," she muttered, looking down at her hands, "but I was given *this*." She cast the watery bits of paper at their feet, snorting in disgust. "Its power has been taken back. You're *nothing* now," she said to Howard. "You're a pitiful weak thing."

"Christ!" breathed Uncle Roy, who obviously recognized what it was that she had thrown onto the ground. He stooped to pick up the pieces and looked at Howard with a horrified face.

Howard winked at him, and Uncle Roy relaxed.

"I'm damned if I'll give her the machine," Jimmers whispered. "Is there a phone inside? We'll call the hospital."

Uncle Roy shook his head. "No phone. Don't be so damned tight-fisted with the machine. Let's crank it up. Give her a taste of it. She's come a long damned way to see it, poor old thing. Look at her."

Mrs. Lamey began jigging the bones at them again, casting some sort of spell. Her mouth worked as if she were reciting something that would confound them all, except that right then one of the bones fell away from the other one and landed in the gravel. Howard was reminded of his adventure with the shotgun in the stone house. He felt suddenly sympathetic, and he bent over to retrieve the bone for her. She warded him off, though, and snatched it up herself, peering at it wonderingly and clutching the two bones in her hand, like chopsticks now, a look of uncertainty in her eye, as if she were watching her power literally fall apart. Like an insane orchestra conductor groping to remember a tune, she began to wave them at Jimmers again, taking up where she had left off.

It seemed to Howard that there was a horrible timelessness to her antics now, that she had forgotten what she was doing and so could see no reason ever to stop. The thought of her going on like that was unspeakable. The tension in the air broke, the tree branches stirred in the wind, and Mrs. Lamey began to cry—a watery snivel at first, which gave way to shuddering and sobbing and wheezing as she pressed the bones to her chest, looking around her with pitiful, vacant eyes but apparently seeing nothing. There was no threat left to her, no magic or power.

Howard felt little satisfaction in that. He felt only the need to restrain her, and then to find her shelter from whatever empty thing it was that her world had become.

"For God's sake," Uncle Roy said to Jimmers, speaking out loud, "let her have a look at the machine. I think you owe it to all of us."

Edith stepped across then along with Sylvia, and they took Mrs. Lamey by either elbow, leading her toward the back door of the museum. No longer sobbing, the old woman glared at Edith, but without any real recognition. It didn't matter who Edith was. There wasn't a living human being on earth, Mrs. Lamey's face seemed to say, that was of any interest to her.

The rest of them followed, Roy and Jimmers still arguing about the machine. But by the time they had gotten around back, and Edith had led Mrs. Lamey into the museum, Jimmers apparently had made up his mind.

"I won't be responsible for it," he said to Roy.

"I will," Roy told him. "Full responsibility."

"It may have serious consequences on the spiritual existence of a very superior human being. There's no telling what will come of it . . ." His warning was lost on Uncle Roy, though, and Jimmers could see that, and fell silent. Then, tiredly, he waved a hand at Howard, Bennet, and Lou Gibb. Uncle Roy stepped across to the paramedics' van, fired up the engine, and angled the van around so that the headlights illuminated the truck bed, where the tin shed sat with its doors gaping open.

Howard climbed up onto the lift gate and then turned to give Mr. Bennet a hand up. Lou Gibb, Stoat, and Uncle Roy followed, although there wasn't room for more than two of them inside the shed. All of them, though, craned their necks to see through the doorway, where the machine sat as ever, half hidden by the fallen aluminum lawn chair. Together Howard and Stoat pulled bags of mulch out, laying them on the truck bed and clearing the doorway. Then they hauled Jimmers' machine out so that the others could get a grip on it, too, all of them easing it across to set it on the lift gate. Bennet lowered the gate to the ground, and they picked up the machine again and lifted it up onto the wooden porch, getting into each other's way.

"Too many Indians," Uncle Roy said, stepping aside and letting the others wrestle with it. They had to tilt the device up sideways, holding on to it awkwardly and bumping their knuckles on the doorjamb. Mr. Jimmers waved his arms and made valuable suggestions, grimacing at the pinging and ponging sounds echoing out from inside the machine.

In the museum, finally, they heaved it up onto one of the redwood tables, which creaked under the machine's weight. Uncle

Roy held a propane lantern over it, and everyone except Mrs. Lamey gathered around to inspect it. Free of shed debris now, it looked like a strange hybrid of sewing machine, harmonium, and vine-entangled shrub. It was studded along the back with what might have been crude vacuum tubes designed to look like bell jars. The frosted glass of the jars was cameo-carved with vines and oak leaves.

There were delicate cylinders, like metal reeds, sprouting from among the bell jars, and India-rubber squeezo bulbs dangling like kelp bladders along the back, making a sort of sighing noise, as if they were breathing.

The entire device was mounted on springs that were tied into what looked at first glance like claw-and-ball feet. Howard was only partly surprised to find that they were actually carved into the semblance of trees, with heavy, twisted root balls at the base, the springs twining out of their upper branches like foliage.

The case of the machine was decorated with more vines and leaves and with the logo of the Guild of St. George. Even the springs and rivets were minutely decorated, so that as he stared at it in the silvery light of the lantern, Howard's vision was confused, and it seemed to him that he wasn't looking at a machine at all, but at something living and growing, like an ancient, tangled garden in miniature, or a carefully contrived archetype of all gardens and deep woods everywhere.

Howard realized that he had seen almost nothing in the darkness of the shed two days ago, when he had foolishly spun the thing's wheel.

Now he saw it clearly, though, and from a better angle, through eyes unclouded by doubt. It was obviously a Victorian-era, gluer-built machine. There was something in the heap of decoration and unlikely gadgetry that suggested, against all reason, a carefully ordered chaos—cosmically arranged doodads mixed up with a deep-woods thicket. Clearly this was the culmination of John Ruskin's work, the great masterpiece of the St. George's Guild, the end product and object of the shadowy Pre-Raphaelite Brotherhood itself.

Edith and Sylvia went back to sit with Mrs. Lamey on her bench against the wall. She still held on to the bones, clutching them in her hands and staring in the general direction of the machine. Her eyes were focused, though, on some distant place, as if the machine were a window on another world. Howard found himself hoping that whatever place it was, it was somewhere serene and safe.

He didn't feel any hatred for her at all, which vaguely surprised him. She was just a lonely, lost old woman wrapped in a blanket now, her life twisted and stunted by witchery and greed. Now that Howard had seen the power of the paper Grail and had gotten a good look at Jimmers' machine, he could understand the ambition that drove Mrs. Lamey.

Jimmers stepped back away from the table and folded his arms. "I can't say with any certainty . . ." he started to say, as if uneasy again with the idea of "cranking it up," as Uncle Roy had put it.

"None of us *wants* any certainty," Roy said, interrupting him. "None of us minds a little uncertainty."

"Just don't let any ghosts steal my damned truck," Bennet said, nudging Lou Gibb in the arm.

Uncle Roy turned down both propane lamps, throwing the room into shadow. "Let her rip," he said to Jimmers.

Mr. Jimmers hesitated for another moment, gathering himself, then he reached out and spun the wheel hard, slapping it faster and faster with the palm of his hand. He manipulated a lever and squeezed the bulbs in among the jars, and the machine made tiny splooping noises like thumb-sized frogs leaping into a pond.

This time Howard could predict what he would see and hear: the fishbowl glow of light, the distant footsteps, the humming, the sound of mechanical men deep in conversation. He thought of the ghosts in the Studebaker and Uncle Roy's spirit woman on the stairs. Was this the same sort of thing? A one-hundred-year-old hoax?

There was a sudden draft, and the temperature in the room fell ten degrees in a swoop, the back door slamming shut with a bang that made Howard jump. The lighted mist became a smoky wraith that swirled and congealed over the picnic table. Everyone still standing around the machine stepped back into the shadows, huddling together almost inadvertently, and Sylvia stood up from the bench and joined Howard, peering over his shoulder, her face full of wonder.

Mrs. Lamey's divining rod clattered to the wooden floor, and Howard saw her stand up then, too, squinting, unable to believe her eyes. She stooped and picked up the bones, then took a half-step forward, talking under her breath. Jimmers held up his arm to stop her, and Edith stood up then behind her, putting a hand on Mrs. Lamey's shoulder.

Through the swirling, machine-made cloud, a vague, nebulous shape appeared, seeming to grow in size and clarity, as if the white mist from the machine were a lighted avenue out of the heavens, and some vast, unruly force were rushing at them along that avenue, out of the void of time and space.

It was a human form that materialized in the light, apparently made out of glittering snowflakes. It seemed to be speaking in tongues, but haltingly, as if with a deficient command of that language.

The myriad voices from the machine fought to become one voice. They were broken apart at first, as if by some aural kaleidoscope, but then they fell together and became whole— the voice of a single, old, enraged man uttering what sounded like a prepared speech in a vast auditorium. "Blanched sun!" he thundered. "Blighted grass! Blinded man!" He paused to gather himself, looking around suddenly with a puzzled face, as if surprised to find himself there. He held out his glittering arms and examined the backs of his hands, opening and closing them stiffly. Then, gesturing with both arms in a broad arc, he went on, speaking in a tone of deep authority: "If you ask me for any conceivable cause or meaning of these things, I can tell you none, according to your modern beliefs; but I can tell you what meaning it would have borne to the men of old time!"

He stopped again and looked around him, right at the little knot of men and women standing just outside the circle of lamplight. It wasn't clear that he saw them, and yet he seemed to be speaking to them directly, with a voice full of conviction and knowledge. Uncle Roy's face was hanging in disbelief, and Mr. Jimmers looked as if the vision before them justified his entire existence. Mrs. Lamey's eyes were narrowed, and she gasped for breath as if she had run a race.

The ghostly face was the visage of John Ruskin himself, white-haired and with the wide-open eyes of a prophet and seer. He fixed those eyes on Heloise Lamey, singling her out. Clearly entranced, she bent forward, hearkening to his words, and she reached out a hand, thinking, perhaps, that he would take it, that the two of them would stride out into the dark and windy night together.

The sound of bees rose on the air of the still room just then, and for a moment the ghost wavered and faded, his voice disintegrating again as the machine lost power. Mrs. Lamey cast Jimmers a look of such wild alarm that Jimmers lunged forward and spun the wheel, and almost at once the image leaped into metal-etched clarity, every hair on Ruskin's head blazing white, as if he were ringed with fire.

346

The sound of a siren rose around them, and the beehive noise faded behind it. Howard thought for a moment that the up-and-down whining of the siren was the noise of the machine, somehow, that it was wound too tight and was spinning out of control.

Then there was the roar of a car engine and tires spinning in gravel. It wasn't the machine at all that was making the siren noise. It was cars outside in the parking lot, police probably, on the trail of Mrs. Lamey and the stolen van.

The museum door flew open just as John Ruskin's ghost, nearly solid now, but still as white as moonlight and moving with the jerky rhythms of an old film image, reached both arms out, gesturing either at Mrs. Lamey or else to underscore some telling phrase, to implore his audience to ignore the three men who stood in the open doorway now, and to pay attention to him and to his passions. "By the plague wind every breath you draw is polluted, half round the world," he told them. "In a London fog the air itself is pure, though you choose to mix up dirt with it and choke yourself with your own nastiness."

Mrs. Lamey moaned loudly, cast off her blanket, and in her muddy, tattered dress she tore away from Edith and flew past Jimmers in a savage rush, knocking him sideways and leaping into the circle of light thrown off by the machine. She scrambled awkwardly up onto the end of the redwood picnic table, still clutching the bones and knocking one of the propane lanterns onto the floor. She stood up, reaching out her arms to grapple with the image of Ruskin, who continued to discourse about plague winds and apocalyptic storms. He seemed to be solid to her touch, and he turned his head and regarded her vaguely, as if *she* were the ghost, just barely visible to him now. His voice faltered and his eyes opened wide.

She teetered there on the table edge, nearly falling backward, but then hanging impossibly in the air, caught in the grip of some indecipherable force that defeated mere gravity. Jimmers shouted and threw out his hand, plunging it into the radium glow of the ghost light in order to steady her, to prevent her from falling. He howled, though, and jerked his arm abruptly backward as if something had tried to clutch his hand and haul him in.

Right then, her face a composed mask, Mrs. Lamey stood straight up on tiptoe and very slowly rose above the table, her head thrown back and her face nearly grazing one of the open trestles that supported the roof rafters. She was washed in an electric-white aura that pulsated and spun, drawing the edges of the illuminated ghost of John Ruskin into herself like water drawn into a whirlpool, until his stretched face hovered beside her own, as if he were hidden behind her, peering over her shoulder. He seemed to be speaking only to her now, into her ear, as if she were the only person present who could hear him.

She shrieked and threw out her hands, casting the arm bones of Joseph of Arimathea into the far wall, where they clattered to the floor. Like a wind devil, the ghost light whirled around her, her hair standing on end as if she would be drawn straight up through the roof.

Uncle Roy's mouth hung open in astonishment, and the three men in the doorway—a policeman and two paramedics—stood gaping, too, as if they were on utterly unfamiliar ground, had found themselves suddenly on the moon and in the middle of some sort of alien ritual.

The ghost from the machine shuddered—a quick convulsion, the light rippling like heat waves—and then exploded, flying apart like a snowball with a firecracker buried in it. Fragments of light showered away in a spiral nebula, as the ghostly voice of John Ruskin shouted one last time and fell silent.

Mr. Jimmers rushed forward now, in an effort to help Mrs. Lamey, who had collapsed, and lay curled on the end of the table now like a sleeping cat, her head resting against one of the machine's feet.

"Stand clear!" commanded the policeman. He stepped into the lantern light. It was the cop from the harbor, looking both suspicious and baffled. The two paramedics pulled a gurney through the open door, then hurried across to lift Mrs. Lamey onto it before checking vital signs. She lay there limp, like a doll with half its stuffing gone.

"Dead?" Jimmers asked in a hollow voice.

"No. Unconscious," one of the paramedics said.

She stirred then, and her eyes blinked open. Her face was empty of animation, though, like a rubber mask. She began to gibber, barely moving her lips, and her hands twitched on the top of the sheet-covered gurney as if she were picking tiny weeds out of a flower bed.

"Mrs. Lamey?" one of the paramedics said to her, looking at her eyes. He passed his hand in front of her face, then snapped his fingers.

She stared straight toward the ceiling, though, or at some point beyond it, oblivious to him, her face limp and her hands still plucking at the sheet. The paramedic shook his head at the cop.

"Finish up and get her out of here," the cop said, "and don't leave her alone in the damned van this time."

"I think the van's safe from her now," Uncle Roy said softly. He stepped across and turned up the lantern that still sat on the back of the table.

The cop looked hard at Roy, then at Bennet and Howard, realizing who they were, as if scattered puzzle pieces had fallen into place suddenly, only to form a picture so weird and complicated as to be beyond his comprehension.

"What's this now?" the cop asked. "The whole damned gang, is it? You're Roy Barton, aren't you?"

Uncle Roy nodded, smiling cheerfully. "Glad you arrived, Officer," he said, shoving out his hand. The policeman looked at it dubiously before he shook it.

"Poor old Heloise Lamey," Roy said. "She burst in here ten minutes ago, right in the middle of all this." He swept his hand around the room, as if to clarify the whole doubtful business. "I don't know if you've met Mr. Stoat. He's a financier. He's underwriting this whole venture."

"Stoat?" the cop said flatly. "What venture is that?" He looked hard at Stoat and then took a closer look at the machine.

"Ghost museum, haunted house," Roy said. "That doggone icehouse was a firetrap. We decided to shift out here when the place burned down." Uncle Roy gestured at the machine. "Stage magic. You know how it is. The kids love this sort of thing. You've got kids yourself . . ."

The cop smiled and started to nod, as if then and there he would pull photos out of his wallet and pass them around. Then he looked abruptly suspicious again.

"Mr. Stoat here is the man who pulled me out of the fire down at the icehouse," Bennet said.

"Good man." The cop caught sight of Sylvia then, who was sitting with Edith on the bench, back in the shadows. "Hi there," he said cheerfully. Sylvia waved tiredly at him.

"How many kids have you got?" Roy asked.

"What? Three. Why?"

"Put the officer down for three tickets," he said to Howard. "Gratis."

"Right," Howard said.

"What happened to your face?" The cop narrowed his eyes at Roy. "Nasty bruise."

"Stepped on a rake up in Caspar," Uncle Roy said. "I've been up there shoveling manure."

"I bet you have. You can quit shoveling now, though. We're knee-deep in it." He smiled for the first time. "Jack MacDonald's been telling me about you," he said.

"Jack?" Roy said, surprised. "You know Jack?"

"We play poker. Saturday nights. Friendly game."

Roy looked at Bennet and winked. "Don't need another couple of players, do you?"

"Well, we are a little short right now," the cop said, smoothing down his mustache.

"Then we'll fit right in," Bennet said. "I'm only five eight and Roy here's nearly a midget when he takes the risers out of his shoes."

Uncle Roy laughed, then looked at Mrs. Lamey and stopped abruptly. She still gibbered and twitched, as if enlivened by a tiny electrical charge, with not nearly enough current to start her up. The two paramedics pushed her rolling stretcher toward the door, maneuvering her through it and down the couple of stairs outside, disappearing from sight.

"Poor old thing," Roy said softly. "She was always delicate. Like a thin piece of glass. Nothing but sharp edges, but it didn't take much to crack her."

The cop nodded. "She had a rough time up at the beach tonight. Freak storm up there did a lot of damage, nearly drowned the old woman, knocked her around pretty bad. She went haywire when they got her down to emergency. These boys left her alone for half a second, and she up and drove off in the van. Took some time to track her down." They heard the door of the paramedics' van slide shut then. The engine roared, and there was the sound of wheels on gravel as it backed out onto the coast highway and motored away north.

"What I wonder," the cop said, "is why she came here. And what was she doing up on the table there?"

Roy clicked his tongue regretfully. "She and Artemis Jimmers here were married. Years ago. She's been pining away for him." He gestured at Mr. Jimmers, who wore a long face, as if this were a personal tragedy.

"You're the one who lives down at the stone house, aren't you?" the cop said.

"Caretaker," Jimmers said, "since Michael Graham's tragic death."

The cop nodded. "My father used to lend Graham a hand, back when Graham was putting up the tower. I even hauled stone around out there when I was a kid. Old Graham was something.

I learned to drink coffee there. He used to haul it out in a big ceramic jug with a spigot. I'll never forget that. Left the place to you, did he?"

Jimmers shook his head. "Just caretaker," he said. "Holding on to the place until the rightful owner came along. Howard Barton here is the owner now. Lock, stock, and barrel. It's all down in Graham's will, giving me power of attorney. We're all supposing Howard will do the right thing and marry Sylvia, and the two of them can hoe chard out there together. Work the garden."

Howard sat down hard next to Sylvia on the bench, looking at her in disbelief, his head swimming. Sylvia widened her eyes at him. "Was *that* your proposal?" she whispered. "Did you put him up to saying that?" Before Howard could utter a word, though, she stood up and rushed across to hug and kiss Mr. Jimmers, then turned around and went after Uncle Roy, holding on to Jimmers' shoulders with one arm and throwing the other around Roy's neck, hugging them both together.

After a moment she let them both go. Grinning, but full of emotion, Roy picked up the knocked-over lantern and inspected it carefully. "Mantle's whole," he said to Jimmers. "Can you beat that?"

"A mystery," Jimmers said. "Better document it."

Roy pulled a book of paper matches out of his pocket and lit the thing with a shaky hand, turning up the knob until the room glowed with the light of both lanterns. Then he spotted the arm bones lying one beside the other on the floor, and he picked them up, looking them over.

"Relics," Stoat said to him. "The genuine article."

"What?" the cop asked, cocking his head.

"Part of the props," Roy said to him. "A haunted house has got to be full of bones. It's standard stuff. Chains rattling in the closet and all."

The cop looked doubtful, on the verge of speaking, when a voice from across the room interrupted him. It was Lou Gibb, his broad face full of astonishment.

"I'll be go-to-hell," he said softly. He and Bennet were both staring at the wall, where the collection of framed photographs had hung.

Uncle Roy, followed now by everyone else, strode across to look closer at the dirty plaster. Two clean white images stood out against it, as if someone had splashed the wall with whitewash. They seemed almost to drink in the light from the propane lanterns. There couldn't be any doubt about what they were.

Roy touched one of the images hesitantly, as if afraid it would rub off, or would burn him, but it wasn't paint or charcoal or anything of the kind; it was shadow and light, captured and fixed onto the wall, a spirit photograph developed when the ghost from the machine had flown to pieces.

Roy turned around, smiling broadly at Edith like a little boy who has just recovered some wonderful lost object. It was John Ruskin's face on the wall, a satisfied grimace tugging at the corners of its mouth. Next to it, like the flip side of a coin from the spirit realm, was the astonished, wild-haired countenance of Heloise Lamey, her face showing jumbled traces of nearly every human emotion, as if her very spirit had departed from her body and was fixed now on the plaster wall.

Uncle Roy gestured grandly at the images, bowing like a maestro.

"Back in business!" he said happily, dusting his hands together before reaching out to clap Howard on the back.